I0612179

Also by

Robert McGraw and Darrin McGraw

Animal Future

Animal Future 2: Party Animals

Not Like Us

Robert McGraw

with

Darrin McGraw

Mondrian Books

San Diego – Riverside

This book is fiction. All names, places, characters, corporations, government entities, and incidents are the products of the imaginations of the authors and are used fictitiously. Any resemblance to actual events, places, locales, or persons, whether living or dead, is purely coincidental.

Copyright © 2020 by Robert McGraw

All rights reserved. In accordance with the U.S. Copyright Act of 1976, the scanning, uploading, and electronic sharing of any part of this book without the express permission of the author constitute unlawful piracy and theft of the author's intellectual property. If you wish to use material from this book for anything other than review purposes, prior permission must be obtained by contacting the author at robert@mcgraw.net. Thank you for supporting the author's rights.

Cover illustration by Robert McGraw

ISBN 978-1-942409-06-9

Mondrian Books

San Diego – Riverside

**With undying appreciation
to**

**Nanci, my lifelong sweetheart
Who never lost hope**

and

**Darrin, my editor/co-author
Who never became boring**

Part One:
Two Worlds

CHAPTER 1
THURSDAY, AUGUST 16, 1934

"Mup hpmp glumup glumunub?" asked President Bernard Shaw Fieldman, tilted back in the barber chair.

"Which carnival's that, Bernard?" As Isaac Cash reached for his Red Imp straight razor on the counter, he glanced at his coat hanging on the nail on the storage room door. From the side pocket, his brother's letter pointed accusingly at him. Soon he would have to face up to replying. But now, the Mercer County Bank President's shave was waiting.

"Wuhmhbump don't know how you missed the handbills nailed all over town," Fieldman said as Isaac lifted off the hot towel. "Elmo Johnson saw carnival trucks on Meekam's Field last night."

Isaac examined the razor's edge in the sunlight streaming through the new window. Last week, the tail end of a tornado had sent a chinkapin limb smashing through the old window. Isaac had nailed one-by-fours across it, gone home, and searched his bankbook, the sofa cushions, and the dresser drawers until eventually he scraped together enough money for a new glass. It was nice to have good light again for shaving the few customers who came in. Soon Isaac would see the Ozark autumn burnishing the dogwood and redbud trees every shade of bronze and copper. That is, provided he hadn't gone bust by then and been forced to go work for his brother out in Texas.

"You're only sheriff part-time, true. But it's still your job," Fieldman said.

As Isaac brushed on the lather, the morning heat was coaxing the odors of Bermarine and Dapper Man pomade from the barbershop walls. The Depression was getting worse every day, and so was the hair-cutting trade. Isaac was grateful for the part-time sheriff job. Even so, having the new window painted—"Isaac Cash Barbershop"—would require several more customers. Paying customers like Fieldman, not those who bartered homemade jam, fresh bread, or ears of corn. The window painting company wouldn't accept homemade jam.

"They'll be setting up today," said Fieldman. "You need to do something immediately!"

"Nothing I *can* do." Isaac stretched the skin on Fieldman's cheek upwards to tighten it. "I don't know the first thing about setting up a carnival."

"You know that's not what I meant! Get serious!"

"Best to keep still, Bernard." Isaac touched the straight razor to Fieldman's throat. "Razor's awful sharp today."

***

America's Fattest Little Lady looked out the window of her trailer as she swallowed the last of her eight-egg omelet and spread jam on her sixth piece of toast. For a carnival fat lady in 1934, cleaning her plate had little to do with enjoying food. America was in the middle of a record-setting depression, and her income depended on staying fat. For Elaine, eating was not a compulsion; it was a marketing strategy.

Similarly, she had chosen the name "Baby Elaine" because of its audience appeal. For some reason, carnival fat ladies were more popular when they went by infantile stage names: Dainty Doris, Jolly Dolly, Baby Ruth. It was as much a requirement as the frilly little-girl frocks they wore, regardless of how absurd such clothing looked on a four-hundred-pound woman. Or maybe because of it.

Demeaning, yes, but also profitable. While the average American's salary was less than $1400 per year, Elaine's trailer boasted oak paneling and plush carpeting nicer than some hotel lobbies. "Mr. Bowlus," she had written to the builder, "you'll see in my drawings that I have designed the trailer to be longer and wider than usual. When it comes to trailers, I take an extra large."

Through the open window, the breeze delivered the clangbang of metal, the shouts of roughnecks, and the dusty smell of one more carnival lot. Looking toward the midway, Elaine noticed the Professor in his powder-blue suit walking down the midway. Considering his height—or rather, lack of it—he was covering ground quickly, a little person with big responsibilities. She had known him long enough to be able to tell when he was feeling under pressure. *Setup,* she thought. *It's taking much too long.*

As the Professor passed the Hootchy-Kootchy tent, he gave it a quick look, apparently satisfied that it was almost completely assembled. In addition to being co-owner of the carnival, the Professor owned the dancing girls' show, and it was the most consistent profit machine of all the Single-O attractions—the independently-owned tent shows.

I should buy a Single-O show as an investment. I don't

5

intend to be a fat lady forever. Elaine was bone weary from fourteen years of hiding her mind behind pink-ribboned dresses and the faked preciousness that amused gawking rubes. Eight years ago, she had established a saving plan that would enable her to stop exhibiting herself by the age of thirty-two. She had missed that deadline this year, thanks to the Depression. Owning a Single-O could allow her to leave the stage after two or three more seasons.

Elaine absentmindedly spun the center deck of the triple-decker Lazy Susan table she had designed herself. As she watched it, a vision twirled up from its surface. *Not a tent show! No! A kiddie ride!* The room always seemed to brighten whenever the cosmos blessed Elaine with a new creative idea. *Something special to make children laugh and squeal!* She smiled and gave the table another spin.

***

Three miles north of Mercerville, a flat-bottomed boat was tied up to the south end of the forty-foot-high White River Railway trestle bridge. A puny breeze skimmed the water, riffled the greenbriers and buttonbushes along the banks, then fell dead. The only relief from the heat today would be here on the river. The sky wasn't green right now, but in North Central Arkansas at this time of year you could never rule out a fast-forming tornado.

On the deck, shaded from the sun by the bridge, a tall dark-haired man used a hunting knife to carve a section from an apple. He watched the juice drip between his fingers, melding into the rushing river current. He cut another hunk from the apple and tossed the core overboard.

Slit someone's throat now, and the flies would be all over you. He popped the apple chunk into his mouth. *Better to do it at night. Cooler.*

***

As he slid the gold watch into the vest pocket of his powder-blue suit, the carnival's co-owner, Professor Desmond A. Pinckney scanned the midway with an expert eye. Above him, roughnecks strained to bolt girders atop the thirty-foot-high Big Eli #5 Ferris wheel. Completing it would require six more hours under the blistering sun. Many of the game booths still weren't assembled either. Setup was behind schedule.

It's this blasted squeejawed lot, he thought as he pulled himself up to his full three-foot-eleven, checked the jaunty angle of his fedora, and gave his silver-topped walking stick a confident twirl. In show business, presenting an air of carefree confidence is half the battle. This season the smiling part kept getting harder.

"Pinckney and Hutchins All-American Shows" was laid out in an elongated horseshoe with the entrance at the open end. The midway extended down the center with large attractions, like the big wheel, at the back to pull carnival-goers through the entire show. It was only fair that every carny get an equal shot at the customers' cash. Unfortunately, this site was a pie-shaped field of parched weeds squeezed between a sycamore-covered hill and a shallow valley with a creek running through it. *No wonder Willie's having trouble fitting things in.*

To prevent customers from wandering off the lot, the concession booths were set close together, forming the horseshoe's perimeter. Carnival-goers needing to answer nature's call could reach the men's and women's donikers outside the horseshoe by going through a narrow alley between the shooting gallery and the string game.

As he passed the gallery, he made a mental note that the paint was flaking. *Shabby is unappealing.* Two dollars worth of paint could mean fifty in profits. *I have to get us into the black somehow. The season's almost over.*

***

"Careful with that thing," Bernard Fieldman said through the lather surrounding his lips. "Don't want to have to call Doc MacPhie."

"Not talking would help," Isaac said, drawing the razor down Fieldman's neck in short strokes. Only once had Isaac allowed a razor to lose its edge. That was after Sarah died.

"Why would a carnival come here anyway?" Fieldman said. "Smallest county in Arkansas."

"Remember that storm last week?" Isaac said. "Smashed my window. Soaked the wood floor."

"What of it?"

"Mountain Home caught the worst part, and that's where the carnival was. I figure their tent got wet, and they plan to spread it out and touch it up with a hot iron."

"Get serious!" Fieldman said.

"If you insist." Isaac wiped lather off Fieldman's face. "Truth is, this depression is hurting carnivals, too, so they're trying to attract folks who can't afford to drive all the way to Mountain Home. Anyway, that's what their man said."

"What man?"

"Advance man. Looking for a field to rent." Isaac rinsed the razor and patted it on a towel.

"You gave him permission?" Fieldman pushed himself out of the chair. "Don't you know what carnivals bring to small towns!"

"Fun?" Isaac put the razor into a jar of alcohol and picked up his horsehair bristle brush.

"Crime! Pickpockets, burglars, grifters! Carnies are all human debris, most of them," Fieldman said. "When I was at that banking conference in Chicago, a carnival was across the street, and they had a woman named Salome with a huge snake, and..."

"Good looking?" Isaac asked, brushing Fieldman's shoulders. "Salome, I mean. Not the snake."

"Look, I know you're joshing. But dang all, you *never* should have allowed a carnival to stop here!"

"Simmer down, Bernard. I'm going out there this afternoon. Let them see that Mercerville does have a lawman. Although part-time, as you say."

"Go right now! Chase them off before they even unpack!"

"That seems a tad extreme. However, I suppose I *could* go now." Reaching for his coat, Isaac noticed the empty Bakelite box on the counter. Young Jeremy Barlow hadn't returned the badge. "It'll only get hotter if I wait."

"Good! I'll organize some men!"

"Whoa! No need for a posse." As Isaac pulled his coat on, he felt Carl's letter still in the pocket. Answering it wouldn't be fun.

"Well, be firm. Mercerville folks can't afford to get cheated by carnivals," Fieldman said. "The bank has a stack of past-due mortgages as high as..."

"Including one on my barbershop," Isaac said.

"You're not the only person I'm letting stall. I'm damned if I'll sit back and watch Roosevelt destroy this town. These are my people, and I intend to help them any which way I can." Fieldman patted his charcoal-gray Homburg onto his head. "The Depression will end by next spring, provided FDR stops meddling. As for your mortgage, just catch up your late payments by the end of the month. If everyone does his part, we can survive this thing."

Great, thought Isaac, *but today's the sixteenth, and I'm*

9

broker than usual. "Say, need any hair tonic?" Isaac mentally calculated, at a profit of eight cents a bottle, how many bottles would equal one late mortgage payment. A lot.

"Mrs. Fieldman buys mine from the beautician in Mountain Home." Fieldman adjusted his necktie in the mirror.

"Fresh eggs?" Isaac pointed to a basket near the front door.

"She buys ours at Hansen's."

"Hansen sells good eggs. Mine are a little cheaper, though. My chickens are non-union. Keeps my overhead down." Isaac took his straw fedora off the peg and opened the door. "Anyway, if you want to stay and read *Police Gazettes,* switch off the fan when you leave. Electricity bill's outrageous. Hottest summer in memory."

"I have too much work to be reading magazines." Fieldman stepped out and started down the sidewalk.

"See you later," Isaac said. "I'll let you know if they have a lady with a snake."

Isaac locked the door, walked around the side of the barbershop, and got into his pickup truck.

Except the truck wouldn't start.

CHAPTER 2

A big man with his belly flopping over his belt dropped the banner he was hanging on the Merchandise Wheel game joint and planted himself, spread-legged and frowning, right in the Professor's path.

"Hold up, boss!" He raised a sun-bronzed hand with stubby fingers like half-smoked cigars. "Your colored field hand put me too far back. I want a better location!"

"Relax. Willie knows how to do layout. I trained him myself. And I'll ignore the field hand remark this time, but never again. Got it, Alonso? Never." The Professor glared up at the man, who glanced away and wisely said nothing.

"The problem, my friend…," the Professor continued, "…is that we're stuck with a lot that's twenty-eight feet too narrow on this side. Yet observe! Everywhere!" He swept his walking stick in an arc. "Carnies coping with a bad situation the best they can. Go thou and do likewise."

"I got a damn tree stump in the middle of my joint. I'll have to jump over it to get to the other side."

"There! You've found your own solution! Do you realize fifty-eight percent of people's fatigue is caused by lack of exercise? As you move more, you'll feel less tired."

"Only thing I'm tired of is one-horse towns. How can I make any money?"

"By using your head! Come with me." The Professor walked toward a nearby booth. "We'll borrow a Kewpie Doll from Brownie. Put it on the stump, and tell the marks they win a prize if they knock

11

it over with a baseball. Two games in one joint means twice the income."

"But a doll is easy to knock over. They'll win every time."

"Alonso! You're running a hanky-pank joint! People pay a nickel and win a keychain or a pocket comb that cost you two cents. Nobody *ever* loses a hanky-pank game, which means *you* make a profit every time they win!"

"Oh, yeah, I see what you mean." Alonso rubbed his chin stubble.

"You'll get rich. You'll be begging me for a tree stump in every town."

"Somebody say 'rich'?" The skinny woman at the Pitch-A-Penny joint dumped a box of Kewpie Dolls onto the wooden counter. "Are we finally going where there's money?"

"We're there, Brownie," the Professor said. "Mercer County, Arkansas. Population only five thousand and twelve, but highly prosperous. Al needs to borrow this." The Professor picked up a fallen Kewpie. "We'll be overrun with tourists. The White River is one of the Greatest Natural Wonders of the Known World," he said. "At least in North Central Arkansas."

"If you say so," Brownie said. "Why does Al need a doll?"

"Explain it, Al. I'm going to the Ten-in-One," the Professor said as he headed toward a large tent near the carnival entrance. In addition to owning the girly show, the Professor owned the Ten-in-One, the sideshow that offered ten exhibits for one ticket price. Local rubes called it simply "the freak show."

"Stringbean," the Professor called out to an emaciated man standing on the stage in front of the tent. "On schedule?"

"Never let you down yet, have I?" The Human Skeleton wiped his brow with his bony forearm. "Oh. Deena pulled a muscle jumping out of the way when the roughies raised the stage, but she's okay. Hey, are we gonna party tonight?"

"If we can get this show set up, yeah. What was Deena doing *in* the way?"

"You know her. Curiouser than a cat. Wants to learn everything. Personally, I think she gets a kick watching young guys with their shirts off."

"Reason number one why I'm glad I don't have a seventeen-year-old daughter." The Professor had a greater fear that he never talked about—passing on the gene of dwarfism. "Tell her to be more careful. I can't afford a contortionist with pulled muscles." He turned and walked away. "I'll be in the office truck figuring out what else I can't afford."

***

At the railroad bridge, the White River turned south, paralleled the railroad tracks past Mercerville, then snaked between varicolored bluffs and thickly-wooded hillsides towards its rendezvous with the great Mississippi.

On the boat, the tall man studied Meekam's Hill two miles west—a limestone runt left over by Mother Nature when she birthed the shale and sandstone Boston Mountains stretching into Oklahoma. Beyond Meekam's Hill was the highway, and beyond that was the discarded pasture called Meekam's Field. Today it was a carnival lot.

Tonight your shame ends. He pulled a rag from his hip pocket and wiped the blade of the hunting knife. A rare wave of the odd feeling he called happiness blanketed him. *I'll do it pure,* he thought. *Even monsters deserve a quick death.*

13

CHAPTER 3

It's not because he's his father's child. That's nonsense!
Rachel Barlow dropped the *Police Gazette* into her purse as she
walked down the floral-patterned carpet runner in the front hallway
of the Russell Boarding House. *Jeremy's a good boy. Only twelve.
Too young to be exposed to lowlifes and criminals.*

She pulled off her apron and tossed it to her son. "Hang it in
the kitchen. Then take off Sheriff Cash's badge. He's paying you a
nickel to polish it, not strut around like J. Edgar Hoover." *These
trashy magazines are inflaming his curiosity, that's all.* "And tell
Miz Russell I'll be back soon to cook lunch."

Outside, she glanced to her right, toward the jail on the other
side of the alley. *The sheriff's never there. I'll go to his barbershop.*
Lately, Mr. Hovchek had taken to parking his farm truck in the alley,
blocking it. *Poor man's so crippled up with arthritis, and this is
close when he needs to cross the street to Hansen's store.* So she had
not complained.

The hot breeze ruffled her butterscotch-brown hair as she
turned left at the gate and headed down Mercer Street. *Jeremy's
going through a phase, that's all. He just needs to be kept busy until
school starts.*

She didn't glance into the window of M'Lovely Lady Dress
Shop as she passed. Anything left from what Miz Russell paid her,
she saved for Jeremy's future. At the Quality Furniture store she
slowed to take advantage of the shade from the awning. The painting
of the frigate *Bonhomme Richard* was still in the show window. In
this Depression, it would likely sit on that wooden easel for a long

14

time. Recently she had noticed Jeremy looking at it whenever they walked by. Rachel was certain Captain John Paul Jones had not deserted *his* wife, leaving her penniless, pregnant, and seventeen.

Jeremy had never known the father who abandoned them three months after the wedding, but that was no guarantee the painting might not arouse boyish fantasies about the adventurous seafaring life. Trashy magazines weren't the only bad influences in the world. *If that blasted sailor ever comes back and I catch him around Jeremy, I'll shoot him in the leg and say, "Git! While you still have one leg to hop on."*

Before she could turn around twice, Jeremy would be grown up. Then what? *A job, a career. It's not too soon to be planning his path.* Maybe Jeremy could work hard for someone and eventually take over the store. *Yes, a businessman. Settled, stable, dependable.*

Ahead, the morning sun silhouetted Mel Frazee's stocky frame as he washed the window of the Frazee Family Funeral Parlor. Rachel nodded. "Morning, Mr. Frazee. No offense, but I hope business is slow."

"The Depression doesn't stop people from dying," Frazee laughed. "The Wall Street morticians probably got rich burying all those suicides."

Rachel smiled at Frazee as she passed. *But not the mortician business. Too grisly.*

She noticed a bolt of blue organza in the dry goods store window. Being slim, average height, and good with a needle, she made her own dresses, but never with such expensive fabric. *Maybe Jeremy could open a dry goods store. Or a hardware store.* Whatever it took, she would make sure her son grew up to lead a decent life.

Inside the store, Pastor Noble Custis was talking to someone. *Probably asking for donations for the poor. He's a good man.* Custis saw Rachel, smiled, and gave a little wave. *A church pastor?*

Jeremy? They barely earn anything. But if Jeremy "felt the call," then I suppose…

Turn around twice, and he'd be grown up and gone. Then what about her? Work for Miz Russell until she passes on? *I suppose. But then…? Can't think about that now.* For now, Jeremy must be her priority. Keep his mind off trashy crime magazines. Keep him busy.

A handbill fluttered on the whitewashed wall of the Purity Drug Store. "Greatest Little Show on Earth. Mercerville. Begins Aug. 17, 1934."

A carnival! Starting tomorrow. She remembered going to carnivals as a child. *All those colored lights! Just everywhere! The banners and flags! The rides and the lively music! People laughing, having fun.* Back then carnivals seemed to be all ice cream and cotton candy, happy feelings and the promise of an exciting future.

She scanned the handbill for the location. *We'll go. It will take his mind off criminals.*

***

Three blocks down the street, on the grassy incline beside the barbershop, Isaac dropped the gasoline can into the bed of his '28 Ford pickup and climbed into the driver's seat. He was thankful he didn't have to prime the finicky carburetor every time he went somewhere. Only sometimes. He stepped on the starter button. The truck fired right up, then quit. He mashed the button again, and the truck started.

Better stop at the filling station and have A.J. or Cyrus put a nickel's worth of gas in the can. Might need it again.

As he shifted into low gear, his sleeve scraped across the envelope in his pocket.

16

"...if you're broke, we could make a place for you here," Carl's letter had said. "It beats starving."

Leaving Mercerville would be tough even if his kid brother owned that ranch in Marfa, but Carl was only the manager. Not that Carl would lord it over him. *But I wouldn't be my own boss anymore.*

In the past, Mercer County had never had a sheriff—or needed one. But it did own a brass badge in a Bakelite box. The surrounding counties—Baxter, Marion, Izard—all had a badge *and* a sheriff to wear it. Apparently that made Mercerville's leading citizens feel humbled, so last year they decided to elect a warm body to pin the star on. The morning after the election, Judge Parmiston and Preacher Custis interrupted Isaac while he was boiling his combs and brushes and handed him the five-pointed star. Everyone agreed Isaac was right for the job of part-time sheriff. He was honest, fair, tough enough and strong enough to have handled rough characters when he was supervising railroad track-laying crews in Texas. Besides, Isaac was the only person they could persuade to accept the office.

It seemed ostentatious to wear his badge in the barbershop and downright arrogant to wear his big Colt revolver. He left that in a box at home, since the job wasn't likely to be dangerous. But if it killed him, so what? Sarah was dead.

Now, even with the sheriff's pay, ends were getting farther and farther from meeting. If he couldn't make the mortgage payments, he'd have no choice but to go work for Carl.

On the other hand, maybe it was time to leave. Every hillside reminded him of a picnic or a romantic walk or an evening in the porch swing with Sarah, planning their future. If he did have to sell the house, there wasn't much that needed repair, assuming he could even find a buyer. When he had finally pulled out of his black pit after Sarah died, he distracted himself for months by repairing and repainting. Anything to keep out of that empty bed.

Abandon the barbershop, sell the house at a loss, and leave? Or stay here with his memories and maybe lose everything anyway. Not many options. None of them good. Isaac let the truck roll down the incline and jump the curb, then he turned right.

In the vacant lot on the north side of the barbershop, the weeds drooped in the heat. Once he had dreamed of buying that lot and enlarging the barbershop. Lots of people lost their dreams in '29.

CHAPTER 4

The tall man stepped inside the boat's dilapidated cabin, picked up his Arkansas whetstone, and wedged it into a small wooden frame nailed to someone's thrown-away table. His grandpa, who raised him, was a hardscrabble farmer who used a Washita stone for kitchen knives. But for a razor-sharp hunting knife, only an Arkansas would do. This knife—*his* knife—must always be razor-sharp. There was not another like it in the whole world. Never would be.

Using his fingertips, the tall man glazed the whetstone with a drop of oil. As he stroked the blade across it, he remembered the first buck he had ever shot, a 150-pound, 8-point whitetail. Missed the head completely. Hit it in the gut. Poor creature stumbled, then ran.

Living alone in the woods, you never use a bullet you don't have to. So he had chased the buck, knife drawn, and jumped on its back. *God'll hurt you if you make an animal suffer. If there is a God.*

He had misjudged the buck's strength and had to struggle to stay on, his legs tight around the flanks, left hand grabbing the rack to keep from being stabbed by the points. Instead of making one clean slash across the throat, he had to jab into the neck again and again. Finally, the blood sprayed out. The buck fell. He stared down at it, shamed by his failure to kill pure.

After a final stroke across the whetstone, he held the knife up at eye level, letting the sunlight play along the edge. Any glint meant a nick. *A blade with nicks ain't nothing but a saw.*

That buck was the last time he ever failed to kill a thing the pure way. *A freak is a live thing, too. I won't make it suffer.*

19

***

As the Professor crossed the midway, a roughneck wearing trousers, a grimy undershirt, and a beat-up fedora trotted over. He was carrying an Egyptian mummy, its burial wrappings dragging the ground.

"Hiya, Professor. Say, could you let me have..."

"Not in this lifetime, Ace. I only give one salary advance in each millennium, and the next advance isn't until 2084."

"How did you know...?"

"Because when I passed the roughies' tent and saw you and Felix kneeling down and heard Barney yelling Hallelujah, I knew you weren't rehearsing Handel's Messiah."

"Aw, Professor, I was hot. I couldn't lose."

"Apparently you *did* lose. Were the dice crooked?"

"Yeah, sort of."

"Then why did you agree to use them?"

Ace looked sheepish. "They were my dice."

"You lost using your own loaded dice? Ace, your options are clear. Either stay out of crap games, or learn to eat grass. I recommend the first option. Grass is seriously lacking in protein." He slid the tip of his walking stick under a scrap of paper and flipped it into the air. "Now finish rewrapping the mummy and get it back to the Ten-in-One."

Ace caught the paper and threw it into a nearby trash barrel. "Listen, Professor, I'm scuffing for food 'til payday. I tried to bum two bucks off your Kraut strongman, but he suddenly forgot all his English."

"Leave Otto alone. Borrowing money you can't repay isn't a wise budgeting strategy. Especially when the lender can bend iron bars across his chest."

20

A short, olive-skinned woman wearing a gypsy skirt, gold hoop earrings, and carrying a black cloth caught up with them. "Hey, Professor. We need to talk."

"Always happy to chat with my favorite mind-reader. Any time at all. How were your profits last week?"

"You and me need to talk, that's how."

"In that case, any time except now."

"I want you to reduce the percentage you charge me," said Freda. "You said that last town would have big crowds. Ha! My Aunt Sadie's rear!"

"There was a near-tornado! An unforeseen meteorological aberration!" The Professor increased his stride and pulled ahead by a nose. "The citizens stayed huddled at home like Neanderthals trembling before the thunder god."

"Feh! Now I'll make *you* a prediction." Freda was neck and neck rounding the turn by the Whirl-a-Way. "Reduce your percentage, or I pack up the crystal ball and head home."

"Don't be rash," the Professor panted as he tried to keep ahead of her. "The Depression's playing in New York, too. Quarter of the nation out of work. Recently the Wall Street Journal…"

"Yeah, but in New York I can get arrested and have free meals," Freda said.

The three were joined by a stray dog that easily took the lead. "Save your breath for the crowd, Freda. As for you, Ace," the Professor said, trying to change the subject, "I'll do you a favor. Tell Cookhouse Lilly to put your meals on my tab until payday. But I'd better see you hustling from now on. And I don't mean hustling crap games."

As the three reached the Pitch 'n Win booth, a sun-shriveled old woman popped her head out and looked at the sky.

"Whaddya think, Professor?" she wheezed. "Another storm?"

"Ask Freda." The Professor stopped to catch his breath.

21

"She's full of predictions."

"I don't do weather," Freda said. "Tell somebody they'll meet a rich stranger, and they'll hope forever. Predict the weather wrong, and they demand a refund."

"Okay everybody, back to work." The Professor mopped his brow with his pocket square as he walked away, followed by the stray dog. "I'll be in my office."

Thelma looked at the mummy. "Sheesh, kid, don't bring that corpse over here. Reminds me of the last time I looked in a mirror."

"It's only carved balsa wood," Ace said.

"Well, cover it with something!"

"Why not?" Ace laughed, grabbed the cloth from Freda and ran.

"Hey, my backdrop!" Freda chased him, screaming "A broch tsu dir, you little vonts!"

True to his nature, Ace tripped over a guy-wire on the Knockem-Sockem-Bumpa-Car ride and stumbled headlong into the tank of water at the Duck Float game, still clutching the balsa mummy.

As the Professor neared the office truck, he called out to a portly popcorn seller wearing a straw boater. "Morris! Chase that stray dog off."

At the top of the steps into the rear of the truck, the Professor paused and looked back. High-rigger roughnecks were scrambling ant-like over the Ferris wheel. Alonso was heaving a baseball at a Kewpie on a stump and missing every time. Morris was clutching his straw hat and puffing after the hound now headed for the hot dog stand. Freda was spreading her curtain over a guy-wire to dry, and Ace was carrying a bucket to refill the Duck Float tank. The mummy was nowhere in sight.

Cookhouse Lilly walked past. "How's setup going, 'fessor?"

"As expected."

"I'm heading to town now," she said, mumbling her shopping list as she shambled toward her own truck. "Flour? Nope. Milk? Yep. Eggs for sure. Always need eggs..."

As he unlocked the door, the Professor took another look at the scurry stretching from the front gate, past the Ten-in-One and the midway rides, beyond the girly show and back to the carnies' living area. *'An ill-favored thing, but mine own.'*

Once again a world was forming from chaos, and behold, it was good.

***

Isaac recognized the woman stepping off the curb to flag him down. It was Rachel Barlow, Miz Russell's assistant at the boarding house. Occasionally Isaac's appetite rebelled against his own cooking, and he would break down and spend forty-five cents for the complete dinner there. Rachel's boy Jeremy would talk Isaac's ear off about gangsters while Miz Russell flitted around the long table, nattering as she and Rachel served the ham or chicken or whatever the meal was for that day.

Isaac pulled over as Rachel strode confidently to the passenger window. She wasn't wearing a hat, although most women wouldn't leave home without wearing at least a pillbox. That supported what Isaac had heard: Rachel Barlow was a bright woman who tended to do things her own way. *She doesn't look cheerful like she usually does. Something's bothering her.*

"Morning, Mrs. Barlow. Is there a problem?"

"Mr. Cash, did you allow Jeremy to borrow Police Gazette magazines from your barbershop?"

"No. And when he's there, I keep him too busy to read."

"Then he's sneaking them out. Twice I've caught him

23

reading under the covers with a flashlight. He claims he borrowed them."

"I suppose if he brings them back, that's true. Sort of." Sitting there was wasting gas, but if he shut off the engine, it might not start again. That would be embarrassing in the middle of town, right in front of God and everybody.

"It certainly isn't true," she said. "And lately he daydreams and doesn't do chores properly. He's had your badge for two days and still hasn't polished it."

"No hurry. I seldom need it."

"The illustrations are trashy enough. Women barely keeping their dresses on." Rachel pulled the magazine out of her purse and dropped it on the seat beside Isaac. "And the articles!" 'Chicago's Own Jack the Ripper' See for yourself! 'Earle Nelson, Gorilla Slayer of Boarding House Ladies.' I mean, really!"

"How about if I speak to him when he brings back my badge? I'll emphasize honesty, obeying your mother, not talking back. That sort of thing."

"Thank you, Mr. Cash. I'd appreciate that. It isn't easy for him without a father." She brushed some stray hairs off her brow. "Anyway, at least he doesn't backtalk."

"Say, does Miz Russell need any fresh eggs? Cheap?" Isaac said. "I could bring a dozen right up."

"That's thoughtful, but I've already done the shopping." She turned and started toward the sidewalk, then called back, "Thank you again for your help."

As Isaac turned onto the main road and headed toward the carnival, he thought about the barbershop and the mortgage. He thought about his brother in Texas and about the possibility of having to go and work for him. He thought about his truck and hoped it wouldn't give any more trouble on the trip to the carnival. And he thought about the carnival and hoped those people wouldn't give him any trouble, either. Amid all of it, the conversation with Rachel Barlow kept weaving in and out. He couldn't get seem to get it off his mind. *I wonder if this heat is starting to get to me?*

CHAPTER 5

"Rube on the lot." Stringbean the Human Skeleton left the door open as he entered the stuffy office truck. "He's just strolling around. Didn't see no badge."

As usual, nothing was out of place inside the truck. Curtains across the cab end shielded the Professor's living quarters. Through the narrow gap, Stringbean could see the child-sized bed and the wardrobe trunk full of fancy suits. Beside it was another trunk with 130 of the world's greatest books, all somewhat worn because the Professor never slept more than four hours a night.

"You finish that Keynes book yet?" Stringbean asked. "Can I borrow it?

"*Monetary Reform*? It's on the chair. Consider it a gift." The Professor was seated at a battered desk cut down to suit his height. "He's clever, but the current situation destroys his business cycles theory."

Other than the desk chair and a loveseat which had both also been made lower, the only seating was a wooden kitchen chair, uncomfortable enough to discourage long visits. String eased his seventy-nine-pound body into the loveseat. His knobby knees came up almost to his chin. Leaning against the loveseat was a long rod with a spring-loaded clamp on one end and a wire running to a grip at the other end. Baby Elaine had invented the device to help the Professor grasp items above his reach. Stringbean used it to lift the book from the chair and bring it to himself.

"Is the guy giving people heat?" said the Professor.

"Naw. Just strolling toward the Ten-in-One, nice as you

please."

"What am I looking for?"

"Typical rube, looking down his nose at us," Stringbean said. "Maybe forty at most. Scots-Irish face. Average build. Straw fedora. Blue suit about ten years old. Didn't see no badge."

The Professor slid off his chair. "Move your bony carcass, String." Stringbean stood as quickly as was prudent for a man with pencil-thin bones. Together they dragged the loveseat away from the wall, revealing a trap door in the floor. The Professor pulled a key ring from his pocket and unfastened the padlock. Inside the compartment was a metal box. He unlocked it, removed one of several envelopes filled with cash, then locked the box back into its hiding place. He lifted his coat off the back of his chair, and shrugged into it. "How's setup?"

"Almost back on schedule," the Human Skeleton said. "Willie's stepping off the layout of the last few game joints. Leroy's helping, so it's going faster. Hutchins says the rides will be ready before dark."

"How about our people?"

"Deena's shoulder is fine. Elaine's staying out of the heat. I saw Ramon, Monsieur Louvre, and Stani at breakfast. Your Kraut friend drove off on another secret mission, probably to destroy America."

"Don't concern yourself about Otto. He's my problem," the Professor said. "How's your wife?"

"Ex-wife. Seesla divorced me again," said Stringbean.

"Again? You two go around almost as often as the Ferris wheel."

"Well, she's still sweet as sugar and busy as a bee. She's at the Hootchy girls' trailer, mending a costume," Stringbean said. "And how's the Professor?"

"The Professor would be a helluva lot better if this outfit

would start showing a profit," the Professor said.

"We've had tight seasons before."

"True, but none of them was our *last* season. This one might earn that distinction." The Professor picked up the bribe money envelope and pushed it into his inside coat pocket. "Time to ice the local constabulary," he said. "Mind the store, will you?"

"Okay. Provided I can stay awake in this metropolis."

"We've landed in a sleepy spot, to be sure." The Professor looked out the doorway over the carnival. "With luck, a carnival will bring some excitement to this town." He went carefully down the steps and started toward the Ten-in-One.

***

Isaac estimated the Ten-in-One tent was about fifty feet long. In front of the entrance was a wooden stage and on either side of the stage, hanging down the tent's sides, were canvas posters with garish cartoon drawings of freaks. The air filtering through the entrance flaps seemed cooler, so he decided to step inside and look around.

As he walked in, he saw a smaller stage directly ahead, about ten feet wide. Onstage at the left stood an upright white board, six feet tall and four feet wide, with the life-sized outline of a human painted in the center. Across the top, in bright red letters, it said "Ramon del Corte ~ World's Greatest Knife Thrower." Then in smaller letters, "With the Beautiful Ramona." There were approximately a million cuts in the board's surface, but not a nick inside the outline, so maybe Ramon was as good as the sign claimed. For Ramona's sake, Isaac hoped so.

Various dumbbells and barbells lay near the back of the stage beside a black case with the name "Ivan the Terrible" stenciled in white on the side.

28

At the far end of the tent, one corner was completely enclosed by curtains. A large sign read, "Astounding Medical Oddity! Half-Man-Half-Woman!" The remaining interior sides of the tent were taken up by areas, each about eight feet wide, separated from each other by curtains. All of the curtained areas contained a small wooden platform, except one. That area had a low wooden fence surrounding it, and instead of a stage, there was only dirt. A sign hung on the fence: "Stay Back! The Drug Fiend Thrashes in Unspeakable Hellish Agony and May Splash You with Filth!"

The curtained enclosure next to that one had a stage like the others, but on this stage was a wide bench with high sides and back, like a throne. It was gold with pink flowers, and was spacious enough to seat two monarchs easily.

"The carnival's closed," said a high-pitched voice. "You aren't allowed in here."

Isaac turned to face a short, petite girl who looked like she might have been in her third or fourth year of high school.

"I was just looking around," he said. "You the owner's daughter?"

"The owner doesn't have children. I perform in here."

"Oh. I guess I thought the show was just, uh..."

"Freaks? You can say the word. We hear it every day. Personally, I think everyone's a freak in some way or other. So depending on how you define freak, maybe I'm one. I'm a contortionist. Know what that means?"

"Sure. You just look a little young to be in a carnival."

"I'm almost eighteen. Old enough to be doing whatever I'm good at." She tilted her head to one side and looked Isaac up and down. "I could put my left heel inside my mouth and my right heel against my spine? Would that be proof enough?"

"No need. I don't doubt you."

"In that case, you can leave now," the girl said, "so I don't have to yell for someone to escort you out."

Isaac smiled. "Didn't mean to alarm you," he said. "I'll be on my way."

As he came out of the Ten-in-One entrance, he saw a carny fastening down the bottoms of the banners. Isaac shaded his eyes with one hand and studied the hand-painted lettering.

ALIVE! * FREAKS! * ALIVE!
10 Attractions for one Price! * See them all!
Only 25 CENTS!

Reckon I could paint the sign on my window myself and not have to pay?

Baby Elaine - America's Fattest Little Lady!
Princess of Pulchritude! Queen of Quantity!
Empress of the Avoirdupois! 575 pounds!

Suppose I traced the letters from the broken window onto butcher paper.

Monsieur Louvre - the Human Art Gallery!
Tattoos Enshroud His Entire Anatomy!
His body is a living canvas!

Then I could tape that on the inside of the new window.

The Evils of Reefers and Dope!
A Once-Wholesome American Youth
His Brain Degraded by Illicit Chemicals!

That is, provided I remember where I stored that half can of leftover paint.

.

Deena -The Human Pretzel!
Twists Her Body into Impossible Shapes!
Stuffs Herself into a Cracker Barrel!

Oh, yes. Beside the trash barrel in the storeroom.

Special ATTRACTION ~ for Adults Only!
Paul/Paulette ~ Half Man-Half Woman!
Male?? Female?? Both!!!

If I do it well enough, maybe I could earn extra money painting windows when barbering was slow. Half barber, half sign painter.

A blank section on the canvas seemed to whisper—

FOR THE FIRST TIME ANYWHERE!
* ISAAC L. CASH *
Prince of the Pigmentary Pallet
Baron of the Barber's Blade!
He'll Astound You by Doing Everything HIMSELF!

Isaac wiped his brow and looked around for water. *Now I'm sure the heat's getting to me*

***

The clank-bang-growl of midway rides being tested was a mother's lullaby to the Professor as he approached the Ten-in-One. He spotted the open-mouthed rube staring at the banners. *Flash grabs them every time. Never skimp on the banner line.*

"Sorry, friend." The Professor switched on his best smile. "Closed until bright and early tomorrow."

Stringbean was right; the towner didn't look like a cop. But who else would show up before opening day except a lawman wanting a bribe?

"Bring your kids to the world's greatest pony ride," the Professor shifted into a pitch. "We have the actual burro ridden by the notorious Pancho Villa while evading heroic General 'Black Jack' Pershing after the cowardly attack on the sleepy hamlet of Columbus, New Mexico, back in Ought-16."

The rube stared at him. Probably never saw a dwarf before.

"Admittedly, it's a fairly old donkey by now," the Professor shrugged. "We also have a thoroughbred descended from the legendary Dan Patch. Tomorrow, this serene Arkansas landscape will have transmogrified into Pinckney's Exposition for Educational Enlightenment and Peripatetic Parade of Natural Wonders."

He thrust a business card in front of Isaac. "I'm Professor Desmond A. Pinckney, the Third, promoter extraordinaire and proprietor of our traveling establishment. At your service."

He slid the card back into his pocket. He never let anyone examine it lest they notice the misspelled word. Once business improved he'd have new cards printed. Until then, a good banner line was an investment, but business cards were merely an expense.

The rube still hadn't blinked. "It's a business card, friend," the Professor said. "All the rage in big cities."

"Oh, I've seen business cards before," the rube said. "I was just wondering about the word 'peripathetic.' I'm thinking it doesn't need the 'h'."

Damn cop. The Professor maintained a determined smile. "And you, sir...?"

"Cash." The rube extended his hand. "Isaac Cash, Mercer County sheriff. Folks wanted me to make sure your show is safe."

The Professor reached into his coat for the bribe. *Cash, huh? He gets right to the point.*

"Some dishonest outfits give carnivals a bad name," Sheriff Cash continued. "Stealing, cheating the marks, attempting to bribe officials. We don't tolerate that."

At the word "bribe," the Professor let the envelope slide back into his pocket. *An honest sheriff? 'O day and night, but this is wondrous strange.'*

"Marks *is* the carnival slang for local people, isn't it?" Sheriff Cash asked.

"Ah...well, low class shows might use that term." The Professor felt in his other pockets for some free passes. "But our employees have the highest respect for our, uh, highly-respected clientele. I hire nothing but honest, hard-working men and women. That includes the Half-Man-Half-Woman, who qualifies on both counts."

He located several passes in an outside pocket. "It's shocking that anyone would offer monetary gratuities to peace officers. However, I hope you'll accept these passes. Good for any ride."

"I suppose if I were wearing my badge," Isaac said, "I wouldn't need a pass."

"Very true," said the Professor. "You're always welcome. Bring your wife and children anytime. Wear your badge and give the passes to your brother or somebody."

"Don't have a wife, and my only brother is in Marfa, Texas." The sheriff peered at two carnies walking past, but showed no indication whether he had seen their photos on any post office wall. "I do know some youngsters, though. So I guess passes would be

33

okay. Thanks."

"Now," the Professor said, "would you like a tour of the Greatest Little Show on Earth?"

"The entire earth?"

"Okay, parts of North America. But substantial parts. The important parts."

"Thanks for the offer," Sheriff Cash said. "But you probably have work to do. I'll just wander around, if that's okay."

"Wander, by all means. If you need anything, that red truck is my office."

"Oh," Isaac said, "there's one thing I promised someone I'd ask. Do you have a snake lady?"

"Seesla. Beautiful girl, except her skin is like a snake."

"Is it real?"

"Absolutely. It's a rare non-contagious condition called ichthyosis. It's painful and makes her joints stiff, but she's brave. Never misses a show."

"So there's no snake in the act?"

"There was, but she doesn't use it anymore."

"Did it die?"

"We don't think so. It seems to change position when nobody's watching. But don't worry, it's not hot."

"Hot?"

"Poisonous. But it isn't."

"No venom?"

"No teeth, either. Too old. Thirty years at least. Seesla has to spoon-feed it mice, which isn't easy. She stopped using it in the act because it kept falling asleep in her arms. A limp snake doesn't impress anybody."

"Thirty years, eh? What's that in human years?"

"A lot longer than you'll live." The Professor tipped his hat and started to walk away, then added, "Or me."

CHAPTER 6

Inside the boat's cabin, the tall man laid his .270 Winchester Model 54 on the table. He removed the Weaver scope, wrapped it in a piece of oilcloth, and slipped it inside his shirt. He wouldn't take the rifle. A killshot in gusting winds, over the four hundred yards from Meekam's Hill to the carnival, was impossible. Anyway, a rifle is a kind of machine, and machines aren't natural things.

Not for this. This death must be pure.

At noon, he started walking the dirt road paralleling the river. After ten minutes, the road ended. He clambered down the riverbank and followed the waterline for another twenty minutes, then scrambled back up and went cross country to reach the back of Meekam's Hill. Ten minutes later he was almost to the top.

Near the top he used the pine trees, black oaks, and leatherwood shrubs for cover as he moved around to the flat side of the hill looking southwest toward the abandoned pasture called Meekam's Field. He wished he were closer, but with the paved county highway between him and the carnival, he might have been spotted. Besides, he needed the altitude in order to get a good view of the carnival below and locate the thing it carried with it.

***

Glancing back to make sure the sheriff wasn't following him, the Professor crossed to the other side of the midway, where a powerfully-built black man was pacing off distances and pointing to

35

the ground. With him was a strapping, well-muscled young white man with a strong resemblance to movie heartthrob Johnny "Tarzan" Weissmuller. He stood in a classic Hollywood pose, left hand on his hip, right hand holding a heavy short-handled sledge hammer.

"This here'll be the flat joint, Leroy." The black man marked the dirt with the heel of his shoe.

"Gotcha, Willie." Leroy dropped to one knee and drove a sixteen-inch stake halfway into the ground. Wham. Wham.

"Flat joint, opposite corner," Willie made another mark. Leroy drove another stake. Wham. Wham.

"Next we got the balloon-dart game," Willie said.

"Or the horse race game would fit, right?" said Leroy. Tomorrow Leroy would be one of the Ten-in-One's most popular performers, especially with young ladies.

"Naw, not the horse race." Willie pulled the red bandana from around his neck and mopped his brow. "The flat joint and the horse joint are both for big spenders. The jointies get mad if you make 'em compete with each other. So I'll put a diddle-e-squat game here."

"Diddle-e-what?"

"Diddle means a nickel. Squat's a dime. After the mark loses his last buck on the high-roller game, the diddle-e-squat next door still has a chance to get his last nickel."

"Willie," the Professor called out as he came closer, "you'll have to finish the layout by yourself. I need Leroy."

"Aw, Professor, I got carnies pitching hissy fits because we're behind schedule telling them where to set up."

"I'll send Ace to help you. He apparently has too much free time." The Professor motioned Leroy over. "Leroy, there's a sheriff wandering the lot."

"Gee, honest?"

"Unfortunately he is. Go around and tell everyone this

36

lawman can't be patched," the Professor said. "Tell Billy B-Ball to hide the oval basketball hoops. And tell Hutchins to hide the rigged Wheel of Fortune. No gaffs on anything. It'll hurt profits, but we have to be one-hundred-percent honest everywhere. At least everywhere we might get caught."

"Strictly legit. Right! Should I hide your rubber Chinese Devil Baby that's in the giant bottle of alcohol?"

"Not *that* honest. This guy's a cop, not a doctor. The pickled punk will fool him like it fools the other marks," the Professor said. "And go to the Hootchy-Kootchy girls and tell them they can't work strong in this town. They have to put away the seven veils and clean up the dance."

"Go back to being Hawaiian Hula Girls, gotcha. Edna has a cold anyway. She won't mind wearing more clothes, even if it's just a grass skirt. On second thought, suppose she has hay fever, then the grass..."

"Get moving! We don't have time to shoot the darn breeze."

The Professor caught himself just in time. If he had used a stronger word than darn to the cuss-free, smoke-free, liquor-free youth, Leroy might have gotten that hurt look in his eyes, like a puppy when you swat it with a rolled-up Saturday Evening Post, and it doesn't know why. Leroy was tolerant about carnies cursing in general, but swearing at him personally was offensive. It might even harm his performance as the permanently-insane drug addict in the "Evils of Reefers and Dope" act. There was nothing less convincing to an audience than a crazed dope fiend moping around with hurt feelings.

"Professor, can't you talk to your girls instead? They always try to get me into their trailer. When I left Duluth, the last thing I said to Mom... well, the last thing was goodbye, but..."

"Just go!"

"Okay, Professor. I'll tell everybody to keep things strictly legit."

"And don't let that sheriff catch you doing it."

"Gotcha. We don't want the sheriff to know we're being honest." Leroy handed the hammer to Willie and trotted away.

Good looks. Talent. Brains. The Professor watched the strong young body moving fluidly across the lot. *Oh, well. Two out of three isn't bad.*

In this case, however, it was the Professor himself who had spent a lifetime being "two out of three." Somebody once said, "Nobody said Life is fair." Somebody was right.

As the Professor headed back to his office truck, Herbert Hutchins, the Professor's business partner, hailed him from the carousel.

"What is it, Hutch?" the Professor said. "Please tell me the Flying Jenny isn't down."

"Relax. Nothing serious," said Hutchins wiping his hands with a rag as he moved around a painted wooden stallion and stepped off the Jenny's circular platform. "Just greasing the connector to the drive motor. Gotta do it more often in this hot weather." He looked around as if making sure no one could hear their conversation. "Naw, it's about Otto. People been talking."

"Carnies, you mean. Who?"

"Let's just say people." He looked around again. "Leave it at that for now. But people are wondering why he leaves the lot at night so often. Even misses the last show in the Ten-in-One."

"Tell these 'people,' whoever they are, to stop thinking about Otto and stick to their own jobs," the Professor said. "I know he needs to leave sometimes, but he's a first-class audience draw, and that's the deal I made with him so he could join us. He's pulling his share of the load. Now, is that it?"

"Naw, there's more. Some of my guys don't like that he's always trying to make time with the women. Especially being a

38

German and all."

"Austrian," said the Professor. "Just tell your roughies to do their jobs and mind their business. The women all know they only have to tell me if some guy is bothering them, and I'll take care of it. That includes your roughies. And you'll back me up with them, right?"

"Yeah, of course! We're partners. I always back you." Hutchins looked around again. "Ain't no good will come from this, if Otto acts like he ain't one of us. The Human Skeleton already hates him."

"Stringbean won't cause any trouble. It's not in his nature," said the Professor. "But okay, I'll say something to Otto. I'll instruct him to be more congenial with the men and less personable with the women. He's a trouper, he'll do what's best for the show. Good enough?"

"Sure. I just want to know that this Otto is with it and for it," Hutch said. "I'll leave him up to you." He turned to leave, then turned back. "Coming to the party tonight. Cut some jackies and have a drink with us?"

"Wish I could, but I have to take a hard look at the bookkeeping tonight. Every ticket counts this season."

Hutchins watched the Professor stride away. *There'll be big trouble if that German ain't with us and for us.*

***

The tall man knelt behind a low crepe myrtle and broke several branches downward to hide his legs. Then he rested the telescope on a limb in the center. A dark cloud muted the sun's glare as he focused the scope on the carnival. Some men were climbing over a giant wheel while others were putting up tents or assembling large machines. At the far end of the field were only cars, trucks, tents, and trailers. A man had propped a large plank against the side of a trailer and was throwing knives into it.

That fellow's crazy to treat knives that way. But he don't look crazy. In fact, everyone the tall man saw through the scope looked normal. There was not a monster among them.

CHAPTER 7

Inside the Hootchy-Kootchy girls' trailer, Seesla the Snake Girl knelt with a handful of silk scarves. Hector the eight-foot anaconda was curled up in a cardboard box nearby, dreaming of sugar-plum rodents or whatever aging constrictors fantasize about.

The ichthyosis that made Seesla's milky English skin red with rows of thick, dark, spiny scales often made her fingers too stiff for the creative needlework she loved—crewel and petit point. Her challenge today, however, was simple: alter Louise Smithson's seven-veils costume so it would cover the ten pounds she had gained during the season. Or at least provide coverage up to the point in the dance when Louise had discarded six of the seven veils. After that, nobody cared if a curve here or there had a larger radius than last season.

"Do try not to wiggle, Lulu," Seesla said. "I don't want to muck this up. There's a good girl."

As Seesla pinned scarves on her, Louise stood on a low hassock in her step-in chemise, as more-or-less motionless as her exuberant nature permitted. Pretty even without makeup, she could easily have passed for a brunette version of movie star Jean Harlow as she gazed through the screen door, hoping to catch a breeze. With luck, she might also catch a glimpse of handsome Leroy, who had joined the show this season. And if he in turn noticed her half-dressed curves...well, that couldn't be helped.

"Leroy," she would say, batting her eyelashes like her movie idol, Claudette Colbert, "the Bible says you and me are God's children, right? So that makes us sort of brother and sister, right?

41

Well, a brother shouldn't feel embarrassed to see his sister in her scanties, should he?"

Then Leroy would put his strong arms around her, like the actor did with Claudette Colbert in "The Wiser Sex." Or maybe that other flick....

"Hey, ladies! Anybody home?" Leroy knocked on the screen door.

Edna Hilliard, the other Hootchy-Kootchy dancer, quickly grabbed a dress on a clothes hanger and held it up in front of Louise. "What is it, Leroy?" Edna said.

"The Professor says you can't do the veils dance here. He couldn't bribe the sheriff. You have to be hula girls instead."

"Thanks, Leroy," Edna said. "Want to come in and chat?"

"Sorry, but I have to warn everybody. Oh, hi, Louise. You look real good behind that dress. You should wear clothes more often." Leroy said as he walked away.

"Dang, Edna! You didn't let me get a word in edgeways," Louise said, stamping her foot. "And I knew something clever to say, too."

"Keep still!" Seesla snapped. "I've wasted half my morning on these bloody veils, and now we can't even use them!"

Seesla's proper British upbringing meant she almost never swore. Edna sat down on the hassock beside her and laid her hand on Seesla's shoulder "This isn't like you. Sees'. Is the heat bothering you?"

"My sweat glands work fine, thank you."

"Leave her, Edna." Louise said, "As they say, it's not the heat, it's the humility."

"Lulu, would you make sense, please?" said Edna.

"Then you *use* some sense." Louise closed the door. "Seesla is a girl, just like you and me, and the best-looking guy in two states was here, and he barely even nodded to her."

42

"Don't blame Leroy," Seesla said. "With my skin, I'm invisible to every man except the rubes in the audience. Leroy looks like Saint George, and I look like the dragon."

"Sorry, Sees'. I wasn't thinking," Edna said. "I mean, standing next to Louise, I don't get looked at much, either. I didn't mean to hurt you, Honey. You're our friend, so we don't even notice your skin."

"Yeah," said Louise. "We love you the way you are. You're one of us."

"It's okay. Really," Seesla said. "I've got String. I'm not interested in Leroy."

"Lulu, you should forget about Leroy, too," Edna said to Louise. "Those polite religious types usually turn out to be the dangerous ones."

Louise giggled. "That's kinda what I'm hoping."

***

Ace snugged up the bolt on the Screamin'-Meemie, laid down the wrench, and pulled his sweat rag from his pocket.

Might as well commit any sin you want 'cause Hell can't be no hotter than this.

No one was watching, so he slipped into the only Screamin'-Meemie gondola that was catching some shade.

The guys from the flat joint are playing cards tonight. I could win back everything I lost at craps. He stretched his legs across the seat and over the side. *But I can't get in the game without a stake. Damn!*

The sweat rag was too wet to soak up any more, but Ace scrubbed it across his face anyway. He felt lucky. Strong lucky. He had to get a stake somehow. Looking through the support girders of the ride, he saw Otto drive his fancy car back onto the lot and stop briefly to talk to Freda.

Damn stingy Kraut. Wouldn't talk to a lowly roughneck, but he's got plenty of time for a Jewess.

Ace picked up the wrench and threw it. It clanged against a girder, then dropped into the weeds. *He could have loaned me two bucks, easy.* Ace picked up the wrench and watched Otto parking his car behind his tent.

Serve him right if somebody snuck into his tent tonight during the party. Probably hides money in his mattress. Or a false bottom in his trunk.

Ace flipped the wrench into the air and caught it as it spun. *Just enough for a stake. I'd pay it back when I won.*

***

The monster had to be somewhere in the carnival below. The tall man drew the scope down the lot from the living area to the front entrance. On the left, people were going into a big tent. A man came out, put something to his mouth, and bit off a hunk. Bread? Meat? Was that tent where carnival people ate?

Monsters have to eat, too. Must be it gets fed somewhere.

Lower down the hill was a tall tree. If he climbed it, he'd have the same altitude, but be twenty yards closer. He stood and aimed the scope at the upper branches. They looked strong enough to support him. Bringing the scope down from his eye, he glimpsed something that gave him a shock like touching a Model A's engine coil with wet hands. Quickly he looked through the eyepiece again. This time he saw only tents, trailers, and the man throwing knives.

Damn! It was there. He scanned the line of booths coming down the far side of the lot, but saw nothing. He lowered the scope and squinted against the baking noon sun. *It was there!*

44

CHAPTER 8

When Isaac returned to his shop, the pickup was low on fuel, so he parked it and walked the four blocks to the Mercerville Sheriff's Office and Jail. Since being appointed sheriff, Isaac had made it a practice to go to the jailhouse on the first day of each month to unlock the cell several times, so the lock wouldn't get rusty. Although today wasn't the first, Isaac wanted the cell in good working order, just in case Fieldman's warnings were justified.

The small brick jailhouse contained one desk, one wooden chair, and one cell, its barred window looking out across the alley to the side of Miz Russell's boarding house. Isaac waggled the door back and forth to shoo out the stale musty air, then plopped his hat on the old desk. He took the cell key from the bottom desk drawer and exercised the lock.

So far, Isaac had only arrested local men who needed to sleep off a drunk. They could be trusted to stay in an unlocked cell without supervision because they understood the rule: If you stay inside, the townspeople won't have to chase you down. Nobody will get hot and sweaty and irritable. Most important, you won't get hurt.

Isaac took his brother's letter out of his pocket for another reading.

"Hey Isaac,

Hope this finds you healthy. Summer here is hotter than a Mexican halapenyo. Awful hard on stock. Sorry to hear about your mortgage. If you lose the barbershop, the owner reckons we could make a place for you here. I told him about your experiences building the railroad and also that you know which end of a horse to

hang the bridle on. Won't pay much, but you'll have three hots and a
cot. Beats starving. Let me know soon if you want the job.

-- Carl

"*P.S. Passenger trains run twice a day from San Antonio. If*
you have to hop a boxcar, drop off in Nopal, before Marfa. The boys
say there's no railroad bull working the yards there. Find a
telephone, and I'll send someone to fetch you."

"Well?" Bernard Fieldman stepped across the threshold into
the jailhouse.

"Pretty well." Isaac put the letter into his pocket. "As long as
my bad knee doesn't flare up."

"You know what I mean. Did you chase that carnival away?"

"Bernard," Isaac took a breath, "folks *need* some fun to take
their mind off their troubles."

"Unless trouble is what that carnival is bringing,"

Isaac explained that yes, he had gone to the carnival, taken a
good look, even chatted with some of the carnies. He had seen
nothing alarming.

"We've known each other, what, twelve years?" Fieldman
said. "Sometimes I get strong impressions about things. I've learned
to pay attention to impressions. That's made me successful. Lately
I'm even getting attention from important people in state
government. The welfare of this town is always my highest priority.
Please listen, Isaac. I'm dead certain you should send that carnival
away *right now*!"

"I appreciate your counsel, Bernard, but I'm sure we'll be
safe from looting and pillaging for the whole time they're here."

"Fine, fine, I won't tell you how to do your job. But seems to
me a real sheriff wouldn't be a welcoming committee for drifters.
Nevertheless, be it on your head." He turned sharply and strode
across the street to his two-story financial empire.

46

Isaac put on his hat, locked the door, and headed back to his two-chair tonsorial emporium. *I imagine a real sheriff wouldn't cut hair, either.* The truth was, Mercer County didn't need much of a sheriff, and that's exactly what they had.

"Afternoon, Mr. Cash." A tall man with horn-rimmed glasses caught up with Isaac a block down the street.

"Afternoon, Elmo. Is it later than I think, or did Bernard Fieldman close up early?"

"Oh, we'd never close the bank before three. That would make people nervous. Uh, that carnival..." Elmo stammered, "Is it going to be dangerous?"

"Been listening to Mr. Bank President, have you?"

"Paying attention is how a man gets successful. I'm fortunate to work for a natural leader like Mr. Fieldman. When I hear him tell people the sheriff ought to run the carnival off, I perk up my ears."

"This time, Elmo, you can just perk up one ear. Bernard's not happy with me, but he's worked up over nothing. That carnival is no worse than any other."

"Great! My boy came home all lathered up after seeing those handbills..." He stopped when Isaac raised a hand.

"Elmo, I just remembered. The carnival gave me some free tickets for rides," Isaac said, reaching into his pocket. "Have fun."

"Say, that's swell! Thanks, Mr. Cash. We'll leave the babies with Grandma and have ourselves a fine time." Turning the corner, Elmo called back, "Thanks again."

Isaac walked on, remembering Bernard's "welcoming committee" crack. Now here he was—a sheriff—handing out passes like some carnival advance man. Not the best way to earn people's respect. He'd better remind Jeremy to bring back that sheriff's badge. Soon.

As Isaac passed the M'Lovely Lady Dress Shop doorway, a hand reached out and grabbed his arm.

CHAPTER 9

"Isaac! I'm glad I caught you," Preacher Noble Custis said breathlessly. "I'm telling everyone about our carnival."

"It's perfectly safe, Preacher." Isaac freed his arm from the preacher's hand. "I went out there today."

"No, no. *Our* carnival. At the church!" Tall, with slightly graying hair and a nice but inexpensive suit, Custis put on his gray trilby hat as he stepped out of the doorway. "I'll explain. In making my visits to comfort and encourage my flock, I'm pained to see how this depression is hurting Mercervillians. No one has a penny to spare. Yet apparently some fool bureaucrat has permitted a carnival to come here. Well, Camilla suggested we organize a free church carnival. And I thought, perfect! We'll give the devil some competition, as Martin Luther said. Or maybe John Wesley. It will raise people's spirits. And!... Bill Berkeley is coming to speak!"

"Bill...?"

"The preacher who's running for the U.S. Congress. His prayer team has been chasing carnivals all summer."

"And when they catch one?"

"They witness! They exhort everyone to close down sideshows that exploit poor feeble-minded people, like fat ladies and dwarves and such. They have armbands and placards and everything. The prayer team, I mean. Not the dwarves."

"Matter of fact, I met a dwarf this morning. Nothing wrong with *his* mind," Isaac said. "Talked like a college professor."

"Brother Bill says they can be trained to seem intelligent. Dwarves, I mean, not professors. He's very compassionate about defective people. It's our duty to institutionalize them, he says, so they can be cared for properly. When he gets to Congress, he'll pass eugenics bills to purify America from the tragedy of disadvantaged births."

"How'd you meet this fellow?"

"Actually, I haven't yet. His Commandant phoned and said Brother Berkeley is in the area chasing carnivals and would speak for free. Except for a love offering, of course."

"Commandant?"

"Of the prayer team. The Emancipate the Exploited and Free the Freaks Rescue Raiders."

"Want to run that by a little slower?" Isaac said.

"They call it the Double-E Double-F Double-R, for short."

"Well, that *is* shorter," Isaac said. "Anyhow, good luck with your carnival."

"It will cheer up the whole town. I'm planning charades and sack races. Camilla's asking people to bake pies for a pie-eating contest. That's why I'm glad I caught you."

"I don't bake pies."

"Actually, I was thinking we could offer...free haircuts?"

"I'd need to give that some thought, Preacher." Isaac nodded and started walking away. "Maybe next time."

***

Somewhere. Somewhere. Somewhere, thought the tall man.

Then he caught sight of it again. Through the scope, he watched the thing weave between tents, trailers, trucks, and cars. He followed its progress until it disappeared into a small tent. *It lives in a tent? They don't lock it in a cage?*

He sat down on a rock and put the scope back inside his shirt. *I've seen it.* His hands were shaking. *It really exists.*

***

As Isaac passed old Judge Parmiston's white two-story house, smells of supper cooking filtered through the screen door. The house had a lawyer's shingle out front and a covered porch wrapping around the ground floor. In all Mercerville, only Bernard Fieldman's house was bigger.

"Isaac! Step up here a minute," the Judge called out from the front porch swing. "Bernard Fieldman tells me you let a carnival come to town without a permit. Is that the whole truth?"

"Yes, Judge, I..."

"Then I believe you. Always were an honest boy. I remember your mother Bessie. Fine lady. Pretty little thing, too."

"Bessie was my aunt."

"I surely did like your mother. Almost asked Bessie to marry me," he said. "Say, if I had married Bessie, I'd be your daddy. Ever stop to think about that?"

"Not really. Rose was my mother."

"That's irrelevant and immaterial, son. Point is, if I'd married your mama, you'd be a lawyer today, instead of a barber. Maybe justice of the peace. See my point?"

"Uh, I suppose if you had married my mother, I'd be someone else, if that's what...."

"You're missing the point. Point is, you're the law around here. You have to enforce the town by-laws." The Judge leaned over the porch railing, and stared down at Isaac. "I helped write them, did you know that?"

"Yes sir, I believe I did."

"But have you ever read the document, is what I'm asking. Just answer the question."

"I have, in fact. It's..."

50

"That's my point exactly!" He pounded the porch rail with his folded-up magazine. "Just tell us, if you would, what the by-laws say about permits?"

"Nothing."

"I'm referring to people being required to obtain permits for entertainment and things. Tell us what it says about that."

"The subject isn't mentioned, Your Honor."

"It isn't?" The old man scowled. "Son, I helped write that document, so be careful how you answer. You're asking the court to believe there is not one word about permits?"

"No sir. It's more a general..."

"This is a gross miscarriage, I have to say. This must be rectified expeditiously. I'll have to rewrite the by-laws. A town can't have people doing things without permits. Who knows where that might lead?" He thought for a second, then said, "What are you going to do about it, Isaac?"

"About the by-laws? Or a permit?"

"The carnival! That's the issue before the court today. The paperwork can wait. What does it take to get you moving, son?"

"Well, Judge, I figured folks could just go and have fun."

"Without permits?"

"No permits required. Just have fun. I'm sure they'll be safe."

"That's why we *have* permits! To protect people from things!" Judge Parmiston sat down and opened his magazine. "Well, all right, but be more careful next time. We can't have order and stability if people can do things without getting permission."

"I'll keep that in mind," Isaac said as he turned back to the sidewalk.

"One more thing," the judge called out. "You're the sheriff. You ought to be wearing your badge!"

The tall man waited all afternoon, hoping for another glimpse of the creature, but it never showed up again. Then at sundown, using bushes and trees for cover, he made his way to the bottom of the hill to wait. He was too focused and intense to feel hunger, but just in case, he had a piece of jerky in his pocket.

There was a shallow dry gully between the hill and the highway. He could hide in the brush there until dark. There was even a small boulder where he could hide the scope, wrapped in the oilcloth and covered with brush. It was as if the whole universe had joined in harmony to provide everything he needed on this most important day. Nature was on his side.

Or God. If there is a God.

CHAPTER 10

"That look round to you?" Billy B-Ball laid down the ball-peen hammer and held the basketball hoop in front of Stringbean's face.

"Round enough for rubes," the Human Skeleton said.

"Took me twenty damn minutes. I still have to do the other one, and it's almost dark," the game operator said. "Forgot to bring the round hoops this trip. Who could predict we'd find an honest cop?"

Stringbean examined the formerly oval hoop. "That'll do 'er. There won't nobody get close enough to see it's barely big enough for the ball to go through."

"The backboard's already two feet lower than standard," Billy B-Ball said. "If the hoops were regular size, I might as well give the teddy bears away for free." Billy B-Ball picked up the hammer. "Then your buddy Roosevelt would have to give me a government job."

"Give FDR some credit, Billy. Making it illegal to own gold was downright genius. Without government controls, wages and prices always compete. That's bad for us working men."

Billy B-Ball shot Stringbean a dirty look and started pounding the other hoop.

"Trust me, I've read a lot about economics," Stringbean said. "That governor Huey P. Long's plan is the right idea. *Share the Wealth. Every Man a King.* Now, you take Baby Elaine. I like her a lot, but I happen to know she's pulling down $250 a week."

"What's wrong with that?" Billy said between blows. "I'd do

53

it too, if I could."

"But would you share it, that's the point. She's making $8000 a year when a family-sized house sells for $3000. She's almost into Rockefeller territory. You should read John Maynard Keynes' book."

"Does it mention rigged carnival games?" Billy said.

"Well, not by name."

***

The Snake Girl loved the late dusk when the sun couldn't damage her sensitive skin. Seesla could barely make out String perched on the wooden rail of the basketball joint. She and Stringbean Samuels had been married and divorced a total of four times, the best she remembered.

Anyway, the divorces equaled or outnumbered the weddings, she was sure of that. Which meant that although String continued to treat his "little English lady" like a child, at least he could never again threaten to divorce her for flirting.

"That you, Luvie?" she called out.

"Naw." The gaunt figure came toward her. "It's Baby Elaine, the Proud Princess of Poundage."

"The knees-up in the cookhouse tent is starting. Let's go." She put her arm around his narrow waist as they walked. "The strongman located some 'snaps' in the last town. Says we can have a nip."

"I ain't drinking beer with no German Kraut soldier."

"You're daft. Otto's Austrian. Anyway, that was many years ago, and he was only a soldier because they made him. He's a good bloke. And snaps isn't beer. More like brandy."

"I don't drink with America's enemies, whatever he calls hisself or his beer. Besides, I'm real tired. You go, if you want. Just

54

behave!"

"You know I'm all talk. But if you recall, I'm also a grown woman and single again." She gave him a peck on the cheek. "Mind how you go, so you don't do yourself a mischief. This ground's treacherous in the dark."

"I won't trip over no tent stake. I was walking dirt lots when you was still a cute little thing in England."

"I was never a cute little thing, but thank you." She patted his arm and broke away. "Don't fret, I'll be home early."

***

The wind shook the concession booths as the tall man crouched between them. Behind him was the open field with the toilets, and beyond that the safety of the woods. When the moon briefly squeezed between the clouds, he looked across the midway for signs of motion in the living area. Everyone was in a big tent up front, yelling and singing, but he figured they wouldn't allow the monster into a party. From the hilltop this morning he had seen the thing enter a tent, but now...? *Which tent was it?*

Some instinct whispered, Go back. Disappear. Forget. Live.

He touched the knife on his belt. *Nature must be cleansed.*

Becoming just another shadow, he flowed down the midway toward the tents.

Again the prompting came, fainter this time. Vanish. Live.

No. Nature demands.

***

The increasing wind was cooling the night's darkness as Seesla pushed through the cookhouse tent flaps. Dinnertime aromas had surrendered to a cigarette cloudbank forming under the canvas

55

canopy. The carnies sat grouped around the tables, each population staying pretty much with their own kind—performers, joint operators, ride operators, or roughnecks.

Otto the strongman was wandering from table to table in a festive mood, a bottle of schnapps in each hand. On the kitchen side of the tent, Cookhouse Lil was opening her portable Victrola while Brownie and Monsieur Louvre looked through the discs, debating whether to hear Duke Ellington's "It Don't Mean a Thing," or a new ballad called "All I Do Is Dream of You" by Ferdinando's Great Northern Hotel Orchestra. Seated at a table near the phonograph, Edna and Louise saw Seesla enter and gave her a come-join-us wave.

Herbert Hutchins, the Professor's partner and owner of most of the rides, sat on top of a table, presiding over an audience of roughnecks. "Hell, this wind ain't nothing. Back in '27, I nearly lost this arm in a blowdown in St. Louie. Old man Kinburg's circus. Tornado hit as we started the slough."

Farther back in the tent, Leroy and Willie sat across a table from Baby Elaine. "The sow?" Leroy said. "A pig?"

"S-l-o-u-g-h," Elaine spelled. "Rhymes with wow."

"It means to take down the show," said Willie. "Slough's circus talk. Carnival people say 'tear-down.'"

Herbert Hutchins raised his arm, a bottle of gin in his grip. "We knew the twister would rip the big top to shreds. The roustabouts was untying tent stakes and pulling wall canvas as fast as they could. Me and the Boss Canvas Man was unhooking the Main Guy from the King Pole."

Instinctively keeping the bottle vertical, Hutchins used it to outline an invisible tent above him. "Then she hit. Guy ropes popping. Quarter poles flying through the air. Down falls the King Pole, straight at my head. Boss Man dives and shoves me to the ground. A thousand pounds of pole hit the sawdust right beside me.

56

Six inches closer, it would have ripped off my whole damn arm. And I don't even have a scar to prove it."

"Six inches? Ha!" Otto set down his bottles and pulled off his shirt. "What think you of this?" He pointed to an old scar extending from his throat to his left armpit. Otto did his act wearing only leopard-spotted briefs and black boots, so everyone had seen the scar. But nobody had ever had the audacity to ask about it.

"English bayonet. But I jump, and the Tommy soldier misses. One inch deeper, and audiences never have the thrill of meeting 'Ivan the Terrible, Laughs in the Face of Death!'"

Otto aimed his fifty-four-inch bare chest at Seesla like a Minenwerfer mortar. "Perhaps, little Snake Girl, you think I killed your countryman? But no, I have ripped the rifle from his hands, and he ran like a schoolboy. I could not bring me to shoot him in his back. Only a boy ordered to die for his country. Like me. Both sides believed they were moral." Otto ran his fingertips along the scar. "I gave him his life. He gave me this souvenir."

"You suppose that's true?" Elaine muttered to Leroy and Willie. "Otto has the best poker face I ever saw."

"That reminds me," Leroy said. "The flat joint operators invited me to play cards tonight."

"If you don't want your money," Willie said, "stuff it in my shirt pocket and go on to bed. Tomorrow you'll be just as broke, but not near as sleepy. But don't you be playing cards with nobody who spends every day running crooked games as a profession."

"They said I don't have to bet," Leroy said. "They'll just teach me some things."

"Flatties?" Elaine laughed. "They'll teach you some things, all right! As soon as they shuffle the deck, you're just another mark."

"But carnies pride themselves on helping each other out," Leroy said.

"On the show, yes," Elaine said. "But when it comes to

money, it's every carny for himself!"

***

Stringbean lay on the couch that was his bed and stared at the ceiling of the long truck he and Seesla shared. Fifty yards away, the wind rattled the Ferris wheel. String wouldn't sleep until Seesla was in her bed on the other side of the curtain.

Otto had joined the show only a few weeks ago. Nobody except the Professor knew anything about him. Otto was muscular, handsome, one of those hateful men who thought every woman wanted him. Hateful because he was right. String had seen it in Seesla's eyes.

Stringbean stared into the darkness, remembering a Luttrell, Tennessee, roadhouse. And Sammy Jameson, the boy he once was.

Sammy and his sweetheart Mary were eating when Jeffers and his sawmill crew swaggered in, fueled partly by bathtub gin, but mostly by pure-dee ol' cussedness.

"Let's play some pool, boys," the big man bellowed. "Anybody seen a skinny cue stick?" Jeffers grabbed Sammy, pulling the painfully-thin farm boy to his feet. "Hell, I reckon Sammy Scarecrow will do."

Jeffers shoved Sammy across the pool table. Sammy's head hit the billiard balls and scattered them to the padded rails as everyone laughed.

Determined not to be humiliated in front of Mary, Sammy jumped up and took a wild swing. Jeffers ducked, grabbed Sammy, and threw him through the plate glass window. Sammy hit the hard ground, stunned. Jeffers jumped through the window and grabbed Sammy, lifting him up. Sammy struck out, barely aware of the shard of plate glass he was holding. Jeffers gasped, looked at the blood spurting from his throat, and fell like a sack of feed. The onlookers

58

scattered when a police car drove up, its red gumball flashing.

***

In that Tennessee jail cell, Sammy Jameson noticed that the middle bars in the window were slightly spread. Weeks earlier, a black man had assumed (wrongly, to his relief) that an evening in jail would end with a lynching party. In desperation, the man had used a rail from the metal bed frame to force the bars. It was futile. The gap was still smaller than any man.

But Sammy was a pool cue, a string bean. He was almost able to force his head through the bars, but the pain was too much. He sat on the filthy cot until he could think straight again. *Better to die here than in the electric chair.*

Feet first, Sammy reasoned. If his chest wouldn't pass through, he could still squirm back inside. Sammy stood on the bed, grabbed the bars, and slid his legs, then his hips, between the bars. His empty stomach passed easily. His chest hurt like hell, but what did cracked ribs matter? His body was outside. Now gravity was his friend.

His temples felt crushed by the bars. *Don't matter if I crack like an eggshell. Being dead is more free than being in prison.* He pushed against the outside wall and struggled. Sammy's brain filled with fireworks, then blackness.

Sammy Jameson regained consciousness face down on the ground. Then, realizing he was no longer inside a cell, he ran. After two nights and a day, Sammy fell exhausted in a field of tall grass. The next morning he was roused by the deep, mellow voice of God.

"Morning, Sunshine. Did you run away to join the circus?"

In the distance Sammy could hear the shouts of men working and smell food cooking. The voice from above was not God, but a little man wearing a crimson suit and a gold watch chain.

"Well, you didn't find a circus this time. You found a carnival." The Professor took Sammy's twig-like arm and helped him up. "For someone like you, a carnival is even better! However, if you want to be a carny, lesson number one is, start every day with a good breakfast."

The Professor led Sammy across the field and toward the carnival. "And if you've somehow forgotten your real name, we'll figure out a new one. What's in a name, anyway? 'A rose by any other name would smell as sweet.'"

Sammy was a little unsteady on his feet, but his brain was clear.

"Stringbean," he said.

CHAPTER 11

If Otto was with Seesla at the party, Stringbean would have it out with him. In spite of the heat today, the temperature in these mountains dropped hard and fast after dark, and with not an ounce of fat anywhere, he could easily catch a chill. He grabbed his hooded mackintosh off the peg as he stepped out of the truck. Maybe tonight he would get a beating for Seesla's sake, but there was no sense catching pneumonia, too.

Reaching the cookhouse tent, Stringbean pulled the mackintosh hood up to shield his head from the wind as he peered through a separation between the canvas sides. He couldn't locate Otto, but Seesla was on top of a table, getting a hot shimmy dance lesson from Louise. Nearby, Stani, the Half-Man-Half-Woman, sat with an artist's pad, sketching Edna.

After several stiff-jointed imitations of Louise's sizzling bump and grind, Seesla broke up in laughter and climbed off the table. Louise kept on grinding, enjoying the yelps of encouragement from the roughnecks gathered around.

The hood over Stringbean's head and the whistling wind kept him from hearing the footsteps of someone returning from the donikers.

"Why you stand in the dark, Skeleton Man? Join with us inside." Otto wrapped a heavily-muscled arm around Stringbean's shoulder. "We talk, have fun."

Stringbean jerked away. "We'll talk when I'm good and ready," he said, striding away. "Not before!"

The tall man could not find a suitable hiding place where he could see all the tents at once and still keep an eye on the big party tent in case someone came from that direction. Someone or some thing. Then he realized he was crouching against something that would serve as a usable den: a long metal trailer with, strangely enough, flowers painted on the side. He dropped to his knees, slid underneath it, and drew his knife. Here, unseen, he could squirm around and watch in all directions, not at exactly the same time, but often enough. Motionless, noiseless, he faded into the dirt and darkness. Tonight had been three years coming. He could wait.

***

The wind was getting colder, so instead of walking around to the cookhouse tent entrance, Deena the Human Pretzel slipped through a ten-inch gap between two side poles. Nearby, Freda sat alone at a table limbering her fingers with a Tarot deck.

"Watch yourself, kiddo," Freda said. "Otto is in his Hello-You-Lucky-Ladies mood."

"Thanks." Deena hitched her canvas bag higher on her shoulder and looked around. "I'll keep my distance." She walked over to Leroy, Willie, and Elaine and sat down beside Leroy. "Anybody like walnuts?" She pulled a sack and a nutcracker from her shoulder bag. Leroy took the nutcracker and began cracking walnuts.

A roughneck walked up to a nearby table and laid down a ratty guitar case. "Hey, Elaine." He lifted out a guitar and strummed a loud chord. "I need your great alto voice."

"In a minute, Skeezix. I want to talk with Deena. And if you expect me to sing, better tune that thing fast. I'm not staying long.

The wind's too scary." Elaine turned to Deena, "How's your family, honey?"

"Better," Deena said. "I send back almost everything I earn, and my brother Ben's in that civilian conservation thing, the CCC, building roads in Missouri."

"Where're you from?" Skeezix asked.

"Ever heard of Boise City, Oklahoma? Or Guymon?"

"Guess not," said Skeezix.

"Well, I'm from a dusty bump partway between them." Deena reached into her bag again and lifted out a fist-sized contraption of gears and levers.

"I lived awhile in Boley, Oklahoma," said Willie. "America's biggest all-Colored town. We had our own electric company, our own telephone company, our own bank. Those were great times."

Leroy pushed some shelled walnuts in front of Deena. "What are you fiddling with?" he asked.

"It's a Sargent and Greenleaf combination lock from an old bank safe. I can open it blindfolded. Watch." She scooted closer to Leroy and held the lock under the table where she couldn't see it. "Doing the Headless Woman act was so boring I almost went crazy. So I started fooling around with locks. With my head inside the mirror box, I had to do it by feel. Nobody noticed. I guess talking to a woman with no head distracts people."

"You were a Headless Woman before you became a contortionist?"

"Yeah. I joined the show thinking I'd be a dancing girl. I'm the only girl in a family with seven boys, so I was used to guys looking. But the Professor said I'm not, y'know, curvy enough. Well, four-eleven and ninety-six pounds, what do you expect? Anyway, I didn't do the headless act long."

"What happened?" Leroy asked.

"I got Mr. Hutchins to teach me some acrobatics and help me

63

work up a bender act. For a contortionist, being skinny and without curves is perfect. I don't earn as much as the Hootchy dancers, but I can leave the goodies covered."

"Wonder if the Professor would consider a Headless Man," Leroy said. "I'm tired of going insane ten shows a day. Rolling in the dirt like a drug addict is ruining my hair."

"Yeah, but on you, messy is kind of cute," Deena said. The lock popped open, and she handed it to him.

"Nice trick," he said. "But opening bank safe locks, what good is that?"

"Nuh-uh," she said. "That's *my* secret."

***

Stringbean took his time going back to the truck, trudging across the midway to stand briefly before the Ten-in-One. Home. Even in the darkness he knew what his banner said.

"ALIVE! Stringbean the Human Skeleton! Watch His Beating Heart!"

Who's the freak? Some poor sap with a defect? Or the rube who wastes his grocery money to gawk. *Next week they'll be back scratching in parched ground, and I'll be socking away their cash.* That day years ago when the Professor sent the nervous young Sammy onstage for the first time, a new world opened up to him. Sure, there was an occasional wisecrack from the crowd, but mostly they stared in awe. And respect. Two reactions he had never before experienced. The feeling was intoxicating, almost like being—well, brave.

It wasn't that he had been afraid of Otto just now. But everyone was there. Suppose he had lost his nerve. Seesla would have seen.

Otto don't deserve to be with natural freaks. He's not a born

64

act; he's only a made act. Seesla and me, we belong together.

Heading back to the truck, String hunched to keep the wind from pushing him into a run. As he snugged the hood tighter around his head, he noticed a light flickering in a tent.

Damned sneak thief. *The stuck-up rubes call us thieves, but then they try to steal us blind.* He opened his mouth to shout the carny cry for help, then stopped. Hell, that's Otto's tent. *It's only that drunk Kraut.*

It was perfect. He would step quickly into the tent, tell Otto to stay away from Seesla, then hightail it out of there before the drunken strongman could even get up off the cot. Stringbean walked over and grabbed the tent flap.

***

Breathing darkness under the trailer, the tall man watched the big tent up front. The wind made it impossible to hear sounds more than a few feet away, so he slithered a semi-circle until he could see the only other approach, a path winding between big trucks parked behind the Midway. Now, as he silently rotated in the dust, he saw a slim figure entering a tent.

There it is! I almost missed it. He slid from his hiding place and moved toward the tent. *I looked just in time. I knew there was a God.*

***

Stringbean pushed through the tent flaps. "Listen, Otto, don't you mess with..."

He stopped, his mouth open. "What the hell do you think you're...?" He quickly stuck his head out of the tent, and shouted "Hey, Rube" into the howling wind.

The tall man was caught off guard by the freak popping back out of the tent so quickly, but his reflexes served him well. His arm swung in one quick perfect motion. Stringbean fell backwards into the tent, clutching his throat.

They say when you die, your whole life flashes before you. Mercifully, Sammy Jameson saw only one vision—Seesla.

Part Two:
The Human Skeleton!! Alive!!!

CHAPTER 12
FRIDAY, AUGUST 17, 1934

At the second or third "Sheriff!" and the eighth or tenth knock, Rachel's eyes popped open. She grabbed her robe and looked out the window. The sun was squeezing over the horizon, and last night's unseasonably cold wind had returned to wherever it lived, leaving the world once again warm and muggy. Across the alley at the jail, a man raised his fist to pound again on the door.

"What's wrong?" Rachel called out.

"I have to find the sheriff! A man's had his neck slit!"

"Where is the man?"

"At the carnival. It's about five..."

"I know where the carnival is. The street behind you is Porter Street. Dr. MacPhie's house is the white one at the top of the hill. I'll phone the sheriff."

"But the man's dead."

"Are you a doctor?"

"No."

"Then don't assume! Get the doctor!"

Rachel pulled her robe on as she rushed downstairs. At the telephone table in the hallway, she scanned the two-page list of telephones in Mercer County. Cash-comma-Isaac was near the top.

"Mom?" Jeremy looked down from the landing. "I heard yelling. Who got stabbed?"

"Go back to sleep. Nothing to worry about." There was no answer at Cash's house.

"Was there a knife fight out at Snyder's roadhouse? Can I go with you?"

"I'm not going anywhere; I'm phoning the sheriff." It wasn't yet daylight. Cash should be there. She dialed again. "Besides, the man's probably dead."

"Great! I've never seen a real live dead man. You can stay, and I'll go with the sheriff."

"I don't have time to argue." She would have to drive out to Cash's house. "Go to sleep."

"No!"

Rachel looked up in disbelief. "What did you say?"

"This is important, Mom. Maybe the sheriff needs me. I'm his helper!"

"In a barbershop! You sweep up hairs! You don't go to murders!"

"There's never *been* a murder! I have to go, Mom. I just *have* to!"

"Whether you sleep is up to you. But if you don't turn yourself around and get back in bed, I'll give you a spanking you won't forget."

"You never spanked me." Jeremy's eyes widened. "Not in my whole life."

"Maybe that's the problem. But it isn't too late to correct that. You will not backtalk and then flaunt it in front of me."

"What does 'flaunt' mean?"

"Bed! Sleep!" She struggled not to shout. "I'll talk to you in the morning. Now git!"

The boy stared for a moment, then went back to his room, mumbling about all the other kids getting to the murder scene first.

Rachel put the phone down. Why wasn't Cash at home?

***

70

In the truck shared by Seesla and Stringbean, Louise opened Seesla's closet and found a robe. "She's probably hung over," she said to Edna. "Let her get awake before you break the news."

Edna shook Seesla's shoulder gently and tried to think of the kindest way to tell her. There wasn't one.

The carnies with living quarters closest to Otto's tent had been the first to respond to Otto's cries of "Hey, Rube." Hutchins and some roughnecks took Otto several yards away and surrounded him, but he showed no inclination to escape.

When the Professor saw Seesla running toward the tent, barefoot and in her thin nightgown, he tried to grab her and hold her back. She shoved him aside, but fortunately Baby Elaine had already arrived from her trailer nearby. She shifted her mass in front of the tent flap just in time.

"No, honey, no!" Elaine wrapped her arms around Seesla and held tight. "You can't go in there. You just can't."

Edna and Louise caught up in time to keep Seesla from falling to the ground, shattered and crying, as Ramona, Brownie, and Freda rushed to help.

***

"Was he really short? A dwarf?" Isaac slid onto the passenger seat and closed the car door.

"Dwarf? He was taller than you." Rachel started the engine and pulled away from the barbershop. "A good-looking young man."

"How did you know I was at the barber shop?"

"Where else would you be?" she said. "You weren't at the jail, and you didn't answer your phone at home."

"I came in to look at my account book."

Actually, he did look at the book, briefly. But that was last night when he pushed it aside to make space on the table in the supply room at the back of the shop. Some nights sleeping with your head down on a wooden table hurt less than going home to an empty house and an empty life.

"I appreciate the lift, Mrs. Barlow. I feel like a fool, letting my pickup run low on gas." Isaac watched the sun breaking free of the mountaintop. *While I sat idling yesterday, listening to her complain about Police Gazettes.*

"Just 'Rachel' is fine," she said. "Nobody calls me 'Mrs.' anymore, and I'm glad. Giving you a lift is no trouble," Rachel said. "I told Miz Russell I was borrowing her car to find you, and I might be gone awhile."

"What about your job?" Isaac said.

"Miz Russell and Jeremy will manage," Rachel said, spurring the 1927 Dodge Four up to speed. "Mr. Fairley is our only boarder right now. A traveling salesman. He's convinced the carnival is a refuge for spies."

"Spies?"

"His words, not mine," Rachel said. "He says carnivals are the perfect hiding place. No one would suspect clowns, snake charmers, and fat ladies of being Bolshevik anarchists."

"It wouldn't occur to most people, that's for sure," Isaac said.

"He says if you don't chase the carnival away, we'll have our hands full."

"I may have my hands full even without Bolsheviks."

"I'd heard you were once what they call a 'bull,'" Rachel said. "A railroad detective."

"Nothing that glamorous, assuming a railroad cop is anybody's idea of glamour. I was a section boss responsible for laying track in East Texas. It's true I dealt with some rough fellows who occasionally got drunk and sliced each other up. But investigating murders, that's out of my league. Mostly I sweep the jail and lock up an occasional drunk." *Anything to hang on to that thirty-five-dollar-a-month sheriff's salary.*

Dust flew as Rachel turned off the county highway onto the dirt road leading to Meekam's Field. She had made the five-mile drive over a winding road in under twelve minutes.

"You handle a car real well...Rachel."

"Daddy taught me when I was twelve," she said. "Farm family. No brothers, three girls. I was the oldest, so I had to help any way I could. He taught me to shoot, too. As wedding presents, Momma gave me her second best set of plates, and Daddy gave me an Iver Johnson top-break revolver. Very cute."

Rachel slowed and pulled onto the carnival lot. "I can ride, too. Had a dapple-gray mare, and wasn't any boy in the county could catch us." She braked to a stop at the entrance. "Here comes the young fellow that knocked on the jailhouse door. I'll stroll around until you're ready to leave."

The young man who opened Isaac's door reminded him of that famous statue of David, if only David had possessed a few more muscles and had been dressed in a plaid shirt and brown workpants.

"Are you the sheriff? I'm Leroy Anderson. Follow me."

As they reached the midway, Isaac smelled food cooking and saw carnies streaming into a large tent. Here and there people gave him a wary glance, but overall everything appeared to be business as usual.

Looks like I may have to question a lot of people. I'd better send Mrs. Barlow home and get a lift back. With my luck, I won't get back in time to give any haircuts today.

They walked the length of the midway and past the Ferris wheel, then threaded their way between some booths at the opposite end of the lot. As they approached the carnies' living area, Leroy pointed to an eight-by-ten camping tent. Beside it, a young woman sat sobbing on the running board of a big car while two other women comforted her. The Professor was pacing in front of the tent, his

73

movements stiff, his face drawn and emotionless. Before Isaac could say anything, the Professor parted the tent flaps and motioned for him to go in.

CHAPTER 13

Before entering, Isaac held the flaps open and looked around inside. To his left was a collapsible cot. The bedding was made with tight square corners, military style, but the blanket was wrinkled. Someone had been lying down.

At the rear, a rope stretched from one side of the tent to the other. On it hung a white shirt, two pairs of socks, and two sets of men's underwear. Yesterday's laundry, apparently, neatly pinned up to dry. In the right rear corner, a steamer trunk covered with stickers from European countries stood open, its drawers pulled out randomly.

Partially hidden by the trunk and lying in a dark spot of dried blood was the scrawny corpse. On the right side of the tent near the entrance was a camp table, and seated in the folding chair was Dr. Shepherd Tingely MacPhie, his old pipe stuck between his lips under his droopy mustache. With one hand, he was writing in a notebook. With the other hand, he was patting his coat pockets.

Isaac stepped inside. "Smoking again, Shep?"

"Nope. It'll be two years next month. Quitting wasn't near as hard as breaking myself of patting my pockets for tobacco. But the pipe helps me think."

"Know who the victim was?" Isaac asked.

"A performer named Stringbean Samuels. Also called the Human Skeleton. Take your pick."

"Who found him?"

"German fellow that lives here. Name's Otto Gieseking. Just before daylight he left to answer the call of nature. When he came back, he saw something in the corner, so he lit his lantern. That's what he's telling everybody. He's pretty rattled." MacPhie stood and walked to the rear of the tent and pointed down at the corpse. "From the way the blood has congealed and settled in the body, my best guess is that death occurred between ten and midnight. Only a guess until I can do a proper postmortem."

"Small tent. Seems like this Otto would have noticed a body," Isaac said, "even back here."

"Says he came back from a party about midnight, drunk. Never lit the lamp. Fell right to sleep."

"I guess that's believable." Isaac squeezed past MacPhie, who ducked under the socks and underwear on the line and maneuvered out of Isaac's way.

"Might be you should hitch up your britches." MacPhie went back to the chair. "So your cuffs don't drag in anything."

"Any other wounds?" Isaac tugged up his pant legs and knelt down.

"One was enough. Severed both common carotid arteries and a jugular. It's real deep."

"He die instantly?"

"Pretty near. Probably lost consciousness within ten seconds."

"Shep, you ever seen anybody killed like this before?"

"Nope," said MacPhie. "Saw a soldier get bayoneted in France during the war. But that was in the gut."

The victim was wearing trousers, a flannel shirt, a hooded jacket that seemed unnecessary in August, and shoes. Isaac emptied the dead man's pockets. A soiled handkerchief. Two carnival ride passes like the ones the Professor had given Isaac. A pocket knife. A three-inch pencil stub. A small folded paper. He placed the items in a neat row on the camp table. "Who saw him last before he died?"

"The killer. Other than that, probably the girl crying outside.

She's pretty tore up about it. They live in a truck you walked past."

"Is she his wife?" Isaac unfolded the paper. It was blank.

"I didn't ask," said MacPhie. "But I plan to get back to her and give her a sedative."

"Okay, I'll come back after I talk to Otto. You can take the body away, but don't let anybody else in here."

"Fair enough. I already had that fellow Leroy send somebody to fetch Mel Frazee and his hearse."

Isaac checked the drawers in the steamer trunk. They held clothes, stuffed haphazardly inside, and toiletry items. The lining of the trunk lid had come undone at the seam for about eight inches, possibly torn by the two-foot-long sword strapped inside the lid. He slid the sword out. There was no blood on it.

He went to the tent entrance. The Professor was sitting beside the young woman on the car's running board, holding her hand. Isaac motioned, and the Professor came over to the tent.

"What's this?" Isaac held up the sword.

"The Fearsome Saber of Ivan the Terrible." The Professor's eyes seemed moist. "Awarded after he single-handedly fought off 176 crazed Bolsheviks and saved the life of Tsar Nicholas the Second." His voice was faintly robotic.

"You're saying this sword came from Russia? About 1917?"

The Professor looked up at Isaac and sighed. "Otto bought it from a pawnshop in Philadelphia about eight years ago. He swallows it. Ivan the Terrible is his stage name."

"Thanks. That's all I need right now." Isaac stepped back inside and pulled the flaps closed.

"Want me to take the sword to town?" MacPhie took the pipe out of his mouth. "For safekeeping?"

"Might as well, but there's no blood on it," Isaac said. "I expect the killer wiped it clean."

"There'll be no fingerprints, either." MacPhie ran his thumb

77

along the blade. "Anyway, it's not sharp enough to cut soft butter, never mind slash a throat."

Isaac looked at the spot on the ground. "How much blood would a skinny man have?"

"About five quarts. But he'd only have to lose two or so. What are you saying?"

"I'm saying, if he was killed right here, shouldn't that blood spot be bigger? Or did somebody drag his body behind this trunk to hide it?"

"Uh-huh. Good point." Doc MacPhie put his pipe between his teeth and patted his pockets. "Should have wondered about that myself."

***

The tall man had earned his knife as a boy, after he finally escaped Grandpa's whippings for good. Never again would he be brought home with a rope around his neck, forced to trot behind the old man's horse or strangle. That last time he ran off, he kept running.

On the third night, he reached a town and hid inside a livery stable. The next morning, the blacksmith discovered him asleep under some horse blankets. He said the boy could stay, provided he worked for his keep. The smith also promised that after six months, the boy would earn a new pair of boots.

The boy didn't need to think about that. He pulled off his battered boots and hung them on a nail so they would still be wearable when he wanted to move on.

"Don't want no boots," he said. "I want me a knife. Not a pocket knife. A hunter's knife. So won't nobody mess with me."

The smith agreed, than asked his name.

"Bert," the boy answered. "Just Bert."

CHAPTER 14

"I have done nothings." Otto's forehead was beaded with perspiration even though it wasn't yet eight and the air was still cool. He was about five-ten, putting him eye to eye with Isaac, but his bulk gave the impression of a water tower perched on two tree trunks. Giant redwoods.

Isaac hadn't wanted to question Otto inside the murder tent, but he wanted the privacy he couldn't have standing outside. So the Professor led them across the midway and behind the Ten-in-One to a small tent used to store props when the performers weren't doing their acts. At one end of the tent was a costume trunk and several crates. Temporary lights were strung overhead, and a single chair sat beside a wooden table holding three jars of makeup. Otto was too jumpy to sit down, so Isaac used the chair. It was going to be a long morning.

"I swear it to Gott im Himmel. I have him finded exactly like that."

Isaac figured the man's English was probably better on a normal day. Waking up and finding a body with its throat slit could rattle anyone, especially if he were the prime suspect.

"Did you check if he was dead?"

"No. I could tell in an eye blink. Man in big blood pool with his neck wide open is not taking a short nap. I am not Brinkley the radio doctor, so what can I do? I run out and yell, is all."

Otto's shirt and trousers were wrinkled in back, consistent with his story of lying face up in a drunken sleep. There were no bloodstains on his clothing, but he might have changed. Isaac

79

checked Otto's shoes and found stains only on the soles. Blood would probably be on the shoes of anyone who had been in the tent, including the Professor, Leroy, and MacPhie. Isaac made a mental note to look at his own shoes the next time he was alone.

"Where're you from, Otto? Tell me about yourself."

As Otto calmed down, he was cooperative, even talkative. He'd come to America in 1926 because the Great War had reduced the opportunities for work in Europe. He went into detail about why he stayed, including the failure of the Austrian banks and the rise of Chancellor Dollfuss, whom he called a dictator.

"Before now, I worked a show based in Illinois," he said. "I know Stringbean very little. Only this season."

Isaac asked enough questions, in enough different ways, to give Otto plenty of opportunities to contradict himself. But he stayed consistent. After forty-five minutes, Isaac let Otto leave, ordering him to stay out of his tent until further notice. Then Isaac went back to make a more thorough search.

Dr. MacPhie was gone, along with Stringbean's body and the sword. Isaac went methodically through the drawers in Otto's steamer trunk, paying close attention to the shaving articles. The man's preferred shaving instrument was not a cut-throat straight razor, but an Enn Werke safety razor from Germany with a half-empty box of Gem blades.

At the back of the trunk was a slim cardboard tube. Isaac opened it and unrolled two posters. One was an art print of a mountain, with a red arrow and the word "Raxbahn." Bahn meant railroad, Isaac thought, but the graphic design was clearly a cable car. He wished he had paid more attention when his grandpa's Austrian second wife kept telling Isaac what various things were called in German.

He flipped the poster over. On the back were the words "Viel Gluck, Otto!" Good luck, Otto. Below was an autograph, "Joseph

Binder," in ink. *Joseph,* Isaac thought, *Not Josef?*

The smaller poster was a cheaply-printed flyer in German. The only English words were a date and the address of a building, Selwin Hall, in Chicago. "Das-something-or-other-verein-fur-something-hilfe-something," meant what? And "Versamlung." Was that the word for meeting? The next line, "Verein" might be "group" or "organization." "Hilfe" was easy – "help." But the rest?

Isaac looked under the cot and dragged out a large suitcase. The contents were mostly clothes, along with a pair of shoes, a photo album, and a leather dispatch case containing letters and a ledger book, probably the strong man's personal budget.

Isaac was sitting on the ground, listing the items in his notebook, when the Professor walked in.

"I gave the lady your message," the Professor said, "and she drove back to town."

Isaac figured it was nothing new for the Professor to look down his nose at small town sheriffs, figuratively speaking. But this was probably the first time he had done it literally. Isaac stood and brushed off his seat. "Has Doctor MacPhie gone?"

"He's with Seesla, calming her down." The Professor looked away for a moment, working to keep his emotions under control. "She's Stringbean's ex-wife. Now, if you're finished, I'll have my assistant drive you back."

"No, I want to talk to her. But first, who might have been close to this tent between ten and midnight?"

"Only Baby Elaine. I was in my office truck doing bookkeeping and looked out the window and noticed her leave the party early." The Professor opened the tent flaps and pointed. "You can't miss her trailer. It's big and pink."

***

The bullet-shaped trailer was metal, like a wingless pink cargo plane with flowery lettering—"Baby Elaine, America's Fattest Little Lady." Isaac slid his fingertips over the polished surface of the open door.

"You must be the sheriff," a woman's mellow voice said from inside. If golden honey could talk, it would sound like that. "Come on in."

Isaac stepped through the wide door that took up the flat end of the trailer. To his left was a small built-in stove, and on the counter sat a one-gallon pickle jar containing more nickels and dimes than he had ever seen. Beside the jar was a stack of postcards with Baby Elaine's photo and autograph.

"My pitch cards," she said. On a bed that filled the far end of the trailer from wall to wall, leaning against lacy pink cushions, was America's Fattest Little Lady. Her frilly white dress had enough material to clothe a family of four, provided they were smallish. "Help yourself," she said. "Ten cents for fair-goers. Free for sheriffs."

Isaac flipped a card over and read the caption. "TAKES SIX MEN TO HUG HER AND A FREIGHT TRAIN TO LUG HER !!"

"Have a seat," she said, motioning toward a small sofa against the wall. "Poor String. Awful. Just terrible."

As he sat down, Isaac noticed long hinges behind the upholstery.

"The seat folds up to store linens. I designed this trailer with lots of storage space," she said.

She doesn't miss a thing, Isaac thought. *Eyes like a hawk.*

On the wall above the sofa were framed photos of her at various ages. One picture showed a pretty youngster who might be Myrna Loy's little sister, except for the baby fat.

"For the record," Isaac pulled out his notebook, "what's your name?"

"Baby Elaine. Proud Princess of Poundage. Queen of Quantity." She fluffed up her sleeves as she shifted into a well-practiced spiel. "Magnitudinous Miss of Mass. America's Hefty Helen of Tr..." She made eye contact with Isaac, who was not smiling. "Aw, hell," she muttered. "Elaine Cranbrook."

"From?"

"Illinois. Peoria. Haven't been back in, oh, twelve years. I'm carny every ounce." She smiled a genuinely sweet smile as she adjusted her lace collar. With arms that heavy, most women would settle for whatever hairstyle heredity and a strong wind gave them, but her hair was quite stylish.

"When did you see Stringbean last?"

"Early afternoon, about two. He didn't come to the party. Maybe if he had..." She broke off and looked out the window.

"What time did you leave the party?"

"Ten-thirty-ish. There's a roughneck who plays guitar and knows the latest songs. People seem to enjoy my singing, so I hung around a while."

"Then you came here?"

"Straight home. The Borneo Wild Man walked me back. I'm nervous about unfamiliar ground at night. Suppose I fell into a ditch and broke my leg! In a circus, an elephant could hoist me up. But a carnival? They'd have to leave me there and frame a new exhibit around me. 'Elaine the Immovable Object.'" She paused. "Seriously, that's why shows never hire a fat person who isn't mobile."

"Did you pass near Otto's tent coming back?"

"Sheriff, look out that window, please."

Isaac looked out past the living quarters and down the midway.

"That big tent near the front is where the party was," she said. "Now in your mind's eye, draw a line from the cookhouse to here. Then look to your right, towards Otto's tent. That's twenty-five feet. Probably more like thirty, if you measured it."

"Thirty feet to what?"

"That's how much farther I'd have had to walk to get within spitting distance of Otto's tent. To an average person like you, thirty feet is nothing. But for someone like me," she continued, "it might as well be a hike in the hills. Especially after walking all the way from the cookhouse. So when I say I came straight back, I do mean 'straight.'"

"So you couldn't have seen if Stringbean was inside Otto's tent."

"Inside another carny's tent? Alone, at night? Everyone would brand you a thief. You'd be lucky to last out the season."

"How long have you known Stringbean?"

"About four years. I was with Higgam and Howard's Great Colossal, but they had a bad fire in Schenectady and closed. I had a run of mud luck for a while, but then I joined the Professor's outfit and things improved fast. He pays me by the pound!" She smiled and smoothed a couple of yards of dress over her lap. "I can't lose. Literally!"

"Were you and Stringbean close friends?"

"I know what you're driving at, and the answer is, not on your life! String was married to Seesla when I joined the show. I'm only interested in someone who's free to stroll down the aisle." Her gaze pinned Isaac like a collector's butterfly. "People think, who'd marry a fat lady?" Her honey voice softened as if she were teaching a child. "Before people even meet a fat lady, they've already judged her. Lazy slob. No self-respect. They don't bother to find out what she's like as a person. Okay then, if rubes want to make fun, they're going to have to pay for the privilege! I work hard to entertain my audience, and if people are in the least bit open-minded, I'll please them, and I *will* earn their respect. And I do!" She gestured gracefully around the room. "This trailer cost a year's wages for the

84

average person, but I don't owe a penny on anything. Never have."

Isaac sensed there was a lot more to this woman than simply being…a lot more woman. She had some special quality. Character? Nobility? After a moment, he said, "You have a really nice voice."

"Carnival fat ladies don't do somersaults or walk the tight wire," Elaine said. "Using my voice is what I'm good at. It makes me happy that people enjoy it."

***

Compared with the luxury of Baby Elaine's trailer, the truck shared by the Snake Girl and the deceased Human Skeleton was spartan. Dr. MacPhie had just left, after warning Isaac that the sedative would take effect in less than an hour. A curtain, now pushed-back, divided the interior in half lengthways. Seesla lay on a bed against one wall, staring out the window. The Professor had said Seesla's skin resembled a snake, but to Isaac it seemed more like bark on a fallen oak. It was a pity to see.

Isaac noticed that Seesla's tear-soaked pillowcase had a hand-embroidered iris. Sarah had liked irises, too, but the only time Isaac ever saw Sarah cry was at their wedding. Later, after they learned she could never have children, Isaac sometimes noticed that her eyes were red. But she never let him actually see her cry.

Seesla's side of the truck was tidy. Her clothing was probably inside the tall cabinet bolted to the wall. Two picture frames hung beside it. The smaller frame held a photo of a smiling elderly couple. In the other frame was the cover from a piece of sheet music, with the image of a girl in Victorian clothing and the title, "Poor Wandering One."

On the other side of the truck, an old couch held a pillow and a rumpled blanket. A small bookcase on the wall had metal lattice in the doors instead of glass, probably to keep the books from breaking

85

the glass if the truck hit a pothole. *A grill would have saved me the expense of a new front window,* Isaac thought. *But I'd feel like a prisoner in my own barbershop.* He looked at the titles. *"Gold and Monetary Stabilization." "In Camp with Theodore Roosevelt."* Clearly, the victim didn't care for trashy novels.

Isaac offered his condolences, then asked the obvious question.

"No enemies." She blotted the tears on her scaly cheeks with a cloth. "It makes no sense." Isaac strained to catch her quiet, English-accented words.

Seesla said she, Louise, and Edna had spent the evening chatting with each other and with various men at the party, which broke up about midnight. "Otto had some snaps, and Louvre brought wine. I got a bit tiddly. I can't manage much alcohol."

"Did you see Mr. Samuels when you came in?"

"Stringbean? No, the curtain was drawn. I got into bed and fell asleep. I thought he was there. He's always been there for me. If you're married, you understand how that is."

"I don't understand the curtain."

"We hung it the first time we got unmarried."

"First time? How many..."

"Four times. In five years." She looked out the window. "The more possessive he became, the more I flirted. The more I flirted, the more he tried to own me. I never followed through. I just... You're obviously intelligent. You understand."

"Not sure I do," Isaac said.

"I'm a woman, in spite of my skin. I like how a man looks at me once he realizes I have the same, well, desires that any woman has."

"Was Mr. Samuels ever violent?"

"Never! It wasn't in him to be aggressive."

"But he did divorce you."

86

"No, I divorced him. Four tries for the brass ring, and we fell off the merry-go-round each time."

"If you're divorced, why live in the same truck?"

"It's a harsh world, Sheriff. For people like us, a sideshow may be the sanest place in it. String and I are not 'made acts'—people who get tattoos or learn to swallow swords. We're 'born acts.' We can't help what we are, and we can't change it. Ever. We need someone who cares about us inside. String always cared about me."

"Then why flirt? Is that caring?"

"Maybe not in your world, but I will never let any man think of me as property." She blew her nose gently. "But I couldn't just leave. Leaving String would have destroyed him. So all I could do was divorce him." She looked at the empty bed. "He already had too much pain. I couldn't bear to give him more."

When Isaac left Seesla's truck, Leroy was standing nearby. "Hi, Sheriff. I just thought maybe I could be of assistance. I mean, you not being familiar with carnivals and carny ways."

Isaac didn't much care for an assistant who might be listening at doors and reporting back to the Professor. On the other hand, Leroy seemed to be the closest thing to normal in this outfit, and if Isaac played the cards right, he might get some useful information from the young man.

"Tell you what," Isaac said as he put on his hat. "First, bring me the fellow who throws knives. Then round up the other Ten-in-One performers. Bring them over to that prop tent, one at a time. But always keep them back about thirty feet. Understand?"

"Gotcha, Sheriff. We don't want anyone overhearing the evidence." Leroy walked away.

CHAPTER 15

In the prop tent, Isaac noticed a long, black wooden case with Otto's name stenciled on the outside. The interior was partitioned, and the padding was indented with three long creases. Clearly, Otto owned more swords than the one Isaac had found in the tent.

Ramon del Corte, the knife thrower, and his wife Ramona walked into the tent. Both were about five-foot-six, with dark hair and medium complexions. Isaac asked them to unlock the case where Ramon stored his knives and tomahawks.

"Were you at the party?" Isaac asked Ramon.

"Only a while. We left early," the man's wife answered. Ramon smiled and said something in Spanish. "He says to tell you we went to our trailer and went to bed early," Ramona translated.

"Did anyone see you?" Isaac asked.

"Shoot no!" Ramona said. "We keep our window covered."

"I mean, see you leave the party?" Isaac said as Ramon opened the case.

"Oh!" his wife said. "I don't know. You'd have to ask them."

"Where'd you learn Spanish, Ramona?" Isaac said. "You sound more Memphis than Madrid."

"I picked it up once I met Ramon. I was born Lucy Beth Hickman over in Black Fox, north of Chattanooga."

Isaac examined the knives. Each was simply a shaped strip of metal with cork grips sandwiched over one end, then wrapped with string to create a handle. The points were sharpened only enough to penetrate the wooden backdrop used in the act. None had the razor-sharp edge indicated by the wound in Stringbean's throat. Ramon said something and Ramona translated.

"Ramon says you're wasting your time. You should be looking for a very sharp knife with a rigid blade. Maybe a long hunting knife. Ramon's aren't made for slicing. His knives have to be perfectly balanced to flip end over end. Ramon constantly figures in his head how many flips the knife has to make over a certain distance. Otherwise the knife could bounce off the wood and hit me. It's kind of a science. Ramon's really smart with that stuff."

Ramon smiled, made another comment, then shrugged.

"Ramon says he has a perfect eye. A gift from God," Ramona said.

"How well did you know Stringbean?" Isaac asked.

"Not well," Ramona said. "We only joined the show this season. We were on the Keith-Albee theater circuit until '31. Talking pictures pretty much killed vaudeville, so we did the intermission act between picture shows for a while, then went to Spain to his family's circus," she said. "We left Spain because his brothers kept trying to s-e-d-u-c-e me. I was raised in the Holiness Church, and we don't allow f-o-r-n-i-c-a..."

Ramon frowned and nudged Ramona with his elbow. "I no understand spelling. Speak American," he said.

Isaac ran his finger along the edge of a tomahawk. It was rigid and sharp, but would it make a razor-like gash in a man's throat?

"You or Ramon ever been in trouble with the police?" Isaac asked. "I can check on that, of course." Ramona said something in Spanish and Ramon shook his head vigorously.

"No, sir. Neither of us," she said to Isaac.

"How'd you two get together," he asked.

"I went to a circus in Chattanooga with friends. Ramon was trying to get a volunteer from the audience because his partner had just run off with a Dixieland cornet player. Well, I thought he was

89

prettier than Valentino and Ronald Colman combined, so I threw up my hand and volunteered."

"Weren't you terrified?" Isaac asked.

"I told you I was Holiness raised. I figured if I could handle poisonous serpents in church, God would surely keep me safe from a beautiful Spaniard with a dull-edged throwing knife. After the show, Ramon had someone tell me that because I kept so calm, he'd pay me to be his assistant."

"So you joined the show," Isaac said.

"I told him my parents would never allow their unmarried daughter to travel with him. Then I looked him straight in the eye and told him that, on the other hand, I was legally old enough to get married." She blushed. "Truth be told, there was no man in Bradley County I would have crossed the road for. But I wanted out of Tennessee in the worst way, and Ramon looked so gorgeous."

"Must be hard to let someone throw knives at you," Isaac handed the tomahawk back.

"Honestly, it's so easy, it's boring. The only part I hate is the end, where he throws spears into my breakaway dress, and I run off the stage wearing just my step-in chemise. Momma wouldn't like that if she was still alive. But if I didn't do it, we wouldn't have a strong finish. He's already outlined me with tomahawks and done about everything a human being can do with a blade. Ramon's the best there ever was."

"Sí." Ramon nodded and smiled. "El major!"

"Well," Isaac said, "I hope you live a long and happy life."

"Oh, I will. As long as Ramon doesn't miss," she laughed.

**

"Pretty girl, no?" Monsieur Louvre said. "I purchased her as a young man in the French navy."

Isaac leaned across the makeup table and looked at the faded mermaid on Louvre's shoulder. Wearing only ballet shoes and bathing trunks, Louvre was the one man in Mercer County who stood a chance of staying cool today. Only his face lacked illustration, and it was partly covered by a large, waxed, handlebar mustache.

"On my other arm is La Statue de la Liberté. Americans forget, but yes, she is the beautiful French woman."

"Actually, I do remember." Isaac said. "A gift from France about fifty years ago."

"Exactament! You are a man who respects tradition. Bon!" A smile erupted under the handlebar mustache. "Tattoo is also a tradition. Very ancient."

Not mustache wax, Isaac thought. *Pomade*. He didn't like the smell. Had they been in the barbershop, Isaac had several jars of Bartwichse moustache wax he'd love to sell to someone. Anyone.

"In the pyramids, the Englishman Flinders Petrie found woman mummies with tattoos. The Greeks and Romans also had tattoos." Louvre grew animated. "You also must have a tattoo, mon ami," Louvre took Isaac's wrist. "A nice cobra. Perhaps a bloody poignard. How you say? Dagger."

"Here in the Ozarks, we don't..."

"Pas de problême. I would not expect to find a skilled tattooiste in this wilderness. I will do it myself!" He started for the tent entrance. "I bring my needles."

"Sit down, Mister Louvre. I don't need a tattoo, thanks. I need to ask questions." Isaac opened his notebook. "What time did you get to the party?"

"I don't know precise. I was first, and also the fortune teller and Hutchins. About nine, perhaps. Very soon everyone else comes."

"Did anyone leave during the party."

"No." Louvre lit a cigarette. "Or perhaps." He took a drag. "Franchement, I can't say. I was talking with the lovely Hootchy girls, and also the snake girl."

"How about Otto?"

"Pfah. I have no time for the Austrian. But he was there, bragging everywhere, loud. You must hit him."

"Hit? Do you mean, 'you can't miss him'?"

"Exactement. You can't miss, you must hit. It means the same, no? So the Austrian was there. Always I wish he would go, but no, he is trying to make the young women feel his muscles. Ma foi!"

"You stayed there the whole time?"

"Yes. Everyone was," the tattooed man paused to think while he scratched an itchy unicorn on his left thigh. "Well, perhaps no. The Half-and-Half leaves, but only for two, three minutes probably to make uriner behind the tent. All humans must, naturalmon, but not behind tent! The Polonais, they are filthy like pigs."

"You don't like Polish people?"

"Perhaps Chopin. His father was French. Some nice music."

"Is it possible Otto also went to the whatcha-call-it?"

"Doniker. Le toilet. Perhaps. I cannot swear he did or he didn't. But your dog is barking at the wrong tree. Otto is not the killer."

"What makes you so sure?"

"Les Boches, they are vicious, yes. But stupide. This was the crime most cunning. To creep silently behind povre Stringbean. Finally to leave his body in the tent, but deny the knowledge. No, cunning is not the way of the stupide Austrian strongman."

"So you don't like Austrians any more than Poles."

"Austrians, Germans, Poles, all the same. Pigs."

"How do you feel about the English? Particularly the English girl, Seesla."

"The little snake girl, she is very sweet. I try to have feelings for her, but mon Dieu, her skin is tres lamentable! Skin should be beautiful, a work of art. You have traveled to England, perhaps?"

"Afraid not."

"If you must go there, do not eat the English food. Révoltant! How do you say? Revolting. In fact, do not go to England at all. There is nothing there."

"Okay, we've covered Austrians, Germans, Poles, and the English. So, how do you feel about Americans?"

"Oh, mon cher ami, I love les Américains. During the war, les Américains and les Français, we have pushed back the Germans and won the war together. Perhaps soon we must do it again, who knows? In Europe now, all things go badly. Much trouble making by Nazis."

"Ever had any trouble with the law yourself?"

"But no. I am the lawful citizen parfait. Only once in my life have the police talked to me. A misunderstanding only. It happened when I got a tattoo in a very nasty place."

"Now you've got me curious. If it's not too personal," Isaac said, "where exactly?"

"The nasty place?"

"Yes."

"Galveston."

***

The carnival opened at ten, even though no townspeople had shown up yet. The riderless grinning horses on the Flying Jenny pumped up and down as *Buffalo Gals* and *Ta-Ra-Ra-Boom-de-ay* blared from a band organ activated by a huge perforated metal disk. Inviting odors rode the breeze out of the food grabs and grease joints, trying to entice customers who weren't there yet. The midway games were open, but the operators were hanging around their joints with no one to con except each other. It was threatening to be a long and profitless day.

At the pony ride, a drowsy burro ignored the painted plywood cowboy with a large hole for a face. The faceless cowboy aimed his six-guns at a painted Pancho Villa, hands held high above his sombrero. Opposite them, a wood and brass view camera sat on a tripod, both held together by black friction tape, ready to capture that momentous occasion when little Johnny stuck his grinning face through a large hole in a piece of painted plywood.

By ten-thirty, the carnival-going crowd numbered sixteen: the Henry "Hank" Clossat family entered first, followed shortly by five-foot-one Agnes Morley, who loved carnivals and circuses, and her six-foot-four boyfriend, Phil "Stretch" Sparmon, whose huge hand held her close, as if to protect her from the odd-looking out-of-towners. Next came the large W.J. Blackmore family, raising the carnies' hopes that perhaps today might show a profit after all, in spite of the aura of violence hanging over the lot. Or more likely because of it. Either would do, as long as the take was good.

CHAPTER 16

Isaac had been questioning people for over three hours and was no closer to identifying the killer. Everyone had an alibi, none of them very strong. Worse, it was clear the carnies were closing ranks, keeping quiet. He knew he was in deep over his head.

Isaac looked up from his notepad as the Borneo Wild Man walked in, a bone in his nose, reddish-yellow streaks on his brown face, and carrying a stick with a shrunken head on top. He was bare-chested, but wore a new pair of gray slacks with sharp creases.

"Leroy says you want me, sir." His accent was not from Borneo. More likely Baton Rouge. "Name's Willie Carter."

"Sit down, Willie." Isaac was sitting in the only chair, so he motioned toward a large trunk. "How long have you known the dead man?"

"Five years, sir. Before that I worked on the Ft. Smith & Western, out of Boley, Oklahoma."

"Railroad man, eh? From the size of your arm and shoulder muscles, I'd guess you were a gandy dancer."

"That's a perfect guess. How'd you know?"

"I used to be section-boss of some pretty big crews in Texas for the International & Great Northern. I've lifted plenty of rails and ties. Even drove spikes sometimes, so as to understand the job better."

"Then I guess you're an honorary gandy dancer," Willie smiled.

"Hardly. But the crew seemed to appreciate a king snipe who treated them fair." Isaac said. "Did you get tired of Oklahoma?"

95

"Naw, I loved Boley. But when hard times hit, I went to my cousin in Chicago. He was courting some gal whose brother did a Stone Age Man act. One night in Springfield, he fell off the stage and busted his back. Had to quit. So I hitchhiked down there hoping to replace him. The Professor gave me a lot of pointers, and after two months he said I'm the best Wild Man he ever had. Also, Baby Elaine pays me to drive her car and trailer from one town to the next."

"How well did you know Stringbean?"

"He never talked about hisself much." Willie said. "Not clear, anyway."

"What's that mean?"

"Well," Willie paused, "if anyone asked, he'd say he was from Nashville. But if that person had been there, then String would say, aw, he really meant Memphis."

"Something bad in his past?" Isaac asked.

"Not my place to ask, sir."

"What do you think of Otto?"

"Seems all right. Hasn't been with us long. Joined after the season started."

"Was something going on between him and Stringbean's lady friend, Seesla?"

"Not my place to know about white people's personal lives, sir."

Isaac backed off. "That's fine wild man makeup. Is that a real bone in your nose?"

"Oh, it's real, but it's gaffed." Willie wiggled the bone out of his nostrils. "A gaff is something rigged so it ain't what it seems. This chicken bone has a hidden metal clip, see? It holds tight inside my nose."

"Carnivals must involve a lot of faking."

"Nothing in a moving picture show is real, either, but people

96

still enjoy them. Anyway, most carnies don't care what you are, as long as you do your job, and I like that. And the Professor is training me to be the lot man."

"The what?" Isaac asked.

"The lot man paces off the layout and decides where everything gets set up. The wrong location can hurt how much money a carny's joint earns."

"Quite a responsibility," said Isaac.

"That's the gospel truth. The Professor, with his short little legs, laying out the lot is hard on him. He decided I have a 'highly-refined sense of spatial relationships' or something, so he pays me a little extra to do the layout."

"What's your judgment of the Professor?"

"Ain't nothing he don't know something about. Always quoting from books and plays."

"I mean, is he honest? Or is he gaffed, too?"

"Depends on if you mean carny honest or towner honest. Yeah, he's got a Borneo Wild Man that's the son of Louisiana sharecroppers," Willie said. "But that's just carnival. Maybe you don't give the crowd what they expect, but you do give them something. They don't get an *actual* wild man, but they get educated about Borneo, and they get a real entertaining show."

"Does he have a temper?" Isaac asked.

"Not like you mean. The Professor might talk somebody to death, but he wouldn't cut anybody."

"Who do *you* think killed Stringbean?" Isaac asked.

Willie shrugged his shoulders and looked down at the ground. "No idea, sir."

"There's a carny code of silence, isn't there?" Isaac said.

"I wouldn't know," Willie said. "But carnies do say you got to be 'with it and for it.'"

Isaac decided to try a different approach. "Willie, remember how it was on a track-laying crew? We had to learn who we could trust. Which fellows held grudges, and who might suddenly get angry and shove a railroad spike into someone's kidney. Willie, I need you to trust me."

Isaac waited. Willie turned the gaffed bone in his hands, but said only, "String was a good man."

Isaac tried again. "Remember those railroad surveyors? We'd have been lost in the desert without them. Well, I'm totally lost in this carnival world. If nobody tells me anything except 'yes sir' and 'no sir,' Stringbean will end up as just another lump in the cemetery grass. His killer will get away scot-free! I don't want that, and I don't think you do, either." Isaac leaned over and laid his hand on the man's shoulder. "Willie, I promise that anything you say will stay just between us. I swear it!"

It was a very long moment before Willie looked up at Isaac. "You're barking up the wrong tree about Otto and Seesla. He's flirty with the other women, but not her. But here's something unusual. Whenever we play a big town, you can bet a shiny nickel Otto doesn't hang around when he's not working. Puts on his good suit and drives out to meet local folks."

"Who?"

"Relatives from the old country, I guess. He talks about Austria a lot. Says this man Hitler... You know about him and his bunch?"

"The Third Reich. Only what I read in the newspaper."

"Otto calls him a disgrace to Austria," Willie said. "I think maybe Otto meets with people who are against Hitler. Maybe he borrows money from them, because sometimes he comes back real happy. Other times, he comes back in a dark mood."

"When he can't borrow any money."

"That's how I figure it."

Isaac thought for a moment. "How about the roughnecks?

Any troublemakers?"

"A couple, but they know if they mess with the Ten-in-One performers, Hutchins will split them like a pine log. Anyway, everybody liked String, so it has to be an outsider. That's all I know."

"Okay." Isaac walked to the tent flap and said loudly, "Dang it, Carter, you're no help at all! Just get back to work!" Then he came back and squeezed Willie's shoulder. "I really appreciate this. Thank you," he said quietly

"Happy I could assist you, Sheriff. Us gandy dancers got to stick together, right?" Willie smiled and stood up. Then as he passed Isaac, he added, "And so do carnies."

CHAPTER 17

As Isaac stepped into the office truck, the Professor motioned toward the wooden chair. Instead, Isaac sat down on the loveseat with the sawn-off legs. He wanted good eye contact, provided the little man would stop pacing in circles long enough. Isaac took out his notebook. "Is there anyone who joined the show recently? Someone you don't know much about?"

"Roughnecks. Nobody knows *them* very well." The Professor changed to pacing figure-eights. "They do the heavy stuff, mostly— setting up equipment and rides. A reliable roughie may get promoted eventually, maybe to relief man for the ride operators."

"Why don't you know them?"

"Hutchins hires whatever muscle we need. Drifters sometimes. He's better with those guys than I am."

"So they come and go."

"Mostly go. Especially if they're allergic to hard work. That's the only kind of work a carnival has. We call those guys 'gazoonies.' You never loan money to a gazoony."

Isaac flipped though his notes. *Seesla flirts. Otto is a ladies' man. String was jealous.* "Let's suppose," he said, "String confronted Otto wanting a showdown about..."

"Ridiculous!" The Professor stopped in front of Isaac. "String's condition kept him constantly uncomfortable. He went to great lengths to avoid pain. A phobia, almost. Otto, on the other hand is the quintessential Teutonic knight—big, strong, and fearless."

The Professor's face was taught and his emotions coldly under control. It was the cold control that bothered Isaac.

"Well," said Isaac, "Jealousy is a powerfu..."

"Furthermore!" The Professor was not accepting comments from the class. "String knew Otto was in the cookhouse. With lots of people who were String's friends, people who watched out for him. Yet you suggest that for some unknown reason, String preferred to confront an inebriated strongman when no one was around. At night! Does that actually make sense to you?"

"Then why was he there?"

"I'm already doing most of the thinking here," the Professor started pacing again. "Do I get to collect a county pay envelope, too?" He kicked the wastepaper basket out of his way.

"I'll try to hold up my end of the thinking, Mr. Pinckney," Isaac said. "But you and I are in the same harness, so we better head the same direction. Is there any reason he'd be in the tent."

"None."

"Looking for something?"

"Being a carny doesn't automatically make someone a thief."

"Never said it did. A man might look for something just to know if it was there. Or if it wasn't there. Or maybe to see if someone was there who ought not be."

"If you mean Seesla, not a chance. Otto is the last man she'd want. Well, the last man next to me. You're barking up the wrong tree."

"I've been told that already. But there are lots of trees, and I have to bark up all of them."

"Quaint. But still wrong." The Professor pulled the gold watch from his vest pocket. "That's all for now. I have a show to run."

"One other possibility." Isaac opened the door and looked across the carnival. "Maybe the killer thought Stringbean was somebody else"

"Are you kidding?" the Professor said. "He was five-seven

and weighed only seventy-nine pounds! Even in the dark, who could a man like that be mistaken for?"

"A woman." Isaac went down the steps and headed for the Midway to talk to Hutchins about roughnecks.

***

Although the carnival was open, the Ten-in-One was still closed. Inside, dressed in the purple suit and brocaded vest he always wore on opening day, the Professor climbed onto the small stage.

"Pay attention, people." Today there was none of the usual joking among the performers. They were grim-faced and silent, waiting for his instructions.

"The sheriff is interviewing roughies," he said, "but he's finished with all of you, so we can open the Ten-in-One while there's still time to make some money. Otto's a little shaky, so he's resting. He'll do the strongman stuff, but leave out the sword swallowing and fire eating until he calms down. The doctor gave Seesla a sedative. I wouldn't ask her to perform anyway. Any reason the rest of you can't work?"

"I believe in respecting the dead, but String was 100-percent trouper." Deena-The-Human-Pretzel was sitting on a towel, limbering up by holding her heels behind her head. "He'd want us to play the rubes for every nickel they've got."

"She's right," Elaine said. "String would tell us to bat away."

Louise stopped unwrapping her chewing gum so she could concentrate. "Me and Edna can do it. It only takes a minute to tie on a grass skirt."

"Absolument raison," said Monsieur Louvre. "The show, it must goes on. No?" Ramon, Ramona, and Stani all nodded in agreement.

"Yes, it must," the Professor said, "if we want to stay in

business. I'll start the opening bally in one hour. Concentrate and we'll get through this somehow."

As the performers left, the Professor motioned to Leroy.

"I want you to skip the first show, Leroy," he said quietly. "Take my car and drive that sheriff back to town. Get him talking. When you come back, tell me everything he said. Everything."

The Professor then walked back to the office truck, locked the door behind him, and removed his coat and vest. He took a leather holster from a locked drawer and strapped it around his waist. Then he put his vest and coat back on, set down at the desk, and loaded a small pistol.

***

"Lost it?" Rachel looked up from polishing the silverware. "Lost it where?"

"If I knew where I lost it," Jeremy said, "it wouldn't be lost."

"Jeremy, that sheriff's badge is county property. Where could it be? You had it last night."

"Yeah. I had even polished it real good, too."

"Get back upstairs and search your room inch by inch. Methodically. Like in those police magazines you aren't allowed to read."

"What about my chores?"

"They can wait. You've lost something that isn't yours, and you must find it immediately. Now go!"

"Okay, okay. I'm going."

"Wait! Tie a damp handkerchief over your face so the dust doesn't make your asthma flare up. In fact, take some damp rags and dust everything while you're at it."

Miz Russell entered the parlor carrying a pile of dish towels. "Cleaning your room, Jeremy? How nice," Jeremy rushed out without answering.

"Goodness, he's in a hurry."

"No," said Rachel, "he's angry at me."

"Why?" Miz Russell said.

"Because I'm angry at him."

"Why?"

"Because I found the sheriff's magazines, and Jeremy lost the sheriff's badge."

"Am I getting confused?" Miz Russell sat down on the sofa. "Or merely senile?"

Rachel sat down beside her and explained about the Police Gazettes.

"He shouldn't lie, of course," Miz Russell said. "But he knew you'd take them away. He felt pushed into a corner."

"I don't intend to let him destroy his mind with rubbish," Rachel said.

"Of course not." Miz Russell patted Rachel's hand. "But you can't just take away something a person loves. You must replace it with something else, or they'll never stop thinking about it. Worse, they'll resent you for winning the battle, and they won't want to be around you any more than they absolutely have to. They'll feel constantly reminded that they lost."

"I can't mother him by walking on eggshells," Rachel said. "Sometimes people lose, and they just have to deal with it. I've certainly had to."

"Very true," said Miz Russell, reassuringly. "One of life's hardest challenges is figuring out what to do when we lose." She laid the pile of towels beside her and started folding them. "Our first loss was learning that I could never have children. Then a year later, Lyman's legs were crushed when the well caved in."

"It must have been awful for you," Rachel took some towels and began folding.

"Much worse for him," said Miz Russell. "Here was this tall, strong farmer, and now he couldn't walk, couldn't work, couldn't start a family. He had lost everything the world says makes someone a man."

"What did you do?"

"You can't curl up and die," Miz Russell said. "You have to stay alive inside and fight. So we sold the farm and opened this boarding house. After a time, we were happy enough."

"It makes my problems seem so unimportant," said Rachel.

"If they were unimportant, they wouldn't be problems." Miz Russell stood and took the towels from Rachel. "Don't worry about that badge. I'm sure Jeremy will find it right where he lost it. Or if not, then very close to there."

CHAPTER 18

Leroy's ability to steer the white 1931 Chrysler Le Baron was seriously hampered by having his knees up on either side of the steering wheel. His gear shifting also left much to be desired. "The Professor needs the wooden blocks on the pedals because his legs are so short," Leroy said. "But I guess you noticed that."

"Hard not to," Isaac said, using one hand to brace himself on the dashboard. "Big car for such a small man."

"Oh, the Professor's not small. That's just his body." Leroy swerved sharply to avoid frightening a squirrel sitting by the side of the road. "Say, do you think the killer might be nutty as a squirrel? An escaped psychopathic maniac?"

"Stranger things have happened," Isaac said. "Careful, okay? These country roads are pretty curvy."

"Why, it's straight as an arrow, Sheriff."

"Funny. Seems awful snaky on this side of the car, Anyway, clarify something for me. You're sure String wasn't at the party?"

"I would have noticed," Leroy said. "I liked talking with him. Economics, mostly. And business. Tell me, Sheriff, any strangers come to town lately? Maybe pretending to be a travelling scissors and knife sharpener? Or a daredevil explorer?"

"Couldn't say exactly," Isaac said.

"Well, does anyone in town have a criminal record."

"Nope. Known most of them for years," Isaac said. "Now, did anyone leave the party early?"

"I didn't notice," Leroy said. "Too busy singing and cutting jackies."

"Cutting what?"

"Cutting up jackpots. That means carnies bragging about their adventures and travels." Leroy said. "Hey, maybe it was a hobo from the railroad tracks. Been any house break-ins lately? Or stolen automobiles?"

"Not to my knowledge."

"Hmm, well, it could be a brain-addled drug fiend," Leroy said. "There's a lot of that going around, you know. People smoking reefers and such. What do you think?"

"Pretty sure someone would have noticed. Town's only five blocks long," Isaac said. "You're not someone I'd expect to be a carny. Your family carnies, are they?"

"My dad's a minister. He wanted me to go to theological college, but I got inspired by the Chautauqua shows that came to Duluth," Leroy said. "The lure of the stage was irresistible, so I headed for Broadway. One evening in a boarding house, I heard a magnificent voice reciting Shakespeare brilliantly next door. When I knocked, the door was opened by a man not much higher than my belt buckle. He said he was producing a new show, so I begged him to hire me as an assistant or errand boy or anything, just so I could learn acting from such a master. Then he told me it was a carnival."

"A carnival in the Ozarks must be as 'off Broadway' as anything gets," said Isaac.

"True, but the Evils of Reefers is still an acting job. Of course, I didn't start out as a permanently insane, drug-addled degenerate. I had to work my way up."

"Have you lived in England, Leroy?" Isaac said. "I believe this is the side of the road they drive on over there."

"I think that's true," Leroy said, steering the car to the right, at least until he was taking his half of the road out of the middle. "England, or maybe Scotland. Would the townspeople have noticed if a funny-talking man wearing a plaid…"

107

"No kilts. He would pretty much stand out in Mercerville society," Isaac interrupted. "Out of curiosity, how does a person work up to being permanently insane?" he said as the car drifted closer and closer to the right shoulder.

Leroy explained that his climb to stardom began as "The Death-Defying Dr. Electro." Ten shows a day he sat strapped to a wooden chair while a generator sent 200 volts (not 20,000, as claimed) crackling through the hidden wiring (not through his body, as claimed). Female carnival-goers screamed, fanned their brows, and fell in love watching Leroy, the brave, handsome "Doctor of Electrical Sciences," gnash his teeth and flail about.

But not on Sundays. Leroy didn't mind physical labor on the Sabbath, if it was necessary. He could justify helping erect a stage or move a tent as a form of community service to his new "family." But sitting in a chair in front of an audience generated income, and income constituted working on the Sabbath. Leroy had to draw the line somewhere.

The Professor threatened to fire Leroy and send him back to New York. (Being a man of culture and refinement, the Professor would never have banished Leroy to Duluth.) Leroy refused to abandon his convictions.

After calculating how much income Dr. Electro was generating, the Professor relented. "I'll compromise. Take Sundays off," he said. "But stay in your tent. I don't want the marks to see you and ask questions about the act. You'd probably tell them the truth."

Dr. Electro retired one day in Enid, Oklahoma, when the switch on the electricity generator shorted during a pre-show test.

"Professor," Leroy held a handkerchief over his nose to filter the stench of scorched leather straps. "Remember me telling you that people will be reunited with their family in heaven?"

"Seems believable." The Professor looked at the smoking

trail of molten wiring. "Even if it *is* taught by a church."

Leroy fanned wisps of smoke away from the now-blackened metal cap that normally rested on his head during the act. "Well, I'm not ready for that reunion yet."

"Understood," the Professor said. "Have the roughies store the chair in the prop truck until I think of another use for it."

The Professor's fertile mind already had another use for Leroy, and after some hasty sign painting, the Professor framed a new act: *The Evils of Reefers and Dope.*

***

"I'm only going to stay permanently insane until my acting improves," Leroy told Isaac. "I've cast my lot with those specially-favored artistes who eschew the workaday world to breathe the heady atmosphere of high adventure upon the sawdust trail of Life."

"Pretty flowery for a drug-addled degenerate," said Isaac.

"I'm practicing to become an outside talker. He does the bally on the Ten-in-One platform and turns the tip. That's carny lingo. It means he convinces the tip—the crowd—to buy tickets for the attractions inside. A good outside talker stimulates business. Hey! Now *there's* a possibility! Maybe it was someone from a rival carnival trying to scare away our customers. What do you think?"

"Wouldn't have any answer to that one," Isaac said. "See that magnolia tree? Make a left onto that street."

"I see it," Leroy said, nearly putting the car into a two-wheel slide around the corner. "My theory is, the killer was a Bolshevik who hates private businesses. Do you know any?"

Isaac turned to look out the back window in much the same way a cat might bid farewell to another couple of lives. "You can drop me off at the funeral parlor down the street there. One more question: Did you hear anything unusual during the night?"

"Not until Otto started yelling. I'm a sound sleeper," he said. "George Washington said, 'Early to bed and early to rise, makes you grow up to be strong and wise.' And look how strong he was. He threw a dollar bill across the Potomac in wintertime." Leroy stopped the car, and Isaac got out.

"Thanks for the lift, Leroy. I can walk to the curb from here."

"Fine-a-ree. But what about my Bolshevik theory?"

"I don't follow politics much. Tell the Professor I'll be back when I know something worth reporting."

Leroy stepped on the clutch and searched for first gear. With a chorus of clashing noises, the big Chrysler lurched off down Mercer Street. By the time Isaac entered the funeral parlor, Leroy had turned the corner. He stopped pumping the brakes to make the car lurch, then shifted smoothly into second gear.

Okay, what did I learn? Number one—the sheriff doesn't suspect his own citizens, which is natural. Number two, there are no travelling salesmen in town. Number three, there have been no sightings of any drifter going through town, nor any evidence of a tramp jumping off a freight train. And four, he isn't dumb enough to bite on any of the nonsense theories. So that narrows his suspect list down to just the carnies. Leroy shifted perfectly into third and drove "straight as an arrow" down the street. *The sheriff believes the killer is a carny—one of us.* Leroy headed back to the highway as fast as he could. *But who does he suspect?*

***

The Professor wanted a fatherly chat with his Hootchy-Kootchy girls. Being a true gentleman, he knocked on the trailer door with one hand as he opened it with the other. Edna was standing in front of the mirror, wearing nothing but a grass skirt and a paper Hawaiian lei.

"Hi, Professor." Edna smoothed down the grass. "Louise ran to the bedroom 'cause she's not decent. She's in her undies." Edna was a little bit thin and not strikingly pretty, but her previous job, before the Crash, was as secretary to a business executive. There she had learned to stand and move with a confident grace and dignity that made her, on the whole, quietly attractive.

"You'll have to wear knickers and brassieres." The Professor picked up some dirty clothes from a low hassock. "Grass and flowers won't be enough in this town. Or any town in this state." The Professor tossed the dirty clothes to Edna and sat down on the hassock.

Louise pushed through the curtain separating the bedroom from the rest of the trailer, wrapping a cotton kimono around her curves.

"When that sheriff questioned you," said the Professor, "what did he ask?"

"Nothing special," said Edna. "Who's friends with who? How well did we know Stringbean? Stuff like that."

"He seemed to want to know if anybody has secrets," Louise said. "I certainly wasn't going to tell the old lecher any of *my* secrets."

"He's not old, Louise," said the Professor. "He just approaches life thoughtfully. You're not used to that."

"He questioned us separately," Edna said. "First me. Then he made me leave while he talked to Louise. He wouldn't let us consult each other about our answers."

"Yeah," said Louise. "It made it real hard to be honest."

"Anything more specific?" the Professor asked.

"He asked where *you* come from," Louise said. "I told him maybe England or Britain, or one of those places." She sat down, crossed her bare legs, and waved the bottom corner of her kimono back and forth to circulate air. "He also wanted to know who was at

111

the party. I said everybody was. Except Stringbean."

"Everybody?" The Professor said. "You're sure about that?"

"Sure I'm sure," Louise said. "I pay attention to people. I have what they call 'a love for all mankind.'"

"Yeah, I've noticed." He pushed himself up off the hassock. "Well, if you think of anything else, let me know."

He opened the door and looked out. "We might get a crowd today, after all. You girls better finish getting undressed for the show."

After the Professor closed the door behind him and walked away, Edna said quietly, "Lulu, did you go to Otto's tent last night?"

"I was with you at the party, Silly." Louise took off her kimono and used it to pat perspiration off her torso.

"But after we came back. After I was asleep."

"No." Louise dropped the kimono on the chair and picked up her grass skirt. "Not last night."

CHAPTER 19

"Everybody expected you'd bring back a prisoner." Mel Frazee ushered Isaac through the faux-painted stained-glass doors of the Frazee Family Funeral Parlor and into the Chapel of Eternal Bliss. "But I noticed your pickup was immobilated all day."

"It's low on gas."

"You going back now to arrest that sword-swallower?"

"Not enough evidence," said Isaac.

"You've got the sword. And the blood inside the murder tent. Toss him in that hot jail of yours. That'll sweat a confession out of him."

"Where's Doc MacPhie?"

"Downstairs in the preparation room, looking at the stiff. Follow me."

"I thought undertakers used terms like 'dearly departed,'" Isaac said. "Or 'mortal remains.'"

"If it was a local person, I'd say mortal remains. A traveling carny is just some stiff." Frazee led the way to a curtained door behind the organ. "But we undertakers do prefer to be called 'morticians,' if you please." He held the door open for Isaac. "The real work is done in the basement. It stays cool all summer," Frazee said. "Gets downright chilly in winter, but the dearly departed don't care. They're going to be underground for the rest of their lives anyway."

Isaac followed him down a narrow hallway.

"When we're finished, we haul them upstairs to put them in the box. It's stupid to carry caskets down the stairs. Of course, this freak is so skinny, we could fold him up and use a child-sized coffin. But someone would probably complain. You know how people are."

As they went downstairs, Isaac became aware of a pungent, sweetly-acidic odor. He smelled his fingers. Even the banister seemed permeated with the stuff. Suddenly an image flooded his mind: Sarah in her casket.

Frazee noticed Isaac sniffing. "Formalin. You get used to it after a few months. Unfortunately, that's also how long it takes to get it out of your pores. Hey, Doc," he called out, "you've got more company. And this one can still talk."

The mortician turned back toward the staircase. "Isaac, before you leave, come by the office. A man your age should think about how you plan to spend eternity. I'll show you a new line of caskets that come with a clear cellophane cover. The family can keep Uncle Harry in the living room for months and never have to dust him." Frazee started up the stairs. "Assuming he was taxidermied first, of course."

"Isaac. You're just in time," Dr. MacPhie said. "I was fixing to go home pretty soon. Did you arrest the strongman?"

"He has an alibi. Everyone saw him at the party." Isaac instinctively offered a handshake to MacPhie, but stopped when he saw the doctor's rubber gloves. "Does the body tell you anything?"

MacPhie picked up a cantaloupe from the table beside the corpse. "I got this mushmelon from Hansen's store. He didn't charge me since it's for an investigation, not to mention being three days overripe. So I won't make you reimburse me."

"Happy to hear it," Isaac said, and meant it.

"Look at the slices on the melon. The first one was made by my best scalpel. Probably the sharpest blade you'll ever find. The next slice was made by my bone-cutting knife."

"For dissecting cadavers?"

"For when I make fried chicken. It's a kitchen knife,"

MacPhie said. "This third cut was made by the sword from Otto's trunk. Now, examine the victim's throat." He handed Isaac a brass-handled magnifying glass. "Which cut on the melon looks most like the wound?"

Isaac looked through the glass at the wound, then at the melon. "I see what you mean. The blade wasn't as thin as a scalpel, but considerably sharper than your kitchen knife."

"Yep. Certainly wasn't done with that dull sword."

"Someone snuck up behind him?"

"I don't think so. The wound is at the top of the prominentia laryngea. What you medically-unschooled barbers call the Adam's apple."

"Seems I recall reading that the first surgeons were also barbers."

"Don't rub it in." MacPhie took the pipe out of his mouth. "Now, if the killer attacked from behind, like this..." MacPhie raised his chin and swiped the stem of his pipe across his throat. "...then I'd expect the cut to be pretty much even across. But this cut is deepest over the left carotid, like a right-handed killer coming from the front. Now imagine this." MacPhie ducked his head and moved his hands as though parting curtains.

"The tent flaps," Isaac said. "You're saying the victim bent over to leave the tent, and when he stuck his head outside, someone caught him by surprise."

"I'm inclined toward that. Or maybe someone hollered, and he came out."

"There should be blood wherever he was attacked," Isaac asked.

"As you pointed out this morning. So I went looking for it." MacPhie shoved the pipe stem between his lips. "There it was, soaked into the ground outside the tent flaps."

"A pool of blood near the entrance?" Isaac sank heavily into

115

a chair. "And I didn't even notice it!"

"Because by the time we got there, it was no longer a pool. It had soaked into the ground. Listen, in medical school, they teach the Occam's Razor principle. The best solution has the fewest assumptions. Assumption number one, we missed the spot in the dirt because we got there early, when the sun was barely up. Lots of deep shadows. Or assumption number two, the carnival people crowded around the tent to look inside, and that stirred up the dust like a herd of cattle."

"Or assumption three, I'm not very good at the detecting business."

"But you *did* point out the lack of blood. Otherwise, I wouldn't have thought to look outside."

"Okay, so the victim put his head through the flaps and was slashed. Then he stumbled backwards and fell where we found him."

"How's this theory?" MacPhie said. "Otto comes back from the party and sees Stringbean enter the tent. He yells. Stringbean sticks his head back outside. Whoosh, Otto slashes his throat."

"Could be," said Isaac. "But it doesn't explain why Stringbean went into Otto's empty tent."

"To wait for him."

"I don't think so. The fat lady told me if someone did that, the other carnies would assume he was a thief."

"But maybe they were good friends."

"Just the opposite. Otto doesn't seem to have what we'd call friends, only people who tolerate him and some who don't. However, I *could* believe Stringbean stepped inside to talk to Otto, maybe warn him to stay away from the snake girl. She told me Stringbean was very possessive."

"But you said he'd never go into an empty tent. And if Otto wasn't there…?"

"Suppose it *wasn't* empty," Isaac said.

116

"Oh, I get you. Somebody else was in Otto's tent, and Stringbean assumed it was Otto. When he saw it wasn't Otto, he came back out, and was killed by an accomplice outside. Or maybe the accomplice was Otto."

"Maybe. Sounds a bit too complicated for Occam's Razor."

"Say, you know, it could have been," said MacPhie.

"Could have been what?"

"A barber's straight razor." MacPhie stuck his pipe into his pocket and dropped the melon into the trash can. "So," he said, "you want to come over for supper? Margaret is at her mother's, but I could whip us up some hash browns and eggs."

"Guess I'll say no thanks this time. Maybe I'll go back out there and talk to Otto again. Or maybe I need to just think."

***

Hutchins looked up from the small table as the Professor came into Hutchins' trailer.

"Herbert," the Professor said, "What did that sheriff ask you?"

Hutchins poured himself another lunch, then set the gin bottle down. "He thinks Otto done the murder."

"He actually said that?" the Professor said.

"Not in so many words," Hutchins said. "But what else could he think?"

"Well, what *did* he say? In so many words."

"He wanted to know who might have a grudge against String. I sure wasn't going to finger another carny, so I said it was probably some bindlestiff hopped off a freight train looking to steal something."

"A possibility, I suppose," the Professor said.

"Here's an idea for you." Hutchins eyed the bottle on the

table. "The killer made a mistake. Eleven p.m., lights shut down, clouds hiding the moon. Maybe Ramon threw his Deadly Dagger of Death at the wrong guy."

"Right. Or Baby Elaine was cutting a pork chop, and her knife slipped," the Professor said. "Get serious, Herbert. I need better ideas than that."

"Don't waste your time looking. If it wasn't a hobo, then it was Otto, plain and simple. Rough stuff happens on a carnival, you know that. I remember one time in East Texas. Three lot lice came back after closing to smash up one of my joints. Piney Woods lumberjacks with ax handles. Thought my agent had cheated them."

"Had he?"

"Hell, yeah. You know how a razzle-dazzle store works. A man's a fool to bet heavy on a game where the agent counts up your score and tells you whether you won or lost. You bet a buck or so. Maybe the agent's got a snappy spiel that entertains you. You have fun, he makes money, nobody's hurt. But you don't bet a week's pay! Naw, those rubes got cheated fair and square. They came back in the mood for some heat, so I cleaned their clocks. I was a hero that night. You shoulda been there."

"I *was* there. But it was Tulsa. And they were oilfield workers with baseball bats. And you were so drunk you didn't have the good sense to be afraid of them."

"Tulsa?"

"Tulsa. Now, back to String. If the killer was one of us, who? Everybody claims they were at the party."

"Naw, not every second. People went in and out, taking a leak or whatever."

"Then it could have been anyone?"

"Including Otto," said Hutchins. "How long would an athlete take to run to the tent, slit String's throat, and run back? Five minutes maybe, and nobody even misses him. I know Otto's your

118

friend from the old days, but he thinks he's God's gift to the female race. And String thought Seesla was his personal property. But Sees' never liked being tied down. You got your infernal triangle right there. Professor, my money is on the Kraut."

"I haven't ruled him out, believe me." The Professor opened the door. "Okay, thanks. I'm going over to do the bally."

Hutchins watched the Professor walk out onto the wooden steps.

"Hey, 'fessor," he said. "Was it really Tulsa?"

"Yes, and they were really oilfield guys."

"I musta been bad drunk."

"Yes, you were." The Professor turned back before closing the door. "But if it makes you feel any better—yes, you were also a hero."

Alone again, Hutchins emptied the bottle down his throat and dropped it into the cardboard box with the other empties.

Makes no difference if one more Kraut dies.

CHAPTER 20

Stepping out of the funeral home, Isaac wondered if Mel Frazee was right. Maybe he should gas up the truck, go back to the carnival, and arrest Otto. Tomorrow Judge Parmiston could organize a trial, and Isaac could get back to cutting hair. Let the lawyers sort it out.

In the distance, he heard the lonesome whistle of one of the freights that often rumbled though. If Hutchins was right, the killer was a hobo who dropped off when the Iron Mountain Express slowed down coming off the railroad bridge. The hobo wandered down the old gravel road and found the carnival completely by chance. After killing String, he hightailed it to the highway and thumbed a ride. Verdict: Itinerant carnival worker murdered by an unknown transient surprised during a robbery attempt. Case closed.

That fit the evidence as well as any other theory. The carnival could finish their stay and leave. Isaac could get back to trying to pay his mortgage.

Whereas if Isaac arrested Otto, the evidence against him was so weak, Judge Parmiston would throw the case out of court. Isaac would look foolish and incompetent.

Isaac decided to buy gasoline anyway and go back to the carnival tomorrow. *I was too patient with those people. Tomorrow I'll push them—hard! Maybe someone will open up and point me in the right direction.*

Reaching the barbershop, he admired the new window. He would miss this place.

If there is a God, God is having a bad week. That's all I can figure. Bert sat on the hillside overlooking Mercerville's five-block downtown area and cut his apple. No one had seen him, and it had been years since he had left tracks that could be followed by anything other than a hungry red wolf. What bothered him was that he had killed the wrong damn freak.

None of this would have happened if she had behaved herself. *It's not like she came from a bad family. She was my uncle's kid.*

In the distance was the White River where he kept his boat. He couldn't actually see the water from here, but to someone raised in the backcountry, vegetation is clearly different near a large source of water. *All those years I lived in the woods and on the river, the only thing I needed but never had was a family.*

Eventually he had saved enough from bootlegging to come back to these mountains where his family had lived for a hundred years. His relatives remembered the troubled orphan runaway, recognized the now-tall woodsman, and gladly accepted him. Blood is thicker than water—especially when accompanied by a large roll of cash.

He built a good cabin deep in the forest—not too rough for a woman to live in—and stocked it with supplies. He would only have to go into town twice a year. When everything was ready, he went downriver to visit his uncle.

A cabin of my own and a wife. Then a son. Bert, like me. She was just fourteen when he took her home, a little older than he had been when he learned to survive alone in the woods. He tried to teach her all the things he knew—how to live off the land, how to be alone, why they must stay away from people,

That first August, only three months in the woods, but already she was complaining about loneliness and isolation. She

121

knew he wouldn't go to town for supplies again until spring, so she begged him to take her with him this time. Finally he said yes, she could go and help load the supplies into the pickup. But in the end, she didn't.

Outside Mountain Home they had passed a carnival, and that got her started again. Please, please, just one hour. She hadn't been with people in so long, and she wouldn't ask for any money to spend. Only please let her walk around for an hour and be with people while he bought the supplies. Then he could pick her up, and she'd be happy again and wouldn't complain.

He felt the sickness of it as soon as he stopped to let her out. Crowds of people. Horrible noise. Unnatural colors. Revolting smells that turned his stomach. The filth and stench of civilization multiplied by a hundred, by a thousand.

When he returned, she was waiting, as he had ordered. She didn't complain, but she wasn't quiet either, babbling about everything she'd seen and how they had a freak show that cost money, but she didn't want to go in anyway because they had some kind of half-human monster. Bert felt sick again, disgusted that people would allow this. Animals flee evil. Humans embrace it, relish it, wallow in it.

It must have been when I was gone hunting for a week that she snuck back to that carnival. He didn't understand how she managed it, but nothing else made sense. *But why? All I can figure is, women don't think normal like men.*

It came every summer, the carnival, regular as deer returning to their wintering grounds. Except, for some reason, it didn't come the next summer, the summer after she died. That confused Bert, until he remembered that deer sometimes abandon an area for one season.

He knew there were other carnivals, but they didn't matter. Nature could tolerate only *one* monster like this, and it lived only in the carnival that had come here. So he would wait.

Last year, he was deep in the woods guiding hunters and didn't learn the carnival had returned until too late. So this summer he had strapped the pickup onto the deck and brought the boat down to Mercerville. Here he could work and earn cash for supplies and still be close enough to drive to Mountain Home when the carnival returned.

A few days ago he had seen a handbill on a post. Running his finger under each word, he almost smiled. This year, after Mountain Home, the carnival would come here to Mercerville.

Bert had gone to find it, to heal Nature. But then he managed to kill some skinny man by mistake. *Ain't no damn God.* He threw the apple core over his shoulder and wiped his knife with an oily rag. On the other hand, maybe Nature needed both of them dead. *That makes sense. That would mean there's a God after all.*

CHAPTER 21

A half-mile south, two blocks west, and five steps down in the church basement, Preacher Noble Custis dropped the smelly Ditto master into the trash can. The three hundred and forty flyers announcing the upcoming visit of Brother Bill Berkeley, candidate for Congress, should be more than enough for the kids to place one on every front door in Mercerville.

Custis riffled the pages to let air dry the ink. True, Berkeley wasn't nationally known yet, but word was spreading fast about the no-nonsense evangelist with strong ideas on lifting America out of the muck. Reportedly, Berkeley had a high opinion of himself, but there was no denying that the man could fill a church.

Full pews would mean, hopefully, a one-time increase of the amount in the collection plate. More important, an attraction like Berkeley might revive the faith of members who no longer attended, their confidence shaken by the Depression.

Sometimes a loving father has to use a firm swat on the behind to get the attention of a rebellious child—or a rebellious nation. This Depression was the firm swat to remind America that jazz-age morals, gangsters in business, and corruption in politics were all symptoms of a national decay that must be cleaned out.

"Noble?" Camilla sang from the top of the stairs.

"In the workroom, dear." Custis wiped his fingers with a rag.

"I just put Mel Frazee and Philo Napker from the hardware store in your study. They say they need your help, and it's urgent."

"Urgent? Goodness!" Custis quickly laid the stack of papers down on the desk. "Of course I'll help them. How could I not?"

124

***

It was almost closing time at Hansen's general store. A tall man walked in and strode down the aisle to where Hansen was stacking a pyramid of pork and beans cans on the counter.

"One tube of Ipana with Ziratol, please," he said.

"Right away, Mr. Fairley. Aron," Hansen called to his sixteen-year-old son, who was sweeping the floor at the rear of the store. "Bring some Ipana toothpaste. Quick now." Hansen smiled. "My oldest. I teach him the business. He's good boy," he said, going behind the long counter. "Twenty-seven cents, please."

Mr. Fairley looked at the blue-mirrored circular front of the radio playing beside the cash register. "Mind if I change the station?" he asked, counting out a quarter and two pennies. "Someone I like is coming on."

"You go right ahead, Mr. Fairley," Hansen said in his lilting Danish accent. With customers getting more and more scarce by the week, a twenty-seven-cent purchase warranted Hansen's friendliest service. "Sometimes I hear Mr. Will Rogers and his Gulf Headliners. But maybe better you like Fred Allen Show?"

"Neither! The Bolshevic-ification of the nations threatens to engulf the world in flames, but all the masses care about is bread and circuses." Mr. Fairley tuned in and out of the static. "Intelligent men feast on the wisdom of the only truly important figure on the political landscape."

"Ah, Mr. President Roosevelt, you mean," Hansen said.

"That mindless tool of international bankers, socialists, and trade unionists? HAH! I'm talking about the savior of the American way of life—Father Charles E. Coughlin."

The hairs rose on Hansen's neck. He recognized the name of the radio preacher whose diatribes against bankers and financiers

125

were sounding increasingly like veiled references to Jewish businessmen. Hansen realized he was caught on the prongs of a moral, as well as mercantile, dilemma. He smiled and walked to the other end of the store, where Aron was taking the toothpaste off a shelf.

"Here is business problem for you," Hansen whispered to his son. "On one hand, a customer wants to pick station on our brand-new Sparton Bluebird. Do we let him?"

"Sure. You can change it back when he leaves."

"Ah, but on the second hand, we will have to hear a demagogue your uncle Max in Detroit says is anti-semitic. Maybe anti-everything."

"But," Aron said, "Mr. Fairley might get angry and not come back."

"Yes, but on the third hand, he is traveling salesman. Maybe he leaves tomorrow anyway and never returns."

"I didn't think of that," the boy said. "Besides, you already have the twenty-seven cents."

"True," Hansen patted the boy's shoulder. "But on the fourth hand..."

Hansen's lesson was interrupted by the entrance of Mel Frazee and Philo Napker, who hurried to the rear of the store.

"Hansen, we need you to join our Citizen's Committee," Napker said as they reached him.

"Aron, take the paste up to Mr. Fairley," Hansen said. "Hello, Mr. Napker, Mr. Frazee. What committee?"

"The Citizen's Action Committee," Napker said. "It's been almost twenty-four hours since yesterday, and Isaac Cash still hasn't caught that killer. Decent women can't walk the streets safely."

"But my wife Annelisa has said nothing to me." Hansen's brow furrowed. "In fact, she is street walking right now, going to make bank deposit."

126

"Yeah, but she's sturdy Scandinavian stock," Mel Frazee said. "Philo's poor wife Lavina is all-American, so she's a nervous wretch."

"We're forming a committee to face up to Isaac and demand a swift arrest of a suspect," Napker said.

"Who?" Hansen asked.

"Whoever's most imminently arrestable," said Frazee.

"I don't think I am right person for this." Hansen said. "Maybe will cause hard feelings, ja?"

"Hell, no," Napker said. "Everybody in town likes you. You represent the Common Man, sort of. Even if you are a foreigner and a Jew."

"What about Mr. Fieldman next door?" Hansen said. "He is important person."

"We can't expect him to join the committee. It would be a conflict of his interest," Napker said. "He gets his hair cut by Isaac every week."

"Hey, what about me?" said Frazee. "Isaac cuts my hair, too!"

"But not every week. Besides, you ain't the town's only bank president."

"Well, I'm the only mortician."

"That's different. You've got a protected clientele. People can't very well be toting dead bodies all the way to Mountain Home to be embalmed."

Mr. Fairley strode down the aisle, stopped a few feet away, and motioned for Napker to come to him.

"The meeting, remember?" Fairley said in a hushed tone. "Very important!"

"Oh, I'll be there," Napker said. "But this is real important, too. We've got to make the sheriff arrest someone for killing that carny."

"The carny doesn't matter. A minor functionary in the greater game. We've bigger fish to fry."

"Okay for you to say. You don't have a wife scared to death and riding your back every time she sees you," Napker said. "You won't even be in town long."

"Nonetheless, you must keep things in perspective," Fairley said. "The carnival is a cog in the mechanism, no doubt. But we are dealing on a much higher level. The civilized world is at stake. Be at the meeting!" He turned, took his toothpaste, and left the store.

As Napker rejoined Frazee, Hansen was still vacillating. "Well, I just don't know," Hansen said. "Isaac, he is good customer. At least now and then sometimes."

"Listen, Hansen." Napker pushed his face close to Hansen's, determined to close the deal. "Did you know Isaac is trying to ruin you? He has started selling home-grown eggs out of his barbershop!"

"Ja?" Hansen's eyes grew wide. "Really? No."

Keeping customers happy was one thing. But a sneaky competitor was an entirely different matter. The die was cast. The Rubicon must be crossed.

"Hokay, fellows." His eyes narrowed with steely resolution as he pulled off his apron. "I join your committee."

CHAPTER 22

Isaac pulled into Mercerville's filling station, a block from the jail, just as Cyrus was rolling a stack of tires into the garage.

"Just in time, Isaac." Cyrus hitched his size-54 pants up above his gluteal cleft. "We're fixin' to close up."

"Afternoon, Cyrus." Isaac tried diplomatically to stay upwind of Cyrus' sweat-saturated apparel. "Fifty cents worth, please."

"I don't think you'll do much hair cutting tomorrow," Cyrus said as he shoved the nozzle into the pickup. "Everybody I talk to is going to that carnival. Matter of fact, I'm gonna close tomorrow afternoon and take Cousin A.J. and my family. You arrested the murderer yet?"

"Working on it."

"Hell, Isaac, nobody here but you and me, and you know I can keep a secret. Who did it?"

"Now, Cyrus, there's a depression going on. You wouldn't want me to endanger my high-paying executive position in law enforcement, would you?"

"Yeah, I guess that's something you *do* have to worry about."

"Not sure I get your meaning, Cyrus."

"Well, not being one to tell secrets, all I can say is that a prestigious leader of our community was at the station this afternoon tanking up his big black Packard. He said people are upset about you letting riff-raff come to town killing each other."

"And did this community leader mention what people he was quoting?"

"Course not, Isaac. That would violate his sacred oath of

129

banker-patient confidentiality. But he did say, and I quote, there is considerable dissatisfaction with the sheriff's performance of his duties. So what's the deal? You must have *some* clues."

"Cyrus, I can't discuss an investigation in progress."

"Got a suspect?"

"Let's just say things are developing."

"Hey, A.J.! Isaac's got a suspect. He don't mess around. He's like Braddock whupping the 'Ozark Cyclone' last month. Bam, bam! The killer's down for the count."

As usual, Cyrus' half-cousin A.J. consisted primarily of two legs sticking out from under a car. His mumble was probably in agreement.

"Mel Frazee says the freak's head was nearly decapitated off." Cyrus teased the gas pump to fifty cents and not a drop more. "He says the murder weapon is a big ol' Confederate officer's sword as long as your arm."

"No, it wasn't done with the sword."

"What then? Arkansas toothpick? Some carnie with a big ol' Bowie?"

"Don't know that it *was* a carny. Could have been anyone with almost any kind of large knife."

"Hear that, A.J.? Isaac's going to make us all line up and lay our pig-stickers on his desk," Cyrus said. "So who's your main suspect, Isaac? Mel says it's the strongman."

"I can't talk about suspects at this point, Cyrus."

"Not the strongman, huh? Well, did the freak have a wife? I always say if somebody ever murders me, it'll be Cinda June. Anybody else would have to line up behind her and wait their turn to murder me."

Isaac handed him fifty cents, and Cyrus hung the nozzle back on the pump.

"Say, Isaac, how about letting me be on the jury. I never been at a murder trial before."

"Jury selection wouldn't be up to me."

"But you'd have influence, right? You know I'm a big supporter of law and order. Nobody more honest than me. Hey, I'll tell you what. If you get me on that jury, I'll give you a couple of gallons for free." He wiped his right palm on his dirty shirt and stuck it out to shake hands. "Deal?"

***

Isaac parked the pickup in the alley between the jail and the boarding house. As he climbed out, he sensed movement in the deepening shadows at the other end of the alley, but saw no one. Was someone playing peek-a-boo?

Isaac walked around the corner of the building, unlocked the jail door, and went inside. He left the door standing open, dropped his fedora on the desk, and sat down. His feet hurt. As he picked up the telephone, he thought he heard the sound of footsteps in the alley. "Come on in," he called out. Nobody replied and nobody entered. He walked outside and looked down the alley. It was empty. He definitely needed some rest.

***

Across the street, the bank was closed, but Bernard Fieldman was at his desk, looking through a box of mortgages. Bernard had grown up in Mercer County and knew everyone whose properties, and in many cases livelihoods, were in that box. Simple people, mostly. Good people. Honest people. Every person represented here was under tremendous pressure.

Until two years ago, Bernard hadn't fully realized how all-consuming, all-destroying, financial pressure could be. Then he picked up the newspaper and read that his best high-school buddy had walked out to the barn and put a shotgun barrel into his mouth. That day Bernard began to understand.

And that day he vowed that Mercerville would have no more suicides because of the Depression. Mercer County depended on him. Unfortunately, this business with the carnival was making him less effective at a time when the pressure on him was greatest. He would demand that Isaac arrest Otto and take him to Little Rock for trial.

Widow Harkens' mortgage caught his eye. The land she inherited would never be valuable. No diamonds (as her father had learned to his sorrow), too rocky for crops, and too far out of town. The only hope was that in five hundred years, Buck Rogers might buy it for a spaceport.

Why not give it back to her? Word would get around and lift people's spirits. That would help the bank's image. A far cry from the humiliation of last year, forced to close for three weeks, beg depositors to forfeit thirty percent of their savings. Roosevelt called it a bank holiday, but that holiday was no picnic.

He pulled Widow Harkens' mortgage out of the box. "Ida Mae," he called through the doorway. "Find the phone number for that Harkens woman."

CHAPTER 23

"Stringbean Samuels," Isaac said into the telephone. "From Tennessee. Sorry I can't give you more to go on, Al. But maybe the Nashville or Memphis police have some record."

He felt lucky to catch Baxter County Sheriff Alsup in his office on a Friday at supper time. Then Isaac remembered that, like Alsup, he was also a sheriff, and he was also working late.

Isaac pushed his right shoe off with his left foot and vice versa. His feet were tired, but he had decided to leave the truck here and make the twenty-minute walk home. Gasoline was too blasted expensive. That fifty cents had only bought two-and-a-half gallons.

"No, Al, I haven't arrested anyone. You're not the first person to ask me that."

He felt his brother's letter in his inside coat pocket. He had almost decided to write and tell Carl to reserve a bunk. No sense kidding himself any longer. The Depression was likely to hang around, and regular haircuts were not at the top of farmers' must-have list. To make things worse, if Cyrus was right that people were upset about his handling of this murder, Isaac had to face the possibility he might not be reelected in November.

"Because I need better evidence, that's why." He took the letter out and picked up a pencil. "My investigation has hit a stone wall." The pencil tip was broken. Isaac tucked the phone receiver between his chin and shoulder, opened his pocket knife, and sharpened the pencil.

"Since you have contacts I don't have, I'm hoping maybe you'll turn something up. Then I can make an arrest and get back to what's left of my real job." Isaac started doodling on the back of the envelope—mostly knives and swords.

"The strongman lived in Chicago. Maybe their police will have something on him. Originally, he's from Linz, Austria. L-i-n-z. A-u-s-t-r-i-a."

He wet the tip of the pencil on his tongue and began to play tic-tac-toe against himself. He figured a sure win would do him good. He'd had enough frustration for one day.

"No, Al, different place. It's Australia where the kangaroos are."

He heard sounds on the sidewalk, coming from the direction of the alley.

"Nope, not even the same continent. Say, Al, a thought occurs to me. This Verein might be like that quasi-Nazi Silver Legion that was in the newspapers, that German-American fascist group over in North Carolina. Maybe Washington keeps track of people like that. Can you contact the State Department somehow?"

The sound was one person, moving slowly, trying not to be heard.

"Well, it was only an idea. Do what you can, will you? Thanks, Al."

Isaac hung up the phone and stood in his stocking feet, facing the door. "Whoever you are, come in," he said. "Now!"

Jeremy stuck his face around the doorframe and grinned. "I was tailing you, Sheriff. I guess I wasn't sneaky enough, huh?"

"You didn't do so badly." Isaac sat down again. "You've never been in here before, have you?"

"No, sir. Only this far. Is that where you lock people up?" Jeremy walked over to the cell.

"That's the place." Isaac pulled his shoes back on.

Jeremy grasped the bars, peering at the cot and wooden stool inside the cell. "Could you lock me up? Just for pretend."

"Sorry. Not supposed to lock people up without fingerprinting them, and my ink pad dried up ages ago." Isaac leaned back in the chair and rested one leg on the scarred desk top. "Anyway, I'd have to charge you with something. You committed any felonies?"

"Does tailing the sheriff count?"

"Nope. That's not even a misdemeanor. Why'd you do it, though?"

"Miz Russell told me to say you're supposed to come to the boarding house for supper."

"I am? How's that?"

"Miz Russell says she'll treat you because you've been investigating all day, so you'd be too tired to fix your own supper and have too much to think about, and anyhow, if you're like most men, you can't boil water without scorching it."

Isaac suppressed a chuckle. The boy leaned against the desk and added, "Mom baked biscuits and cherry pie."

"In that case, let's go have supper." Isaac put Carl's letter back into his pocket and picked up his fedora. "I admit I've had a hard day. I don't believe I'm up to withstanding the wrath of two spurned women."

Before they reached the door, the telephone rang. Isaac never got any phone calls in the sheriff's office, so he knew it had to be a wrong number. Except that he never got wrong numbers either.

"Hello?" He realized he probably should have said something official sounding, like Mercer-County-Sheriff's-Office, Sheriff-Cash-Speaking. But it was too late now, and he wasn't in the mood to apologize.

"I'd like Sheriff Cash, please," a man's voice said.

"That's me. Who are you?"

"This is Clement T. Samuelson, editor of the Mountain Home Sentinel. I understand you had a knifing death last night."

135

"A man was killed, yes." Isaac realized he didn't know how to handle this part of being sheriff. "I'm investigating it."

"Killed is an understatement, Sheriff. Reports are that the man was nearly decapitated. Any murder is news, but this sounds like a slaughter. Have you arrested the butcher yet?"

Isaac wondered why everyone seemed to think he should already have a killer in custody. Didn't these things usually take more time? "Like I said, I'm investigating the incident. I have some suspects."

"Incident? Only an incident? I like that. It demonstrates a subtle, understated sense of irony. How many?"

"How many what?"

"Suspects. You said *some* suspects. That means more than one."

"Look, Mr. Clemson, it's too early to be writing about this."

"Are you telling me to back off? Reporting news is my job. I don't have to explain the First Amendment to you, do I? And it's Samuelson."

"Sorry. Look, Mr. Samuelson, you write whatever you want, but honestly, I don't know anything to tell you."

"Fine, I'll write 'Sheriff Says Investigation at Standstill. Mercer Maniac Terrifies Town.' That'll work."

"You wouldn't..."

"Unless you start cooperating, I will. Now why don't you tell me about your suspects? You can be an anonymous source. I'll keep it quiet until tomorrow's paper."

"I'm going to hang up now, Mr. Samuelson."

"Okay, how about this headline? 'Slasher Stalks State. Cash Can't Cope.' How'd you like to see *that* in print?"

Isaac looked in disbelief at the phone in his hand.

"Excuse me, Mr. Samuelson, I'm going to go eat my supper now. And you can quote me on that."

***

"Jewish-Red-Bolsheviks," Mr. Fairley said through his mouthful of mashed potatoes. "The Great Anti-Christ World Power, that's who. The Hidden Architects of World Domination."

Isaac had no desire to deprive Miz Russell of her only boarder. Times were hard. But he couldn't help wishing this traveling salesman would finish his rounds in Mercer County and keep traveling.

"A carnival is the perfect hiding place for agents of subterfuge, stratagem, and sabotage," Fairley continued. "They travel around making contact with their secret spies in every town. Identify the spies and arrest them all! This may be the last chance to preserve our national superiority."

"Now, now, Mr. Fairley." Miz Russell came in, carrying a plate of hot biscuits. "I've known almost everybody in Mercerville since I was a baby. But I can't think of a one who strikes me as being obsessed with dominating the entire world. Seems like an awfully big chore for people who have to stay pretty much focused on scratching out a living."

"My point exactly. Our adversaries are deceitful and devious in all their ways. They know what you expect to see in people, so that's the image they present. It's all a front."

"More biscuits, anyone?" Miz Russell placed the plate on a folded-up tea towel and sat down beside Rachel. Mr. Fairley reached out and took three without breaking his conversational stride.

"Honest people think the government will protect them," he said. "But I have been to Washington, D.C., and I'm here to tell you our nation's capital is the most awful sinkhole of moral depravity you can imagine. We can't expect protection from that quarter. The Constitution has been usurped. The enemy owns Washington. Lock,

137

stock, and barrel!"

"Last year President Roosevelt recognized the Stalin government." Isaac attempted to aim the discussion in a more logical direction. Any logical direction at all. "But he..."

"Roosevelt. Pfah! Stalin. Phooey!" Mr. Fairley explained.

"Should we assume you aren't a strong supporter of the President?" Rachel asked.

"Roosevelt, Stalin, Ramsay MacDonald—Bolsheviks all." Mr. Fairley buttered his biscuit so viciously that Isaac feared the man might accidentally slash his own wrist. "Cut from the same cloth, by the same pair of scissors. Not a dime's difference in any of them. Not that it matters."

"Uh, why doesn't it matter, Mr. Fairley?" asked Jeremy.

"They aren't the real leaders. Our real masters are unknown. Secret. Hidden."

"Then how do we know they exist?" Jeremy replied.

"You look at the signs, that's how. You can't see the wind, but when trees are blowing down..." The salesman paused to bite a biscuit in half and give the less incisive minds time to catch up with his reasoning.

"Goodness, Mr. Fairley, you would have liked my dear Lyman," Miz Russell said. "He used to sit right there where you're sitting and complain something awful about the carpetbaggers coming back. Heavens, there hadn't been any carpetbaggers in Arkansas for thirty years. Didn't matter, he still worried. I miss dear Lyman so much." She spread a napkin across her lap. "But I surely don't miss his political prattle."

"The signs are all around us," Fairley continued, unfazed. "Bank robbers roaming the countryside. Murders at carnivals. The enormous increase in the..." he lowered his voice almost to a whisper. "...white slave trade!"

"Jeremy, go fetch some more jam," Rachel said.

138

"It's okay, Mom. We learned about slavery in school."

"Just go fetch the jam. Now skoot!"

"Mr. Fairley," Isaac said firmly, "I believe the tone of this discussion has reached..."

"It has reached your own backyard, Sheriff! The tentacles of international evil are even now strangling Mercer County! Remember that young girl who disappeared last year from Tucker?"

"The Skrogins girl? Yes, I remember. She and one of the McWhorter boys ran off to Joplin to get married. Her daddy followed them up there with a shotgun and brought her back."

"But how do we know?" the salesman asked mysteriously.

"We know because she came home, finished high school, married Cleave Tyler's son, and now she's six months pregnant," Isaac said. "That's how we know."

"You don't get it, Sheriff." Mr. Fairley leaned over his plate so far that his necktie slid across the gravy. "A substitute. A highly-trained look-alike inserted into your community, just waiting until time to do her part in The Plan."

"The Plan?" Isaac said. "Are you referring to the violent overthrow of Mercerville, Arkansas? By a worldwide conspiracy of pregnant eighteen-year-olds?"

"Think about it, Sheriff. How do any of us know we really are who we think we are? Hmmm?"

139

CHAPTER 24

After dinner, Mr. Fairley went upstairs to write his sales report, Jeremy and Miz Russell went to the kitchen to wash dishes, and Rachel walked Isaac to the front door. As she reached for the doorknob, she noticed moving shapes through the door's twin panels of frosted glass.

She opened the door to find Preacher Noble Custis on the porch, knuckles raised to knock. Behind him were Mel Frazee, Hansen the grocer, Philo Napker, and Miss Pardus Ann LaBane, principal of the Mercer combined junior and senior high school.

"Mr. Hansen saw Isaac come in earlier," said Preacher Custis explained. "Could you spare a few minutes to chat with a friendly citizen's committee?"

"If this is a formal delegation," Isaac said, "let's go next door to my office."

"Nonsense," Rachel said. "That place will give everyone heatstroke. Let's get comfortable in the parlor. Besides, I'm a citizen, too, and I'd like to listen in."

When they were all seated, Preacher Custis hemmed and hawed a bit, but the meaning was clear. The town wanted an arrest.

"Lavina had to close up M'Lovely Lady early," Philo Napker said. "She was that terrified of going to her car."

"That's pretty terrified, I guess," Isaac said. "Won't be dark for another hour, and she parks beside the back door."

"Easy for you to say, sitting on your rear doing nothing," Napker shot back. "But if you were a woman..."

"Philo, calm down," Miss Pardus Ann LaBane said.

"Lavina's in no danger. I'm barely one hundred pounds soaking wet, and I'm not afraid to walk down the street, murder or not."

Nobody in the room doubted it. Everyone knew that many years ago, Pardus LaBane had spent three days tracking the bear that had killed her fiancée. Her rifle jammed after the first shot, but that didn't matter to the bear, which by then was lying at her feet with a hole in its left eye and a bullet in its brain. Miss LaBane then field dressed the beast with her hunting knife, made a travois out of tree limbs, and dragged the meat back to town to feed poor families with children.

"However, Isaac," Pardus continued, "you must make certain the children are safe. The children are my first concern." Nobody doubted that, either.

"You have to admit," Mel Frazee said, "knowing a slasher might be in the alley sharpening his sword, well, it makes people ask whether they're prepared to meet eternity."

"The sword is safely locked up in your basement preparation room, last I saw," said Isaac.

"He'll have another one. Slashers always do."

"Perhaps you could arrest the strongman for tonight," Hansen said. "Then tomorrow..."

"Tomorrow?" Napker said. "You don't let a madman loose! You keep him locked up until the trial."

"Now hang on," Isaac said. "There's not enough evidence to even hold a trial."

"It happened in the strongman's tent," Frazee said. "Plus, it's his sword, and he's a German. That's proof enough!"

"If you offer," said Hansen, "perhaps he might enjoy to spend the night in jail. His tent must be very unpleasant now, I think."

"I'd get my baseball bat and go with you," Napker said, "except Lavina made me promise to come home soon. She doesn't want to be alone."

"You *have* four big sons," Miss LaBane said.

"But not grown men. Oldest one's only nineteen."

"Isaac, I'd help," Preacher Custis said, "but as a man of the cloth, I have to set a non-violent example. Perhaps Mel...?"

"Hell, yeah, I'll go," Frazee said. "I'll load my 12-gauge and bring that strongman back tied across a pole."

"That's enough of that kind of talk," Isaac said. "I spent a long time questioning the man, and I don't believe he's a danger to anyone in this town."

"That's a good point," Hansen said. "Maybe the killer hates carnival freaks only. Maybe he likes us."

"I wish Brother Bill Berkeley were here," Preacher Custis said. "He'd know what to do."

"I can manage without him, thanks," Isaac said. "Now everyone go home and calm down. I'll go back tonight and talk to the strongman again. I was thinking about it anyway. If I decide he's a threat, I'll lock him up. Fair enough?"

"Hold on," Napker said. "How do we know we can trust you?"

Isaac stared hard at Napker, unblinking. Napker looked at the others for support, but found none. Pardus LaBane mouthed something that appeared to be "Shut up!"

"What I mean is," Napker sputtered, "if you swear it, then we'll leave it to you."

"Absolutely," Preacher Custis said. "We're very blessed to have you as our sheriff."

"Even if I *am* only part time?" Isaac stood and walked to the parlor doorway. "Thank you all for coming."

"Well, ah... I have to meet Bill Berkeley's team at the church." Preacher Custis stood and put on his hat, and the committee members followed him out of the room.

"If you change your mind about the shotgun...," said Frazee.

"Don't believe I need it," said Isaac, "but thanks."

"And if the carnival doesn't have a casket for that dead freak, I can give them a good price on one. Never been used."

"I'll keep it in mind. Goodnight, everybody."

After Rachel had let them out the front door, Isaac said wearily, "Guess I'll head back to the carnival,"

"I'll tell Miz Russell we're leaving."

"I don't need a lift this time, thanks. I bought gas today."

"Now listen. You may have to bring back a possible killer, a very strong man, sitting beside you in the pickup while you steer around five miles of hills and dangerous curves at night. Not to mention, the wind's getting strong again, and I'm sure a storm's going to hit later. You need a driver and a car with a back seat. And tell me this, do you have handcuffs?"

"Well, there's a roll of twine under my driver's seat." Isaac hesitated. "I think."

"I have a brand-new skein of stout clothesline. I'll get it. And a wrap. That wind may get chilly after dark."

"Hold on, Miz Barlow," he said to her back, which was already receding down the hall. "I don't believe he's dangerous, but even so, you shouldn't..."

"My name is Rachel, remember? Grab your hat." She gave him a quick glance over her shoulder. "And in case you're wrong about Otto, I'll bring my revolver, too."

***

It was 9 p.m., barely dark, when Preacher Noble Custis unlocked the church recreation hall and held the door for his wife. To his left he could see headlights washing the side of the chapel as a caravan of four late-model black sedans pulled into the parking lot.

143

Custis waved a welcome while Camilla went in to turn on the lights.

Crowd-thrilling orator and Congressional candidate Bill Berkeley jumped out of the first car, wearing a spotlight white suit. He walked briskly up to Custis and gave him a quick bear hug. The top of his head barely reached Custis' nose, yet he seemed so...well, formidable.

"Beloved brother in the faith, I'd know you anywhere." Berkeley's voice was deep and resonant. "The sincerity in your eyes. The character in your countenance!" Berkeley slapped Custis' shoulder, at the same time looking past it into the recreation hall. "No welcoming dinner? Well, I understand. You must have a very small congregation." Berkeley's permanent smile displayed his brilliant white teeth, but the smile didn't quite make it up into his eyes. "No sense incurring expense feeding humble servants who ate lunch. The Good Book says travel without purse and scrip, right? "

Custis flushed. Nobody had told him he was supposed to organize a church dinner for that late at night!

"No matter. We'll have a snack once we're at the assigned homes," Berkeley said. "Commandant! Outline the plan!"

A man got out of the first sedan, wearing a black uniform with a wisp of white shirt between the lapels. He was taller than Custis, but a pronounced stoop made his hunched shoulders almost level with his ears. His thrust-forward head, sharp nose, and the way his tiny unblinking eyes scanned Custis were reminiscent of a vulture deciding whether its next meal had rotted enough to be tasty.

"Carnival tomorrow noon." The Commandant said. "Ladies picket entrance with placards. Men suppress opposition and secure public address system."

"Opposition?" Custis said.

"Nothing we can't handle," said Berkeley. "My scouts say the surviving freaks are only females, a dwarf, and a couple of older males. Once I control the microphone, I'll give some brief remarks.

144

Urgent need for eugenic purity! Keep our national bloodstream undefiled! Institutionalize defectives! That sort of thing. If it isn't immodest to say, audiences always give me an *excellent* response. But now, about our sleeping quarters...?"

"Oh, yes, sorry. The church members offering their homes are..."

"Aha! This must be your lovely wife." Berkeley saw Camilla's still-youthful silhouette coming through the doorway and extended his hand to her. "Commandant, get the housing information from Pastor Noble!"

"Um, it's Custis," the pastor started. "Noble is my first..."

But Berkeley had chivalrously offered his arm to Camilla and was guiding her in the direction of his car. "While they're talking details, Sister Noble, we'll get to know each other. My staff will be thrilled to meet you. Please call me Preacher Bill."

Preacher Noble Custis watched Berkeley and Camilla walk off, their steps illuminated by the glow from Berkeley's dazzling white shoes. For some reason Custis couldn't identify, an old saying drifted into his mind. Something about taking a viper into one's bosom.

CHAPTER 25

The wind whipped the prop tent as Isaac and Rachel followed Leroy inside. They could hear the Professor inside the Ten-in-One a few yards away, giving his spiel for the blowoff act.

"Ladies and gentlemen, our last exhibit is amazing, remarkable, and only for adults who desire to see it. Inside this private booth you will meet an astounding medical curiosity, Paul/Pauline, the world's only true hermaphrodite. That is the scientific term for a person with the anatomy of *both* male and female on the same body. Paul/Pauline will remove *all* outer clothing, not in any vulgar way, but merely to demonstrate that Paul/Pauline is indeed a genuine Half-Man-Half-Woman. Because this attraction is so extraordinary, we feel it fair to require a small extra charge of twenty-five cents, a mere pittance for the privilege of viewing a phenomenon that the greatest medical experts..."

Leroy held the chair for Rachel to sit down. "Sorry I look filthy. It's only makeup. I still have to go insane one more time tonight."

"We're looking for Otto," Isaac said. "He isn't in his tent or in the Ten-in-One."

"Gone. Drove off about eight. I was walking to the cookhouse for a snack when he passed me."

"Has he done this before?" Isaac asked. "Leave at night?"

"Sure. Maybe once in every big town. I think he has a deal with the Professor to skip an evening show when he wants to. But he doesn't do it in hamlets like this."

"Where does he go?" Rachel said.

"He never says. I guess he has relatives in America."

"What do you know about him?" Isaac took out his notebook.

"Well, he was in the Austrian Army during the Great War. An artillery loader. That helped him build his strength. After that, he developed his act in circuses. Eventually he decided he'd make more money in America. He took the carny name Ivan the Terrible because we were mad at people with German names. He says he won't be using it much longer. Says there are more important things in life than showing off for hayseeds. No offense intended."

"None taken," said Isaac. "He's retiring?"

"I guess. Maybe his age is catching up. In Europe he used to pull a two-ton truck with his teeth. Now he uses Cookhouse Lil's pickup. But he's still strong. He's given me lots of muscle-building tips." Leroy pounded himself hard in the belly. "When he was younger, he let rubes hit him in the stomach. They could never make him double over."

"Rubes?" Rachel said.

"Local people. No offense intended."

"None taken," Isaac said. "How old is he?"

"Hard to say because he's so fit. At first I thought he was younger than he is, but later I decided he must be older than he was when I thought he was younger."

"Uh, how old would that be in years?"

"Way past his prime, for sure," Leroy said. "About your age, I guess. Not that you're old for a sheriff. But physical stuff? Let's face it, that's for younger men. No offense intended."

"None taken." Isaac made a mental note to start taking brisk walks. *Not much, anyway.*

***

147

Normally the drive back to Mercerville through the rolling hills would have been pleasant, perhaps even romantic, with the moon playing hide and seek in the clouds. Tonight stiff gusts abused the car, and Isaac noticed Rachel tightening her grip on the steering wheel.

"If this wind gets too unruly," Isaac said, "I guess Miz Russell wouldn't mind me driving her car."

"Sheriff, I learned to drive fighting the winds through the Ouachita Mountains. Had our share of tornados, too. But if you're frightened...?"

"No, no. You're doing fine. Just offering, that's all."

When Sarah was alive, he did the driving. Sarah didn't enjoy driving a car even in good weather. She preferred sitting close and resting her hand on his leg or the back of his neck, sometimes leaning over to kiss his ear.

"You're very quiet," Rachel said.

"Just thinking."

"Think Otto's taking it on the lam, as they say in the movies?"

"Otto doesn't strike me as a man who runs from trouble."

Rachel hugged the shoulder as a truck passed. "I can't think where he might have gone," she said. "Mercerville's dead. Even Mountain Home rolls up the sidewalks by now."

"I don't think he's looking for entertainment. I think he's attending to something personal." Isaac watched dark shapes flow by. Which shapes had substance, and which were mere shadows? And what was Otto?

"I'm sorry about this wild goose chase," he said. "You'd have done better to stay home and put Jeremy to bed."

"He won't sleep much anyway. Too excited about the carnival tomorrow. His father didn't hang around long enough to take us places."

148

"It must have been awfully hard, raising a child without a husband," Isaac said.

"Looking back, I realize he never really seemed like a husband. But I was so naïve. Three months after we married, his clothes skipped town with him in them. Not even a note on the pillow saying 'you were fun, honey, but it's over.'"

"I believe I heard he was a sailor."

"Had been. Got tired of the sea and came home. Said his people were farmers in Baxter County."

"So he was a farmer."

"Only if you mean cash crops. By the time he disappeared, Otis had won money in card games from nearly every man in Mercerville. What he couldn't win, he'd borrow. He could talk the hind leg off a Missouri mule. You never met him, did you?"

"No. When Sarah and I came back from Texas, Jeremy was starting school."

"You remember when he was little? Well, I suppose we did attract notice. We were the pity of Mercerville for quite some time. Did you also hear that while we were married, my husband made serious efforts to bed half the women in town?"

"No, I never knew that."

"Neither did I, at the time. It came out after he was gone. I felt a right fool, I can tell you. Oh, but Otis was gorgeous to look at. And me not yet eighteen, and very sheltered concerning men. Truth is, I was plain stupid."

"Everyone makes mistakes," Isaac said. "Did you try to trace him?"

"Definitely not! I did get an envelope shortly before Jeremy was born. The postmark was Boston, but no return address and no letter. Only a blank paper wrapped around thirty dollars. Guilty conscience money, I guess."

"At least it helped with expenses."

"Oh, I didn't keep it. I parceled it out to the people he owed money to. A dollar here, two dollars there. Not much of a repayment, but I didn't want any part of that man or anything that was his. Except Jeremy."

"Didn't you have anyone to help you?"

"Mama wanted me to come to her. But Daddy was dead by then, and she was living with my sister's family. I didn't want to intrude. I had made my bed, and I intended to lie in it."

"Pretty hard bed, I'd say."

"Yes, but about that time, Miz Russell decided she couldn't handle the boarding house by herself since Mr. Russell's death. So one morning I showed up on her doorstep, stomach as big as a barn. I said, give me a place to live and three meals a day, and I'll do whatever work needs doing."

An oncoming vehicle rounded a curve, and Rachel steered closer to the shoulder. "As for Otis, maybe he went back to the sea. Maybe he started another family. Two, for all I know. He never knew what a mistake he made leaving me. And I guarantee he'll never get a chance to find out."

"Rachel, slow down." Isaac twisted in his seat to watch the passing car. "Turn around!"

"What? Did you leave something behind?"

"The car that passed by. That was Otto!"

CHAPTER 26

Fighting strong gusts on an unfamiliar road, Otto wasn't driving particularly fast. Rachel and Isaac caught up and flagged him down in the parking area. Isaac had the door open and his foot out before they were completely stopped. "Stay here!" he told her.

"Whatever you say." Rachel reached into her purse. "But if he tries to jump you, make sure you're not in my line of fire."

Isaac met the strongman getting out of his car and asked why he'd left.

"I left, yes," Otto told him. "Is no crime."

"Where'd you go?"

"Putting a note under your jail door."

"About what?"

"I said only that first I must do something important. Then I come and tell you everything."

"What was Stringbean looking for in your tent?"

"How would I know? I wasn't there. But I am no murderer."

Over Otto's shoulder, Isaac could see Rachel in the car. He took a step to the side. He didn't know how accurate her aim might be. From now on, he planned to carry his own revolver.

"You're coming with me." Isaac grasped Otto by the arm. Otto made no attempt to pull away. He also didn't budge.

"This helps no one." Otto said. "Even if you arrest me, I cannot speak tonight. Give me tomorrow only. Then you shall know everything."

"Why should I trust you?"

"This is vital to many good people's lives. But for you, you

151

should trust not even people you think are good."

"If you're lying..."

"I do not lie. But I say no more now. Tomorrow you know everything. You must trust me, is all. Please."

Is this carny playing me for a mark? Isaac felt like a fool for believing Otto. Can you see honesty in a man's eyes? "You just told me to trust no one," Isaac said.

The strongman smiled and patted Isaac's shoulder. "No one is Otto the Great except me. Therefore, I am the no one you can trust."

***

Rachel parked behind the boarding house, and Isaac watched as she went up the back steps, gave him a last wave, and went inside. Then he bucked the headwind up the alley to the front door of the jail to get Otto's note.

By not arresting Otto, he was sticking his neck out for Mercerville to chop off. But apparently there was something going on behind this murder, and he meant to root up the whole mess, starting with what Stringbean saw in that tent. Or who.

If the citizens wanted his job, fine. Let them pin the badge on Big-Mouth Philo Napker. Then Isaac realized that, with the distraction of the Committee's visit, he had forgotten to get the badge from Jeremy. That was probably symbolic of something.

His feet hurt, and he was too sleepy to walk home, but thankfully the pickup had some gasoline now. He opened the door, flipped the light switch, and looked down. There was no note.

Had Otto said under the barbershop door? No, he said jail, Isaac was certain. Perhaps a gust had blown it under the desk. Isaac got down on his knees. Nothing. Maybe when he opened the door, the wind sucked the note outside. He went out and looked up and down the sidewalk. *With my luck, the dang thing's halfway to Cotter.*

He was staring at the gutter wishing he had a flashlight when a fast-moving car turned onto the far end of Mercer Street. As it drew closer, he recognized the Professor's big white Chrysler. A head showed well above the steering wheel. That meant the Professor wasn't driving.

The car braked hard to a stop, and Leroy leaned over to the passenger window. "Sheriff," he said. "The Half has been murdered."

Isaac wasn't sleepy anymore.

CHAPTER 27

Inside the viewing booth of Paul/Pauline, the Half-and-Half, Isaac didn't have to search for blood this time. The world's only genuine hermaphrodite lay twisted and contorted in a wide pool of it. The calves and feet were still on the low four-by-five-foot wooden platform, and an overturned stool lay across the ankles. The sky-blue evening gown had slipped up to the knees, exposing one hairy male leg and one nicely-shaped female leg in a nylon stocking. The stocking wasn't held up by a drab round elastic thing like ordinary women used, but an honest-to-goodness French black lace garter. Isaac started to pull the skirt down and provide the victim a last moment of modesty, then stopped. *Best not to disturb the body.* Isaac stepped back. He had told Leroy to fetch Mel Frazee and the new flashbulb camera Frazee used for the "Final Rest Portraits" he tried to sell bereaved families. Photos might bring out something Isaac had overlooked. He continued to search the booth until Frazee arrived.

After Frazee had photographed the scene and removed the body, Isaac walked over to the office truck. The door was open. The Professor was at his desk, wearing a crimson suit and vest, but no shoes. The little man looked smaller than Isaac remembered, and older. He looked up as Isaac entered. "You have any clues?"

"No," said Isaac. "But somebody does."

"I have no patience left for cryptic cleverness."

"Otto admitted something's going on in this carnival. He won't tell me what."

"Damn right something's going on." The Professor reached

down for one shoe. "Some lumpen flagitious hillbilly is butchering my people while the sheriff picks his nose."

"Ooo, big words." Isaac dragged the wooden kitchen chair close to the Professor and sat down. "I figure that's what educated folks call a scintillating rejoinder. Jocose repartee. A fulgurating parry and riposte."

The Professor looked up, his shoe only half on, his mouth half open.

"Yes, I know some fancy words, too," Isaac said. "Read an entire book once, all by myself. Didn't even have any pictures." He leaned back and crossed his legs. "Having thus expounded on my educational qualifications, I will ask you one more time. Who's killing your freaks?"

The Professor dropped the shoe and closed his eyes. His shoulders slumped. "Sheriff Cash," he said quietly, "If I knew who this killer was, you would now be hauling away his bullet-ridden, lifeless carcass. Even if I spent the rest of my life in your jail." He released a deep breath, sat up, and looked at Isaac. "How can I help?"

"Start by showing me the Half-and-Half's personal possessions."

***

When they were inside the tent belonging to the dead Half-and-Half, the Professor unfolded a document and handed it to Isaac.

"You're a lawman, what does that look like to you?"

"Explosion in a print shop?"

"Polish. It's Stani's identification document from Poland." said the Professor. "Stanislaw Chrzaszczyk Zbigniewski."

"I see why it was easier just to say 'Stani.'"

"In Poland, the government requires everyone to carry

identification," the Professor said.

"National identification documents? Waste of time. Criminals will only forge them anyway."

"That's a refreshing concept, Sheriff. Not progressive, perhaps, but refreshing."

Isaac looked at the things they had spread out on the bed. Makeup. A watch. Sketch pads. A wooden box with drawing pencils, water colors, and brushes. "This all?" he asked.

"Couple of bottles of whiskey. Wad of cash hidden under the mattress." The Professor rolled the cash up and took a rubber band out of his pocket. "Maybe enough for a casket and funeral."

"Anything in German?" Isaac remembered Otto's poster about a meeting. "Letters? Documents?"

"Stani spoke only Polish and a smattering of English."

"Okay, I'll be back tomorrow to examine the murder scene in daylight. Don't let anyone into that little booth." Isaac held the tent flaps for the Professor. "I took photos, and I'll know if anything's been touched."

"I'll rope it off and post a guard. And here, too." The Professor started to walk out.

"Hold on," Isaac said. "What's the bulge under your coat. Is that a pistol?"

Though words rarely failed the Professor, he paused, then flipped his coat aside. "It's registered, I promise. In New York they'd call it a belly gun."

"So inaccurate you almost have to push it against a man's belly to hit him," Isaac said. "Well, the Sullivan Act doesn't apply here, so I'll ignore it for now. But make darn sure you don't draw it without a very good reason."

"Good reasons seem to be piling up."

"Why would Otto kill the Half-and-Half?"

"He wouldn't. They barely knew each other."

"Would he kill Stringbean?"

"Once I'd have said impossible. But the world has become as distorted as a funhouse mirror. Otto's not the same man I knew years ago. He seems preoccupied. When he isn't doing his act, he stays in his tent writing letters."

"He sometimes leaves at night, I'm told."

"The man's not my brother, and I'm not his keeper," the Professor said.

"In that case, I guess I'll be his keeper," said Isaac. "I'm arresting him on suspicion of murder." Either Leroy was lying about Otto's excursions, or the Professor was. "And if you people don't break your carny code of silence before someone else gets attacked, you may all be joining him."

"I get the point. Well, perhaps I've underestimated you."

"You thought I was another typical rube."

"I thought you were another typical sheriff. I of all people should know better than to judge a man by his appearance."

***

Isaac located Otto just coming out of the cookhouse. Over Otto's shoulder Isaac could see several carnies having an agitated discussion. The news of Stani's murder was spreading across the lot.

"I need you to come with me to the sheriff's office," Isaac said.

"For what reason?"

"I want to know why Stringbean was in your tent, and I want you to tell me everything you know about certain people. I don't want anyone snooping around and overhearing." Isaac gestured with his head toward the group gathered near the cookhouse entrance. "Let's go."

"Ah. But there is not a need," Otto stopped in his tracks.

"Here on the lot we can find a place to talk. No need to take me back to town."

"Okay, then." Isaac thought quickly. "We'll sit in my truck out in the parking area."

When they reached the truck, Isaac opened the driver's door. "Get in the driver's seat. You're going to drive us back to town, like it or not." He pushed on Otto's shoulder and felt the same response you get from pushing any two-foot-thick stone wall.

"You are arresting me?" Otto said. "For what?"

"Let's not call it arrest. Let's just say you're being detained in order to assist me in my official inquiries." The phrase had seemed impressive when Isaac had read it in the Police Gazette, but now it sounded hollow and more than a little desperate. He braced himself, expecting Otto's powerful right hook, but it didn't come. Instead, the strongman's shoulders perceptively slumped a little.

"Please, Mr. Sheriff," Otto sighed. "Tomorrow I must do something urgently important. I swear..."

"Save your breath. Get in the truck and drive!" This time when he pushed on Otto's shoulder, it yielded, and Otto slid behind the wheel.

"After questions you bring me back, yes?" Otto asked.

"Provided I like your answers." Isaac shut the door. "I'll give you the ignition key once I'm in the passenger seat."

For the first few minutes of the trip, neither man said anything. His pulse racing, Isaac sat in the passenger seat turned uncomfortably to the left to keep a constant watch on his prisoner.

The wind was dying, but halfway through the sharp turn south of Meekam's Hill, a gust took Otto by surprise. The pickup swerved, throwing Isaac against the passenger door.

"Almost a carnival ride, eh?" Otto said, quickly regaining control. "Perhaps I tell Professor to build a thrill ride with little farmer trucks on a bumpy track, and an airplane propeller making the wind blow. Ah, but what name for it? Tornado Alley perhaps?"

It was too dark to spot a funnel, but Isaac's reflex was to scan the sky. That name wouldn't be too popular around here.

When they reached the jail, Isaac motioned Otto into the cell. Otto balked. "What about your questions?"

"Tomorrow," said. "When we can get you a lawyer. Now move!"

"Then be early," Otto said as he stepped inside the cell. "Earlier is better. Much earlier."

Isaac locked the door quickly and took the first solid breath he had had in more than an hour. "Get some sleep," he said.

***

The lights were off in the boarding house next door, except for two rooms upstairs. Isaac knocked on the door, and soon Rachel opened it. He apologized and gave her the jail keys in the unlikely chance there was a fire.

Driving home, Isaac thought about Rachel's run-away husband. Why hadn't she gotten a divorce in all these years? Isaac didn't figure she was Catholic. More than once he had seen her walking to church with Jeremy, and there sure wasn't any Catholic church in Mercerville. Not that there couldn't be. Hansen's family was doing okay in spite of them being Jewish, so probably a limited number of Catholic families could also become accepted. Eventually. Maybe the answer was that Rachel didn't really want a divorce. Maybe, in spite of what she said, she secretly held out hope her husband would return.

Or maybe she simply didn't know how to go about getting a divorce. After all, she had no idea where her husband was. If that were the case, Isaac might be able to help. Someone like Otis Barlow would probably have brushed against the law on occasion. Sheriff

159

Alsup had resources Isaac didn't have. He had connections with other sheriffs and police departments, maybe even the G-men in Washington. Isaac planned to phone Al tomorrow anyway to ask about any new information on Stringbean's or Otto's past. He could also ask Al to trace one Otis Barlow, sailor. Last known address, Boston.

Not that Rachel mattered, except as a friend. But it's natural to help your friends. After all, when he confronted Otto, she had kept the strongman in her gunsights the whole time. Any woman who is willing and able to shoot a man dead to protect you deserves your appreciation.

Isaac waggled his head occasionally to clear the cobwebs from his brain until finally he reached home. He pulled around back into the shed with no door that he sometimes honored by calling it a garage.

Too tired to go inside, he shut off the engine and sat there appreciating the nighttime coolness filtering through the August heat. He looked up and studied the clusters of gathering thunderheads. *Rachel's right. Going to rain tonight. Probably a lot.*

At last count, he had two murders, no weapon, no witnesses, no fingerprints, no monogrammed handkerchief dropped at the scene, not even a torn-off button clutched in a dead man's hand. His future as a sleuth was not promising. He wished he could wake up tomorrow in a new town, with a new job. Except *that* would mean Marfa, Texas, and the job would be shoveling horse manure.

With citizens forming committees to complain, his reelection as sheriff was increasingly doubtful. Worse, his barbershop might be foreclosed on by this time next month. After careful consideration, it occurred to Isaac that being knee-deep in horse manure might actually be a step up in the world.

The only sounds he could hear outside the pickup were the crickets, the wind whipping through the cedars and chinkapins, and someone's dog barking a long way off. The only sound he could hear inside the pickup was the whisper of his soul asking how he had ended up so far off target from where he had once aimed his life.

Isaac went inside, pulled off his sticky shirt, and washed up. Then he knelt beside the bed where they used to kneel each night and Sarah would say a prayer. Reaching under it, his hand hit Mason jars full of jam, payment for haircuts that couldn't be afforded in cash. He shoved them aside and felt for the pasteboard box containing his Colt .45 hogleg revolver with the seven-and-a-half-inch barrel. It was wrapped in oilcloth to keep out dust and damp. He would need to clean it before loading it, but it was midnight, and he was whipped. He'd do it tomorrow.

Part Three:
The Amazing and Astonishing
Anatomical Aberration!

CHAPTER 28
SATURDAY, AUGUST 18, 1934

Isaac dragged himself out of bed about six, figured out which shoe fit on which foot, then remembered that pants should go on first. He pulled his suspenders up over his undershirt and headed toward the kitchen.

As he neared the kitchen, his growling stomach reminded him of chickens. Feeding them, not eating them. They hadn't had seed in twenty-four hours and by now were probably launching a raid on his vegetable patch.

On the back porch he picked up the dented tin saucepan, and scooped it into the bag of feed. He was more generous than usual. He felt inclined to reward whatever friends he still had left, even if they were only poultry.

Back inside, he rinsed his hands with water from the pitcher that always sat in the sink under the dripping faucet. The water wasn't wasted, because the pitcher reminded him to water the flowers in the window box he had built for Sarah just before she started having headaches. A tumor on her brain, the hospital said. Two weeks later she was gone.

Isaac cleaned his revolver, dressed, and drove down to check on his prisoner. The pavement wasn't as wet as he expected, but last night's high winds had scattered limbs, branches, and debris in the streets. A block from the barbershop, Isaac braced himself for bad news. Happily, the new window was still in one piece, with the morning sun reflecting off the spot where the sign would be painted, if he could only solve these murders and get back to cutting hair.

When he reached the jail, he half expected to find the bars ripped out and Otto scaling a tall building with a blond damsel under one arm. As it turned out, the most serious threat Otto posed was the assault on human eardrums caused by his snoring.

Isaac went next door to the boarding house and found Rachel baking fresh bread. He asked her to take breakfast to the prisoner when she had time.

"Do *not* use the cell key," he told her. "Take your gun with you. Stay by the front door and tell Otto to stand in the far corner of the cell and face the wall. Then have Jeremy put the tray on the floor and move away. Otto can bend down and reach through the bars, or stay hungry."

Before leaving the boarding house, he used the phone in the front hall to call Shep MacPhie.

"He's already gone," said Margaret MacPhie. "He got Mel to open early so he could start the autopsy first thing. Shep is turning into a regular Sheerluck Holmes."

*   *   *

The Professor was lacing his shoes when Willie and Leroy entered the office truck shortly after daylight. "Anything?" he asked.

"Naw," Willie said. "I slept in a bedroll at the murder place. Nobody anywhere close."

"I stayed in Stani's tent," said Leroy. "Hutchins had roughies walking the perimeter of the lot all night. Everything normal. No strangers."

"Okay. This nut is targeting Ten-in-One performers, so tell everyone that from now on they stay in pairs, especially after dark." The Professor reached for his necktie. "Deena can sleep with the dancers tonight, and Seesla can sleep in Elaine's trailer. Leroy, you sleep in Louvre's trailer. Willie, you sleep in here."

165

"Some of the carnies are afraid you'll close and leave us in the lurch," said Willie.

"Obviously people who don't know me well," the Professor said. "Sure, I wish I were back in New York, but yesterday was the first day all season that the carnies earned a good wage. Today, once the rubes learn there's been a second murder, they'll be on us like flies on roadkill. Somebody remind me why I'm supposed to love my neighbor."

"In Matthew," said Leroy, "Jesus tells us..."

"My comment was rhetorical," the Professor said. "Oh, one more thing. Tell everyone that if they see a guy today that they saw yesterday, that could be the killer. Honest farmers are too poor to come to a carnival two days in a row."

***

Ace looked at the ground three hundred miles below. "It looks fine," he yelled down to Hutchins.

"You can't tell from there," Hutchins yelled back. "You got to climb all the way to the top."

Damn. Another fifty miles. Ace tightened his arms around the steel upright and used the exposed ends of the huge bolts as steps to inch his way toward the top of the Screamin'-Meemie.

"Go on! That harness belt is strong. It'll hold you," Hutchins yelled. "When you get there, whack that spinner with your wrench to loosen up any rust. Then take that rag out of your pocket and wipe off the shaft."

"That's my sweat rag," Ace yelled. "I ain't using that."

"I don't care if you use your damn drawers. Just wipe it!"

A hot gust ruffled Ace's shirt, and the upright swayed as he neared the top. He closed his eyes and held on.

"Quit sightseeing," Hutchins yelled. "We got other jobs need

166

doing."

Shut up, old man. I swear I'll drop this wrench on your bald spot. Crack you like an egg.

Baby Elaine saw Hutch and Ace yelling at each other, but having come this far, she didn't intend to turn back. Today even her normally reassuring aluminum cocoon seemed vulnerable. After a murder only thirty feet from where she slept and another one twenty feet from where she performed, she needed to stay close to people she knew.

"Hi, Hutch. Whatcha doing?" she said.

"Hi, Babe." Hutch continued looking up at the top of the ride. "Trying to get that lazy Ace to check the hold-down spinner."

"What's that?" she asked.

"See up at the top, that washer the size of a dinner plate? It needs to spin free. If it ain't clean, the ride will jerk a little when a passenger seat goes over the top. If dirt clogs it up, the ride might stop completely, and there was a lot of dirt blowing last night."

"Okay," yelled Ace. "I'm coming down now."

"You ain't wiped off the bolt yet," Hutchins yelled. "You stay up there 'til you do."

"Okay, okay! I'm doing it!" Ace pulled out his rag. "Then I'll stuff this rag down your throat."

"Oh, that's the way it is, is it? Well, whupping some kid's tail wasn't on my list today, but you come on down, and I'll show you how it's done."

"You fellows are only joking, right?" Elaine said.

"Like hell." Hutchins spat into the dust. "Don't know why I hired that kid. Claims he worked for Sparks Circus before they closed. If he did, he's probably the reason they closed."

"Hutch, I was wondering, if I designed a kiddie ride, who would be a good company to build it? I have an idea for something

167

really unique that kids will love. If it's successful, I have some other ride ideas. Maybe I'll switch from performing to management and let my rides bring in the income instead of me having to do the same show eight times a day"

"You dreaming up more inventions? Well, I would have said Clapham, but they almost went bust. Now they only make bleachers for damned circuses."

"I've noticed you don't like circuses," Elaine said. "Why did you work in them so long?"

"Aw, I was a wet-behind-the-ears acrobat, and I fell for a bareback rider named Dee Solter. She could do a three-horse Roman stand at full gallop. Longest legs I ever saw. Whoo-eee. But her and me only lasted six years, then she took up with a clown. If she had left me for a big cat trainer, or a high wire walker, fine. But a clown? That really hurt! Some women got no class."

"So you switched to carnivals?"

"Started drinking, then bounced around a lot. Carny life is better for me. Things aren't so controlled and regimentated. Anyhow, it's not circuses I hate. It's the attitude of some of the owners. Think they're hotshots just because they got a trapeze and an elephant."

"Awright, old man," Ace yelled from above. "I'm coming down to have a talk with you." With the flexibility of youth—and the stupidity—Ace shimmied down the upright a lot faster than he went up.

"Babe, see me tomorrow," Hutchins said. "I'll think of somebody to build your ride for you. Right now I got things to do." Hutchins picked up a two-foot lead pipe lying on the ride platform.

"Is that pipe part of the Screamin'-Meemie?" Elaine asked.

"Naw, it's more of a tool," Hutchins said as he started toward Ace. "I use it for straightening out roughnecks."

168

Edna snugged up her kimono and pulled the chair over to the trailer door. Closing the door on a morning like this would make the small trailer heat up quickly, but she needed to use the mirror mounted on the back.

Edna had slept with her mom most of that last year as the sickness gradually stole away her mother's mind. Now she didn't care that she had to share the small trailer's bed with Louise. It helped dull the edge on Edna's emptiness.

Louise came out of the little bathroom, carrying the hairbrush. She took a quick look out the side window, but saw nobody she was interested in, only women. She turned to Edna, waiting patiently in the chair.

"Tell me what else you miss, honey," Louise said, beginning to brush Edna's hair. A little extra attention usually helped soften Edna's bouts of melancholy.

"Another thing I miss? Edna said. "Cranking the old ice cream freezer for family picnics. Hard work, but I could do it."

"Yeah, picnics were fun," said Louise. "In high school, the boys always wanted me to skinny dip. I never would. But now, compared with Hootchy dancing, it seems downright innocent." She paused to pull a few hairs off the brush. "What else do you miss?"

"Sundays with Mom. Before she got sick," Edna said. "She'd take me to church and on the way home, we'd sing silly songs she made up. Until when she got senile at the end. She was my good buddy."

"Well, I'm your good buddy now," Louise said. "I guess you and me could go to church sometime."

"You'd go to church with me? Really?" Edna looked at herself in the mirror. She seldom cried anymore, yet her eyes always had dark shadows. She was beginning to look too much like her mother. "That's sweet, Lulu. I'd like that. I wonder what kind of churches are in this burg."

"Let's go to that kind Leroy belongs to. He could sit between us, and I could wear my good dress. He said he likes to see me with clothes on."

"The show is closed tomorrow because of the blue laws," Edna said, "but I don't know if they have his church in Arkansas. Maybe that's only around the Great Lakes."

"Oh, I'd love a little cottage beside a lake. I'd skinny dip every day."

Edna looked into the mirror at her reflected friend. "Do you think Leroy would do it?"

"Skinny dip?"

"Take us to church," Edna said.

"With a maniac creeping around? Sure he would." Louise looked back at Edna's reflection. "We say we want to get right with God, but we need a brave man to drive us. Then we smile and bat our eyes."

"Then start batting." Edna pointed out the window. "Because here he comes."

CHAPTER 29

"Morning, Isaac," MacPhie said as Isaac walked into the preparation room. "You awake enough to examine the famous Half-Man-Half-Woman?"

"No. But I guess I have to."

"Then we'll take it slow." MacPhie pulled the sheet down to the shoulders. "The throat was slit, but not like the first victim. See this abrasion under the chin? The killer came from behind, threw his arm around the neck and jerked the head upwards. Slash, it's over. Fast and quiet."

"That's why the audience didn't know anything had happened until they passed through the curtain into the viewing booth," Isaac said. "Same knife in both murders?"

"Can't tell. But it gets more interesting medically." MacPhie pulled the sheet down to the navel. "Know what you're looking at?"

"Well, strange things happen in nature," Isaac said. "But I don't know the medical term."

"Pectus carinatum. Pigeon breast. One side of the thorax protrudes noticeably more than the other because the sternum and clavicle have grown more on that side. In this case, the upper ribs stick out, too. It's sometimes caused by childhood rickets. It's not especially rare. Nobody's perfectly symmetrical. However, in this case, the asymmetry is greatly exaggerated. That *is* rare."

"How do doctors treat that?"

"No reason to treat it. It isn't a problem. Normal is a range, not an exact point. One human is six-foot-six, another is only five-foot-one, but both are normal human beings. Atypical, but normal.

We shouldn't label people 'abnormal' without a serious reason. God—mind you, I don't concede there is one—but if there is, God loves variety."

"What makes, uh… one breast larger?"

"Not really breast tissue. It's flabby muscle, possibly caused by lifting weights with one arm. Combined with the enlarged thorax, it makes the chest look female on one side."

"Now you've confused me," Isaac said. "Is this a male, a female, or what?"

MacPhie removed the sheet completely. "What's your verdict, Sheriff?"

"He's a man, I'd say," said Isaac.

"Yep. Nothing to shout about, but definitely male. No female development at all."

"Then he wasn't...what's it called?"

"Hermaphrodite. Nope, nor anything like unto it," said MacPhie. "Only a fellow who turned a skeletal asymmetry into a show business career. He also used a sticking bandage to flatten his privates under his body."

"Plus growing long hair on one side and half a beard on the other." Then Isaac pointed to the abdomen. "These stab wounds, they're more like shallow slices."

"Those were made after the victim's heart stopped. They didn't bleed much because he was on his back. Gravity pulled the blood toward the ground, away from his front. The evening gown has matching slashes from the waist to the thighs."

"Maybe the killer wanted to cut the gown open quickly, before anyone came."

"So he could see a hermaphrodite, you mean?" MacPhie said. "He could have done that for twenty-five cents. I sure wish I knew how this killer thinks."

"I don't care how he thinks. I just want to catch him."

172

"Maybe it's an obsession." MacPhie stuck the pipe into his mouth. "The killer didn't get satisfaction from the first killing, so he's compelled to repeat it. If only we could peer inside an abnormal mind and understand it."

"What happened to not labeling people abnormal?"

"Normal minds don't slash throats." MacPhie said. "You have to stop him, of course. But I can't help wondering how much science might learn if we could capture this guy and study him."

"Keep on wondering, Shep. When this is all over, I promise I'll be in the front row at your first lecture. But right now I intend to hunt him down."

"Fair deal, Isaac. You keep hunting, and I'll keep wondering. In fact, I already have a thought about it."

***

When Isaac reached the carnival, he saw that last night's storm had snapped most of the pennants off the top of the Ten-in-One. Roughnecks were re-hanging the fallen banner line, leaving empty spaces where two banners had been removed. The Human Skeleton and the Half-Man-Half-Woman were no longer "with it and for it."

Isaac examined the murder scene again, then questioned all the performers who were in the Ten-in-One when Stani was killed. Deena the Human Pretzel was last. She looked frail and birdlike perched on a chair in her exhibit space in the Ten-in-One, her feet drawn up under her.

"We're all looking over our shoulders." She shuttered and pulled her robe tighter. "I was the last one to see Stani alive, huh? It could have been me."

"So you were coming back from the toilet?"

"Doniker, yeah. Before the last show. I passed Stani's

173

viewing booth. She was drawing in her sketch book. I stuck my head in and waved. She smiled."

"See anyone else?"

"Louvre walked past, wearing his cloak. The others were at the far end. Near the curtain that opens onto the bally stage."

"What happened then?"

"The Professor started his bally, and I went to the curtain."

"But not Stani?"

"She never goes out front. She's the blowoff act. She stays hidden so the rubes have to pay the extra twenty-five cents to see her."

"You say 'she' and 'her.' Didn't you know Stani was a male?"

"Yeah, I guess. I knew Stani was originally a carpenter's apprentice in Krakow. But she always seemed female to me. Very quiet and gentle, you know? I liked her. I didn't understand her, but I liked her."

After Deena left, Isaac sat and thought. When the Professor started the bally, two performers were onstage with him, and Stani was still alive. The others were inside, grouped more or less near the curtain, listening for their cues to come out.

Isaac stepped through the curtain to the narrow backstage and quickly walked the length of the Ten-in-One, his eyes on his railroad pocket watch. Twenty-six seconds. Add a liberal two minutes waiting for the opportunity to slip unseen into Stani's booth and kill him. Then maybe one minute or so to slit the costume open. Assume another twenty-six seconds to walk back, and the total was under four minutes.

However, with the show beginning, if Otto had slipped away even for four minutes, the others would have noticed. Add that to the carnies all giving each other alibis for the time of Stringbean's murder, and it suggested a conspiracy involving many—perhaps all—of the carnies. Fifty-some people, all keeping the carny code of silence about the murders of two well-liked performers by a newcomer carny who was not generally known, much less liked. It didn't ring true.

Isaac needed that Occam's straight razor MacPhie mentioned. The simplest explanation was Hutchins' theory about a hobo from the tracks, but that had its problems. The killer had not stolen anything, so why murder someone? And why would a hobo target only "born acts," people who were physically atypical?

A hobo? Very unlikely. A powerfully-built strongman viewed by scores of people daily? Almost impossible. An outsider tracking this particular carnival? Quite possible, if it was someone with the skills to get in, kill quickly, then blend in with the crowd. And worse, someone capable of seeing other human beings as nothing more than "freaks" worthy of destruction.

CHAPTER 30

Isaac held out two dimes and a nickel to pay for Otto's breakfast.

"Wait until the county reimburses you." Rachel handed him the jail keys. "It's easier if you pay by the week. Assuming you hold him that long."

"Don't see how I can hold him, period," Isaac said. "Based on Deena's statement, although the body wasn't found for another twenty minutes or so, the actual murder happened during a fifteen-minute window. The only performer not there was Otto, and he had the best alibi of all. That window was about the time he was out front with you and me."

"So even if he murdered Stringbean, he couldn't have killed the Half-Man," Rachel said. "Are there two killers?"

"I doubt it. And if there's only one, then I've locked an innocent man in jail." He put on his hat and started out the boarding house door. "I'm letting him out."

"Isaac, think this through," Rachel said. "Word has already spread about the second killing. People are saying you don't know what you're doing, that you took too long to arrest an obviously-guilty man."

"Twenty-four hours. Good grief, do they expect miracles?"

"They're not realistic, I agree. But they're scared," Rachel said. "There hasn't been a murder in Mercerville as far back as anyone remembers. People can understand some drunk shooting off a gun in Snyder's Roadhouse. But a throat slashed in the same big tent where local families were enjoying watching the other

176

performers? And then they step through a curtain and see the body lying in a pool of blood? It's too bizarre for average people to cope with. One misstep and they'll take it out on you."

"I can't stomach keeping a man in jail when there's no evidence except that it happened in his tent."

"Keep him just until the carnival leaves. Anyway, it's probably the safest place for him. He's caught between frightened citizens who think he's guilty and a murderer who may have Otto's name next on the list."

"Listen, it's not angry citizens that bother Otto, or even a killer. It's that important duty of his, something he absolutely *has* to do. And today!" Isaac said. "So I plan to watch him like a hawk."

"Okay, now *you* listen. What if he runs?"

"Don't start in on me, Rachel. I know it's a gamble. Anyhow, I already told Leroy to come and pick him up. The decision is made."

Walking to the jail, Isaac told himself he ought to feel flattered that Rachel was concerned about him. But dang it all, if the responsibility was his, then the decision was also his. It was time people saw him as the big dog in this fight. Come to think of it, maybe he'd better think the same way—before he got cold feet. What kind of sheriff releases his only suspect?

Isaac entered the jail, pulled his chair up to the cell, and sat down facing Otto, who was lying on the cot. "Sit up!" Isaac kicked the bars with his foot. "Time for a chat. What do you know about Stringbean's murder?"

"For certain? Only that a criminal was in my tent."

"How do you know?"

"How could I not know? Did you look how my clothing was disturbed?"

It did seem inconsistent that the clothes had been stuffed into the drawers, while everything else in the tent was organized with

177

near-military precision.

"I'm not convinced," Isaac said. "Last night you talked about a crime worse than murder."

"I can say nothing yet."

"You promised to tell me today."

"No, I said I must do something first. But you would not allow me. I must still do it. Then I tell you all."

"You have a good idea who killed them, don't you?"

"Not anymore, no," Otto sighed. "I thought I did, about the Stringbean. But now my idea makes no sense. I have made a mistake."

"I'll decide if it's a mistake. Just tell me who you suspect."

"Who I suspected is now not possible. Besides I still have my important duty. Give me until tomorrow afternoon. Then you learn all."

"Sorry, no dice." Isaac pushed his chair back to the desk, walked to the door, and looked out. The Professor's car was coming up Mercer Street.

"Wait!" Otto's pleaded. "I never in my life have begged. You cannot realize how important this is. Only twenty-four hours, please! Then if you don't believe me, arrest me."

"You're already in jail, in case you hadn't noticed." Isaac watched the car slowing down.

"Even if the killer *is* who I thought, you couldn't possibly prove it," Otto said. "Give me until tomorrow. What I do will help you!"

Otto was pleading to an empty office as Isaac walked to the corner and motioned for Leroy to pull over in front of the boarding house and stop. Then he went back into the jail.

"You lied to me once, Otto. About leaving a note."

"No, I swear. Perhaps the storm last night. Yes, the wind."

"Maybe." *Well, that's what I thought, too.*

He took the key from his pocket and held it up. "I'm probably crazy to stick my neck out for you, so listen close. Tomorrow you *will* tell me everything, or you're back here waiting trial for murder!"

"Yes, yes. If I run, you get the state police, the Army, anything." said Otto. "I promise I will not disappoint you,"

"Good, because lately I get disappointed real easy. By the way, Arkansas doesn't have state police. But if you run, me and Pardus LaBane will track you down, and I promise I'll shoot you myself."

***

Shep MacPhie hung up the phone. This was getting irritating. A man should stay home when you're trying to phone him. Even if he doesn't know about it, and even if it's Saturday. Making you phone again and again, with no answer, that was just plain rude. Especially when he knew something you really, really needed to find out.

***

Isaac watched Leroy drive off with Otto, then went inside to phone Judge Parmiston.

"Sorry to trouble you, Judge," Isaac said, "but I don't want to make a mistake. Do I need a warrant to search the tent…"

"Of course you need a warrant for a tent! A man's tent is his castle. That goes all the way back to English law, 1628. Or maybe it was 1826. Whose tent is it?"

"The carnival strongman. Where the murder…"

"That human skeleton fellow? You should have searched that tent yesterday!"

179

"I did investigate the scene. But now I want to examine the strongman's trunk."

"Why didn't you say so? Don't make me drag everything out of you, son. Of course you need a warrant!" the judge barked into the telephone. "Now get moving before there's another murder!"

"Actually, Your Honor, there *was* another murder. Last night."

"Two murders? I've been county judge for nineteen years, and that whole time we never had a murder in this town, and only two men murdered anywhere in the county. They were drunks who shot each other in a fight, so I guess that counts as a double murder."

"How soon can I pick up the warrant?"

"You already got one. I told you to get on out there, didn't I? And I'm the Court, aren't I? That's all the warrant you need. I'll do the paperwork. Right now I've got more important things to do than talk on the phone. I'm rewriting the town by-laws."

CHAPTER 31

Isaac spotted the Professor talking to a grandmotherly woman in the Ten-in-One ticket booth. "Keep an eye on the new guy that relieves you," the Professor was saying. "I think he's holding out."

"Of course he's skimming," she said. "We all skim. You don't pay us enough."

"Only because you'll hold out anyway, no matter how much I pay you. But this guy's stealing more than his fair share."

"Got a problem?" Isaac said as he walked up.

"No, no. Merely discussing...ah, bookkeeping procedures," the Professor said. "How can I help you?"

"I want to ask Willie something."

The Professor pulled his gold watch from his vest pocket. "According to my precision chronometer, he'll show up any time now."

Isaac heard yelling and turned to see the crowd part as the Original Wild Man from Borneo ran down the midway waving a half-eaten hot dog and screaming "Yagoona wanna walla woggie." Or words to that effect.

"It's called a 'wild man escape,'" said the Professor. "It always generates interest in the show."

The Wild Man grabbed the framework of the moving Ferris Wheel and was lifted into the air while stuffing the last bite of hot dog into his mouth.

"Willie's going to break his neck!" Isaac said.

When the Wild Man was ten feet in the air, he let go and

dropped about four feet, landing on the roof of the small lean-to that housed the Ferris Wheel's motor. He slid down the slanted roof and hit the ground running.

Willie charged through the scattering crowd, then ran up the stairs onto the Ten-in-One stage and through the curtains. Herbert Hutchins was right behind him, swinging his lead pipe and yelling, "Get back in there, you brute! And I don't mean maybe!"

As they disappeared backstage, the Professor shouted, "Everything's under control, folks. The Original Wild Man from Borneo is being locked up again. In ten minutes you can see him as close as you like, safely behind steel bars. Step over to the platform for a free sample of the edification and enlightenment you'll receive in the Ten-in-One. Yes, *free*! Hurry, Hurry!"

The crowd began ambling toward the Ten-in-One stage.

"Time to do the bally. Walk with me," The Professor said.

"That chase was impressive," said Isaac. "Carnivals are all about showmanship."

"No, just the best parts. And for a good purpose. Illusion brings reality to life."

"Seems to me life *is* reality," said Isaac.

"Then allow me to enlighten you. Suppose you find a genuine three-legged boy in an orphanage. You can't simply tell people the truth."

"Truth is always best," Isaac said.

"Not always. You'd have to tell them the child's own mother abandoned him. And when a carnival came along, even the orphanage was glad to get rid of him. Say that, and people would think it's the most heart-breaking tragedy they'd ever heard."

"They'd be right," Isaac said.

"So you would send people home despairing and forlorn? Nice guy!" the Professor said. "But wait! Tell them the boy was shipwrecked on the Island of Lost Souls, a victim of Dr. Moreau's

182

evil experiments. However, he overpowered the mad doctor and helped everyone escape, and now he's honored by the crowned heads of Europe."

"Why invent a fable?

"Hope! People don't need to be told that life can be harsh and ugly. They *already* know that!" the Professor said. "We show them a *different* reality, filled with the hope and inspiration that they too can conquer their fears, carry on, and endure life's dreariness. My Ten-in-One performers demonstrate that any dream is worth dreaming and that *every* life can have meaning! We're not simply putting on a show, we're creating a sublime work of art. To you, the Ten-in-One is only a sideshow," he pointed with his walking stick. "But those so-called freaks can lift people's spirits as much as any Shakespeare play. Humans can't survive without at least *some* hope of overcoming obstacles and finding happiness. We give them that hope."

"What do you give that poor deformed child?"

"We give him a future! And a home for life with people who will accept him as he is, help him, maybe even love him. Most important, they'll show him that a so-called accident of birth has as much right to life and happiness as any other human."

"Do people always believe the illusion?"

"They always *want* to." The Professor looked up at Isaac. "It isn't harsh reality that people need, it's uplifting dreams. Never forget that. Dreams keep us alive!"

When Isaac and the Professor entered the prop tent, Willie was sitting on a trunk, wiping perspiration with a towel.

"Willie," the Professor said, "what was that nonsense with the hot dog?"

"Aw, I was talking with Elaine and didn't finish my lunch. But I know I can't be late building the crowd for the next show, so I ate on the run. I didn't think it would spoil nothing."

The Professor rolled his eyes. "I'm going out front to start the bally," he said, walking out. "Don't miss your cue."

"You were great, Willie! Very impressive!" Isaac sat down in the chair and paused a moment. "Remember my comment about surveyors keeping us from getting lost in the burning desert? Well, I'm feeling more heat every minute."

Willie took a sack of apples out of the trunk. "You hungry?"

"Now you mention it, yes. Thanks." Isaac selected an apple and took a bite. "What is this killer's motive? Revenge? Hate? Love? Money?"

"Stani never had any money. Spent it all on art supplies and booze," Willie said. "String kept all his in banks. He didn't care about money as long as he had his books to read. Now with Otto, yeah, I suspect money is a big thing."

"Why, do you think?"

"You seen his Lincoln Phaeton?"

"What about it?" said Isaac.

"Most performers got their own trailer. Sleeping in a tent, that's what roughnecks do. Or somebody who just joined the show, like Leroy. Not a seasoned trouper like Otto."

"I don't follow."

"My guess is, Otto can't afford a trailer because he bought that fancy car to make himself look successful to rubes. What if he's running a con on people in every town, and then moving on. And what if String and Stani figured that out."

"Blackmailers getting murdered? Certainly possible," Isaac said. "Willie, I'm sure Otto's going to do something soon, but I don't know what. An extra pair of eyes would sure help. Will you keep watch on Otto as much as you're able?"

"If it helps find the killer," Willie said, "that Austrian just got himself another shadow."

CHAPTER 32

On the bally stage in front of the Ten-in-One, the Professor picked the microphone up off a small table and laid his walking stick in its place. "Ladies and Gentlemen! Step close to the platform. I'm Professor Desmond A. Pinckney, the Third, and you are about to meet some of our very special performers, free of charge." In the space between the stage and the row of rides stretching down the midway, people slowed, then stopped to watch the dwarf in the lemon-yellow suit.

"Yes, I did say completely free! Move closer, please. Keep the lane behind you clear so others can pass." Most of the "tip" shuffled forward—cautiously. A freak show was something alien and demanded extra vigilance.

Standing near a ride, Bert waited until the crowd had settled, then moved up to the rear. He was never comfortable around groups of people. You might be able to predict what an animal would do, but never a human.

Bert had walked around the carnival for nearly an hour without finding any trace of the unnatural thing. Maybe it was like those Florida fish he had heard about—hamlets. They could change from male to female whenever they wanted. But fish don't come back to life once they're dead. Bert had to make sure the unnatural thing hadn't come back either, and he reasoned that if it *were* still alive, the freaks would bring it out as proof it hadn't been killed last night.

"Coming through the curtain now," the little man was saying, "is the world-famous Tattooed Man, Monsieur Louvre, from

185

Paris, France. A Living Canvas of Incredible Indelible Images rivaling the greatest art museums!"

Louvre swirled his scarlet cloak above his head as he crossed the stage, clad only in swimming trunks. He struck a pose, allowing the crowd a quick look at the Eiffel Tower stretching from the base of his neck all the way down to a Paris street scene that disappeared into his trunks. Then he covered himself and left the stage.

"Seated to my right," the Professor gestured, "...bigger than life, is Baby Elaine, America's Fattest Little Lady."

"Hi, everybody!" Baby Elaine waved a pink hankie. "Come inside and ask me anything you want." She hid her face behind the hankie and giggled loudly. "And I *do* mean anything."

Bert watched closely as the dwarf brought the freaks out one by one. The first one was clearly not the thing Bert had killed, just an old sailor with tattoos. Then there was a fat lady, but Bert had a cousin almost as fat. Maybe they would like each other.

"Inside you'll also meet Seesla the Snake Girl," the Professor said as she came onstage, "whose scaly skin has what medical experts agree is true dermal papillae, just as reptiles have. And she speaks fluent reptilian!"

The snake girl looked normal, except for her rough blotchy skin. Bert had killed probably a hundred snakes in his lifetime, and this was no snake, only a short woman wearing no shoes or makeup. She was thin, obviously not a big eater, although her dress revealed too much for Bert's liking. This Seesla woman could probably handle life in an isolated cabin just fine, especially if she could talk to snakes. Bert wished his wife had been more like this snake girl.

"Following her are Hilani and Luilani, the beautiful Hawaiian maidens, here to give you a free sample of their own show, which begins soon in the red tent just thirty yards down the midway to your left. Look! They shimmy, they shake! They're like jelly in an earthquake!"

186

As Louise and Edna set their grass skirts into vigorous motion, the crowd cheered, and no one noticed the Professor point the microphone at the loudspeaker, and then slide his thumbnail across the top of the microphone. The piercing feedback screech from the loudspeaker brought everyone's eyes back to him. He faked a surprised look at the microphone, but continued his spiel.

"Once inside our tent, you'll witness an amazing performance by Ivan the Terrible, a modern Hercules..."

Otto bounded onstage, shaking both fists above his head, and joined Louise and Edna at the front of the stage. Each girl clasped her hands around one of his impressive biceps and hung from his arms.

"...lauded and applauded by the Crowned Heads of Europe for..."

Otto began to spin, swinging the girls from his massive arms as easily as two sacks of flour. The crowd let out a collective "Ohh!"

"...his magnificent muscular mastery." The Professor scraped his nail across the microphone even harder, making it squeal more horribly than before.

*＊＊

In the prop tent, Isaac watched Willie check his makeup in the mirror, making sure the orange stripe down the center of his nose was straight. If Life forced Willie to play the role of a savage, then he intended to be the best-looking savage these rubes had ever seen. Outside, the noise of the audience suddenly swelled.

"Hear them squealing?" he said to Isaac. "That means Otto is swinging the Hootchy girls around the platform. Time for me to go over and get inside my cage."

"Even with a murderer on the loose, the show must go on. Right?"

"You're catching on, Bossman." Willie adjusted the fake bone in his nose. "We'll make a performer of you yet."

"Fair enough," Isaac laughed. "I just might need a new job."

***

On the stage, the Professor made the microphone squeal once more, then glared angrily at it and laid it on the table.

"Ladies and gentlemen," he said, "we seem to have a microphone problem, but I want to do my favorite magic trick for you, so come as close as possible, please. I have a normally unimpressive voice," he said, lowering the volume of his normally impressive voice. Obediently, the tip pushed forward, eager not to miss a word. People who might be tempted to leave and spend their money elsewhere were now hindered by the bodies pressing against them.

"My favorite magic trick is that I will turn you all into little boys and girls again. Yes, for the next five minutes, the ticket seller will sell *only* children's tickets, no matter whether you are one year old or one hundred years. But this is only for those of you who buy your ticket right now, at the reduced price of twenty cents, one-fifth of a good old American dollar..."

It was time to end the bally and "freeze the tip" with something dramatic to capture their attention completely. Otto, who had gone backstage, now strode quickly back on stage, carrying a flaming torch.

"...and that reduced price begins," the Professor said, "...RIGHT...NOW!"

At that cue, Otto blew a mouthful of flammable lamp oil vapor across the top of the torch, sending a blast of flame six feet out, and above the heads of the shrieking crowd.

Bert watched from the back of the crowd as the Russian blew

188

fire from his mouth. Strange, Bert thought, but useful. He wondered if the man could do it in the rain, or only in dry weather.

The more important reason for packing the crowd—the purely psychological reason—now came into play. When you pack people together like sheep, they begin to think like sheep. And sheep follow their leader.

"Dang all, this is amazing!" shouted a man with a large handlebar moustache, who was in the center of the throng. "I mean to get me a ticket right now!" He quickly squeezed through the crowd, heading straight for the ticket booth. By the time he reached it, carnival-goers were pushing to line up behind him, digging into their pockets.

(The sheep with the handlebar moustache was named Felix. Once inside the Ten-in-One, he would slip out a side exit, put the fake moustache into his pocket, and return to his regular job maintaining the rides.)

The bally show now finished, Edna and Louise moved to either side of Baby Elaine's big chair to steady it so that Elaine could stand up safely. Otto went backstage to prepare the swords and weights in his exhibition booth.

Although the Professor had packed the crowd into an easy-to-influence flock ready to be fleeced, he noticed a small group of people remaining off to one side of the stage. They wore black armbands and were listening to a man in a snow white suit.

Has Hutchins hired an ice cream salesman? the Professor wondered as he picked up the microphone, now miraculously free of static. *And those black armbands. Have they all been to a funeral?*

Suddenly, the man in white jumped onto the stage and grabbed the Professor's hand that was holding the microphone.

"Citizens, freeze where you are! I command you!" the man yelled into the microphone. "I'm putting a stop to these crimes in the name of your God and mine!"

189

Watching this, Bert was surprised to learn that freak shows had preachers. But then, he had expected that a carnival would be nothing like the normal world. All that mattered was that the unnatural thing had not been brought out or even mentioned. That meant it really was dead and could never again reproduce. Bert was glad he had come back today to make sure. He had never killed one of those before.

***

Inside the prop tent, Isaac and Willie heard an unfamiliar voice over the loudspeaker. "I'm putting a stop to the crimes of inferior births and defective offspring!" the voice yelled. "I am Brother Bill Berkeley, candidate for United States Congress and a humble shining sword in the hand of the Almighty. I proclaim this sideshow officially closed and these wretched freaks free from servitude. Enjoy the rides and games, folks, but this freak show is finished!"

Then a different voice shouted, "Get the hell off my stage!"

"That's the Professor," said Willie. "Something's bad wrong." He tried to go around Isaac, but Isaac pushed him back.

"Stay right here," Isaac said.

"Boss, you don't want to mess with no carny brawl. They get nasty real fast."

"Listen to me, Willie! This is not like that peaceful all-Black town. This is an Ozark village with a killer loose, and these people are scared and panicky. This situation could explode. Now, please, just stay put safely until I find out what's happening."

***

"I want you off this stage NOW!" The Professor held onto

190

the microphone as tightly as he could, but Berkeley twisted it out of his grasp.

"You see, folks?" Berkeley said. "A dwarf's limited mentality can't understand that we're freeing him from bondage."

The audience didn't know whether to be respectful to a reverend, attentive to a political candidate, or just envious of someone who could afford the cleaning bills for a white suit.

The Professor kicked at Berkeley's shins, but Berkeley dodged, grabbed the Professor around the waist, and lifted him off the ground. "Be still, little brother. Let your dwarfish heart rejoice."

The crowd laughed, thinking the action onstage was part of the show. (After all, treating a dwarf like a sack of potatoes has long been an acceptable form of comedy among some classes of society.) Baby Elaine began shouting "Hey, Rube!"

"Citizens," Berkeley said. "Every fifteen seconds Washington spends one hundred of your tax dollars on feeble-minded defectives from bad bloodlines. Useless eaters! Congress wastes your money supporting drooling, slack-jawed dregs of the dependent class." Berkeley was finding it difficult to preach with a swearing, struggling dwarf in his arms.

The black armband people began to clap and chant, "Cleanse this place! Perfect our race!" over and over. Standing with them was Preacher Noble Custis, who was *not* clapping or chanting. He was looking on, horrified.

"What a tragedy we didn't arrive in time to save the deformed half-creature that was murdered last night." Berkeley exclaimed. "He or she would now be safe behind the walls of a charitable institution." The Professor wiggled free and tried to run, but Berkeley caught him by the back of the coat. "That's where we'll take all these victims of inherited biological deterioration. And that pathetic creature," he pointed at Baby Elaine who was yelling the carny call for help, "will be spared from the public humiliation that

191

has made her feebleminded."

"Cleanse this place! Perfect our race!" the chant continued.

The Professor managed to twist around enough to punch Berkeley hard below the belt buckle and the man squealed, "Commandant, I need you!" The craggy-faced man in the black uniform shouted "Hallelujah," leapt onto the stage, and lunged toward Seesla, trying to pin her flailing arms behind her. Louvre ran onstage and pushed in between Seesla and the Commandant.

"Every forty-eight seconds," Berkeley shouted in an increasingly frantic voice, "a baby is born who is in some way abnormal. Born to be your burden! It costs money to care for mentally and physical malformed misfits! My Prayer Team will now pass…" He interrupted himself to hiss "Hold still, blast you!" at the Professor. "…will pass among you. Every dollar you donate to eugenic science helps stamp out the tragedy of tainted blood lines. Some lives are not worth living, but we can't solve those people's problem without your generous contributions."

Seesla broke free and ran backstage as the Commandant shoved Louvre off the edge of the platform.

The Commandant now made a grab for Louise, but Edna jumped on his back and wrapped her arms around his neck in a choke hold, losing part of her grass skirt in the process.

A woman near the stage gasped, "That girl's nearly stark naked!"

"Simmer down, Wandene," her husband said. "You know carnivals are all fake."

CHAPTER 33

As Isaac elbowed through the rear of the crowd, Berkeley was again lifting the Professor off his feet. "Hey, Rube!" Elaine was yelling over and over. Edna was piggyback on the Commandant, while Louise kicked his shins and worked her way higher.

"Cleanse the nation's germ plasm!" Berkeley yelled, "Promote the godly cause of eugenic purification! Look how insane these freaks are! Help us tear this sideshow down right now! And vote Berkeley for Congress!"

"No! Everybody stop," Preacher Noble Custis shouted, separating himself from the Rescue Raiders group. "Remember Corinthians six. Longsuffering! Kindness!"

Edna's weight dragged the Commandant off balance, and he fell on the stage. Baby Elaine slid off her chair onto the man's body, pinning him down.

As Isaac pushed through the astounded townspeople to the edge of the platform, Preacher Noble Custis yelled, "Matthew five, nine. Blessed are the peacemakers!"

Isaac reached the stage, faced the crowd and yelled, "I'm Sheriff Isaac Cash. I order you to disperse."

Someone grabbed Isaac's arm and spun him around.

"Isaac Cash?" The small man with the pencil mustache had a surprisingly powerful grip. "What do you say about this?"

"Leave me alone, and you'll find out," Isaac jerked his arm free. "Citizens of Mercer County, I..."

"Would you characterize this as a riot?" The man adjusted his horn-rimmed glasses as he squeezed in front of Isaac. "Is it accurate to say 'Chaos in Mercerville. Citizens on Rampage'?"

"Who the hell are you?" Isaac said.

"Clement T. Samuelson, editor of the Mountain Home Sentinel."

Berkeley shouted "Peace, little brother," as the Professor clawed his way up Berkeley's shirt front.

"Matthew ten," Custis' voice came from somewhere in the crowd. "I come not to bring peace, I came to bring a sw...Oh no, not that one, not that one! I didn't mean that."

"This damn elephant's crushing me," the Commandant groaned loudly.

"How about a quote?" Samuelson pushed his face inches from Isaac's. "Something pithy and succinct."

Isaac ignored him, calling out to the crowd, "I'm the Sheriff. I order you to go home."

"Pithy, yes, but clichéd."

"Samuelson, let me do my job, or I'll put you under arrest."

"Oo! Suppression of the press!" Samuelson's eyes grew bright. "You're trampling my First Amendment. Can I quote you?"

"I don't care what you're the editor of, you can..."

"Editor?" Berkeley moved as close as possible to the edge of the stage and clamped his hand over the struggling Professor's mouth. "Which one of you? I can do an interview with you just as soon as...Yeeeaaa!" Berkeley said as the Professor bit his hand.

Four "Free the Freaks Rescue Raiders" saw their leader's plight and pushed roughly through the crowd. They began scaling the stage shouting "Perfect Our Race." In response, the crowd hollered "Get off so we can see the dancing girls!" Several husky farmers peeled the Raiders off the edge of the stage as easily as shucking corn.

"We can still have our own carnival at the church," Preacher Custis pleaded. Then he bravely but foolishly jumped between the farm hands and the raiders. He was quickly knocked to the ground.

Isaac shoved Samuelson aside, pushed his way over to Custis, and yanked him free from the scuffling men.

Suddenly Leroy rushed through the doorway, his face streaked with brown makeup and his hair standing out in all directions. He grabbed the Professor and tried to pull him from Brother Bill's loving arms.

"My gun, Leroy," the Professor said. "Help me get my gun!" Berkeley and Leroy tugged in opposite directions for possession of the Professor, who managed to draw his derringer. Unfortunately, he lost his grip. The gun fell to the platform and fired into the air.

"The freaks have guns!" the Prayer Team screamed. "They'll slaughter us all." The crowd surged backwards ten feet, knocking over the low barrier surrounding the Screamin'-Meemie.

At the rear of the crowd, Bert was pushed hard against one of the Screamin'-Meemie gondola seats. *You'd think these fools had never been shot at before.* He got up and walked away quickly. The half-human freak was dead, so there was no reason to stay.

Several roughnecks responding to the "Hey, Rube" cries ran past him. They waded into the crowd like a farmer's wedge splitting a fence rail, shoving citizens aside or throwing them to the ground as the roughies worked their way up to the melee in front of the platform. Bert didn't look back. *Wonder if carnivals have a place to buy an apple.*

***

On the platform, Leroy abandoned his peaceful religious upbringing and gave Brother Bill a solid right to the jaw. The freak saver dropped the freak he was saving, and staggered backwards. The Professor grabbed his walking stick, swung it around his head, and let it fly directly into Berkeley's face. Berkeley swore and clutched his nose. Bright red blood streamed onto his snow-white suit.

(For weeks thereafter, he would wear the bloodied suit in the pulpit as he told of his near martyrdom by a secret cult of freak masters. "They tried to destroy *me*, a patriotic American crusading against their exploitation of simple-minded misfits." Then, looking to the heavens, he would gesture toward the crimson stains and silently mouth, "Forgive them not.")

The Rescue Raiders in front of the stage had managed to punch free from the fun-loving farmers and now faced the greater threat of oncoming roughnecks. Their only avenue of escape was to try again to climb onto the stage.

As Berkeley pressed a handkerchief to his nose, Otto jumped through the doorway, his feet making a deafening thud as his 240 pounds hit the stage floor. In his hand, he held the torch, which he had relighted backstage. Behind him came the Wild Man from Borneo, screaming "Boogedy-wahkata-yakaty," and waving a spear in one hand and a rubber shrunken head in the other. Together they charged the man in white.

Afterwards, it was debated around Mercerville whether Berkeley fell, fainted, or flew off the stage, hindquarters first, onto the heads of his own Rescue Raiders.

Breathless, the Professor picked up the microphone and tried to carry on. "All part of the show, folks...(pant)...Just a sample...(pant)...twenty-five cents...(pant)... Aw, the hell with it." He headed toward the curtained doorway with Leroy, Otto, and Willie protecting his retreat.

(Berkeley was last seen being escorted away by the Double-E Double-F Double-R team, his formerly angelic clothing streaked with dirt, blood, and an unidentified wet streak down one leg. Trotting alongside was editor Clement T. Samuelson, attempting to conduct an interview. However, the Reverend Brother Berkeley was

196

no longer feeling talkative.)

"Damn," said Hutchins, peering through the curtain. "Look at 'em lining up for tickets. This'll be the best sales day ever."

Leroy grabbed a chair and helped the Professor sit down. "Professor," he said, "this would be a great promotional gimmick. I could play the preacher's part. We'd do it twice a day. Maybe more."

"Leroy," the Professor wheezed, "I love you like I'd love my own son if I didn't hate children. But just this once—Shut the hell up!"

***

Twenty yards away, Bert ignored the ruckus and looked at the apple. Normally he would never pay money for an apple. He knew several unguarded backyards, but none were nearby.

Nature had depended on him to correct its mistake and restore balance. He had done that and done it pure. Last night was the reason that Nature—or maybe God—had demanded Bert sacrifice the one thing he had needed to complete himself—a family. Now his long probation was over. His diligence deserved a reward.

Bert took his first bite of candy apple on a stick and savored the morsel briefly. It was sweet, sticky, and disgusting. He spit it out violently. His first carnival would be his last. There nothing about carnivals worth wanting.

If I cut the sugar junk off, maybe there'll be enough apple to eat. He reached for the big knife on his belt.

It was gone.

CHAPTER 34

As things settled back to normal, or at least carny normal, the crowd dispersed, either entering the Ten-in-One or filtering down the midway. Isaac helped Preacher Noble Custis to his car and made sure Custis wasn't too shaken to drive home. Then he went back to the Ten-in-One. A young man had replaced the elderly woman in the ticket booth.

"Twenty-five cents, buddy," the man said. He looked two meals and a face wash away from his last ride balanced on the rods under a train.

"When does Ivan the Terrible start his act?" said Isaac.

"About twenty-five minutes into the show. Show's starting now. Only a quarter, buddy."

"How long does his act take?"

"I dunno. Ten, twelve minutes. Buy a ticket, and time it yourself."

"When he finishes, does he stay here? Or does he go to his tent?"

"How should I know? Listen, buddy, you buying a ticket or not?"

"No thanks," said Isaac. "I'll pass."

"No thanks to you too, buddy. Come back to this show when you've got a steady job."

Isaac ignored him and started down the midway. He wanted a closer look at the things inside Otto's suitcase. A voice called, "Hey, Sheriff," and Isaac turned to see Jeremy trotting toward him.

"Thanks for the passes you gave us," Jeremy said. "I rode the

Screamin-Meemie! It's real scary! You go real high, like a roller coaster, except you're in your own bench seat, and it's always rocking and jerking, and you feel sick and almost throw up. I'm going again!"

"Hello, Sheriff." Rachel walked up, energetic but graceful as always. "I hear you really saw the elephant today."

"They have an elephant, too?" said Jeremy.

"It's an old-timey expression," Rachel said "It means you've experienced everything there is to experience."

After Leroy's comment last night about men who were past their prime, Isaac wasn't sure how to take the "old-timey" remark. "There was a short spate of vigorous proselytizing by an itinerant preacher, yes," he said. "But the carnies handled it without my help."

"That's sort of how I heard it," she said. "Jeremy, go read those Ten-in-One banners and decide which one you'd like to see. I want to chat with Sheriff Cash."

As Jeremy ran off, Rachel turned serious. "Isaac, the whole town's talking about the second murder. Some folks are upset that you arrested Otto, then turned around and released him. Bernard Fieldman says he warned you the carnival would bring trouble, but you wouldn't listen."

"Guess I can't dispute that."

"Philo Napker was at the boarding house talking with Mr. Fairley. They're furious. Napker says you should close the carnival immediately because two murders is more than Mercerville can handle."

"Meaning more than the sheriff can handle. Well, he may be right."

"So are you closing it?"

"Nope. You don't pack up the suspects and the evidence, and ship it all someplace else. That's running from a problem, except in reverse. Best to have everything here where I can watch it."

"I'm sorry about pressuring you this morning. I didn't mean to." She slipped her arm through his as they strolled toward the Ten-in-One. "If a boarding house helper's opinion matters, I think you're a good sheriff. I support your decision."

"Your opinion *does* matter. I really appreciate all you've done to help. In fact, I'm beginning ..."

"Mom, guess what!" Jeremy ran up to them. "The ticket man says he'll let us see all ten attractions for only two bits each."

"Well, I suppose we can afford that. Won't you join us, Sheriff?"

"Wish I could," Isaac said, "but I want to check something in Otto's tent while he's busy onstage."

Isaac watched as they walked to the tent, bought their tickets, and entered. Then he went over to the ticket booth. "That lady gave you two quarters. You dropped them inside your undershirt, didn't you."

"Wha...? How did you know?"

"Never mind, just stick them in that cash box."

"Hey, buddy, you got a beef?"

"Yeah. You're skimming the take. Embezzlement is a felony."

"Listen, buddy, I don't know who you are, but I'm pretty sure you're not carny."

"I'm pretty sure I'm the Sheriff of Mercer County, that's who. And I know for a fact we have an empty cell exactly your size."

"You'd arrest me for two lousy quarters?"

"Times are tough. Now put them in the cash box. And don't do it again. You may not see me, but I'll be watching you. Buddy!"

The man shook his head in disbelief, then slipped his hand inside his shirt, pulled two quarters out of a small cloth bag hanging around his neck, and dropped them into the slot in the top of the metal box. As Isaac turned, he gave the man one last glare and said, "Come back to this town when *you* have a steady job."

***

Isaac looked around to check if anyone would see him go into Otto's tent. Then he remembered he wasn't a burglar. He was the sheriff, and the judge had approved a warrant.

Inside, reaching under the cot to get Otto's suitcase, he noticed something beneath the thin mattress. He lifted it and found a blue suit sandwiched between the mattress and the cot to keep the creases sharp. No-iron ironing. It was a trick Isaac had used himself since Sarah died.

Yesterday the suitcase was unlocked. Today it wasn't. In detective books, Philo Vance would bend a paperclip into a lock pick. Isaac didn't have a paperclip. He also had no idea how to pick locks. Instead, he opened his Barlow knife, slipped the slimmest blade behind the suitcase's loose hasp and into the shackle slot, then applied wiggly pressure.

Several futile tries later, he made a frustrated, somewhat-vicious jab, and the lock popped open. Inside the suitcase were the same items as yesterday—mostly underwear, some with mended places. Otto was so organized, he even folded his underwear.

Isaac looked over at Otto's trunk. Someone had searched it on Thursday night. Stringbean? Or did Stringbean catch someone else, who then killed him?

Turning back to the suitcase, Isaac took out a pair of impeccably-shined shoes wrapped in cloth. Cardboard had been fitted inside each shoe to make the innersoles last longer. A closer look revealed checking on the leather. Willie was right. Otto had once had money, but now he was struggling to keep up appearances.

Under the shoes lay a leather dispatch case and a small album with about twenty photos. Some showed a younger version of Otto beside a somber, bearded old man wearing a black suit and hat. Except for the beard, the man might have been a preacher.

The dispatch case contained a gray notebook and two stacks of letters tied with twine. Some were typed, but most were handwritten and from different writers. All were in German. Several pages of the notebook had numbers in neat, precisely-aligned columns.

Was this Otto's expense book? The amounts might be dollars, German marks, or Austrian whatever-they-use-over-theres, assuming the figures even represented money. They might as easily be a secret spy code.

***

Inside the Ten-in-One, the audience grew silent as Otto looked up at the sword above his face. At dawn, he had been in jail for murder. Tomorrow he might be there again. His perspiration today was not the honest sweat of lifting barbells, but the kind of sweat he hadn't experienced since he had earned his chest scar in 1918.

Swallowing to lubricate his throat, he concentrated on overcoming the body's gag reflex. Holding the cross-guard with his right hand and guiding the blade with his left, he slid the blade between his lips and past his tongue. When it was totally down his throat, he bent at a forty-five-degree angle and held his arms away from his body, allowing the audience to see for themselves that nineteen inches of steel was well and truly inside his esophagus. Some of them moaned, but none looked away. Otto straightened up and drew the sword out more slowly than he'd ever done before. It was Otto's fist shake in the face of Death.

202

Swords didn't frighten Otto. Tomorrows did. In the smoke, noise, and gore of those four days on the battlefield at Soissons, Otto had grasped the most important fact in life: No matter what you do, each sunrise brings you one day closer to the ultimate nightfall.

But today, as on so many other days, Otto had stared at his fear without blinking. As people applauded, he held the sword out, offering it to a farmer with his family near the stage.

"Here, you try," Otto smiled. "Is easy."

The man declined, waving it away.

"No? Ah! He is wise to say no," Otto addressed the audience. "This sword is very dangerous." He paused for effect. "It has my germs all over it." The crowd laughed.

Standing nearby were two boys, about ten years old. "Say, listen," one boy said to his buddy. "I know how he done that. It's a trick. The blade goes into the handle."

"But the blade's a lot longer than the handle."

"It folds up. All this stuff is hooey."

Whatever stupid comment a rube thinks is original, the carny has dealt with more times than he can remember. Today, however, Otto was not in the mood to tolerate arrogance. Staring at the boy without blinking, he held the hilt with both hands and in one powerful motion, stabbed the sword down through the top of the wooden prop table beside him. The board screamed *Krazack!* as eight inches of blade splintered through its other side.

The audience gasped. The two wide-eyed boys gulped. Otto gave them a withering glare. Then he smiled, bowed formally, and walked offstage while the audience applauded wildly.

Otto hadn't been in the mood to laugh at much of anything since Black Tuesday, 1929. Especially not today.

***

203

Isaac couldn't take the ledger or letters because that would tip Otto off. Right now, it was important to give Otto room to maneuver and watch what he did. Besides, there was no guarantee they had anything to do with the murders. He pulled out his notebook and began copying the few words in the ledger. He could borrow the high school's German-English dictionary from Pardus LaBane.

As Isaac concentrated, he blocked out the midway squeals and screams. He had become so accustomed to the carnival that the roar of the "Screamin'-Meemie" was almost as soothing as the rush of the White River on a summer afternoon. Isaac never heard the confident footsteps nearing the tent entrance.

Ivan the Terrible had come home from work.

CHAPTER 35

"Are you crazy?" the Professor barked at Leroy, who was standing with Jeremy in the doorway of the office truck. "Willie, is this guy certifiable?"

"Leave me out of this." Willie was in front of the full-length mirror, or rather, the Professor-length mirror. But it was tall enough to let him admire the sharp-looking gray slacks he had recently bought in that last town.

"Leroy," the Professor said, "it's almost time for the next show. You should be in the Ten-in-One, getting ready! You can't be playing nanny to some towner kid."

"Oh, Jeremy's not just any kid." Leroy said. "Remember the lady who told me to get the doctor for String and she'd find the sheriff and..."

"YES! I remember the lady who brought the sheriff up here! I remember it all like it was only yesterday. Which is exactly when it was! And Leroy, do you know what?"

"No, what?"

"I don't bleeding care!"

"Well, I sort of promised her. I didn't think she'd be gone this long. She should be back any minute."

"Leroy," the Professor sighed. "The boy can jolly well take care of himself until his mother comes back. This is a carnival! Kids *love* carnivals."

"But will he be safe? You know what people say about carnies."

"*WE* are the carnies, Leroy! Us!" The Professor managed to

get his volume back down. "We are good people! Maybe a little weird, some of us. Okay, a lot of us. But basically good."

"But considering the murders, I thought a child should be with an adult and not…" Leroy began.

"Hang on, you two," Willie interrupted as he crossed the room. "I'm leaving anyway. I'll handle this." Willie laid his hand on Jeremy's shoulder. "If you're not afraid to go with an out-of-costume wild man, I know somebody you can stay with and have a lot of fun. Have you ever wanted to hit some guy really hard?"

Jeremy grinned and his eyes grew wide. "You betcha! Let's go!"

***

"Yoo-hoo. Mister Ivan the Terrible. Wait!" Rachel called out loudly. Otto turned as she caught up with him.

"How can I help the lovely lady?" he said.

"Oh, Mister Ivan, I am such a fan of yours," Rachel said breathlessly, but even more loudly, as she pulled Otto's large hand away from the tent flap and took it in both of hers. "We both are. My son, I mean. Oh, it's such a thrill!"

"I am very enchanted, dear Madam. But I am much tired, and I get only a short rest." He gently separated her hands to free his. "Please excuse me."

"Ooo, I had no idea your biceps were so large." She slid her hands up his arm and hoped she was doing it the way a real femme fatale would. "I bet I couldn't *begin* to get my arms around your big, manly chest."

"Some other time we must try. But now, excuse…"

"Oh yes, but first give me your autograph. My son will be so sad he missed meeting you."

"Yes, of course. I cannot refuse the lovely lady."

206

"Just a minute more," she said even louder. "I have a pencil in my bag."

"Madam does not need to speak so strongly. My ears hear very well."

"Sorry. I'm so excited. Here's the pencil. You can write on the back of this."

"You want Ivan to autograph the back on an envelope?"

"The last thing I received from my dear mother right before she...you know. It's very precious to me."

Otto looked at both sides of the envelope. "Mountain Home Butcher Supply?"

"Mother's place of employment. Oh, I wish she could be here to see this, the Great Ivan autographing the last invoice she ever sent me."

Otto quickly wrote, "Good luck, Ivan the Terrible," and handed the envelope back.

"Oh, his name," she said, her voice again rising. "My son will be devastated if you don't write his name."

Otto sighed. "Naturally, Madam. What is?"

"Just write 'To Jeremy.' That's capital G, small e, small r...Oh, no. You wrote the letter G. It's Jeremy with a J. It's an old English name."

"Madam, you have told to me 'capital G.' I have it very good geheard," Otto said, trying to hide his irritation.

"Oh, I couldn't have."

"Aber, ja. Das haben...I mean, yes, you did that."

"Oh, I'm so flusterated, I can't think straight. Please, write J-e-r-e-m-y. Yes, that's perfect. Thank you so much."

"Madam is very welcome. And now, I must..."

"Yes, you must need a lot of rest, being so strong and all. Tell me, how many hours of sleep..." But she was speaking to his back as he pushed into the tent.

"Good day, madam," came the voice from inside.

***

As Rachel walked between the trailers and tents, she heard a man clear his throat. Isaac stepped out from behind a trailer.

"Can't even spell your own son's name?" he said with a straight face. "I call that mighty poor mothering."

"You shush, Isaac Cash."

"Where is Jeremy, by the way?"

"After we left the Ten-in-One, we saw Leroy going to the prop tent. I asked him to talk to Jeremy while I went to find you."

"Don't know why you wanted to, but I admit I'm grateful you showed up when you did. If Otto knew I was searching his things again, he'd destroy any evidence he might have hidden elsewhere."

"Thanks for not being angry that I followed you, but I was really curious whether you found what you were looking for."

"Don't know, but that reminds me of something that might be right down your alley. Can you tell if a seam has come loose by itself, or if it was cut open deliberately?"

"I'm not sure. Why?"

"Otto has a steamer trunk. It's where MacPhie and I found the sword. There was a seam open in the lining. I didn't think anything of it yesterday, but now I realize it's the only thing in that tent that isn't in perfect repair."

"I suppose I might be able to tell, as much mending as I've done. As soon as Otto leaves again, we'll..."

"No. I'm not even sure it matters. If I decide it's important, I'll confiscate the trunk and bring it to you," Isaac said. "Up yonder is the ice cream stand. I'll buy you one. We'll get Jeremy first, of course."

"No, let's take a minute for ourselves," she said. "Just to calm down. Then we'll find him."

***

"Jeremy's not here, Mrs. Barlow." The Professor rose from his desk. "I traded him to gypsies for three tins of Romanian caviar." He crossed the truck floor and extended his hand. "So nice to meet you. Come with me, I'll show you where he is."

"Then you didn't actually trade him?" said Rachel. "Pity. I've never eaten caviar. You *were* going to share, I hope."

"To be honest, the tins looked a bit rusted. Otherwise you would now be searching for a missing son. Which, come to think of it, is exactly the situation, isn't it?"

He led Rachel out of the office truck and saw Isaac waiting outside. "Nice to see you, Sheriff. Sorry you couldn't make it earlier."

The words stung. There had almost been a riot, and Isaac had been helpless to stop it. "I hope Jeremy was no trouble," was all he could think to say.

"He's a bright lad. I've never enjoyed talking to any child more. On the other hand, I've never enjoyed talking to any child, period." He shaded his eyes from the sun and pointed. "Do you see the one, two...the third booth? The Pitch 'n Win baseball booth. Jeremy is with Thelma and her husband, Killer. Don't let Killer's face alarm you. For years he boxed in traveling athletic shows, and his once-handsome countenance displays considerable wear and tear. In more than two-thousand-three-hundred matches, he never lost a single bout." The Professor turned and stepped back into the truck. "Unless instructed to do so by his manager."

***

Nearing the booth, Isaac and Rachel saw a man holding his hand up while bobbing and weaving in front of Jeremy.

"Hit the hand, kid. Come on, stay focused....Hey! Good one! You got in a good shot. Hit it again."

"Goodness, Jeremy" Rachel laughed. "What's all this?"

"Hiya, mom. Hiya, Sheriff. This is Killer; he was the world's champ. He says I have great reflexes. One time Killer whupped eight men in a single day."

The man pulled off his flat cap and seemed embarrassed. "Had my work cut out for me that day, so I did. You a sheriff? I don't fight anymore, but they was all honest fights. Did he say sheriff?"

"Name's Isaac Cash," Isaac extended his hand to shake. "Just enjoying the carnival, that's all."

The boxer's bald head had numerous scars, his nose was flattened like a stepped-on yam, and his three-day stubble was uniformly gray. Nevertheless, his calloused hand was as hard as marble and his grip so firm it made Isaac wince. "Nothing official, then?" the man said.

"A little, I admit. There have been two murders, of course." Isaac tried to read something in Killer's eyes, but they seemed as black as a well and twice as deep. "Did you know String and Stani very well?"

"Naw. Hello is all. Just to talk. Skeleton was smart. He was a good talker, so he was."

"What do people call you when they don't call you Killer?"

"Mostly 'hey, you!'" Killer laughed, showing one gold front tooth and several missing side teeth. "Back in Boston they called me the Kid."

"But your real name." Isaac took a ball from the counter and threw it straight at one of the rings hanging near the back canvas. It missed the ring completely.

"Real name, you mean? Kid Callahan, so it was. Yeah. Real name was O'Callahan. With an 'O.' But it don't sound as good. So Kid Callahan. Yeah."

"When you and String..."

"Give it a try, kid." Killer handed Jeremy a ball and seemed not to hear Isaac. "Honest game. No gaff. Free throw."

"No free throws," said a wizened little woman walking up to the booth. Her skin was leathery and wrinkled from her sparse hairline all the way down to where her bosom had once been before it drifted south. She extended a tiny claw-like hand to take the ball from Jeremy.

"Lazim gain, Thelma." Killer softly mumbled the carnies' coded warning that this mark could cause trouble. "Sheriff."

"Like I said..." Without losing a beat, Thelma picked up another ball and handed it to Jeremy, "...no free throws for anybody except the law. Here you are. Show Dad your stuff."

Jeremy gave the ball a half-hearted toss and it went straight through the ring without touching the sides.

"Killer says you knew the murdered..." Isaac began.

"Way-hey, whoa-ho," shouted Thelma. "We got a winner. Step right up and win a prize! Three balls for one nickel. Easy-breezy. Throw it and show it. Right here, right here, right here!"

"Like I said, great reflexes." Killer grinned and handed Jeremy a small kewpie doll, "Honest game. No gaff."

Isaac motioned Thelma down to the far end of the booth as a young man stepped up to the counter with his girlfriend and handed Killer a nickel.

"Just wondering how well you knew Stringbean," Isaac said.

"The skeleton man?" Thelma said. "Didn't know him. There's a pecking order on a show. Jointies don't talk to ride operators. Ridies don't frat'ranize with roughies. And performers

211

only hang around with other performers. Me and Killer work hard. We're independent operators. We rent space for a fee plus points. You know, a percentage of the take. If we had time to associate, it wouldn't be with freaks."

"How about the Half-and-Half? Same answer?"

"Same answer."

"That's not what Killer says."

"Killer says whatever Killer says. His brain's Mulligan stew. Too many right jabs to the head. Sorry, but we don't know from nothing about the freaks. Nothing."

"Well then, thanks for nothing."

"Any time. But I will give you some advice."

"Work on my pitching arm, right?"

"Naw, don't waste your time. The game's designed so the more experience you have, the worse you do. The distance fools people, and the ball's not regular. Some guy like that one," She threw a look over her shoulder, "...on the hometown team. Wants to win a prize for his girlfriend. He'll spend fifty cents before he ever gets the ball through."

"But Jeremy..."

"Cause he's a kid never had a lesson in his life, that's why. He don't have any preconceived training about how he's supposed to throw. The more you teach him how to throw a ball right, the better he'll play baseball, but the worse he'll do in a carny joint. It ain't no gaff, it's only human nature." Thelma picked up a bseball. "Play ball with your son more often. He's a nice boy."

"Maybe I will," Isaac said. "Thanks for the advice."

"That wasn't it. Here's the advice. Watch the Kraut. I grew up around them people back in Pennsylvania. Never saw a one of 'em I'd trust from here to that post. I'll lay even money Otto done the dirty work. And three to one says he'll make a run for it. Soon."

CHAPTER 36

As Isaac said goodbye to Rachel and Jeremy, afternoon was heading quickly toward evening. He walked to the Ten-in-One exit and peeked through the flaps. Otto was inside, doing his act again. Isaac returned to the midway and asked a roughneck where to find Herbert Hutchins. The roughie pointed toward the Ferris wheel.

"Yeah, I guess I've got a minute," Hutchins said when Isaac caught up with him. "Let's go behind the floss wagon, where we can talk in private."

"The floss wagon...?"

"The grab joint that sells cotton candy. Fairy floss."

"I understand you're in charge of the roughnecks," Isaac said as they walked, trying to establish rapport. "I used to boss a railroad track crew. Rough guys can be a handful."

"You can't cut 'em no slack." Hutchins spat into the dust. "If you ain't hard as a brick, they'll walk all over you."

"Yeah." Isaac decided it might help if he spat too, so he did. "Some of them would disappear right when I needed them most."

"They don't have much affection for work, that's for sure." Hutchins laughed and spat again.

"Any of your roughies disappear around the time String was killed?" Isaac asked, trying to work up enough saliva for a second rapport spit.

"Naw, last gazoony who walked was in that other town, Mountain Home. Left with a broad."

"A local woman?"

"Could have been anybody. An old girl friend, a wife.

213

Sometimes guys join the show so's they can get to some town we're heading for. Maybe he was fresh out of stir and trying to get back home. Or maybe she was some working woman he took a shine to. These roughies ain't like you and me. They ain't got any class."

"Yesterday you thought the killer was some 'bo who dropped off a train. But what about that gazoony? Maybe he came back."

"I got a new theory now. Whoever it was, he was looking for Freda. I've gave it a lot of thought."

"The fortune teller?"

"Yeah. I figure he went to the mitt camp first, but she had gone to the doniker or maybe to grab something to eat."

"Mitt camp...?"

"Her palm reader booth. She practically lives there. See, here's my theory. The guy thought she cheated him, and he was all het up about it. Wanted to beat up on her, maybe cut her. But he saw Stani from the back, and the long dark hair on one side confused him. He thought it was the gypsy, cause she has long dark hair. So the guy followed Stani into the Ten-in-One."

"Had anyone threatened Freda?"

"You kidding? She was raised in East Harlem. Nobody messes with Freda."

"Let me sort this out. You think someone wanted to kill Freda, who is almost always in her mitt camp. But he ended up in the back of the Ten-in-One, where Stani is sitting under a banner that says Half-Man Half-Woman. And has short hair on one side and half a beard."

"You never know about murderers. I guess they might make a lot of mistakes."

"Probably, but does this seem likely?"

"Like I say, it's a theory," Hutchins said. "I'm still working on it."

"One other thing," said Isaac. "Was there any reason Otto

might have a grudge against either String or Stani?"

"How would I know? I stay away from the Ten-in-One. Freaks give me the heebie-jeebies," Hutchins said. "If the Professor's people want to slice each other up, that's their business. My business is running rides and games for decent people to have a little fun. And that's what I need to be doing now." He spat again and walked back toward the midway.

***

"Sure, I knew both the deceased." Freda stood in the opening of her fortune-teller tent, buffing her nails. "I've been working the Professor's outfit for six seasons." She went inside and motioned for Isaac to sit at the opposite side of the small round table. "Five, if you don't count the season I got sick and nearly died for two months. My enemies should only know."

"Sorry to hear it," Isaac said. "What was the illness?"

"You're a sheriff, right? If it's all the same, I'll share my body problems with a doctor, thank you very much."

"Sorry again." Isaac's standing as a Mercer County official clearly didn't impress Freda. He doubted anything did. "Herbert Hutchins thinks the murderer wanted to hurt you, but killed Stringbean and Stani by mistake."

"Yeah?" She used the sleeve of her gypsy blouse to polish a spot on her crystal ball. "Well, Hutchins also thinks eternal peace and joy reside at the bottom of a gin bottle. I pay no attention."

"How well did you know Stani?"

"To nod hello, that's all."

"Stringbean was with the show before you joined, right?"

"*He* was, but Seesla didn't come along until, I think five years ago."

"Before her, did you and Stringbean have a relationship?"

215

"HAH! My mistake. You're not a cop, you're a comic. Which one, Wheeler or Woolsey? Listen, emaciated and cadaverous, I do not find handsome. I'll stick to men with body on their bones."

"Like roughnecks?"

"Are cops naturally insulting, or do you take classes? I'm nice-looking, if I do say it myself. Should I be desperate? If I'm interested, I can attract. But roughies? Hah!"

As she pulled a lipstick tube from a pocket in her peasant dress, Isaac noticed her foot pat once on the Turkish rug. An eerie glow came from somewhere behind her head. She patted her foot again and the glow increased. Freda gazed intently into the crystal ball and used her reflection to apply the lipstick.

"How long have you known the Professor?"

"Worked with him six years. I told you."

"I'll repeat the question. How long have you *known* him?"

"Maybe a little longer, I guess."

"How little?"

"It's no crime to know somebody. We're both in show business. I'm around, he's around. You meet, you say hello. How much knowing is that? Maybe I met him about two years before I signed on."

"That makes it eight years. And how long have you known Otto?"

"Why should I know Otto?"

"You're both in show business. You're around, he's around. You meet, you say hello. Just answer the question. Otto lived in New York, and you're from New York. I hear the accent."

"*You* hear an accent? Listen to yourself in a mirror sometime. Don't talk accent to me. Right now, I'm one of the few people in Arkansas who talks normal."

"I asked if you're from New York."

"Yeah. Ever been there?" She dropped the lipstick in her

pocket and pulled out an eyebrow pencil.

"I've heard of it." Isaac said. "It's a big place."

"So most recently I'm from Astoria, to be exact. That's in Queens. Ever heard of Queens?"

"I've heard of that, too. Now stop the runaround, and give me some straight answers."

"All right already!" She stroked her eyebrow with the pencil, but quickly put it away. Her hand was shaking slightly. "Otto and I shared the bill in a vaudeville house in Canarsie in '26. I suppose you've heard of Canarsie, too?"

"No."

"Aha!" A smirk crossed her lips. "Other than that, I don't know the man from Adam's pet monkey. Nothing social."

"Shouldn't be hard to check. What was the name of the vaudeville theater?"

"Okay, so maybe a little social. But not personal-social, if that's what you mean. Business-social."

"What kind of business-social?"

"I was the front girl with a mentalist. Mystro the Magnificent. Real name was Izzy Slotkin. He's blindfolded with his back to the audience. I put a black velvet bag over his head. Then I work the audience and get some object. I ask Izzy what I'm holding, and he tells them."

"I don't believe in mind reading."

"A cop who's cynical? My dream is shattered."

"Nobody can read people's minds. What's the gaff?"

"Code words. I had to memorize scores of them. Where you put the word in the sentence is important, too. It all means something. It's a secret language only the front girl and the mind reader know. But you're right, it almost *is* impossible. Toughest act I ever did."

"How did Otto figure into this act?"

217

"He didn't. He opened the show with his muscle stuff. Back then, vaudeville always opened with some kind of silent act because people were still coming in, talking, finding their seats. Mystro was the fifth act. We closed the first half. To give it a strong finish."

"Then Otto was just another performer."

"Otto was never just another anything. He's always been special. Women loved him. Of course, back then his body was younger. Oh my, yes! Anyway, we'd talk backstage, but that's all. Mystro the Magnificent was a magnificent bore, is what he was. So I talked to other people any chance I got. No law against it."

"Did you ever see any indication that Otto could be violent."

"Only if he had good reason. One night me and a belly dancer came out the stage door, and three guys in the alley started putting their paws all over us. Otto heard us scream and came out the door like a lion. Took on all three of them and nearly handed them their heads. You should have seen them scatter. But if you're talking about murder, the answer is no. Not Otto. Otto's a mensch."

"You ever been in his tent?"

"A couple of times, sure, but only to talk. Not what you think. We're friends, is all."

"Were you there last Thursday night?"

"No. Never at night, and never with a knife, and never with intent to kill. Boy, you aren't very subtle with this cop business, are you?"

"M'am, I'm trying to make some sense of these murders."

"What sense can *anyone* make? America's rotting. Europe's practically on fire. Germany picks antisemitism over republican democracy. The world is going crazier every day. That's what sense! Look, Sheriff, I hope you catch the guy, I really do. But I don't know anything."

Two high-school girls poked their heads in, wanting their fortunes told. It didn't matter. Isaac had already decided he wouldn't

218

get anything useful from Freda. Either she knew nothing about mysterious attackers in the night, or she was the best liar he'd ever met. Considering her present occupation, that part seemed almost a certainty.

CHAPTER 37

As Isaac passed the Screamin'-Meemie, approaching the Pitch 'n Win, someone yelled, "Hey! Cash!" He turned and saw Philo Napker walking quickly toward him.

"I got a bone to pick, Cash," he said loudly. "Why in hell's name did you let a murderer out of jail?"

"I'm not convinced I did." No one was paying attention to them yet, but if Napker kept shouting, people soon would. "Calm down. No sense attracting a crowd."

"Fine! Maybe they'll bring tar and feathers. I couldn't believe it when Lavina told me she saw the murderer going down the street, free as a bird. Are you simple-minded or just plain crazy?"

"Philo, the law requires evidence."

"What *we* require is a *real* lawman who knows what a jail is for. Not some hair-cutting amateur!" Napker's face was so close his whiskey-laden spit flecked Isaac's shirt. "Mercerville needs a sheriff, and you sure *are... not ...it!*" He punctuated his words by jabbing his finger in Isaac's chest.

As people stopped to watch, Isaac saw faces he recognized. None of them looked supportive. "Philo, you've said enough."

"Not near enough! You get your tail over to that sideshow and arrest that killer!" Napker grabbed Isaac's lapels and jerked him forward.

Isaac had had enough. As the intoxicated man jerked him closer, Isaac lowered his head, butting Napker forcefully on the nose. Quickly he put his hand against Napker's chest and shoved hard. Napker staggered backwards, eyes wide. Since the third grade,

220

no one had ever fought back. It was a new experience and Napker didn't like it.

Napker rushed Isaac and threw a round-house right. Isaac snapped his head back so hard his fedora flew off as Napker's fist swooshed past his chin. He grabbed for Napker's arms to subdue him, but Napker's fury only increased, his fists battering Isaac's head and chest. Isaac tried to jump backwards, but the crowd, mostly men, didn't allow much room to maneuver. They were cheering for a good fight, and Napker's name was being shouted twice as often as Isaac's.

Napker outweighed him by a good forty pounds, but Isaac was taller and had a reach advantage. His left fist connected hard with Napker's already-sensitive nose. When Napker instinctively raised his guard to protect his face, Isaac drove his right fist into the man's stomach. Napker doubled over and dropped to one knee, gasping.

"All right, everybody," Isaac turned to the crowd. "Show's over. Get on your way."

One of the men pointed over Isaac's shoulder. Isaac turned just as Napker came up fast, a large jagged rock in his hand.

Isaac jumped to the side and kicked toward Napker's crotch. His aim was off and the kick landed on Napker's knee. Napker stumbled, but caught himself and lunged again, striking out toward Isaac's head with the rock. Isaac managed to deflect the blow with his arm, and it connected instead with his left shoulder. The stone's edge sent a searing pain down Isaac's arm, but his right first landed hard on Napker's jaw, knocking him backwards .

Suddenly Napker headed for the ground again, sprawling across a long leg that had kicked his feet out from under him. Two large, calloused hands caught Napker as he hit the dirt, jerked him up, and spun him around. Killer Callahan now had Napker from behind, his right arm behind Napker's neck and his left arm

221

squeezing Napker's throat in a choke hold.

"Settle down, Mister," Killer said in a voice not loud, but commanding. "Management says you're creating a disturbance."

Napker swung the stone vainly and tried to spit out a curse, but his compressed larynx would not cooperate. Isaac yanked the stone out of Napker's hand.

"Sheriff," Killer said, "should I boot this drunk out the front gate? Or would you rather throw him in jail?"

"What's your choice, Philo? Can you control yourself, or shall I do like that 'real lawman' you mentioned and jail you for assault with a deadly weapon?"

His oxygen supply nearly depleted, Napker apparently decided that discretion was the better part of getting throttled by a heavyweight carny with cauliflower ears. His mouth formed something that came out as a groan, but his watering eyes clearly said, "I'll be a good boy."

"If you go home right now, Philo, I won't lock you up." Isaac nodded to Killer, who released his grip. As Isaac watched Napker walk sullenly toward the front gate, he noticed a bright yellow movement on the red office truck thirty yards away. From the top of the steps, the Professor looked toward Isaac and tipped his hat, then went inside. Isaac turned to thank Killer for the help, but the boxer was gone. The crowd had evaporated, too, replaced by one familiar face.

"Masterfully done, Isaac," Bernard Fieldman said with a broad smile. "I couldn't follow how you knocked him down. It all happened so fast."

"Didn't it, though." Isaac picked up his hat and brushed it off.

"Well, everyone was rooting for you, I guarantee that."

"Uh-huh. I saw it in their eyes." Isaac put his hat on. "So, were you looking for me?"

"Not at all. Merely enjoying the sights with Mrs. Fieldman," he said. "I noticed you earlier showing Rachel's boy how to throw a baseball."

"Bernard, let's not play games. Napker talked about tarring and feathering me, and I suspect you'd gladly furnish the supplies."

"Now hold on, Isaac. That's not true. Oh, I admit I *was* upset. But now that I'm here, I see it's only a good old-fashioned carnival. Look how everybody's having fun. I admit I was wrong."

"You're not worried about a lunatic slaughtering us in our beds?"

"Oh, a killer's running loose somewhere, but he's run halfway to Oklahoma by now. With everybody on their guard, a lunatic would have to be crazy to hang around."

"You still want Otto arrested?"

"If there's evidence, yes. But you're convinced there isn't. I guess because I lost friends in the war...well, never turn your back on the Europeans. But if you're sure Otto is innocent, I trust your judgment. Now I'll find Mrs. Fieldman and ride some rides." Bernard smiled and waved as he walked off. "Maybe you'll do the same with Rachel and Jeremy."

***

Inside the truck, the Professor eased into his desk chair, aware of the bruises from his struggle with the crazy man in white. After a moment, he pointed to the magazine on his desk. "Man, I'd *love* to get that Bonnie and Clyde car. It has 167 bullet holes."

Leroy was stretched out wearily on the loveseat, playing with the grabber device Elaine had invented. "Yeah, you could patch the holes and repaint it."

"Patch the...? Do you say these things just to annoy me?"

"Okay, my second guess is, you'd put it in the Ten-in-One."

"Better still, I'd make the car a separate tent attraction. 'The Wages of Crime! Deluge of Death! Nearly 200 Bullets!'"

"Only 167." Leroy squeezed the grabber, lifted the magazine off the desk, and moved it slowly through the air.

"In show business, 167 *is* 'nearly 200,'" the Professor said, leaning back and closing his eyes.

"Can you buy it from Bonnie and Clyde's family?"

"It's disappeared," The Professor said. "Right now half a dozen scoundrels are loading their shotguns to shoot holes in Fordor Deluxes."

"And next season half a dozen carnivals will all claim they have the one-and-only Death Car."

"Exactly. Rubes will believe whichever carnival they see. The public's demand for spectacle is met, and everybody makes money. At least in that carnival." The Professor opened his eyes and sat up. "Look, Leroy, here's some advice. You're not without talent. You have a natural sense of timing. But to survive in show business you need financial sense! In the arts, it's chicken one day and feathers the next. Actors, dancers, musicians—especially the classical guys—might spend as long learning their craft as a doctor spends in medical school. So why aren't we paid like doctors?"

"Because we don't tell people, 'Buy a ticket or you might die,'" Leroy said.

"No. Because the world says, 'Since you love what you do, you shouldn't expect to be paid well, too.'"

"Art is its own reward." Leroy contemplated the magazine dangling at the end of the grabber
device.

"And inside that cliché there is truth. All the arts are somehow sacred, even my lousy little carnival. But you can't eat sacred. And most people see art as an optional extra and the artists as hired help. Even a genius like Mozart had to use the servants'

224

entrance."

Leroy smoothed out the magazine on the desk. His fingers brushed a glossy photograph of Clark Gable. "Did Mozart get rich? Or famous?"

"He died young, which is often helpful with the fame part, but in the meantime he chased commissions like crazy. Show business is called *business* for a reason. Leroy. You want to make it in this business? Find new ways to generate income, new ways to attract an audience."

"How about I hide a sponge in my mouth and fall out of the death car spitting fake blood."

"You're catching on! Next point: never spend everything, and when you –"

"Professor, I may not understand finances," Leroy said. "But I do understand about pulling in audiences." He flipped back to the Bonnie and Clyde article. "What I'm saying is, my dad and I used to practice with our shotgun on the side of an abandoned boxcar. I'm very accurate."

The Professor's eyes widened and a smile crept across his face. "Leroy, I've been underestimating you," he said. "Now, suppose I buy a second-hand Ford..."

CHAPTER 38

All afternoon and evening Isaac stayed in the shadows and watched Otto. The man's movements consisted of doing his act, then resting in his tent until the next performance. Isaac checked with Willie often enough that words became unnecessary. A raised eyebrow from Isaac was answered by a shrug of Willie's shoulders or a shake of his head. If Otto was doing anything out of the ordinary, neither of them could spot it. "Surveillance" was the term *Police Gazette* magazine used for this sort of activity. "Waste of time" seemed more accurate.

Nearing the Screamin'-Meemie ride, Isaac saw Rachel and Jeremy talking.

"...because I don't want you falling asleep in church tomorrow, that's why," Rachel was saying. "It's almost your bedtime."

"You're not fair! I only rode the Screamin'-Meemie twice," Jeremy pleaded. "When we got here, you said..."

"Whoa there." Isaac held up a hand as he joined them. "How's about a compromise, Rachel? I'll treat him to one last trip on that fool thing. Then, Jeremy, you'll go home to bed without complaint. Fair enough?"

As they watched Jeremy climb into one of the Screamin'-Meemie gondolas, Rachel asked Isaac, "Learn anything important tonight?"

"If I did, I don't know what. I realized something, though. When I questioned Otto yesterday, I didn't catch on at the time, but now I think he was manipulating me. There was something he didn't

226

want me to think of, so he distracted me with things like European politics."

"Maybe the Professor could help," Rachel asked.

"He's evasive, too, a bit. But he covers it with wit and charm. He can convince people of almost anything."

"It's a kind of armor, I think. He won't allow anyone in," Rachel said. "Life must be terribly frustrating for someone in his situation who's also so intelligent and competent." Rachel watched the bench holding Jeremy climb higher up the Screamin'-Meemie. "Isaac, if Otto was evasive about something, maybe the Professor is being evasive about the same thing."

"Good point. I hadn't thought of that."

"That's because you don't live with someone who's always twisting you around his little finger to get what he wants. In fact, I see my little manipulator waving to us from the top of the ride. We'll be able to go home to bed soon. At least when the ride starts moving again."

***

At the east side of the Screamin'-Meemie, Hutchins peered up at the top of the main girder. *I'm gonna kill that Ace! He didn't wipe off the hold-down spinner.*

***

Standing at the south side of the Screamin'-Meemie, Bernard Fieldman patted his wife's arm. "I'm sure there's no problem. They probably stop it so people at the top can have a panoramic view," he said while thinking, *If a citizen is hurt on this ride, I swear I'll haul every one of these degenerates into court.*

227

***

"See the engine running this ride, Cuz'?" Cyrus said to A.J., standing beside him at the north side of the ride. "That's an ol' Emerson-Brantingham tractor engine. I betchu the damn fool carnies ain't overhauled it since Noah."

***

"That poor child!" Elaine stood looking out the doorway of the Ten-in-One. "He must be terrified. I think the hold-down spinner is stuck. Find Otto. He can climb up and hit it hard with a hammer."

Looking over Elaine's shoulder, Edna said, "Otto's too old to climb that mast. But Leroy is really strong."

"Not Leroy!" Louise said from behind Edna. "What if he got hurt?"

***

On the west side of the jammed Screamin'-Meemie, Rachel stared up at the little bench swinging in the wind at the top. She shivered in spite of the August night's heat. Isaac felt an urge to put a comforting arm around her shoulder, then thought better of it. He was the one who had talked her into letting Jeremy have one last ride.

***

Fifty feet above the carnival, Jeremy held tightly to the safety bar as the wind increased. From here—top of the world—Meekam's Hill didn't seem very large at all. He could see a curving slice of the White River, but the water was now just a black strip. The dark area to his right would be Mercerville, closed for the night. Moving carefully, he slid halfway around on the bench in time to see the last bands of sunset fading below the distant hills. *Wow! I bet the people down there can't see the sunset the way I can.*

His gondola rocked slightly as he looked over the side at the crowd gathered far below. A few people were scurrying about, but most of the little figures were motionless, human dots in the fading light. *Probably looking up at me.* He could see people helping people out of the gondolas at the bottom, but he couldn't locate his mother and the sheriff. All the human dots looked the same from his viewpoint. The only things he could see clearly were the tops of the tents and the rides, their cheerful lights speckling the night. He was holding tight to the safety bar of a rocking gondola high above the world. No one was up there but him, as blackness engulfed the world. There was no ladder long enough to reach him. He was stranded. All alone.

Gosh! I hope they don't fix it too soon.

CHAPTER 39

Bert walked around to the other side of the ride, wishing he had his rifle scope, so he could be sure. But it all made sense. His knife was gone. This was the ride he had been knocked into when the crowd surged. And as the last rays of sunset painted the Screamin'-Meemie orange, his hunter's sharp eye had seen the glint of unpainted steel on the side of one, but only one, of those wooden seats. It made perfect sense.

***

It didn't make any sense for a knife to be there, but it was. Along the outside of the passenger bench Jeremy was in, at the bottom, was a thin metal crosspiece holding together two wooden planks that formed the right side of the bench. Jammed between the crosspiece and the wood was a hunting knife.

His mom had refused to let him buy one, even if he saved all his money from working for Mr. Cash. "Not until you're sixteen," she had said. "Be satisfied with your pocket knife."

Sixteen was a very long time away from twelve, and she hadn't actually said he couldn't *have* a hunting knife. She only said he couldn't *buy* one. This knife was free. So he wouldn't be disobeying. Not exactly. And once he had it, she'd probably let him keep it. Maybe. Anyway, he wouldn't tell her immediately. He'd keep the knife hidden for a while. The problem now was how to reach down far enough to grab it.

***

"Pump up the tank all she'll stand, boys." Hutchins picked up the emergency fire hose and closed the nozzle down to a pinpoint. "The pressure has to be high enough for the water to reach the top of the upright. If I can blast the gunk off that spinner, it'll slip, and the ride will move again." He pulled the hose along as he moved close to the base of the upright. "At least, I hope so."

***

Jeremy knew his mom was down there somewhere, but the ground was too far away to make out people's faces. *If I can't see her, then she can't see what I'm doing either.*" He leaned over the side of the bench and stretched as hard as he could. His fingertips were still a good four inches from the knife. But if he could twist around and get his right knee up on the seat, he should be able to reach it.

The seat rocked as he lifted his foot off the footboard, and he quickly put his foot down again. This would be tricky.

***

The last sunlight was gone, and the top of the Screamin'-Meemie was above the carnival lights. The bench with the boy in it was illuminated only by the few small lights strung around the ride.

Bert wished he could see the knife better. It looked like the kid might be reaching for it. *Damn, I wish there was more light.*

***

The bench was built to rock back and forth, Jeremy reasoned, not tip over completely. At least he hoped so. He wrapped his left

231

arm around the safety bar and slowly lifted his right foot off the footboard. The bench rocked, but only slightly. He twisted his body to the right and slid his knee up onto the seat. Suddenly the seat tipped backwards. Instinctively, Jeremy leaned forward to balance himself. The seat responded, tipping forwards even farther than it had gone backwards. Jeremy slammed his body back against the seatback and threw his right arm over the side, grabbing to latch onto any part of the bench he could. The bench was now rocking violently back and forth. This whole thing was turning out to be not such a great idea.

***

"Sit still!" Hutchins yelled upwards. Town people had no common sense at all. "Damn!" The roughies pulled the portable spotlight over to the ride. Hutchins called out to Skeezix, "Aim the light at the very top of the upright. I need to see the spinner so's I can aim the water. We barely have enough pressure as it is, and I got to keep the spinner wet and moving until the ride gets back down again. Okay! Switch the light on!"

***

Bert stood looking up, his mouth twisted into something approaching a smile. All he'd had to do was wish for more light, and there was light. *Maybe there's a God after all.*

***

The spotlight and the water hitting the top of the upright combined into a blast of dazzlingly bright fog. The spray coming off the upright was like a hard rain, wetting Jeremy and the seat. Jeremy

232

kept his eyes tightly closed, hoping the urge to vomit would go away as the bench gradually stopped rocking. At least he had his right knee up on the seat now. He opened his eyes and leaned far over the side until he could wrap his fingers tightly around the handle of the knife. It was stuck, but the water spray made it possible for him to wiggle it a little.

I haven't done all this just to quit now. He braced his left foot against the footboard and jerked the knife as hard as he could. As he yanked, his foot slipped on the wet footboard, the bench rocked wildly again, and Jeremy lost his balance. His right armpit slammed down on top of the end piece. Pain shot down his arm, but he managed to keep his fingers closed around the jammed knife's handle. Both his feet shot off the footboard and dangled in space as the gondola rocked. The blade stayed stuck between the boards and the crosspiece. It was now Jeremy's only solid connection with the safety of the Screamin'-Meemie gondola.

Below, the crowd screamed. To Jeremy, it was not a reassuring sound. *I can't hold on. I have to do something, and right now, even if it's the wrong thing.* He pushed on the safety bar with his left hand while pulling on the knife with his right, hoping to drag his body up enough to get one foot onto the footboard. He pushed and pulled, and his rump scraped hard across the edge of the seat as his body inched upward.

Like a garden of statues, the moaning crowd stared up, trying to see through the blinding spray.

Suddenly the Screamin'-Meemie gave a loud metallic scream as it lurched once.

The sudden jerk torqued the gondola, and the knife came free as the ride began to move slowly. Safely back on the seat, Jeremy looked down at the knife in his hand and smiled. *You saved my life. We're gonna be friends. But now what do I do with you?*

A cheer went up from the crowd as the ride moved smoothly

downward, but their breathing wouldn't become normal until the boy was once more safely on the ground. In the shadows behind them, one figure moved around for a better look. Bert's eyes, long accustomed to peering through the spray of fast boats running bootleg down black rivers at night, picked out what others missed. The kid still had the knife and was wrapping something around it, probably a handkerchief. Then he reached behind him, maybe sticking it under his belt at the small of his back. For Bert, the suspense was over. His special knife was no longer lost. It was his, and he would have it back.

***

As they walked, Rachel put her arm around Jeremy's shoulder. "I'm thankful the worst you suffered was a good soaking. Your clothes will dry soon in this heat. But tuck your shirt in."

"It's all wet and clammy." Jeremy reached behind him to make sure his shirttail still covered the knife stuck under his belt.

"Does it really matter, Rachel?" Isaac said, hoping she was still speaking to him. "You're going home anyway."

"Oh, I suppose not. He's had a terrible experience. Anyway, Jeremy, now you can say you've truly seen the elephant."

Pacing them from not far away, Bert recognized the boy who had his knife. *It's the kid who hangs around the barbershop. I know where to find him.*

***

Later, as Isaac walked toward his pickup, he heard a noise and turned. He was being followed by a dark figure wearing a long black duster. Isaac recognized the chicken bone.

"I gotta hurry back," Willie said when he caught up, "but

234

here's something that might be interesting. Coming back from supper I passed the Professor's truck, and I heard him and Otto arguing. I thought maybe he wanted Otto to pay for a table he smashed with his sword today. But then the Professor yelled, 'I want to know everything!' Otto said relax, he'd have it all under control tomorrow, and then it wouldn't matter who was arrested." Willie looked around to see if anyone was near. "So what do you think?"

Isaac paused, then said, "I think 'interesting' is probably an understatement."

Part Four: We're Dark Today

Sunday, August 19, 1934
CHAPTER 40

Otto waited in his car on the isolated dirt road. Yesterday's rendezvous hadn't happened because he had been locked in jail. Today, however, he would get what he had come to Mercerville for. He checked his watch again. The delivery was now one hour late.

In exchange for a large amount of American cash, he would hand over ten pages from his ledger as a good-faith token. The incriminating ledger itself would stay locked safely inside the Professor's hiding place until the rest of the money had been wired to Otto's bank on Monday. From now on, Otto was taking no chances. A man had been killed in his tent, and yesterday someone had jimmied his suitcase, but escaped while Otto was distracted by the lookout woman.

A fast-moving vehicle appeared over a hill. Otto was surprised to see that it was a pickup truck. In American movies, criminals always drove big black sedans. The truck barreled down the long hill, picking up speed, then disappeared below a rise. Suddenly it appeared at the top of the rise, coming fast, and almost on top of him. "Zu schnell, Idiot," Otto muttered.

As it sped past, the truck sprayed dust over Otto's car. The driver was an old lady with gray hair and heavy jowls. Her passenger was a dog bearing a strong family resemblance. Otto turned and watched out the back window as the truck disappeared over another hill. He scanned the nearby woods for movement, feeling for the walking stick on the seat beside him. Grasping it, he twisted the handle to unlock the two-foot-long blade hidden inside. There was nobody in sight. After a few minutes, he decided he was not in immediate danger. Nonetheless, something had gone wrong. He had to find out what.

***

Although he hadn't slept much in two days, Isaac stood at the chipped porcelain bathroom sink, rinsed soap off his shaving brush, and dropped it back into the mug. After Sarah died, he eventually stopped going to church, but he still shaved, even on Sundays. He couldn't afford to slide back into that pit he'd wallowed in during those first weeks. Self-discipline was good for anyone, but for him it meant survival.

Not that Isaac had become an atheist. That wasn't why he stopped attending. At first, everyone fussed over him, pitying him, saying how sad it was about Sarah, and if there was anything they could do, don't hesitate to ask.

After a while, the sympathizing dropped off and they started asking, tactfully, what his plans were. Then they would casually mention a single cousin they had in Little Rock, or a sister, or an aunt, or a best friend. And always about how well she could cook. Apparently every unmarried woman in Arkansas was the world's greatest cook, at least based on what every unmarried woman's cousin, brother, niece, or best friend told him. Nobody else, they swore, could match her apple pies. Or her fried chicken. Or her potato salad.

Did they think he couldn't fry an egg? Or that he even cared what he ate anymore? Did they think cooking could fill his soul's emptiness?

Isaac drew the razor down his cheek. Exhausted though he was, he felt something he had not felt in three years—a reason to go on living.

***

"Little Rock last March? My lecture on placental abruption? Of course I remember you, Dr. MacPhie. Big mustache. Always had a pipe, but never smoked it. What's so important on a Sunday morning, my friend?"

Dr. Schneider, Professor Emeritus, dragged the telephone across his desk and smoothed his bathrobe as he sat down. From the kitchen, the odor of bacon and eggs called to him. But colleagues mustn't be ignored.

"Hermaphrodism? Yes, I've seen it," he said. "Very rare. The textbook I'm writing will have a section about it."

He pulled on the phone cord, which was caught under a stack of reference books.

"Really? You mean an adult? Not a newborn? That's remarkable."

Schneider grabbed his pen and reached for a nearby pad of paper.

"Oh, not a true case. A carnival fake, eh? Too bad. That's hardly something I'd put in my textbook, Dr. MacPhie. How did he die?"

He laid the pencil on the desk and eased back in his chair.

"How ghastly. Did they catch the killer? No? Well, that's a tale worthy of a pulp magazine, I'm sure. But I don't see how I can shed any light on it." The Professor Emeritus sniffed at the aroma of breakfast waiting, but listened with professional courtesy.

"No, the obstetrics division hasn't had a case even remotely like that in well over a decade." Schneider said. "But hang on. You said somewhere in Baxter or Mercer counties? As it happens, I had dinner last fall with a retired colleague, Dr. Polk. He used to practice in Mountain Home. He mentioned an unusual birth that occurred

241

about three years ago, I think. But the baby wasn't hermaphroditic. More like cryptogenitalia."

Schneider ran his finger down the stack of reference books, trying to remember which one discussed the condition. He located it, second from the bottom. He decided against trying to pull out one book without upsetting the whole stack.

"Yes, Dr. MacPhie, I may have Polk's phone number. Provided, of course, Dr. Polk is still living."

CHAPTER 41

In fifteen minutes, Isaac would be at the carnival for a showdown with Otto and the Professor. This time they would tell him what they knew, or he'd lock them up and charge them both with murder and conspiracy. He glanced down at the fuel gauge. Running back and forth to the carnival had used up much of that fifty cents worth of gasoline.

Isaac pulled up to the stop sign at the corner of Church and Mercer streets. If he hadn't known it was August, the large number of worshipers streaming into the church would have suggested Christmas or Easter. Apparently, double murders not only boost carnival attendance, they also spur a healthy increase in church-going. He was about to shift into first gear when Preacher Noble Custis came striding out to the street.

"Wonderful to see you, Isaac," he smiled. "I have great news. Widow Elsie Harkens is back home to stay. The bank's letting her have her house back. She's talking with her sister Dulcie over by the rosebush. I know she's eager to see you."

"Oh, she already has. She smiled as I drove by," Isaac said. "I smiled back. I believe that's all I'll have time for today."

"Oh." Preacher Custis was at a loss for words, not a helpful condition in his profession. "Well, we miss you. And if you see Dr. MacPhie, tell him we miss him, too."

"Preacher, you know the only time MacPhie's been inside your church was when Pete Peterson had a heart attack on top of the Jell-O salad at the potluck dinner. Shep is agnostic."

"In that case," Preacher Custis said, "tell him that we miss agnostics, too. On Sunday, God misses everybody."

The sound of a loud male voice drifted from inside the church. "Goodness! I must hurry," Custis said. "Brother Bill Berkeley has started without me. He's very...uh...dynamic."

As Custis hurried away, Isaac shifted into first, then saw Mel Frazee and Phil "Stretch" Sparmon crossing the street, flagging him down. He shifted into neutral and let the truck roll up against the curb.

"You joining us, Isaac?" Frazee said. "Plenty of room for sinners begging to be spared another day from throat slashers."

Isaac shook his head. "It appears there'll be an abundance of the faithful without me. I'd better keep working on the case."

"Damn right you better," Stretch Sparmon said testily. "People are sick and tired of a murder every night, regular as clockwork."

"Aw, don't ride Isaac so hard," Frazee said. "There hasn't been a throat-slashing for almost thirty-six hours. Anyway, it's good for the funeral parlor industry. Makes people consider their future prospects."

"I heard there's talk about a recall election," Sparmon said. "If you're smart, you'll jail the strongman and send the carnival packing!"

"Can't do it," Isaac said. "If the carnival leaves, the killer will, too."

"Well, that's exactly what we want," Sparmon said.

"There's not enough evidence. But I'm on my way now to question him again."

"Then I recommend you watch your back," Stretch Sparmon said. "Don't expect this town to come to your rescue now that you've become bosom buddies with those carnies."

Isaac was about to reply when an explosive "Boom!" came from inside the church. Isaac jumped out and ran up the path with

Stretch Sparmon and Mel Frazee close on his heels.

***

"Yes, I remember that baby." Ermaline Polk raised her voice to be heard over the static on the telephone line. "It happened just before my brother retired. Terrible tragedy."

"Because it was born with a defect, you mean?" MacPhie said into the phone.

"No, that was tragic enough, of course, but my brother hushed it up. The general public didn't need to know that. Although he said the specialists in Little Rock could have corrected it if someone had taken the baby to them."

"Then what tragedy?"

"The way the baby died. It shocked the whole town, even though none of us really knew the couple, them living way out in the woods like that."

"Miss Polk, I haven't heard about any of this. What happened?"

"Well, the young mother—just a girl, really. Still in her teens. She killed herself! Jumped off a bridge holding the poor baby in her arms."

"What was their name?"

"Gracious, I'm not sure I ever knew."

"But you could find it in your brother's notes, couldn't you?"

"Dr. MacPhie, I'm surprised you would even ask such a thing. I'd never touch his notes without permission."

"When will Dr. Polk be back?"

"Not for two days. Maybe three."

"Miss Polk, two people have been brutally murdered, and we think this incident with the baby might help us identify the killer and stop him."

245

"If it's that important, you'll have to beat the bushes. Literally. My brother is camped somewhere north of here, fishing on the White River."

CHAPTER 42

Isaac, Sparmon, and Frazee ran inside the church just as the Commandant grasped the bass drum mallet in an interlocking mashie-niblick grip and struck another explosive blow on the drumhead. BOOOM!

"Otto the Giant threw a fire bomb at me! The Drug Addict shot at me! But here I am"—Brother Bill Berkeley patted the lapel of his replacement white suit—"preserved and aflame with holy preaching power!" He raised his arms high and trotted in a circle on the stage while, dotted throughout the congregation, people wearing the armbands of the Double-E Double-F Double-R Prayer Team hallelujahed vigorously.

Back at the pulpit, Berkeley said, "That sideshow is a perfect example of defective human breeding. Just as physical strength requires physical hygiene, a strong America requires pure racial hygiene."

Sparmon and Frazee went to sit with their families, leaving Isaac standing at the back of the church. As he scanned the congregation, he was surprised to see Louise, Leroy, and Edna seated in the center section.

"Was Adam some grotesque half-man-half-woman?" Berkeley said. "Was Eve a feeble-minded fat lady the size of a barn? No! God created Adam as the purest male specimen ever, and Eve was the ideal woman. It isn't God who's responsible for deformed, misshapen freaks, is it?"

"It's the Devil!" the Commandant shouted, waving his drum mallet and almost leaping to his feet.

"Any honest freak would admit that deformed, feebleminded people would be better off if they had never been born. Wouldn't a loving God provide a way to cleanse humanity? Yes!" Berkeley's right arm shot up, finger pointing to the heavens. "The word eugenics means 'good birth.' Eugenics is the way!"

The arm-banders hallelujahed even more loudly. They, too, had trouble staying seated.

Louise leaned across Leroy. "Look around," she whispered to Edna. "We could start our own sideshow with some of these people."

"Friends," Berkeley smiled, "I've spotted in our midst two beautiful examples of what America's offspring will become, once Congress passes my eugenics laws. I mean that magnificent young man…" Berkeley pointed straight at Leroy. "…and his beautiful bride." He motioned toward Louise. "Both of you stand up!"

Leroy and Louise looked at each other, unsure what to do, but people nudged them, whispering, "Stand up, brother. Stand up, sister."

"Look at these inspiring results of good breeding and pure Arkansas bloodlines!" Berkeley said, beaming.

Leroy glanced around, saw Isaac, and shrugged. Isaac suppressed a smile.

"Oklahoma passed a eugenic sterilization law in '31," Berkeley continued, "and your neighbors in Mississippi have sterilized the dependent class since 1928! Kansas has practiced health-promoting sterilization for over twenty years! As your Congressman, I'll sponsor laws to guarantee that *all* American children will be as flawless as this young couple. Thank you, Friend. You and your lovely bride may sit down."

As the organ music began a soft seduction, Berkeley's voice seemed to develop audible teardrops. "Believers, God needs your generous offerings so that soon no sweet, innocent baby will ever be born into a life not worth living, the victim of an impure bloodline." Ushers were passing wooden plates among the congregation. "Let every eye close as you make your offerings. God sees your generosity, and so do I. A brother is slipping a two-dollar bill into the plate. Bless you, brother. An elderly sister is sharing her widow's mite. Bless you, Sister."

Isaac lowered his head, but kept his eyes open and didn't see any widow or any mite.

"In these hard times, everyone needs God's blessings." The tremor in Berkeley's voice joined the tremolo of the organ, and he brushed away his tears with a handkerchief. "Don't let selfishness steal your blessings. I keep only enough for my ministry's expenses. Plus a modest stipend, of course." Oddly, his cheeks became wetter each time he passed his handkerchief across his face. "Ah, a small boy is contributing his allowance. Bless you, son!" Isaac spotted several small boys in the congregation. One of them was wiping his nose on his sleeve, but none of them was contributing anything except squirming.

As the ushers brought the offering plates forward, Berkeley resumed his theme. "Just as you can *see* that someone is a dwarf, you can tell instantly when someone is stupid, can't you! You know instinctively when a family's misfortune is their own fault because they're just plain lazy. Inspiration warns you when a foreigner looks shifty and dishonest. Your good judgment tells you that a certain woman probably has loose morals. To decent folks like us, inherited weaknesses are as plain as the nose on your face. Eugenics doesn't decide that someone is defective! Your God-given discernment tells you that! Eugenics merely supplies the solution!"

Berkeley picked up a sack from behind the pulpit and held it high. "Luke 6 says a corrupt tree cannot bear good fruit! Every wise farmer *knows* you can't produce healthy stock by breeding your best animals with the worst ones." He shoved his hand into the sack and brought out a handful of red wheat. "And just as wise farmers cull out defective animals, they also plant only healthy seed." He let the grain stream through his fingers back into the sack. "Americans must have only the purest of seed. I will pass laws to banish moral weaknesses like insanity. Epilepsy. Depression. Malicious asthma. Astigmatism..." The congregation stared hypnotically at the red waterfall against the white suit. "...Sinister left handedness. Promiscuity. And people who—you can recognize them just by looking—are simply not fit for decent society."

Suddenly the rust-colored drizzle ceased, and the bag disappeared behind the pulpit. "Until science can weed out unborn humans the way you farmers weed your crops, government-provided sterilization is mankind's *only* hope! Eugenics..." Berkeley smiled and stretched his arms wide, "...promises to free future generations from all inherited impurities—forever!"

A smile brightened Berkeley's face. "Believers, John eleven, verse fifty, says one man should die, rather than our whole race be defiled. But nobody intends to eliminate sub-standard individuals who are *already* born. Those unfortunate mistakes of nature will be taken to humane institutions where their basic needs can be provided for as long as they remain alive. And where compassionate doctors will perform a safe surgical procedure to cancel the reproductive ability of anyone who is judged—by a competent government panel, mind you—judged to be physically, mentally, or socially unacceptable. More than one year ago, the German National Socialists passed their Law for the Prevention of Genetically Diseased Offspring. The Nazi government is showing us the way to spare humanity of the un-normal and the unfit, including those with unfit character. Friends, the dependent class is draining the U.S. Treasury dry! My laws will require mandatory sterilization before anyone who is unfit or unwilling to work can receive *one penny of public aid!* Elect me in November and put humanity back on God's

Eugenic Gold Standard!"

Brother Bill scanned the room and for a brief moment locked eyes with Isaac. "Human husbandry will end the mongrelization of the human race, including that worst of all defects"— he slammed his palm on the pulpit—"Crime!"

Leaning over the pulpit, he pointed to the back of the room. "There is your brave sheriff. He courageously arrested the freak killer, but iron bars could not hold the monster. He escaped and slaughtered another freak that very night. Beloved...," Berkeley's face contorted in anguish. "...what shall we *do* when the law is helpless to punish crime?" Berkeley motioned to a man wearing a EE-FF-RR armband. "I have eyes and ears at that carnival. Stand and report, Deacon Wademeckler!"

"First," the deacon said breathlessly, "we spotted a stranger sneaking into the carnival, with—" he paused for effect "—a leather holster over his shoulder! And second, the carnival strongman drove away this morning and *still* hasn't returned."

"The killer has escaped!" The Commandant yelled, so excited that he dropped the bass drum beater.

"Wait!" Pardus LaBane shouted from the congregation. "Let Sheriff Cash speak!"

"Of course," Berkeley said. "Sheriff, please reassure us that you've arrested Otto again."

"No, and that's because..."

The Commandant leapt to his feet yelling, "Arrest the killer!"

"Now hold on!" Isaac shouted. "I can't arrest somebody without any..."

"The sheriff needs helpers!" Berkeley shouted even louder and had the benefit of a microphone. "I will shoulder the mantle of leadership!" He jumped from the platform and ran up the aisle. "Everyone follow me to the freak show! Today we'll tear down evil forever!"

251

CHAPTER 43

Elaine walked out of the cookhouse and looked at her silver trailer ninety yards away.

There's no reason fat can't be fit. Granny Plunkett did farm chores until she was eighty, and she was fat. Elaine began her long trek. *Not as fat as me, but pretty fat. And lots older.*

Usually Willie brought her breakfast to her trailer. But last night at dinner she had told him not to do it anymore.

"I'm still young. I want to stay healthy," she had said. "I need to walk more, get fitter so I can breathe easier. Tomorrow I'm beginning a fitness regimen."

"You do realize," Willie had said, "that for someone like you, exercise can be risky."

"Yeah, I get paid by the pound," Elaine had replied. "Well, if I start losing weight, I'll eat more dessert to make up the difference." Elaine had then pointed to the slice of pie on Willie's plate and asked, "Are you going to eat that?"

Now here she was, actually trudging back from breakfast. Not that she was there yet, but her goal was getting nearer with each trudge.

As things are now, she thought, *if I got hurt, my income would end right quick. But if my ride ideas work, I could lease them to ride operators like Hutch. Two rides in each of six carnivals, and I'd be earning more than I earn now and the investment risk would be spread out. I need to get fitter; my brain will work better.*

As she passed Otto's tent, the flaps moved in the breeze. "Yoo-hoo, Herr Otto. Guten Morgen. How are you?" There was no

252

answer, but Otto was often preoccupied with writing letters.

Only twenty feet to her trailer now. Somewhere ahead she heard a musical tinkle. Elaine was breathing harder, but proud of her resolve to become fitter.

The tinkling sound was not so much musical as metallic, like someone scooping coins out of a large pickle jar. *Her* pickle jar! And the trailer door was slightly open!

Elaine's first reaction was to yell for help from Otto. As she turned, she saw that the spot where he parked his fancy car was empty. Never in recorded history had Otto allowed anyone to drive his car. If the car was gone, so was Otto. It must be an intruder in Otto's tent, and his accomplice was in her trailer. She was surrounded.

"Hey, Rube," she tried to shout, but her normally beautiful alto voice was only a panicked screech. That screech was followed by the sound of the pickle jar crashing on the trailer floor and coins splashing against the wall.

Elaine realized she had enough breath to run or to call for help, but not both. If she stood there yelling for help while some madman slit her throat, yelling wouldn't have done her a bit of good. So, for the first time in thirteen years, Elaine ran. Not fast. In fact, not much faster than she could have walked. But it felt faster.

Inside Elaine's trailer, Ace heard her shout for help. He panicked and dropped the pickle jar. He grabbed with one hand for the falling jar and with the other hand for the coins spilling out. He succeeded only in catching three dimes, two nickels, and a vision.

The vision was of himself sitting in jail nursing the results of the beating he would receive from the carnies who would soon chase him down. Ace jumped through the open doorway and, seeing Elaine running in one direction, he ran the other.

***

Beat the bushes, Miss Polk had said. Well, why not? MacPhie wrote a note telling Margaret where he was going and left it on the table for her to find when she came home from church. If he could help Isaac understand the killer's motivation, maybe they could predict his behavior. And if they could predict his next move, they could catch him.

MacPhie slid into the driver's seat of his Dodge Victory Six, fired up the engine, and headed towards Mountain Home.

***

Leroy, Louise, and Edna rushed out of the church and ran to Edna's car. Louise hopped in the back as Edna said, "I can't drive fast on winding roads, Leroy. You drive!"

Hearing that, Louise hopped out of the back seat and into the front. "Step on it, Leroy!" she said. "We gotta beat those crazy preacher people back to the lot."

Brother Bill Berkeley's call for action was responded to by his own team, plus perhaps twenty locals. In the calmer air outside the church, most of the congregation looked at each other sheepishly, then slipped away and headed home. As Isaac strode quickly across the parking lot, Bernard Fieldman's Packard pulled up on his right side. "Isaac, I'm taking my family home where it's safe," he said. "Get this insanity under control before somebody's hurt!"

Fieldman pulled away as Pardus LaBane's sensible black 1927 Chevrolet Capitol Coach pulled up on Isaac's other side. "I'll follow them and try to calm people down," she said, leaning across the seat, "but I advise you to hurry. I don't want to teach my students about mass hysteria and crowd delusion using their own hometown as an example!"

254

Heat waves radiated off the asphalt as cars streamed out of the parking lot. Isaac ran to his pickup. Down the street, he saw Rachel walking quickly toward the boarding house with Jeremy trotting ahead of her. It would have been nice to enjoy a peaceful Sunday with them at the boarding house. Oh, well.

***

Leroy and the girls had an eight-minute head start on the Rescue Raiders, but their lead was shrinking fast. Even with the pedal down to the floor, Edna's little car slowed going up the long hill south of Meekam's pasture and the carnival lot.

"Come on, Leroy!" Louise bounced on the seat more than the fairly smooth road warranted. "Push this baby!"

"If we aren't lucky, we'll all have to push," Leroy said. "We're running low on gas."

***

Turning the car onto the main road, Preacher Noble Custis was frustrated for two reasons. First, after the horrid events of yesterday, he had no desire to return to that carnival, especially not as part of a stage-managed protest. But he felt he must protect his flock from wolves in shepherd's clothing. His second frustration was that the leader of the wolfpack was now seated comfortably in the back seat.

"Genesis 45 says, Tarry not," Brother Bill Berkeley said. "My highly-motivated team won't move a muscle until I get there to inspire them. In other words, get a move on, Custis!"

"But as Paul counseled. Let us run the race with patience." Custis turned his head and smiled at his wife beside him. "Hebrews, chapter twelve. Right, Camilla?"

255

Berkeley laughed and said, "Yes, if we're going to swap scriptures, we mustn't forget your lovely lady. For her lips are a thread of scarlet and her speech is comely. Yea, her lips drop as the honeycomb. Song of Solomon, chapter four."

Song of Solomon? Custis caught a sharp breath. *How dare he quote the Song of Solomon about MY wife!*

Berkeley leaned forward, reached over the front seat, and patted Camilla's shoulder. "I'm proud to have your husband working under me, Camilla. The superiority of his Nordic breeding is obvious." He turned his head toward Custis. "None other than our recently-departed President Calvin Coolidge said that biological laws prove that we Nordics deteriorate when mixed with other races. You can't get a much higher authority than that. Except the scriptures, of course."

He patted Camilla's shoulder again, letting his hand remain there. "I'm sorry there wasn't time for your husband to preach, Camilla. But there's so much to be done, and I'm reluctantly forced to accept that I am the chosen mouthpiece God has called forth to speak for Him. When I'm elected, I'll invite you up to Washington to visit me." He smiled at her. "Both of you, of course. It's a pleasure to mingle with such a fine Nordic couple."

"Actually," Camilla Custis said softly as she moved Berkeley's hand away from her, "my family is from Italy. Both sides. But you're right about my husband's family being fine Nordic people. Even his grandpa, who has a hunchback, and his aunt, who was mentally ill."

Still smiling, Brother Bill slid back in his seat, looked out the window, and silently watched the scenery go by.

CHAPTER 44

Inside the cookhouse, Freda used her fingernails to strip the crust from her egg sandwich. "I know it sounds good, Willie. But owning a game joint isn't for you."

Sitting across from her, Willie looked up from his chili. "Beats working for somebody else."

"Not necessarily. Look, since you joined, have you ever been too sick to work?"

"Naw, I eat healthy and don't drink," Willie said. "Although once in my second season, I wasn't much good for two days."

"So did the Professor drop you by the side of the road, wish you luck, and drive off? Of course he didn't. If you'd needed medicine, he would have gotten it for you." She mashed the crust into a ball and dropped it into her empty cup. "You know why? I'll tell you why. Because the Ten-in-One performers make money for him, that's why. To him, you're all business assets, and a smart businessman maintains his assets. I'm telling you, you're all inventory."

"Well, I don't..."

"Inventory!" She took another bite of her sandwich. "Which isn't totally bad, just partly. Now, suppose you *did* own a Single-O joint. You could be 'Zambesi the Witch Doctor.' Throw some bones. Tell fortunes. It could be a good schtick. But suppose you got sick and couldn't work. What would the lot man do? You lay out this show, what would *you* do?"

"Well, I'd have to leave the witch doctor's joint packed up, and I'd move the other joints so there wasn't a hole."

"Exactly. And how much would the boss pay the witch doctor for not working?"

"Nothing."

"Right! And if you stayed sick, eventually you'd be out of the show. You want to own a business? Fine, but not in a carnival! Settle down in some town where there are lots of black people. Open a barbershop or a grocery store or something. Believe me, carnival life can very easily become a dead-end. Me, who could have married a jeweler or at least a guy in the garment trade. But no, I had to get stars in my eyes about vaudeville. So now, at my age, I'm schlepping a tentful of fortune-telling gear from town to town. Not to mention hoping I'm not the next one with a slit throat."

"He hasn't killed any women," Willie said.

"Well, he killed the Half." Freda stood and picked up her cup and plate. "So he's fifty percent closer."

As Freda and Willie walked toward the cookhouse exit, Louise popped her head inside. "Get to the front gate! They're coming!" she said. "We split up to warn everybody."

"Who?" said Willie.

"Me and Edna and Leroy. We split up when we…"

"No, Louise! Who is it that's coming?"

"The crazy preacher people! They're going to destroy the carnival!"

***

After leaving the church, Rachel had told Jeremy to run ahead and get the key to Miz Russell's car for her. Now she was headed for Old Farm Road. It was a narrow dirt road, little used, and a short cut to Meekam's Field—the carnival lot. With luck, she might get to the lot before the Berkeley caravan did, but she had no intention of meeting up with them.

If they managed to tear down the Ten-in-One, they would probably also locate Otto's tent and wreck it, too. Isaac wouldn't approve of her investigating on her own, but if Otto's steamer trunk did hold some clue to the killer's identity, it mustn't be destroyed.

Rachel stopped the car on the dirt road at the bottom of the hill. Somewhere in the trees to her right was Shallow Creek, where she and Jeremy had picnicked a couple of times. Perhaps they should have another picnic before school began. Maybe it wouldn't seem too bold to invite Isaac to join them.

As she climbed the hill, she picked up a stick the right length to be a hiking staff. If any carny stopped her, she could claim to be a lost hiker. At the top of the hill, she paused to look around. The lot seemed oddly vacant. Perhaps some of the carnies were inside avoiding the afternoon heat, but more likely Berkeley's people had begun to arrive, and the carnies had gone to the entrance to confront them.

She reached Otto's tent without meeting anyone and ducked inside. Her eyes located the steamer trunk immediately. It was secured with a new lock. *Darn! He must have noticed the tent was searched yesterday.* She knelt and examined the lock, wondering what to do.

"If you're thinking of stealing that trunk," a voice said, "it looks a bit heavy, you being so slim and all."

***

"Go straight to the freak tent," Berkeley said, once his forces had assembled near the entrance. "Those with baseball bats, move to the perimeter of the group and ward off resistance."

"We have to wait for Sheriff Cash," Preacher Noble Custis called out. "He's the one with authority to close things."

"We don't even know he's coming. Ecclesiastes says there is

259

a time to rend, and a time to cast stones. Well, today is the time to tear down a sideshow. Right, believers?"

The Prayer Team gave a mighty cheer, but the local citizens seemed less confident, perhaps because Preacher Custis had a valid legal point. Or it might have been the fact that some tough-looking carnies were gathering on the opposite side of the entrance.

"Divide into two teams." Berkeley spread his arms the way he might part the Red Sea, if that became necessary. "Team One, overturn the ticket booth and pull down the stage. Team Two, tear down tent canvas as fast as you can."

"We *must* wait for the sheriff!" Custis said. "Ecclesiastes says there's a time for peace!"

"What *you* must do, Brother Custis, is learn your scriptures better. Joshua 10, God hath delivered your enemies into your hand."

"Yes, but Matthew 5," countered Preacher Custis. "Blessed are the peacemakers."

"Psalms 94. Rise up against evildoers," Berkeley parried, then riposted with, "And also Deuteronomy 7, Smite them and utterly destroy them!"

The Prayer Team cheered their leader on. "Shame that amateur, Brother Bill! Devastate and humiliate him!"

"John 8," Custis countered. "He that is without sin, cast the first stone."

The Mercerville-ites moved away from Berkeley's people and sided with Custis. "Chew him up, Preacher. Go for the scriptural throat!"

"Proverbs 11," said Preacher Custis. "The hypocrite with his mouth destroyeth his neighbor."

"Hypocrite?" Berkeley drew himself up to his full shorter-than-average stature. "How dare you, Custis!"

"Because all men are created equal, endowed with unalienable rights, that's how!" Custis responded.

"That's not even *in* the Bible, you ignorant Philistine," Berkeley said.

"Well, this one is! Deuteronomy 5:21."

"Deuteronomy *what*?" Berkeley squinted, trying to recall it.

"Thou shalt not desire thy neighbor's wife!" Custis yelled.

"You accuse me of coveting Camilla?" Berkeley's face grew red. "You JUDAS!"

"If the sandal fits, wear it, you King David!"

"TRAITOR!" Berkeley cast his snow-white, pocket-sized New Testament directly at Custis' forehead. Custis ducked and leapt for the man in white. They fell to the ground, grappling.

"I'll lay even odds on Berkeley. Two dollars," Philo Napker told Mel Frazee. "He's younger and fitter."

"I'll take that bet. Custis is clothed in the Armor of Celestial Righteousness," Frazee said. "Not to mention, he's six inches taller and was on his college wrestling team."

261

CHAPTER 45

The downhill slope wouldn't have challenged a casual Sunday hiker. But Elaine wasn't hiking; she was running for her life. Once she made it into the trees, she looked over her shoulder to see if the killers were gaining on her. That's when she tripped and started her long roll down the hill.

It wasn't much of a slope, but to a 490-pound woman rolling down it, every bump and pebble deserved a comment, and none of them were polite. When her tumble ended, she found herself at the bottom of a hill, the foot of a tree, and a turning point in her life.

Oh, Lordy, I hurt in places where most people don't even have places. She rubbed some of those places as she sat up and leaned back against the tree, listening for anyone chasing her.

They'll find me easy. They only have to follow my skid marks.

When they finally caught her, what would they want? All her life Elaine had been doing what some man wanted. First it was her creepy stepfather, damn him and his little games. Next was the tractor salesman who had promised to sweep her away from her miserable life. Instead of a castle in the sky, he had taken her to a hay loft in the barn.

Her subsequent miscarriage made her hormones go haywire. As her weight problem became increasingly serious, she listened to (and unfortunately believed) the doctor who called her shameless and pathetic. Her own fault, he said. No self-respect, he said. He told her to eat less and pray more—for self-control.

The next man who told her what to do was the manager of a shabby carnival that came through town. He told her to go home. But this time Elaine was sick and tired of doing what men told her. This time she decided to do things her way.

"I thought I told you to get lost," the manager said when she returned the next day.

"Not exactly. You told me to come back another day when I was old enough to leave home. Well, today's another day, and this time I brought my suitcase."

"You ain't fat enough to be a fat lady. You're just regular fat, not carny fat."

"You don't have anybody fatter, do you? Tell you what, mister. I'll use my mouth to eat big, and you use your mouth to talk big. Between us, we'll make people believe I'm the best fat lady in the business. Or at least the youngest."

The man looked her over, then grinned and said, "Now I'll tell *you* what! If you stick it out two weeks without running home to mama, then I'll start paying you. Any questions?"

"Yeah," she said. "Where do I sleep, and when do we eat?"

Are the killers about to catch up with me? She listened carefully, but heard only the leaves rustling and somewhere through the trees, a creek gurgling. No one seemed to be chasing her. After all, she hadn't actually seen them. She could never identify them. They must have been looking for something in Otto's tent. *They couldn't find it, so they broke into my trailer because it was closest.*

Elaine grabbed a low-hanging limb and managed to slide herself up the tree trunk into a standing position. She leaned against the tree, catching her breath. There were still no sounds except the peaceful murmur of nature. She look up toward the top of the hill. Climbing it would be impossible without a great deal of help

Quiet! she commanded herself. *I can solve this problem. Calm down and think.*

Elaine studied the hill. A third of the way up was a flat boulder. When she made it that far, she could sit and rest. Half way up, there was a large fallen tree. That would be her second resting place. *I got myself down here, and I can get myself back. Just not nearly as fast.*

Somewhere a songbird was singing. A good omen. When things get bad, a pretty song can cheer anybody up.

Elaine froze. Something large was crashing through the underbrush behind her. She tried to pull a limb off a tree, but it barely bent. In desperation, she grabbed a small branch and flexed it back and forth quickly. "Break! I don't have time to go buy a damn ax."

It snapped and she waved the broken branch in the direction of the noise. "Keep away, or I'll brain you! I'll split your skull like a pumpkin after Halloween."

"Stay where you are," a voice called out. "Don't move!"

***

Rachel looked up at the woman silhouetted in the sunlight as the breeze moved the tent flaps.

"Well, I'm a hiker," Rachel said. "I got lost and stumbled on this carnival."

"Actually, you're the sheriff's friend," Seesla the Snake Girl said. "I saw you and your son with him yesterday."

Rachel blinked. *Never try to con a carny.* "The sheriff doesn't know I'm here. I wanted to help him learn about something inside Otto's trunk, but it's locked. It might help explain why Stringbean was killed. Rachel stood up. "I promise I'll..."

"Not yet, please. I want to ask something." Seesla motioned toward the camp chair. "First, how's your boy doing? Okay?"

Rachel sat down slowly. "He's fine, thank you. A couple of bruises, that's all."

"He's a brave lad." Seesla sat down on the cot. "Most kids

would have been crying."

"I don't mean to pry, but how are *you* doing? I'm sorry for your loss."

"I'm all right, I suppose," Seesla replied. "Time will tell."

"He was your…husband, I think."

"Carny style. A townie wouldn't understand." Seesla brushed her hair back from her face. "Do you have a husband?"

"No. But I'm glad I lost mine," Rachel said. "He abandoned me when I was seventeen and pregnant. Sneaked out of town without a fare-thee-well."

"That's cold-hearted."

"If you weren't married to Stringbean," Rachel said, "were you and Otto...?"

"Otto? Heavens, no!" Seesla said. "But who knows what String thought. He wouldn't tolerate his wife flirting, but I can't seem to stop. I suppose I'm still a schoolgirl in that way."

"So then, you actually *were* married."

"Often. We rode the Flying Jenny four times."

"What is...?"

"The carousel," Seesla said. "Some night after closing, a man takes his woman to the Jenny with a few witnesses. The couple rides together, and then that means they're married."

"Is that legal?" Rachel said.

Seesla smiled. "In our world, legal is whatever carnies agree is legal."

"But is it considered—until death do you part?"

"Or maybe only until the end of the season. That's up to the couple. Anytime they want, they can have the operator run the carousel backwards. They ride it, and they're officially un-married. Even in your world, marriage is only as permanent as you choose to make it, right? Or as happy." Seesla brushed her hand across her eyes. "We were both too stubborn. Being married kept spoiling a

265

beautiful friendship."

"I can understand that." Rachel patted Seesla's forearm. It was hard and scaly, but not off-putting. "Sometimes a woman thinks she's in love because she hasn't learned to recognize the real thing. I found something that seemed close, so I accepted it. Foolishly."

"Well, if there *had* been an only man for me, String would have been him," Seesla said. "Only a man who's lived through what he had and hasn't become hard could sense the scared little girl hidden under this skin." She watched the tent flaps moving in the breeze. "Maybe I'll take what we saved and go back to England. The southwest, where it's damp. I'll stay indoors and sew, and if I have to go out, I'll wear a veil and say I'm a widow. It's true, in a way. At least it should be."

Seesla went to the tent flap and looked toward the front of the carnival. "Normally I'd fancy some more girl chat, but those religious fanatics are back and everyone has gathered at the gate." She turned toward Rachel. "I need to know something. Tell me honestly, does the sheriff think Otto killed Stringbean?"

"No, he doesn't. Everyone in town thinks Otto is guilty, though."

"He hasn't exactly earned our confidence, either. If a carny is evasive with other carnies, we're tolerant. We don't pry. But it's different when carnies are getting murdered."

"I should leave," Rachel said. "Berkeley and his people seem very unstable."

"Don't worry. This time they haven't taken us by surprise. They'll never get past carny men. And no carny will bother you while you're with me," Seesla said. "Although they might push me a little for helping an outsider. That is, if you still want to get inside Otto's trunk."

"Oh, yes! Can you help me?"

"No," Seesla called over her shoulder as she slipped out

through the tent flaps. "But I know someone who can."

***

Normally, Isaac would have thought the rolling hills on the way to Meekam's Field were lovely and scenic. But normally he wasn't behind the pickup, pushing it up one of them.

I'll have to start carrying a stick with notches on it. The dang gas gauge says there should still be an eighth of a tank.

On this narrow stretch, there was no safe place to stop on his side of the road. However, there was a wide shoulder on the opposite side, provided his strength held out another twenty feet. As he pushed, sweat soaking the back and sleeves of his shirt, he passed the final road sign in the series he'd been seeing for the last mile.

When life has put you
Up a creek,
It's hard to turn
The other cheek.
— Burma Shave —

Isaac finally got the pickup across the road and onto the dirt shoulder. He kicked a rock behind the front wheel to keep the pickup from rolling backwards down the incline. Then he sat on the running board and mopped his sweaty face with his handkerchief. He was three miles from Mercerville and two miles from the carnival. The only option was to hike to the carnival. Once he calmed the mob down and sent everyone home, he'd have Leroy bring him back with a can of gasoline.

Lucky there's no creek here. I'd be up it without a paddle.

***

"Bingo, bango, bongo," Deena giggled as the lock popped open.

"How did you do that with only two little metal strips?" Rachel asked.

"It's all in the wrist," Deena laughed. "That and the fact that the metal strips are lock-picks. I can now say I've opened exactly twenty different locks with them. Nothing is safe from The Great HouDeena. Hooray for me!"

"It's only a wardrobe trunk," Seesla asked Rachel. "Are his things suspicious?"

"Not the contents. The lining," Rachel said. "The sheriff wants to know if it's just torn or if it has been cut deliberately."

"Let me take a close look," said Seesla. "Rachel, you keep watch and warn us if Otto drives back in."

CHAPTER 46

By the time the Commandant broke up Custis and Berkeley's fight, the roughnecks and joint operators gathered at the front entrance were about equal in number to the citizens congregated outside. About twenty feet behind the roughies and jointies were the male performers. Leroy stood guard beside the Professor, in case the mob once again tried to grab him. Right behind them stood Ramon, flipping a knife up into the air several turns and catching it by the handle every time.

For the freak-savers, the odds were intimidating. Each roughie and jointie was carrying some handy household implement such as a monkey wrench, ax handle, baseball bat, or a two by four. All of the carnies had hard, determined looks on their faces, with the exception of Alonso, who was sporting a grin almost as big as the huge ball peen hammer resting on his shoulder. At the group's head stood Herbert Hutchins, tapping his lead pipe against the side of his leg.

"I don't know what you people had planned," he welcomed the visitors, "but I expect to see your fat backsides going down that road, starting ten seconds from now. And take your trash with you."

He motioned and two roughnecks came forward frog-marching a man with a pencil mustache and horn-rimmed glasses. Hutchins said. "We caught him trying to take pictures inside the Ten-in-One tent."

"If you hadn't spoiled my time exposure," said newspaper editor Clement T. Samuelson, "I'd have run it on the front page. 'Mysterious Mercerville Maniac's Murderous Marquee: Austrian

Assassin's Ambush Arena.'"

Hutchins tossed the leather shoulder case containing Samuelson's No.1-A Kodak camera into the dust. The roughnecks did the same with Samuelson.

"Don't ever come back, neither." Hutchins shook the pipe at him. "If I ever see you here again, I'll bust more than your little Brownie."

At the back of the cluster of townspeople, Philo Napker turned to Mel Frazee. "I've been tossed out of bars and ejected from speakeasies," he said. "I was even forcibly escorted out of a political rally. But getting banned for life from a carnival? That's got to be a new low!"

***

Elaine gripped her broken branch tightly as the crashing noises in the forest came closer. Suddenly Willie broke through the bushes to her right. "Elaine! Are you okay?"

"Willie! The killers came back! Not Otto. His car's gone."

"Slow down. What happened?"

"Someone was in Otto's tent. His partner was in my trailer. I ran as fast as I could. Then I fell down that hill. How did you find me?"

"Leroy said the preacher's mob was coming to cause trouble," said Willie. "So him and me and the Hootchy girls ran around warning people. But I couldn't find you, so I followed your footprints like an Indian tracker."

"But you didn't come the way I came."

"I got lost," he said sheepishly. "I'd better stick to being a Wild Man, not an Indian."

"Doesn't matter. You still rescued me." She looked at the hill she had rolled down. "Now we have to get back. Is your way

270

flatter?"

"Worse. You don't want to go the way I came." He looked at the hill, then at Elaine. "I'll go back for help."

"No, it's okay." She started slowly up the grade, then looked back at him. "Stop worrying! You won't have to carry me. I made a plan for climbing this thing. Besides, I need the exercise."

***

As Otto turned his car onto the open field in front of the carnival, he saw a crowd at the entrance. *Was ist?* The Professor had said local laws required the show to stay closed today, so why were people there?

Overwhelming demand, perhaps? Otto slowed as he neared the group. A man pointed toward him, and a shout went up from the crowd. *Meine gute! Arkansas must be my best fans ever!* Normally, Otto was happy to stop for autograph seekers, but today he had important responsibilities. He decided to smile, wave, and keep driving.

Suddenly the crowd surged, forcing him to stop. Several women rushed to the car and pounded on the hood and fenders. Behind them, some men were shaking baseball bats above their heads.

A man in white raised his fists and shouted, "Citizen's arrest! Drag him out!" Otto recognized the preacher who had attacked the Professor yesterday. He slammed the gearshift into reverse and hit the gas pedal, sending the car backwards.

"After the killer!" Berkeley yelled. As the car sped backwards, Otto spun the steering wheel hard, throwing the car into a 180-degree moonshiner's J-turn. At the midpoint, Otto shifted into first gear. The car leapt forward and raced across the field and away from the shouting crowd.

I was wrong. They are definitely not fans.

***

Standing beside the pickup, Isaac congratulated himself for remembering that there was indeed a creek nearby, and he wouldn't need a paddle. A large field lay in front of him, and on the right of the field was Meekam's Woods. Running through the center of the woods was Shallow Creek, which in summer was usually little more than a trickle. The carnival was on the other side of the woods, a walk of, at most, ten minutes from the creek.

When he reached Shallow Creek, Isaac saw that Friday night's storm had raised the water level several inches and widened the creek by a few yards. He quickly removed his shoes, stuffed his socks inside, and rolled his trouser legs above his knees.

After reaching the opposite bank, Isaac sat down to put his socks back on, but his wet feet made it almost impossible. He pulled off his shirt and was drying his feet with it when he heard horns honking. Isaac looked toward the road as Otto's car rounded the bend and clipped the bumper of Isaac's pickup parked on the shoulder. The pickup jumped over the rock and began rolling backwards down the incline. Otto's car skidded across the soft shoulder and one wheel dropped into the ditch, bringing the car to a stop. Otto leapt out and ran into the field as the pursuing drivers slammed on their brakes.

Isaac splashed across the stream, his shoes and socks in his hand and his trousers above his knees, struggling to get one arm into a shirtsleeve. *With my luck, I won't be able to stop Otto or my truck.*

Brother Bill Berkeley's car screeched to a stop, and the Commandant jumped out of the driver's seat, ran to the trunk, and took out a rifle. Pardus Ann LaBane pulled up beside him and got out just as he swung the rifle to his shoulder. His shot was wild, kicking up dirt thirty feet in front of Otto. But it did manage to flush a bevy of bobwhite quail.

The Commandant glared at his rifle. "The sights are off." He worked the bolt and was taking aim on Otto's back when Pardus grabbed the forestock and pushed the barrel up into the air. "You idiot! That's a human being out there!"

In the center of the field, Otto was heading for the cover of a long fallen log near the top of a rise.

"He'll get away! Shoot him!" Berkeley yelled as he got out of the car. The mob parted like the Red Sea, and Berkeley passed through the multitude on dry asphalt.

A shot from the woods made everyone turn. Isaac was running towards them, bare-chested, shirt and shoes in one hand, his big revolver in the other. He fired a second shot above his head. "Put down that rifle!" he yelled. *Dang! My wrist will be sore tomorrow. I should practice with this thing once in a while.*

"Isaac!" Pardus yelled. "I can stop that man without hurting him. Say the word."

"Do it!"

Pardus jerked the rifle out of the Commandant's hands. "Let me have that before you give all the quail heart attacks." She rested her elbows on the hood of the car and centered the iron sights on the fallen log. She squeezed the trigger and popped off a branch to Otto's right. He immediately swung to the left and ran toward the end of the log.

"You didn't hit him!" Berkeley said.

"I don't *want* to hit him! I want him to surrender. And these sights are perfectly fine!" Pardus then shot off a branch at the left end of the log, and Otto changed direction back to the right. He was only twenty yards from the log when she shot off another branch. Otto swung left again.

"Look at that," Mel Frazee said to Stretch Sparmon. "She's

got him running back and forth like a damn painted bear in a shooting gallery."

Pardus fired again, kicking up the dust ten feet in front of Otto. Exhausted and still yards from cover, the strongman froze and raised his hands above his head.

CHAPTER 47

"The path down to the river is six miles from here." The man at the filling station took the nozzle out of Dr. MacPhie's car. "Watch for where the red barn was before it burned down. The path's on the opposite side. Two dollars, please."

MacPhie handed the man two dollars. "If it burned down, how will I see it?"

"Can't miss it. It's right there on the left. Or on the right, depending if you're coming from Skeeter or from Three Sisters."

"I'll be coming from here, of course."

"On your left, then. This is Skeeter, Arkansas, ain't it?"

"A filling station and four houses?"

"Three. The Hoskins house is vacant. Population took a big drop when they moved to Hot Springs. Had nine kids and a grandma. Made a big percentage difference in the census count."

"And the path is how far past the barn that burned down?"

"It ain't. It's a hundred yards this side. When you get to the barn, you've already missed it."

***

"I'm grateful you gals saw Willie and me coming back," Elaine said. "It wasn't in my plans today to roll through a patch of poison ivy. But it hasn't started to itch. Yet."

"If you're lucky, maybe it was just Virginia Creeper. Let's hope." Rachel finished washing Elaine's legs, then stood up.

"Will soap prevent itching?" Deena asked, stretching her left arm up along her spine to touch her right ear.

"If poison ivy is what Elaine rolled into," Rachel said, "Fels-Naptha is the best thing to get the oil off. I'll also make a soothing oatmeal and baking soda poultice, just in case it *was* poison ivy."

"I hope not. I can't scratch my ankles. They might as well be in Iowa," Elaine said. "Come to think of it, I played Iowa six years ago. I'm pretty sure it's longer than that since I could reach my ankles."

"You'd make a good nurse," Seesla said to Rachel.

"I'd like to think so," Rachel said. "I always wanted to be one."

"Maybe it was Otto in the tent," Deena said. "He came back to get something."

"Nope. Otto's car was gone," Elaine said. "Then I saw my door was open, and then the jar crashed. Time to run!"

"With the coins scattering all over the place," Deena said, "the thief sure wasn't going to hang around picking them up."

"Or maybe he was a carny," Rachel said, "and knew Elaine would recognize him."

"Carnies don't steal from other carnies," said Seesla. "You town people don't respect our way of life, but we *do* look out for each other."

"Town people look out for each other, too," Rachel said. "At least in small towns."

"But as a town grows," said Deena, "strangers start moving in, and that changes things."

"Fear of the unknown," Seesla said. "If someone looks like you and lives the way you live, they're probably not a threat. But if it's someone unknown, someone who is different—then you tend to wonder, are they a threat? Will they hurt me?"

"The world is naturally a dangerous place," Elaine said. "Plus, there are bad people who prey on others. Good people will always have to be careful."

"Y'know, maybe it was a man and a woman," Deena said. "Or even two women. You didn't actually see anyone."

"Didn't matter if it was the governor and his wife going to a tea party," Elaine said, "my priority was to protect myself. Besides, what kind of person goes into another person's tent without permission?"

Rachel looked down and dried her hands with the towel, hoping she wasn't blushing.

"It makes sense that both murders are connected," said Seesla. "String was killed before Stani. Stani's tent is only a few yards from Otto's. Maybe the killer went to the wrong tent."

"Personally, I think Otto's tent had something someone wants," Deena said. "But what? And who?"

CHAPTER 48

Distant thunder rumbled as a cloud darkened the hillside overlooking Mercer Street. Bert sat on a stump halfway up the hill, oiling the leather of his empty knife sheath. He had no regrets about the thing called "the Half." That killing was pure, and necessary to keep Nature in balance. However, Bert never lied to himself. *The skinny man was a mistake. I did it hurried and sloppy.* It was impossible to know why Nature should care a bit more about human flesh than about a raccoon hit by a truck, rotting by the side of the road. Nevertheless. *It wasn't pure. Nature might make me pay. Or God might. If there is one.*

Earlier that day, Bert had seen the salesman drive out of town. Soon after that, the mother and the boy came home from church, and almost immediately she drove away. Bert waited an hour, planning what to do next. He was just climbing the hill when he looked back and saw the sheriff's pickup sitting in front of the jail. After about five minutes it pulled away, heading for the county highway.

Now he looked down from up on the hillside. He liked sitting on a hillside, just thinking about Nature and things. But he didn't much care for remembering.

***

Grandpa had favored extended whipping sessions with his brass-buckled belt. The blacksmith, on the other hand, was a businessman and understood the value of time. A work-hardened fist to the side of Bert's head was the time-efficient way to teach any lesson the boy needed.

If the teaching required more emphasis, the smith would jerk the boy off the ground and hold his head over the flames of the forge. Not so close as to sear his face, but close enough to singe off Bert's eyebrows as the struggling boy stared into Hell and screamed.

One afternoon, lying in the sawdust with blood seeping from his ear, Bert wondered: W*hy*? If other people could have eyebrows, why shouldn't he? He decided that, like his grandma's Book said, it was time to put away childish things and become a man.

The blacksmith had made an excellent hunting knife. The seven-inch blade was crafted from a broken U.S. Marine Corps Mameluke sword, its engraved pattern still intact. The full tang was layered with walnut to form the handle.

"That knife's good advertising for me," the blacksmith had said. "Not another one like it in the whole world."

A few days later, as the blacksmith once again raised his fist to beat the boy, Bert baptized the blade in the blood of its maker. *I didn't know nothing yet about doing things pure. So I just buried my knife in his gut.* As the blacksmith lay twitching and jerking, Bert grabbed two oilskin slickers off the wall pegs and a box of matches from the workbench. It was time to run.

He hid in the hills all summer, moving south, living off the land. Eventually, sick of eating blackberries, serviceberries, and wapato baked in embers, he learned to approach ground-nesting birds, then freeze until they hopped closer. Guinea hens, peafowl, maybe chukars, when he could run them down in rough country, even the occasional squirrel. Bert could be a statue as long as necessary. Then, quick as a rattler, he'd throw the oilskin like a net, pounce on the creature, and kill it. Eventually, he could sneak up on almost anything. It kept him alive.

As the nights chilled, he crept into barns for shelter.

Sometimes he could hear farm families chatting, but humans seemed like a different breed. Solitude was the only companion he could trust. When winter forced him out of the mountains, he hid on an isolated farm. Two spinsters discovered him, but didn't ask who he was. All they cared about was whether he would do their lifting and toting.

Come spring, they introduced Bert to their brother Alvin McCoy, a moonshiner, bootlegger, and smuggler hoping to get rich off Prohibition. For six years, Bert rode the inland waterways with McCoy, running Cuban rum up from Florida and white lightning down from the Ozarks. And most important, becoming expert in living on the river.

***

It was Sunday. The streets would be empty all afternoon, although if someone had a need for medicine, Hansen was willing to open up his store. The boarding house was empty now, too, except for the kid and the old landlady. Then they came out the back door into the back yard and started hanging up wet clothes. Now Bert could act.

Stuffing the oily rag into his back pocket, Bert hurried down the hill. His knife was the one link between him and the killings, and no other knife looked like his. That meant the boy hadn't shown it to the sheriff yet, or the sheriff would have already come for Bert. If he could find the knife quickly, he wouldn't have to use it on anyone.

Bert walked quickly down the alley beside the boarding house and slipped through the front door. Looking down the shotgun hall and out the back door, he could see the boy and the old lady. Two overflowing laundry baskets would keep them busy a while, but he would have to search quickly. The knife wouldn't be lying around. The kid would keep it safe. *Where? Bedroom.*

When he reached the landing, he saw a door standing open. He looked around the edge of the doorframe and saw lace doily things everywhere. *The old landlady's room.*

Silently, he moved into the second bedroom. Beside the door stood a large cedar chiffarobe. The right side was a long door. The left side held drawers. He opened the door and saw shirts and trousers hanging on the wooden pole. *Too small for the salesman. Boy clothes.* Bert jerked open the drawers. Two were filled with clothes. The third had only trash; a long metal tube with a slot at one end and six holes spaced down one side. A cloth bag filled with little colored glass balls. A round wooden thing with string wrapped around a grove and a man's name on it—Duncan. None of it made sense. Junk. His knife wasn't there.

No. A mother wouldn't let her kid play with a big knife. She'd keep it in her own room.

In the room next door, a dress was draped over a treadle sewing machine. *The mother's room.* Quickly he pulled out every drawer and dumped the contents. He opened the closet and threw the clothing on the floor. He moved faster now, pulling the bedclothes back, kneeling to look under the bed. *Nothing.*

Bert sat down on the edge of the naked mattress. He could think better if he sat quietly and controlled his breathing, like when he used to catch birds. *It has to be here somewhere.*

A sound. The noise seemed to have come from inside the staircase. Mice? Insects? The old house settling? It could have been anything or nothing. *Where do town-people keep knives? Kitchen.* He moved noiselessly to the doorway and looked out. Nobody was on the landing or the stairs. Nature might overlook his mistake with the skinny freak, but he didn't want to kill normal people. Not if he had a choice. *But if there's no God, then killing a kid is no different than killing a raccoon.*

281

"How come we get a carnival here in Mountain Home," Sheriff Alsup shifted his six-foot-two, two-hundred-forty-pound frame toward the back of the chair and rested one foot on his desk, "and the best we can do is a couple of drunk fights and a pickpocket? But Isaac Cash gets the self-same carnival in a little ol' town no bigger than a rabbit's rear, and he gets two murders in two days. Messy ones, at that. Don't seem quite fair, somehow. You mind explaining that to me, Isaac?"

Isaac sat down across from the Baxter County Sheriff, and shrugged his shoulders. "Diligent police work, I guess. Attracting the scum of the earth so you don't have to deal with them. Matter of fact, I just put the strongman behind bars again. With the help of an elderly school teacher, that is. I'll probably be the laughing stock of three counties by tomorrow. And no, I'd rather not tell you the details."

"I wasn't asking for any. You just keep right on locking up suspects. You won't hear any complaints from me." Alsup took a sip from a tin cup with the stamped identification "Ark. St. Pen." and the cellblock number 3-B. "Seriously, Isaac, I notice you're walking a little bit lopsided. I never knew you to carry a firearm before. If you need more manpower on this thing, don't be bashful about asking. I'm stretched kind of thin for deputies, but I'll do what I can for you. Now what's so important that you made me come back to the office on a Sunday?"

"I appreciate all your help so far, Al. But I need you to do some more research." He handed Alsup the identification papers of the dead Half-and-half. "Can you get me any details on this name?"

"Get details? I can't even read it. Is that Mexican or something?"

"Polish. That's why I drove over to give you these papers personally. It wouldn't have made sense over the phone."

"Hell, it doesn't even make sense in person."

"A telegram would probably be best. Send it to this line at the bottom. That's the police station in Krakow, Poland."

"Poland? Hoo-ee, you come up with some weird stuff, Isaac. First it was kangaroos, now it's gonna be polar bears. I'll give it a try, but no promises." He opened a drawer and took out a notebook. "We had some pretty good luck with your boy Barlow, though. We found out that he did go back to Boston. Worked as an AB on merchant ships."

"An AB?"

"Able Bodied Seaman. He shows up on the records of a charitable outfit called 'The Seaman's Aid Society' in Boston. I get the impression he wasn't what you'd call financially secure. They gave him a bed to sleep in quite a few times between 1924 and '27."

"I think I'm about to hear the word 'but.'"

"Actually, I was going to say 'however.' However, he dropped out of sight six years ago. Probably got himself thrown in prison, but my contact didn't know for sure."

"Nothing since then?"

"No, but—there's your word 'but' you were waiting for—the guy in Boston is checking out Coast Guard records and such. He'll contact me soon as he knows anything."

"Well, it's a good start."

"Wish I could say as much for Otto Whats-it, your German strongman."

"Austrian."

"Oh yeah, the kangaroo place. Well, the New York police

don't have a criminal record for him. Neither does Chicago. I haven't had any luck with that 'Verein' group, either. But I do have two things I can do for you."

"Much obliged. What are they?"

"I happen to have a Chicago telephone book that's only three years old. And over there on the other desk, I have a telephone nobody's using." He took a thick phone book off a high shelf and plopped it on the desk. "Enjoy what's left of your Sunday afternoon, Isaac."

***

Miz Russell didn't normally wash on Sundays. But when a leak in the upstairs cupboard has left all the sheets and towels rain soaked and getting mildewed, you can't delay, not even if the sky is threatening another storm. In the summer heat, they should be dry by nightfall.

Once the heaviest items were hung, Miz Russell sent Jeremy back to the kitchen to fish the first batch of fried chicken out of the skillet, then ease the rest of the chicken pieces into the boiling grease. "Be careful not to let it splatter on you!" she said.

Jeremy was thrilled for a private chance to test the sharpness of his new hunting knife on the uncooked chicken on the counter. Once inside, he moved as silently as any Indian in a Tom Mix movie, in case his mom or Mr. Fairley had come home. He didn't want anyone to see him retrieve the knife from the little storage cubbyhole under the staircase.

When he got back to the kitchen, steam was rolling out from under the lid of the deep, cast-iron skillet sitting on the front burner. Jeremy laid the hunting knife on the table, picked up a thick hand towel, and used it to lift the skillet lid and lay it on the counter. The hot melted lard was bubbling and popping in the skillet as he used the metal tongs to take out the fried chicken pieces and lay them on a platter beside the stove.

If Jeremy had kept his back to the door, Bert could simply have taken the knife off the table and slipped out the front door unseen. But something told Jeremy he wasn't alone.

He turned and looked into the face of a tall, expressionless man holding the knife.

When Jeremy opened his mouth to yell, Bert thrust toward Jeremy's throat. Jeremy instinctively swung the cast iron skillet to block the thrust. The iron handle was searingly hot, and the pain made him let go. The skillet flew into Bert's chest, coating his face, neck, and chest with boiling grease.

Bert's scream rang like a wildcat. He dropped the knife as he fell on the grease-smeared floor, at the same time catching Jeremy's arm and pulling him down. Jeremy kicked wildly until Bert slammed a fist into the boy's chest, sending him sliding across the floor. Bert lunged for the knife, but Jeremy kicked it under the table, then scrambled through the doorway into the hall. Looking over his shoulder, Jeremy realized his attacker would catch him before he could reach the front door. His only chance was to make it upstairs and lock himself in his room.

He was halfway up the stairs when his ankle was gripped by the man's hard hand reaching through the banister columns. Jeremy fell, hitting his chin on a stair step, but he kicked with his other foot. In the man's other hand the knife flashed. Then there was motion behind the man as something swung down and smashed into his elbow. The knife clattered on the floor. Jeremy's ankle was free again, and he scrambled up the steps.

Bert turned and grabbed the old lady by the shoulders and threw her against the wall. The skillet in her hand and the cloth wrapped around the iron handle went flying down the hall. She lay moaning on the floor, but he would come back to her. Now he must finish off the boy, so neither of them could identify him.

He looked up just as the boy disappeared into his bedroom and slammed the door. By the time Bert got to the top of the stairs, the door was locked. He stepped back, then threw his weight against the door. There was a cracking sound. He did it again.

Inside, Jeremy put his shoulder against the heavy cedar chiffarobe and strained to slide it across the door. Slowly it moved, then stuck, only half blocking the door. The wood around the door lock was splintering. Jeremy knew he'd never move the chiffarobe enough. There was no place left to run.

He could jump out the window, but it was a two-story drop to the alley below. If he could lower himself out the window, the drop would be shorter. A quick glance down gave him hope. Old Mister Hovchek had parked his truck in the alley, and the bed was filled with bales of hay.

As rain began falling, thunder rippled counterpoint with the noise of the doorframe splintering. Nothing protected Jeremy except eighteen inches of chiffarobe, and it was now sliding under the pressure of Bert's crashing assaults against the door.

Jeremy put his legs out the window, twisted around to grab the sill with both hands, and slid out. The pain in his burned palm caught him off guard and made him let go of the sill with that hand. With rain drenching the clapboard siding of the boarding house, it was impossible to hold on long with only one hand.

In the bedroom, the noise of furniture being overturned was accompanied by increasing grunts and shouts. Jeremy looked down at the bales of hay and prepared to release his grip. Then he saw it.

Wedged between two of the bales, the farmer's pitchfork was pointing up at him.

CHAPTER 50

Before starting the pickup, Isaac took a moment to review the notes he had taken in Alsup's office. Nobody was answering phones late on a Sunday afternoon, and he had been about to write the exercise off as a waste of time. Then one phone call led him to another, and then to a third, which finally gave him some useful information. The Chicago meeting advertised on the poster in Otto's trunk was held by a legitimate organization, a social club for immigrants from German-speaking countries. There seemed nothing mysterious about Otto attending their meetings and nothing that suggested a motive for murder. He made a note anyway, because good law enforcement demands giving as much credence to facts in a suspect's favor as to those pointing to his guilt. Exculpatory versus inculpatory, his Police Gazette had called it.

Thunder rolled in the distance, but the shadow that fell on Isaac's notepad was not from a cloud. Out of the corner of his eye, he saw a big man's hairy hand reach for the door handle.

"You Isaac Cash?" the man said.

"Reckon I am. Why?"

"I'm Deputy Tom Love. Sheriff Alsup wants you back in the office."

"Not under arrest, am I?"

"Should you be?" The big man opened the pickup door and waited for Isaac to climb out. "He didn't say anything about arresting you. Just said he has a present for you."

***

Jeremy's fingers were slipping as the rain came down harder. He couldn't hold on much longer with only one hand. He tried again to grasp the window sill with his burned hand. The pain brought tears to his eyes. If he could twist his body as he dropped, he might miss the pitchfork. He had no other choice.

Across the street, the door of the general store flew open. Hansen had looked out the window and seen Jeremy.

"Jump!" Hansen shouted over the downpour as he came running. "You land in hay only. You be fine."

The feeling in Jeremy's fingers was almost gone now. "I can't," he yelled. "There's a pitchfork."

"Pitchfork?" said Hansen. "Ah! I see pitchfork. You stay up there until I move pitchfork!"

Jeremy felt a powerful hand clutched tightly around his wrist. He was being dragged back into the room.

***

The late afternoon sun was hot, but to the south a thunderhead seemed to be showering southern Baxter and much of Mercer County. At least it wasn't another tornado. Dr. Frederick Polk waded out of the river and trudged up the steep hill toward his car parked in the clearing at the top. True, he hadn't caught much worth keeping, but that's not what fly fishing is about. At least, not entirely. Relaxing, contemplating, and enjoying the solitude far from any other human being.

"Hello," a voice said.

Polk looked up and studied the man at the trailhead. He wasn't dressed for fishing and had no rod. He was dressed casually, not for serious hiking or boating. There were no houses around for at least five miles, so what was a non-fishing, non-hiking stranger doing out here?

"Hello, yourself," Polk said. "I'm afraid they're not biting today."

"Can't say I'm any great shakes as a fisherman anyhow. But I'm a pretty good tracker. I finally located Dr. Frederick Polk, didn't I?"

"Yes, that's me. Who are you, some kind of game warden?"

"No. I'm a doctor, like you. I need you to tell me about a baby you saw three years ago."

"What? Right here and now?"

"Um-huh." MacPhie smiled, pulled the old pipe out of his pocket, and stuck it into his mouth. "I figure right now is when it needs to be. And right here is where we are."

***

"Hey, little buddy," came the voice from above. Jeremy twisted his head upwards and saw the sweaty face of the Borneo Wild Man.

"I might can lift you by myself," Willie said, holding Jeremy's wrist tightly. "But it'll help if you'd put your feet against the building and scramble. I got myself all tired out fighting with that guy. Come on, scramble!"

Moments later, they sat on the floor, their backs against the wall, and caught their breath. "Where did you come from?" Jeremy asked.

"Some people chased Otto the strong man off the lot, so the Professor told me to take Baby Elaine's car and follow them." Willie used his torn shirtfront to wipe blood from a cut on his bruised face. "When I caught up, the sheriff had arrested Otto. He said I could go back for food and fresh clothes and bring 'em to Otto in jail. Anyway, as I drove past the alley, I saw you hanging out the window. So I came running."

"Where did the guy go?"

"Out the back door. You needed help, or I would have chased him. On second thought, maybe I wouldn't have. Fighting him has about used me up." Willie grimaced as he stood.

"Is Miz Russell okay?"

"I'll check. She was sitting on the floor looking dazed when I ran in. She pointed up here, but I had already seen the guy breaking through the door." Willie said. "You lie down and rest." He lifted the side of Jeremy's overturned bed and set it upright again.

"My gosh!" Jeremy said, pointing toward the crumpled bed sheets. "It must have been stuck to the bottom sheet all this time."

Willie looked toward the shining thing Jeremy was pointing at. "What's that?"

"Sheriff Cash's badge."

***

As Hansen opened the door, he heard a woman moaning. He peeked around the door cautiously and saw Miz Russell sitting on the floor near the staircase, rubbing her back. As he stepped inside, Hansen noticed the umbrella stand near the door and pulled out the largest umbrella. He heard voices upstairs, then the sound of footsteps coming quickly down the steps as a black man practically jumped down to the floor near Miz Russell and reached for her.

"You stop!" Hansen shouted, jerking the umbrella up near his shoulder like a baseball bat. "You stop now!" He advanced slowly toward the black man. "You run out the back door right now, or I murder you with this umbrella!"

Willie put his palms up toward Hansen and tried to keep his voice calm. "It's all right, sir. I just wanted to help her get up."

"You better run away right now!" Hansen advanced a little

faster and much more resolutely. "I mean it. I kill you dead!"

"Stop, Mr. Hansen!" Jeremy yelled from the landing. "He's my friend. He rescued me when I was out the window. He's the Wild Man from Borneo. Put the umbrella down! Please!"

Totally confused, Hansen stopped and looked up toward Jeremy, who seemed to be perfectly safe and sound. *Why is a man from Borneo in the Ozarks?* he wondered, not having been to the carnival yet. *And why would a wild man rescue Jeremy.*

"We're all right. I can explain everything," Jeremy said.

And why is a wild man wearing such nice-looking gray slacks?

CHAPTER 51

Isaac walked quickly out of the Baxter County Sheriff's office, trying not to stumble down the steps as he read for the second time what Alsup had facetiously called "a present."

"Wait up, Sheriff Cash!" Deputy Tom Love stuck his head out a window and called to Isaac. "Some doctor's wife is on the phone for you. Says it's real urgent!"

***

Slowing only when the curves demanded it, Isaac drove the seventeen miles back to Mercerville at a pace that would have made even auto racer Barney Oldfield jealous. On the phone in Sheriff Alsup's office, MacPhie's wife Margaret had told Isaac that when MacPhie returned home, she had been waiting by their front gate, bouncing with nervous tension because she had no way to contact her husband or Sheriff Cash. As MacPhie had pulled up, she had yelled for him to go straight down to the boarding house. She had also told him she couldn't locate Isaac, and MacPhie had instructed her to phone the next nearest lawman, the sheriff in Mountain Home.

In their brief phone conversation, Margaret had told Isaac what little she had learned about the attack when Jeremy phoned, trying to reach the doctor. She had also assured Isaac that Jeremy and Miz Russell believed their injuries were not serious, and that Rachel had not been in the house at the time.

Comforting though that assurance was, it didn't make Isaac's foot any lighter on the gas pedal, or his feeling of self-reproach any lighter on his conscience. The maniac was no longer specializing in carnival performers that Isaac barely knew. He was now striking out at people Isaac cared about deeply, and Isaac had left them alone and vulnerable. He had failed them.

As he parked his truck at the jail, a car pulled up in front of the boarding house. It was driven by what appeared to be a little old lady—a little *very* old lady. Isaac was sprinting toward the boarding house when the front door opened and Dr. MacPhie came out, helping Miz Russell down the steps.

"Shep, is she…?" Isaac said to MacPhie.

"Don't have time to explain," MacPhie said. "Go on in the house. Rachel will tell you everything."

Rachel was standing at the foot of the staircase when Isaac rushed in. "It's all under control," she said. "Jeremy's bruised and shaken, and his hand got burned, but that should improve a lot in twenty-four hours. I told him to keep it in a bowl of cold water and rest a little while, then get his pajamas and toothbrush."

"Miz Russell? Is it her heart?" Isaac asked.

"No, just banged up. Nothing's broken. Shep says Tincture of Time will do the rest. Two or three days at her mother's place, and she should be up and around."

"That old lady in the car is her mother?" Isaac said. "She would have to be…"

"Ninety-one years old and still driving. Yep, that's her," Rachel said. "Listen, I'm closing the boarding house for a few days. MacPhie convinced me that Jeremy and I should spend the night up at his house. It didn't take much convincing. He has a gun there, and I'm taking mine, too. I phoned Mr. Hansen and he agreed to let Mr. Fairley sleep on the sofa in the back of the store for tonight." She told Isaac what little she knew about the attack, then gave him a quick version of her experience in Otto's tent examining the trunk.

"What!" The stress of this afternoon was beginning to boil

293

over inside Isaac, but he managed to keep his voice down. "Otto could snap you like a twig! Never mind that a maniac was chasing your son down this very hallway while you were playing detective."

"I couldn't foresee that! I didn't know Jeremy had any knife. Now do you want to know about Otto's trunk, or would you rather scold me for being a bad mother?"

"I'm sorry," Isaac said. "Tell me."

"Well, I couldn't open it. It was locked with..."

"Meaning you took a big risk for nothing. What if you had gotten caught?"

"I did get caught, but it was only Cecile. Seesla."

"The Snake Girl?"

"Her real name is Cecile Hampstead. It turns out she and I have a lot in common, and..."

"And she might be a killer."

"Calm down! She wouldn't *steal* a boyfriend, much less kill one. Anyway, it was locked, but Deena the contortionist picked the lock."

"That little girl? She picks locks?"

"Pretty fast, too. She wants to be the world's first female escape artist. Anyway, I couldn't tell whether the trunk lining was torn or cut, but..."

"So it *was* for nothing."

"Stop interrupting! *I* couldn't tell, but Cecile could. She has much more sewing experience, and she said if the seam had been torn, you'd see mostly longish threads, broken in a few places. But if it was cut, there'd be short threads, all the same length. It's logical when you think about it."

"And?"

"Cut. Somebody searched that trunk very thoroughly."

"I thought so. Well, thank you. But from now on, leave the detecting to me and just concentrate on keeping you and Jeremy

294

safe."

"By the way," Rachel said, "he found something he wants to give you. There on the table in the parlor."

Isaac went into the room and saw a small bowl covered with a folded piece of stationery. Printed carefully on the paper were the words "Dear Sherif Cash." Inside, it said—

"Here's your badge. I polished it good as I could. Thank you for everthing. Your the best man I ever new. —
Jeremy Barlow"

At the bottom of the bowl was Isaac's badge, shined to a fare-thee-well. Isaac folded the note and put it and the badge into his pocket. He remembered that the pocket already held what Sheriff Alsup had called "a present." He hated being the one to deliver it, but it had to be done.

"Rachel, could we sit down? There's something you need to read."

***

Miss Pardus Ann LaBane looked around as she entered the funeral home's chapel. The scarlet satin brocade curtains weren't merely worn, they were also tasteless and tacky, especially the naked cherubs. Mel Frazee had probably purchased them for next to nothing from some Little Rock speakeasy raided by the police. Even as a student in her third-grade class, Mel never had good judgment about anything except making money. He would win marbles from the other boys at lunch, sell them back for a penny a marble, then win them again at recess.

"Everyone take a seat around the table, please," Judge Parmiston said "The Mercerville Town Council, meeting in extraordinary Sunday session, will now come to order. Where is our fifth member?"

"Preacher Custis asked to be excused, Your Honor," Bernard Fieldman said. "He was injured."

"All requests to be excused from a Council meeting should be submitted in writing two days in advance," the judge said.

"Two days ago he wasn't planning to get injured," Mel Frazee said. "Anyway, you only called the meeting today."

"Well, what happened?" said the judge. "Slip and fall accident? Those pulpits can be dangerous."

"Some kind of altercation, I believe," Bernard said.

"Pants?" the judge asked. "Or coat?"

"Pardon?"

"The alterations. Did his wife poke him with the scissors? I always thought she was near-sighted. Italians often are. Poor vision runs in their blood." Judge Parmiston polished his glasses with a handkerchief from his breast pocket.

"No, your honor. I'm told it was a fistfight."

"I don't believe it. Preacher's wife wouldn't hurt a fly." He finished wiping his glasses and folded the handkerchief. "Although you never can predict what women will do. With all due respect to Miss LaBane, of course."

"Thank you," Pardus said, "but surely we don't need to rehash today's disturbance. We're here to discuss a petition that's been circulated about Sheriff Cash."

"No discussion needed." Philo Napker said. "The sooner we send Isaac Cash back to barbering, the sooner we can haul Otto down to Little Rock for a speedy trial and execution!"

CHAPTER 52

Isaac motioned towards the sofa. "Sit down please, Rachel." If she fainted, he could holler for Shep to bring smelling salts from his little black bag.

"I asked Sheriff Alsup to try tracing your husband. As I was leaving today, he received a telegram. Unfortunately…well, here." Isaac handed her the telegram. As she read silently, Isaac reviewed it in his mind. She took enough time to read it twice.

Re inquiry Seaman Otis Barlow. Stop.

Fishing trawler Anne Marie out of Gloucester, Mass, sunk during storm 1931. Stop.

All hands lost. Stop.

"I'm sorry, Rachel," he said as she folded the telegram up again. "I know how it is to lose someone you love."

"You're very kind. But I lost the man I loved the day I realized Otis wasn't who he pretended to be. And that I didn't mean anything at all to him." She took out a handkerchief, but didn't dab at her eyes. "What I lost was a foolish girl's dream. I stopped crying about that long ago." She looked up at Isaac. "Isaac, losing our dream can happen to anyone. It's a risk we take in living life."

Isaac wasn't sure what to do next. Sit down beside her on the sofa? Hold her hand? Keep his distance and give her space?

Uncertain, he sat down at the table, remembering he was wearing his revolver just in time to keep the holster from banging against the table. The only sounds were the clock ticking and MacPhie's footsteps coming down the hallway and into the parlor.

297

"I gave Miz Russell a small dose of chloral to mix in with her valerian root tea tonight. It'll help her get a good night's sleep," MacPhie said as he put his black bag on the table. "Isaac, that Jeremy is quite a boy! Burned, banged up, hung out a window, and all he cares about is, can he help capture the 'Knife Guy'?"

"Request duly noted and denied," Isaac said.

"About that knife," Rachel said. "I looked around and couldn't find it, and Miz Russell is certain the man picked it up and took it with him."

MacPhie sat down in the armchair. "Rachel, does the description Jeremy gave you match anyone?"

"Not really. Tall. Dark hair. Strong," Rachel said. "the carny that saved him—Willie—swore the man's not a carny, but maybe he couldn't tell, because he also said the face was blistered and dark and blotchy from the hot grease. Bleeding, too."

"Second-degree burns. Maybe even third-degree in spots. He'll stand out in a crowd, that's for sure," MacPhie said. "I'll phone the hospital to alert us if he shows up. That man's hurting bad."

"Let's assume Willie is right, and the guy isn't a carny," Isaac said when MacPhie returned from making the phone call. "That means he could be anyone from anywhere."

"Anywhere is a big place," Rachel said. "Let's start locally. Who fits the description?"

"Lots of fellows," MacPhie said. "What became of Kimmey's oldest son? He was a troublemaker."

"Still is," Isaac said. "But he's in prison in Oklahoma."

"The oldest Willetts boy is built like a water tower," MacPhie said.

"But Jeremy knows him," Rachel said.

"Taylor Fustby? He's tall," said MacPhie.

"Out of town," Rachel said. "Left last week to visit family in West Memphis."

"Assuming he didn't sneak back to town. How about Cyrus Jenkins' cousin?"

Isaac listened as Rachel and MacPhie volleyed names like a tennis match.

"Might be tall," Rachel said. "I've only seen him on his back under Miz Russell's car."

"Stretch Sparmon?" Isaac said.

"Tall, but I don't know if he's strong. Could be," MacPhie said. "Elmo Johnson?"

"The bank teller," Rachel gasped. "He's tall. Dark brown hair. Well built. And Jeremy's never met him."

"Okay," said Isaac, "if Elmo doesn't show up at the bank tomorrow, I'll go after him. But I've been thinking. These murders were bold, vicious, and merciless. I don't believe anyone we know is capable of that. Not our people."

"Me either, really," MacPhie said. "So let me tell you about my odyssey today. Isaac, you thought maybe the killer was examining the Polish man's body. That set me to wondering, so I phoned an obstetrics professor at the Medical School in Little Rock. I asked about cases similar to that Polish carny, except real. From there I tracked down Dr. Frederick Polk at his favorite fishing spot."

"He's the professor?" Rachel asked.

"No, a friend of his. Polk is retired in Mountain Home, but he practiced in Cotter and served as Baxter County Coroner. The last inquest before he retired three years ago was a young woman who threw herself off a railroad bridge north of Three Sisters. When she jumped, she was holding her newborn baby."

"How awful," said Rachel.

"Gets worse. She was very young, her first pregnancy, and she had to deliver the baby alone. Her husband was a hunting and fishing guide, and they lived way back in the woods. Anyhow, the verdict at the inquest was that the baby was stillborn because the umbilical cord got wrapped around the neck. The mother's mind became unbalanced when she realized her baby was dead, causing her to take her own life."

"How does this tie in with the murders?" Isaac said.

"Hold your horses. We have two interesting points. First, when Polk examined the baby, he found something unusual about the baby's…uh...privates."

"Doctor, I've had a baby and helped deliver several others." Rachel said. "Discussing genitalia won't shock me."

"The baby was like the Polish fellow pretended?" Isaac asked. "Herma-whatzit?"

"No," MacPhie said. "In this case, there were no genitals visible at all. Genital aplasia, Polk called it. He said it sometimes occurs when husband and wife are too closely related and both have the recessive trait."

"When I was twelve," said Rachel, "our cow had a calf like that. It was disturbing."

"Your parents allowed you to see that?" said MacPhie.

"I not only saw it, I was with Rosie when she dropped the calf. I was the oldest, so I helped nurse the animals. Now, you said there are *two* interesting points."

"Point two. A week after the inquest, a fifteen-year-old girl admitted privately to Polk that she and some other kids had been swimming upstream and had seen the woman jump."

"Why didn't she come forward at the inquest?" Isaac asked.

"A group of girls and boys were skinny dipping together. Her daddy would blister her hide if he found out about it. Anyway, Polk went back to his notes and photos and decided the baby's death was not caused by the umbilical cord. Those were actually finger marks on the neck."

"You're saying she strangled her own newborn?" Isaac frowned. "Polk should have reported it to the authorities."

"The verdict would still have been insanity," MacPhie said. "Besides, suppose it wasn't insanity. Maybe she was mentally defective. Polk felt there was no sense adding shame and scandal to the tragedy. You see, she and her husband were first cousins. That sometimes causes hereditary problems. It's sad, but unforeseeable."

"That Bill Berkeley says it can be prevented, but I don't care for his solution," Rachel said. "He would allow bureaucrats to declare that one family is defective and another is normal. Why should politicians control child-bearing? They can't even manage the banking system!"

"You're talking about the eugenics movement," said MacPhie.

"That's the term Berkeley used, yes. Label a whole family as degenerates because one member was born handicapped," Rachel said. "Or one became a criminal. You'll never convince me a child is destined to commit crimes just because his father did!"

"There *have* been studies of hereditary defects," MacPhie felt his pockets for his pipe. "The Jukes family. Another named Kalikakos or something."

"But Berkeley wants *forced* sterilizations! Of whole families!" Rachel said. "Based on what evidence?"

"Getting back to these murders..." Isaac began.

"I admit I'm not comfortable with forced sterilization," MacPhie said, "but apparently the law is. The Supreme Court decided the Bucks case years ago."

"What's legal should be what the citizens agree is legal! Not what a few judges invent and interpret! 'Malicious asthma' indeed!" Rachel said. "Berkeley would let doctors terminate unborn babies that a committee only suspected *might* be defective. He compares it to pulling weeds!" Rachel leaned toward him. "Dr. MacPhie, everyone knows you're a free thinker. What if some politician decides your opinions might damage society? And therefore *you* are

301

a defective human!"

"Ridiculous," MacPhie said. "Maybe my opinions make people uncomfortable, but science can't be subverted that way."

"Don't be so sure!" Rachel slapped the sofa cushion. "I saw it right here in Mercerville today. In the church!"

"That's one good reason I don't go to church," MacPhie laughed. "But look at it this way. If science could predict a baby would be born incurably deformed, wouldn't parents be glad to bypass that defective birth and try again? Isn't that kinder than saddling the whole family with a lifetime of misery?"

"That depends on who gets to define 'defective,'" said Isaac. "But back to Stringbean and..."

"Exactly!" Rachel interrupted. "Who decides? Even scientists can have poor judgment. Or be corrupt. I don't want anyone playing God, no matter who!"

"Rachel, when I give a cancer-ridden patient morphine to ease the agony, I'm playing God," MacPhie said. "God decided that patient would die a horrible death. But I come along and say 'No, you don't! I can't stop you from taking his life, but I won't let you torture him as well.'"

Isaac tried again. "Suppose Stringbean went to Otto's...,"

"That's different!" Rachel gestured vigorously toward MacPhie. "You're an honorable, ethical man, willing to take that decision on your conscience. You're not some politician who could arbitrarily decide which children can be born, then go off to play golf with his cronies."

"If I could jump in here," Isaac said. "Except for Stani's genital deformity, I don't see how this baby relates to two murdered carnies."

"Maybe *I* do. It's obvious doctors can be wrong," Rachel said pointedly. "Suppose Polk is wrong, and the mother didn't do it."

"They lived alone," MacPhie said. "If it wasn't her, then it must have been..."

"You're saying the husband killed the baby?" Isaac said. "Why didn't she go to the police?"

"There wasn't time. He told her she was about to be next!" Rachel said. "So she ran!"

"Hmm. Possible," MacPhie said. "The girl who witnessed the suicide swore she saw a man lurking in the woods. But she couldn't describe him."

"Tall. With dark hair," said Rachel. "And a big knife."

"Okay, let's assume," said Isaac, "that a backwoodsman's wife has a deformed baby. The husband's tall, strong, and healthy, so he can't believe he's the father. Conclusion? His wife must have slept with a deformed man. Enraged, he chokes the baby. The mother grabs the baby and runs. He chases her, to kill her for her infidelity, but she jumps. Later, he decides to kill the freak he thinks she slept with."

"And if a carnival had been in that area recently," Rachel said, "there's your connection."

"Isaac, remember our conversation about getting inside the mind of a killer?" MacPhie said. "I think maybe you're in there."

"What was the couple's name?" Isaac asked.

"Polk didn't remember. When he gets back on Wednesday, he'll locate the records."

"Not good enough," said Isaac. "I need it now."

"Phone the Mountain Home Sentinel tomorrow," Rachel said. "They probably printed the woman's obituary."

MacPhie took his pipe out of his mouth. "There's something else to consider. Suppose that woodsman is *not* our killer. I've thought all along this was a case of obsession, but suppose we're wrong about who is obsessed. According to Sigmund Freud, our obsessed killer *could* be someone with an intense self-hatred. In other words, it might be another deformed person."

"So we can't rule out the freaks," Rachel said.

"Except Otto isn't a freak," Isaac said. "Performers like him and Deena and Willie are what carnies call a 'working act.' Baby Elaine and the tattooed man are 'made acts,' because they intentionally did something to themselves in order to be sideshow performers. To carnies, 'made acts' and 'working acts' aren't freaks. The word 'freaks' means people who were born the way they are. They're special—and carnies understand that."

"So then, the only so-called freaks still alive in this carnival are the Professor and the Snake Girl," MacPhie said.

"'Deformed person' certainly doesn't sound like the tall, powerfully-built man Jeremy saw and Willie struggled with," Rachel said.

"No, it doesn't make sense, but the backwoodsman theory does," Isaac said. "The big problem, how do I find him? He could be anywhere."

"He was in this house today. Keep your eye on the hook," Rachel said. "It's already baited."

"I don't like the sound of that," Isaac said. "The bait you're referring to...?"

"Jeremy saw the man before his face was burned. He can identify him," Rachel said. "That maniac has to kill Jeremy. We won't be in the house, but he doesn't know that. He'll be back. Tonight."

"I don't believe he will, as bad as he's injured," said MacPhie. "I believe he'll go to ground. But as Rachel says, even doctors can be wrong. So we're going to my place, and I'll load my shotgun. The recoil knocks Margaret off her feet, but she can shoot my revolver more or less straight."

"And I'll have mine, too," Rachel said. "Tomorrow I'll figure out what to do next."

"You won't need to," Isaac said, "because tomorrow I'm

putting you and Jeremy on the train..."

The sound of a gunshot made them jump. Upstairs, Jeremy was yelling even before they reached the stairs.

CHAPTER 53

"Sheriff," Jeremy yelled as they rushed into his room, "a man shot a gun in the alley!"

Isaac pulled his revolver as he looked out the window, but saw no one.

"Was it the man who attacked you?" Rachel sat down on the bed and hugged Jeremy.

"I only got a glimpse as he ran away. Too dark to tell."

"You hurt anywhere, boy? Let me look." MacPhie pushed Rachel's arms aside and pulled up Jeremy's shirt. "Isaac, you better check on your prisoner."

But Isaac was already down the stairs, heading for the door, his revolver still in his hand. A minute later they heard him yell for MacPhie to come quick.

When MacPhie reached the jail, Isaac was in the cell kneeling beside Otto, pressing a towel against the man's throat. "He's been shot in the neck. He can't breathe!"

Rachel rushed through the office door, holding Jeremy by the hand.

"Isaac, take the boy to my house fast as you can," MacPhie ordered. "Tell Margaret to give you my emergency surgical kit! Rachel, I need your help."

Rachel held Jeremy's hand tighter as she looked down at Otto. Then she let go.

As Isaac and Jeremy ran out, MacPhie yelled, "And tell Margaret to phone Mountain Home for an ambulance." He turned to Rachel. "Does blood make you faint?"

"When Daddy chopped his foot really bad with an ax," she said as she knelt down, "I held it closed all the way to the hospital."

"In that case, put your thumb and finger right here on his neck. Pinch it and make that wound open up so I can see the hole. Fortunately the bullet cut across the front of the throat instead of going straight into the neck and hitting the spine."

MacPhie patted his pockets and quickly found his pipe. He pulled the pipe stem from the shank and snapped the shank off the bowl. Carefully he worked the shank into the hole in Otto's throat. Otto's chest moved upwards as air once again reached his lungs.

"That'll do until Isaac gets back with the kit. Nurse Barlow, you have just assisted with an emergency tracheotomy. Now we need to control the bleeding. By the way, how old were you when your daddy..."

"Not quite fourteen."

"Somehow that doesn't surprise me," MacPhie said.

***

Isaac watched the ambulance pull away from the jail, grateful that it was Otto and MacPhie on their way to the hospital, not Rachel or Jeremy. He was tempted to hug her, but he was afraid that might seem too forward. Besides, the sleeves of her dress were soaked with blood.

"Why would this guy, injured like he is, come back a few hours later to shoot my prisoner." Isaac said. "None of this makes sense."

"No, unless there's some connection between the attacker and the carnival. That's where Jeremy found the knife," Rachel said. "On the other hand, suppose it wasn't him. Maybe he has an accomplice."

"That's an excellent point," said Isaac. "If so, I now have two killers to track down."

"It complicates things, that's for sure. Well, I need to go to MacPhie's and check on Jeremy." Rachel said. "Then I'll come back and tidy up things in the hallway where Miz was shoved down. Won't take me long."

Isaac ignored her blood-soaked sleeve and put his hand on her arm. "Rachel, you're not thinking clearly. You already said you're closing the boarding house for a few days."

"Oh, you're right, of course. The mess will just have to wait," Rachel said as she started across the street toward MacPhie's house. "See you tomorrow."

"Good!" he said. "I want you and Jeremy to go and stay with my friends in Little Rock until I can catch this killer."

"Thank you for saying that," she said, turning back to Isaac. "It's been a long time since anyone except Miz Russell has cared about us." She put her hand on his upper arm and gave a little squeeze.

"I'll pick you and Jeremy up at ten-thirty," Isaac said. "The train leaves at eleven."

"No, Isaac. I've never run from anything in my life. I certainly won't teach my son to live that way."

"Well, tomorrow, after you've had a good night's..."

"Tomorrow I'm taking Jeremy and a bag of tin cans to the opposite side of that hill behind the boarding house. I'm going to teach him how to shoot my gun."

"You can't expect a boy to learn to handle a gun in five minutes."

"You're right," she said. "I'll need a lot more bullets. I'll go to Hansen's store first."

"Jeremy is only twelve!"

"My daddy taught me to shoot when I was eleven."

"Yes, and I started when I was nine, but that was a long time ago. And on a farm. We live in a town now."

"Makes no difference."

"Certainly does. This is not the wild and woolly frontier. We have laws."

"The law didn't stop a madman from dumping my underwear on the floor and chasing my son with a knife."

"I can't be everywhere. I was in Mountain Home trying to solve a crime."

"I'm not blaming you. But I intend to protect my son."

"Now listen, Rachel. I admire you for being a modern woman and independent. But I'm serious. Tomorrow I'm putting you and Jeremy on the train to Little Rock, like it or not!"

"How exactly do you propose to do that? Arrest us? You don't even have handcuffs! Are you planning to march a woman and a twelve-year-old boy into the train station tied up with twine?"

"If that's what it takes! I *am* the sheriff, you know."

"You don't have to tell me that! I'm the person who's been standing up for you when nearly everyone in town says you can't handle the job."

"Who? Mister Bank President? Idiots like Napker and Fairley?"

"Others, too. Meanwhile, you fall all over yourself apologizing for only being a barber. Well, I intend to protect my son."

"With what? That peashooter you had in your purse the other night? If I were the killer right now, you wouldn't have..."

When the pistol appeared in her hand, Isaac's first thought was, *How come I didn't notice her apron pocket sag?* Fortunately, she had it pointed at the ground, not at him. His second thought was, *Hey, she can draw pretty fast.*

"Give me that thing!" he said. "You're going to shoot off your big toe."

"Yours maybe. Not mine. I'm very accurate."

"Did Judge Parmiston give you a permit for that?"

"A permit? People are getting their throats slashed every night at bedtime, and all you ask is whether honest citizens have permission to protect their children?"

"That's not true. Nobody got killed last night."

"Maybe you just haven't tripped over the body yet!"

"That's it!" He reached out. "I order you to give me that gun right now!"

"Don't you dare touch me!" she said. "You're not taking away my only protection without a fight."

"You think that toy would be any help in a real fight? Against a real gun?" He patted his Colt .45.

"You leave that hogleg where it is, Isaac Cash. I could drop you before that ridiculously long barrel cleared the holster."

"Yeah? Well, I'd still get off one round, and that's all it would take to blow you and your little toy gun to kingdom come."

"Right now this toy in my hand is more dangerous than that cannon in your holster!"

"Well...," he groped for some logical retort. "My gun is a lot more powerful than yours!"

"Oh, for heaven's sake! Don't men ever stop thinking like little boys?" Rachel spun around and started across the street again. "I'm going to check on Jeremy and then go to bed. Good night!"

Isaac watched her striding across the street. *That is one confident woman! Don't believe I ever met one like her before.*

CHAPTER 54

At first, Isaac wished he had a tall stool. But that wouldn't have a back on it. So this was the best solution. Push the desk inside the cell and set the wooden chair on top. The other end of the desk would keep the cell door propped open. Not that it mattered, since he had the key in his pocket. But after this weekend, he was ready to believe that anything that could possibly go wrong was just about to.

He climbed up on the desk, sat down in the chair, and leaned forward against the brick wall. Now he could look out the barred window and keep watch on the boarding house. He couldn't see the front door, but he could see enough of the street that no one could reach the front door without being spotted.

The back door was a problem. If the killer came from the north, Isaac would see him crossing the far end of the alley. But if he came from the south, from behind the buildings farther down the block, Isaac would not see anything until the killer reached the back screen door. Determined to stay alert, Isaac splashed his face and neck with a handful of water from the bucket beside him on the desk.

***

"I just hate for you to go back there tonight," Margaret MacPhie said. "You don't need your toothbrush! I could use Shep's alcohol to sterilize his toothbrush. He never needs to know. As for a nightgown, unfortunately, mine are all too large for you and miles too short. But if you didn't mind being, well, a little bit exposed…"

"It will be fine, Margaret, really," Rachel said. "It isn't just my toothbrush and nightgown I need. I've realized that Mr. Fairley still doesn't know what happened, that it might be dangerous to spend the night in the house. That's not fair to him, so I'll write a note telling him to go across and knock on Hansen's door. I'll only be gone a few minutes."

"Then take the revolver with you. I'll still have the shotgun."

Rachel remembered what MacPhie had said about the recoil, and suppressed a smile as she visualized short, round Margaret firing a shotgun and ending up on her backside.

"I have my own revolver. You must keep yours close by you at all times," Rachel said. "Don't worry. I'll be back in a few minutes."

***

It had been a long and exhausting day. Isaac's back ached from pushing his truck up the incline, his legs ached from running from Shallow Creek all the way across the field near the carnival, his wrist ached from firing his big revolver into the air and now, worst of all, his heart ached with disappointment over his failure to protect his town from a maniac.

Isaac got off the desk and shook the kinks out of his bones. He was climbing back onto the desk again when a light came on in the boarding house, upstairs. *Is that Jeremy's room? No. Rachel's.*

Out of the corner of his eye, he saw the hood of a car slowly drift into view in the alley behind the boarding house.

I didn't hear it. He must have put it in neutral and coasted.

Isaac slipped out of the jailhouse, flattened his back against the side wall of the boarding house, and moved silently down the dirt alley, his Colt .45 in his hand.

Ten feet from the rear of the house, Isaac heard the click of a car door opening, then a light kerchunk as it was carefully closed.

Isaac didn't hear anyone going up the back steps, but the next sound was the squeak of the screen door. He ran around the corner to the foot of the stairs and yelled, "Freeze! Or I'll shoot." No one was there.

He's inside already? Doesn't anybody lock their back door around here?

Someone jumped out of the car and swung a tire iron. It missed Isaac's wrist and hit the revolver, which flew onto the back porch and clattered down the steps.

Isaac grabbed the man's arm. As they struggled against the front of the car, the assailant tried to beat Isaac over the head with the tire iron, but lost his grip, and it smashed into the windshield. The two men fell to the dirt, each grappling for a better hold. Rolling over, they came to a stop with Isaac on top, pummeling the man with his left hand while strangling him with his right hand. The other man was trying his best to gouge Isaac's eyes.

"Stop it!" Rachel shouted as she turned on the porch light.

"You see, Miz Barlow?" yelled Mr. Fairley from behind her. "I told you! You see?"

"Isaac! Let go!" Rachel rushed down the steps. "You're strangling Philo Napker."

"I knew the sheriff was the killer," Fairley said. "Never trusted him. Damnable Roosevelt-ite!"

Rachel grabbed Isaac's shoulders and pulled him backwards. He fell sideways into the dirt and quickly came up on his knees in a defensive crouch. Napker lay on his side, coughing and sputtering.

"Will someone tell me what is going on?" Rachel demanded.

"He attacked us, Miz Barlow," Fairley said. "As I got out of the car, I told Philo I saw a shadow in the alley. So I slipped inside to fetch you." Fairley left his place of safety behind Rachel's back and leapt down the steps to help Napker up.

"If it hadn't been for Philo's bravery," Fairley said, "the

sheriff would have slit our throats like sacrificial lambs on the unholy altar of the Anarchist World Conspiracy."

"Why were you two sneaking around back here?" Isaac demanded.

"Nobody was sneaking," Napker sputtered. "Can't citizens come home quietly from a patriotic meeting?"

"Quiet," Fairley hissed. "Don't tell him anything."

"What meeting?" Isaac said.

"No torture you can inflict," Fairley said, "will make us betray our fellow patriots."

"Speak for yourself," Napker rasped. "I'm the one who got choked."

"You were coming home from a meeting?" Isaac said. "Some kind of anti-Bolshevik thing?"

"It's all right, Isaac," Rachel said. "I think it's five or six men sitting around Seth Walkip's table, talking politics."

"How did you know that?" Fairley gasped. "*You're* a spy, too!"

"Mr. Fairley," Rachel said, "when you use the telephone in the hall, your whisper is so loud I'd have to be a deaf spy to miss it." She handed him a piece of paper. "Now, this note explains why I'm asking you to spend the night in Hansen's store. It could be dangerous to sleep here tonight. And Mr. Napker, please go home."

"Danger? What danger?" Fairley said, backing away from the house. "Is it the maniac? Hansen's store has a big front window. I'd be a sitting duck! An unwilling scapegoat!"

"Get your stuff, Fairley! You're staying at my house tonight," Napker said. "We can't expect this pretend sheriff to keep anyone safe! We'll barricade ourselves and take a stand, if it comes down to it." Napker climbed into his car and slammed the door. "I'll send you the bill for my broken windshield," he told Isaac as he started the engine.

314

Fairley stumbled up the steps and through the doorway, not taking his eyes off Isaac until he was safely inside. "Three minutes," Fairley called out. "That's all I need!"

"Sheriff Cash," Rachel said, going up the steps to the back porch, "if you would wait until they leave, I'd like a word with you, please." She leaned against the door frame and watched Isaac brush the dust from his clothes and pick up his revolver.

When the two men had driven off, Rachel looked down at Isaac and said, "It's late, Sheriff Cash, and I have a big day planned, so please tell me plainly and clearly—what's this all about?"

"Well, I saw the light go on in your bedroom, and then this car pulled up in back…"

"Why were you watching my bedroom?

"I wasn't. I was in the sheriff's office."

"Then how could you have seen a car at the rear of the house?"

"I was looking out the window," he said.

"The window of the cell?"

"Yes, m'am. But then I had to get down off the desk and limber up."

"Why were you on the…? Never mind. Go ahead," Rachel said.

"Well, when I got back on the desk, I saw your light come on."

"You were standing on the desk, watching my window? Is that correct?"

"I was sitting in a chair," Isaac said. "The chair was on the desk."

"But you were in fact watching my bedroom."

"Not your bedroom, exactly. The whole house."

"You thought you could see the whole house from the top of a desk," she said wearily. "Inside the cell."

"More or less." Isaac wished he wasn't so tired and could express himself better. "In case the killer came back. What I mean is…"

Rachel sighed as she straightened up. "Never mind. You are the sheriff, you can do what you think best. But I am going to gather my things, go back to MacPhie's house, and try to get a few hours of sleep." She closed the screen door behind her as she went inside. "I recommend you do the same."

"Yes, m'am," Isaac said.

But he didn't. He went back to the chair on top of the desk.

Part Five: The Blow-off

CHAPTER 55
Monday, August 20, 1934

A little before daylight, sleep conquered Isaac, and rather than fall off the chair, he stretched out on the hard, thin cot. An hour later, a hideous ringing woke him. He staggered out of the cell and managed to say hello into the correct end of the telephone.

"Already at work? You must have gone to sleep quickly last night," MacPhie said. "Personally, I only got about five hours on a sofa in the doctors' room at the hospital. I figured you'd want to know about Otto."

"How is he?"

"Out of surgery and resting well. Fortunately the bullet passed across his neck without hitting the spine or the major blood vessels. But he won't be gargling swords for a while."

"I spent some time in the cell last night," Isaac said. "My guess is Otto saw someone and dived into the corner. The bars kept the gunman from getting a clear shot. Any idea what kind of gun it was?"

"The surgeon thinks probably a .22 pistol or something similar. I'm thinking maybe one of those German millimeter things. A lot of our boys brought them home as war trophies. Or maybe the shooter is one of Otto's countrymen."

"Any way to find out the caliber for sure?"

"Isaac, we don't have the gun, and we don't have the bullet. All we have is a throat wound with stitches. You want to catch a murderer from that, you better hire Charlie Chan or Dick Tracy from the funny papers, because it's beyond me."

"I'll search the cell for the bullet, now that the sun's up. This afternoon I'll go to the hospital and question him."

"You won't get much conversation. Could be a month before he can talk again. He'll never be any threat to Rudy Vallee."

"He can write notes. This can't wait."

"Okay, here's a thought. You told me Otto is a ladies' man. A small caliber pistol is something a woman might carry."

Or a very small man, thought Isaac.

***

Leroy would have preferred to go to breakfast, but the Professor needed someone to think out loud to. So Leroy stretched out on the loveseat, folded his arms behind his head, and watched the Professor pace around the office.

"First," the Professor said, "let's assume Stringbean and Stani were killed by whomever shot Otto last night. And that it was the same guy Willie fought with. What does that give us?"

"I don't know. What?"

"I don't know either, but it must give us something," The Professor stared at the floorboards. "Let's start with the murders. What did String and Stani have in common?"

"Their names begin with S."

"*Leroy…!*"

"Sorry, Professor. Okay, they were both skinny. Both about the same height. Both were Ten-in-One performers. Both men. Well, at least men if you take into account…" Leroy stopped. "Hey! Maybe the guy only kills freaks."

"Otto isn't a freak. He's a made act."

"Maybe the guy hates freaks, and he considers you all to be freaks."

"That would include you."

"I'm only an actor. Nobody hates actors," Leroy said. "Except directors."

"Your logic is irrefutable." The Professor said. "Never mind. Get up and move that loveseat. I'm going to show you something nobody knows about. String knew. I trusted him. I believe I can trust you, too."

The Professor unfastened the padlock on the hidden compartment. In it, beside the cash box, was Otto's leather dispatch case. The Professor opened the cash box, pulled out three envelopes, and handed them to Leroy.

"Drive my car to the Mountain Home hospital," the Professor said. "Tell them whatever treatment Otto needs, he gets. If necessary, give them that cash. But only if they ask for money. Get back here as soon as you can."

"Should I carry the cash in your briefcase?"

"That's not my case. It belongs to Otto, and you never saw it. Understand?" The Professor grew quiet and ran his fingertips across the soft leather. "I beginning to think that sheriff is right."

"Meaning?"

"I have no choice but to break the carny code of silence." The Professor lifted the dispatch case out of the compartment, laid it on the desk, and picked up his letter opener. "But first we have to break the lock on Otto's case."

CHAPTER 56

Inside Elaine's trailer, Elaine was at the far end of her big bed, sitting with her back against the wall to make room for Seesla to sit on the corner at the foot the bed. Willie stood just inside the trailer, leaning against the doorway so he would notice if anyone approached. As the Professor laid the leather dispatch case on the bed near Seesla, Freda pulled her chair closer and examined the case with a critical
eye.

"Here's the situation," the Professor said. "Cookhouse Lil arranged with the local store to open early and sell her things she needs fresh. Eggs, milk, and such. When she got back here, she told me she had learned that Otto was shot last night. It's very serious, a throat wound. That's all she knows.

"The word is already going around the lot," Elaine said. "Have you talked to the sheriff?"

"No," said the Professor. "Anyway, the only person he ever arrested was Otto, and he let him get shot. People, we're going to stop being sitting ducks. *You* are the ones I trust, and I need your brains to help figure this out. Especially Elaine, because she sees things in creative ways. Now, I believe whoever shot Otto also killed String by mistake because String was in Otto's tent."

"But why Stani?" Seesla said. "Did he witness it?"

"That's a possibility," the Professor said. "The question is, was Otto shot by the guy Willie fought with? And is that guy a towner?" The Professor paused. "Willie, you said the guy's face was burned and hard to recognize. That gazoony who quit the show last week was tall. Was he the guy?"

"Pretty sure it wasn't him," said Willie. "I remember him."

"Ace was tall," Freda said. "And Hutchins fired Ace yesterday and banned him from the lot."

"Naw, definitely wasn't Ace," said Willie. "Ace isn't that muscular. I'm sure it wasn't anybody with the show."

"It gets more complicated," said the Professor. "Saturday night, Otto came to my office. He told me someone had searched his tent the night String was killed and again on Saturday. He asked me to lock this case in a safe place. It contains letters and a book. When I heard Otto had been shot, I read everything." He emptied the case onto the bed. "Don't give me that look, Elaine. You know I normally hold sacrosanct anything my people trust me with."

"It's okay," Elaine said. "This situation is special. Murder changes everything."

"Seems to be mostly numbers," Freda said, flipping the book's pages.

"I saw a local address on one page," said the Professor, "so I sent Leroy to find out who lives there."

"These letters look German," said Seesla. "You read German?"

"And several other languages," the Professor said. "The letters are from people in Austria. About money they received from a fund. A few letters contain cancelled checks."

"That's nothing new," Freda said, laying the book on the bed. "As long as I've known Otto, he's helped family and friends in Europe. He was making good money before the Crash. He had investments."

"When he joined the show," said the Professor, "he said he wanted time off occasionally to meet with people from Europe. Well, he's a first-rate act, so I agreed."

"This is starting to add up," said Willie. "More than once

323

Otto said he's against Hitler. I told the sheriff maybe that's how Otto gets people to give him money."

"I hope you're right," the Professor said. "But it may not be so innocent."

"Is Otto involved in something crooked?" Elaine asked.

"Maybe. This could be the key." He handed her the book.

Elaine flipped the pages. "It's an accounting ledger."

"Some of the amounts are the same as in the letters," the Professor said. "I'm not sure what that means."

"Ask Edna." Seesla said. "She did bookkeeping before she started dancing."

"I thought she was some executive's secretary," the Professor said.

"She was, but he was the head accountant."

The Professor turned to Willie. "I want you to get..."

"The Hootchy gals. On my way." Willie headed out the door. "I read your mind."

***

"Embezzling?" Freda looked at Edna. "Otto? Then why do so many of those letters wish him luck?"

"I only said it's possible." Edna flipped to another page in the ledger. "I wish we had his side of the correspondence."

"How do detectives catch embezzlers?" Louise asked.

"It's real tough sometimes." Edna said. "With big money like this, the guy would keep double books. If you had the other ledger, an auditor could compare it with Otto's records."

"If I were embezzling," Elaine tipped her head back and closed her eyes. "Where would I hide a double set of ledgers?"

"How about in a bank?" Leroy stepped through the door of the trailer. "Number 62 Mercer Street, the address you sent me to locate? It's the Mercer County Bank."

"What? Are you sure?" the Professor said.

"Yeah, are you sure?" said Louise. "I know banks lose people's money, but I don't think they embezzle, do they?"

"Did you double-check the address?" Willie asked.

"Hey, why does everyone think I can't get an address right?" Leroy said. "Sure, I say stupid things sometimes, but only because it's fun acting like an idiot."

"Well, it's the most convincing act you do," Freda said.

Louise shot Freda a dirty look. "Leroy, I think you're a swell actor."

"Listen, I'm six-two, handsome, and blessed with an excellent body. Believe it or not, lots of people feel threatened by that," Leroy said. "So I let them think I'm dumb, and then they relax. It's crazy that people would hate someone they don't even know, just for the way they look."

"I don't hate you, Leroy," Louise said. "In fact, if..."

"Not now, honey," Edna said quietly.

"Edna," Elaine said. "What Louise said about banks—Could a bank be involved in this?"

"Well, look." Edna flipped over the cancelled checks. "One of them has a rubber stamp that says, 'MCB,' a date, and 'ARK.'"

"MCB," said Willie. "Mercer County Bank. Arkansas."

"But if somebody at a bank was embezzling," Seesla said, "they wouldn't keep the fake ledger there."

"Why not?" said Edna. "Banks have lots of ledgers, and they all look the same. Also, in a small town like this, a bank might store a customer's ledger as a service. One more ledger wouldn't be noticed."

325

"We need to have a look inside that bank," said the Professor.

"Already did. It had just opened," Leroy said, "so I went inside and asked them to change a five. Somebody was ahead of me, and I had plenty of time to look around."

"How many people work there?" Willie asked.

"Three. The teller, an old lady at a desk, and a middle-aged man in an office up front."

"Was there a walk-in vault?" Edna asked.

"Only a safe in the back corner. It's a really small bank."

"Elaine?" The Professor noticed her lean her head back against her pink pillows. "Is that fertile brain of yours designing something we can use?"

"Maybe." She closed her eyes. "But I wish I knew more about that safe."

"Willie," the Professor said, "go find..."

"Deena." Willie started out the door. "Read your mind again."

"You know, Professor," said Freda. "I think you two guys could develop that into an act."

CHAPTER 57

Isaac found the bullet in less than two minutes. The fresh nick in the wall suggested a ricochet, and as he knelt to search the floor, he spotted the hole in the mattress. *Today's going to be a better day.* He dug the slug out of the stuffing with his pocket knife and a pencil. Unfortunately, it was deformed from hitting the wall. Matching it to a specific weapon would be impossible. He dropped it into an envelope and put it in the desk drawer. Then he phoned Sheriff Alsup and explained what had happened in the past twelve hours.

"Hell's bells, Isaac, you're busier than a one-armed paper hanger," Alsup's low, resonant voice came over the line. "Two dead, one wounded, and now you want to locate some river guide?"

"Can you help me?" Isaac pushed his hat to the edge of the desk to make room for his feet.

"Maybe. I do remember that girl's suicide. The husband was a real backwoodsman. Went by the name of Bert, as I recall. First-rate hunter and stalker. You want to get yourself a deer, he knew right where they would be, and he'd get you up real close. If you heard even the slightest noise, it would be you or the deer, because Bert never made any sound at all."

"Still live there, does he?"

"Nope. Moved about a year after she killed herself. Don't know where he went. But I imagine he'd find work of some kind. He was a handy fellow, this Bert. He could fix almost anything from your boat motor up to your John Deere."

"Al, what was he like personally?"

"Didn't know him too well myself. He didn't spend much time in town. Seemed honest enough. Kinda had this way about him like he felt aloof from other people. I guess spending so much time in the woods by yourself, you can start thinking other people aren't as in tune with nature as you are."

"Being a hunter is one thing, but do you think this fellow could kill another human being?"

"Isaac, if a man fills himself with enough hate, he can find some excuse to kill. It's even easier if his target happens to be wearing a badge. So you take care now, hear?"

Isaac hung up the phone, then stared at it. He didn't want to make the next call, but he needed information fast, and he wouldn't hesitate to do what had to be done.

***

"Did you see the name painted on the safe?" Deena asked.

"I thought that might interest you," Leroy winked at her, pulled a dollar bill out of his pocket, and read the words he had penciled in the margin. "Cary Safe Company. Buffalo, N.Y."

"Is there a back door?" Elaine asked.

"No, and the bank doesn't have one either," Leroy waited for a laugh, but none came. "Sorry. Anyway, there's an alley behind the bank, and I walked down it. No back door, no windows."

"Bad news. The only way in is the front door," the Professor said. "No way to reach the safe during the day, and tonight may be too late, with a killer still at large."

"Well, there *is* a small panel screwed onto the wall in the alley," Leroy said. "It's maybe seven feet off the ground. I don't know if it goes into the bank."

"One story building?" Deena asked. "Or more?"

"Two stories. Why?"

"That would be a panel that lets you clean out the duct running from the boiler in the basement up to the higher floors. Kind of like sweeping a chimney, but metal. How big is it?"

"Pretty squeezy. About sixteen inches wide by fourteen high."

"Squeezy for you is only snug for me."

"It doesn't matter," Elaine said. "Unless it opens somewhere inside the bank, we're still out of
luck."

"Now that you mention it," Leroy said, "I remember seeing a grill on the inside wall, but in a slightly different place."

"It's still the same shaft," Deena said. "The grill allows hot air into the bank. Usually it's not screwed down. They pop off to make cleaning easier. I guess people figure nobody's small enough to get into the shaft anyway, so they're not as careful inside as they are with the outside panel."

"Deena, how is it a farm girl knows so much about banks?" the Professor said.

"I was hoping you wouldn't ask."

"I *am* asking. And I want to know," said the Professor. "Tell me."

"Well, um..., maybe when we play small towns, I might have left the lot after midnight once or twice. Or maybe more."

"You rob banks?" Elaine gasped.

"On second thought, *don't* tell me." The Professor covered his ears. "I don't want to know."

"No, no. I never take anything," Deena said. "But you all know my dream is to become an escape artist. Well, you can't learn about safes sitting in a Ten-in-One. Banks are where the safes are. Leroy, can you describe the combination lock?"

Leroy drew a quick sketch. "There's a lever handle here, and over here is the lock."

"But describe the center of the dial," Deena said.

"Dark. Maybe black."

"Perfect. That means it's an old model." Deena said. "At least thirty years. This is a cakewalk."

"This is crazy, is what it is," said Freda.

"Certifiably," said the Professor. "Forget it, folks. We don't even know the fake ledger is
there."

"I wouldn't bet on it," Willie said.

"Honey," Louise patted Deena's knee. "It's too risky. You're a sweet youngster...."

"Stop it!" Deena jumped up. "Everyone listen to me! I've already *done* stuff like this. Except at night. Daylight will only make it easier."

"Easier for somebody to waltz you across the street to that jail," Willie said.

"If that happens, we'll claim it was a promotional stunt for the carnival, and we'll hire the best lawyer in the state," Elaine said. "I've been wondering what to do with my money."

"Everybody stop treating me like a fool just because I'm young!" Deena said. "I've been on my own for two years. I know what I can do and what I can't do. And I can *do* this! Just keep the people in the bank distracted."

"I shudder to think what these yokels would do," Freda said, "if she were locked up here."

"Deena's a grown woman," Seesla said quietly. "Grown women should be respected and allowed to make their own decisions."

"Thank you, Sees'," Deena said. "Everybody, this could be my big break as an escapologist. Even if I was arrested for breaking into a bank, think how the publicity would advance my career!"

"Edna and me won't let them see you," said Louise. "Even if we have to pull off our clothes and do the Hootchy right there."

Willie turned to Elaine. "Let's think this over. Break into a bank that's straight across from the jail. Open a safe in one minute, maybe two. Find a ledger book we're not even sure is there. Then get out without anyone knowing they been robbed. All in broad daylight."

"Hmmm," Elaine thought for a moment. "Yes, I believe that about covers it."

The carnies looked at each other with expressions ranging from uncertainty to complete disbelief.

"Well, people?" said Elaine.

"I'm in," said Freda, shaking her head sadly. "I guess."

"We both are," said Edna and Louise.

331

"In for a penny, in for a pound," said Seesla.

"I guess it isn't exactly stealing, under the circumstances," Leroy said. "I'm just glad today's not a Sunday."

"If it were anyone else," the Professor said, "I'd say absolutely not. But Elaine, you've never disappointed me yet. Tell us your plan."

"Wait." Deena said. "How will I know which ledger?"

"It will have some of those German names from Otto's letters," Elaine said. "Write them on a strip of paper you can stick up your sleeve. Professor, Louise will need a twenty-dollar bill. And Seesla's skin has to be covered up. Do we still have a widow's outfit in the costume trunk?"

"I have it." Seesla lowered her eyes. "I've been wearing it when I'm alone." She looked up and saw the others staring at her. "It makes me feel...at peace, somehow."

"We understand, Honey," Elaine said gently. "Okay, everybody listen. You'll take two cars. The Professor drops Leroy, Seesla, and Deena in the alley behind the bank, then drives to the side street and waits. The other car, with the distraction people, waits down the block. Seesla will signal when Deena goes into the shaft."

"Willie, you'll drive Elaine's car," said the Professor, "and while they're inside, keep the motor running, just in case."

"No. Willie must stay here," Elaine said. "In an Ozark town, a black man attracts attention. Willie, tell him what you told me."

"There wasn't many plantations up here," Willie said. "Too hilly. And the few slaves there were, well, they left after the South surrendered. But that doesn't matter. I'll drive."

"Excuse me, everybody." Elaine looked at them firmly. "Either I'm planning this raid, or I'm not. And if I'm in charge, my decision is, no unnecessary attention. Period!"

They all looked at the Professor. "She's right," he said. "The last thing we want is to attract attention. Willie, I'll spread the word to everyone that you're boss of the whole carnival until I return. Hutchins will drive Elaine's car."

"Hector!" Seesla said.

"Hutchins would be better," said Leroy. "Hector's a snake. No opposable thumbs."

"No, I mean we need someone to take care of Hector while I'm gone."

"Why is everybody looking at me?" Elaine said. "I signed on to be the brains for this thing, not a boa-sitter."

"I have a really big purse," Freda said, "but I don't know about an eight-foot snake. Especially not carrying it into a bank. What if it got out?"

"He'd make a great distraction," Leroy said. "You could ask about keeping him in a safety deposit box."

"Leave Hector in his cardboard box," said the Professor. "We'll put him in the car's trunk."

"Nooo," said Seesla. "He'll get too hot. Snakes can't perspire. He'll die."

"Well, back in the purse," said Freda.

"Oh, all right!" Elaine said. "I'll keep him here in the trailer. But at the other end. Waaay at the other end. Does he have a leash?"

"Carnies!" the Professor muttered and shook his head. "Okay, people, I'm glad the snake problem is settled. Now, could we please go rob a bank?"

CHAPTER 58

"Mountain Home Sentinel," said the woman on the other end. "Serving North Central Arkansas with all the news we know that's new to you."

"This is Isaac Cash, Sheriff of Mercer Country. Let me talk to Mr. Samuelson, please."

Samuelson was downright friendly until he realized that Isaac was asking for information, not giving it.

"Yes, I remember the case," Samuelson said. "We published the woman's obituary. Rather well written, if I do say so."

"When exactly was that, do you recall?"

"Sorry, can't help you."

"What was the woman's last name?"

"Sorry."

"Do you recall the name of the husband?"

"No dice."

"I'm only asking if you remember the name."

"Of course I do. I wrote the obituary."

"Well, would you tell it to me, please?"

"Most assuredly not. No sir-ee. That's privileged information. I can't release that."

"Mr. Samuelson, this could help us catch a killer before he murders someone else."

"And I'm telling you that this is more important than any one person, dead *or* alive. This is a First Amendment issue."

"I'm a sheriff, for heaven's sake. I'm sworn to uphold the Constitution. And I'm investigating two murders and an attempted murder."

"I don't care if it's ten murders and a regicide. I don't give information to every Tom, Dick, and Isaac who's curious."

"But on Saturday you yourself called this man a maniac!"

"Listen, Cash, maniacs have rights, too. The Constitution was written to protect even crazy murdering scum. And it's my duty as a journalist to protect the murdering scum's rights from abuse by the unbridled excesses of overzealous authoritarianism."

"All I want is the man's name, for Pete's sake!"

"No, it wasn't Pete, and don't think you can fool me into revealing confidential sources with an old trick like that."

"Confidential sources?" Isaac heard himself shouting, but didn't care. "It was an obituary published for anyone to read! It's in your files!"

"Get this straight, Cash. If you want files, you'll have to subpoena them. That's the legal, constitutional way!"

Isaac sighed, then took a long, calming breath. "Okay, Mr. Samuelson. You win. I'm going to phone Sheriff Alsup now. His office is right down the block from yours. I figure it will take him maybe ten minutes to phone the judge and get a warrant authorized. Then another five minutes to get to your office. A total of twenty minutes at most. Then he and his deputies will pull every filing cabinet you have out of that building, onto the sidewalk, and into the back of somebody's pickup truck."

"You can't do that! I haven't broken any law."

"Well, you wanted a warrant. Fine. And since you don't recall any details of the incident, we'll have the warrant include searching your house for any files you may keep there."

"You can't bully me with your fascist strong-arm tactics!"

"Tell me something," Isaac said. "How come when *you* play by the rules, you call it the Constitutional way. But when *I* play by the very same rules, I'm a fascist, strong-arm bully? You want to

335

play by the rules? Fine, but it's a two-way street! So okay, let's play."

The silence was so profound that for a moment Isaac thought the phone lines had gone down somewhere. Finally, the newspaper editor spoke up.

"Uh, look, Cash, the truth is, I don't actually remember those people's names. But I do remember writing the obituary. The old obits are in a pasteboard box down in the basement. But I'll find it, I promise. Then I'll phone you back. Give me twenty minutes, okay?"

"That's fine, Mr. Samuelson. I'm going to walk down the block, but I'll be right back. And for the record, my name is *'Sheriff'* Cash. You can quote me on *that*, too."

***

Leroy got out of the car, looked up and down the alley, then motioned for Deena to get out. Then the Professor drove slowly down the alley to the street and stopped again. Seesla lowered her black veil, got out, and stood at the end of the building. The Professor pulled the car around to the corner where he could watch the sidewalk and warn Seesla if any locals came from either direction. Seesla looked down the alley toward Leroy and Deena and folded her arms across her chest, the signal for all clear.

Leroy didn't have to unscrew the wooden panel. His screwdriver was big enough to use as a pry bar, and the panel popped off when he applied muscle. Deena, dressed in her leotard, kicked off her slippers and wrapped the rope around her waist. "Give me plenty of slack."

"Don't worry. It's a fifty-foot rigging rope." Leroy quickly tied his best Boy Scout bowline knot at the small of her back. Then he interlocked his fingers in front of him to make a stirrup for her foot. She took a little hop into his hands, and he boosted her

336

headfirst into the opening. In another second, all Leroy could see was the rope disappearing into the darkness. Leroy signaled to Seesla, who then walked to the corner and signaled for the second car to unload the distraction team.

After a couple of minutes, Leroy realized the rope was no longer feeding into the shaft. Soon Deena's feet reappeared as she backed out and dropped to the ground.

"Serious problem. Got any axle grease?"

"No," Leroy said. "Will oil do?"

"It'll have to. Hurry."

Leroy ran down the alley and around to the corner to the Professor's car. "Slight delay," he said, taking a can of Sinclair Opaline motor oil from the trunk. "Don't worry."

When he returned, Deena took the can and said. "Turn your back and close your eyes."

"Why?" Leroy asked as he turned around.

"The duct makes a little turn, then it narrows. My leotard gets caught on the sides and keeps me from moving. So I'm going to strip naked and oil myself."

"The paper with people's names...?"

"I'll fold it up and carry it in my mouth. Now close your eyes. If you open them, I swear..."

"I won't. I promise."

Leroy closed his eyes and waited. Soon Deena's voice came from in front of him. "Keep 'em closed, and hold out your hand."

"Boy, I sure hope my mom never finds out about this." Leroy felt warm oil on his palm.

"I've turned my back," Deena said, "Rub some oil between my shoulder blades to make sure I didn't miss a spot."

"With my eyes closed?"

"Unless you want me to poke them out, yeah."

Estimating her height, Leroy put his hand out until it bumped something. It was her right shoulder.

"Sorry, Deena. I've never oiled a girl before." He slid his hand across to the back of her neck, then down.

"I hope you realize this is a first for me, too," Deena said. "Okay, that's enough. I'm going in now." She pushed Leroy against the wall. Eyes still closed, he clasped his hands and felt the momentary pressure as Deena bounced into the shaft.

338

"You know what, Leroy?" she whispered from inside. "You're the first real gentleman I ever met. You never peeked once. Bye."

Leroy waited a moment, then opened one eye and saw Deena's feet again disappear.

CHAPTER 59

Isaac didn't see the envelope wedged between the door and the doorframe until he was leaving the jail. He went back inside and sat down to read the letter.

"To Sheriff Isaac L. Cash:

"Pursuant to Article 7, Section C of the Bylaws of Mercer County, you are temporarily suspended from the office of Sheriff and relieved of all authority, responsibilities, and privileges as of midnight tonight, Monday, August 20, 1934.

"This action is the result of a citizens' petition citing gross neglect of duty and misfeasance stemming from your failure to protect the citizenry from recent capital violence by person or persons unknown. This matter will be resolved by a recall election for the position of Sheriff, to be held no later than ten days from this date.

"You are hereby instructed to surrender all keys, documents, and other county property to me, first thing Tuesday morning.

"Signed this day, Judge Alva E. Parmiston.

"P.S. Dang it all, Isaac, I told you that you better throw somebody in jail quick. It's what people expect of a sheriff. But no, you had to go and do it your own way. Well, I wish you luck. — Judge P."

Isaac laid the paper down and looked out the open door. For some reason, the thought of losing that monthly salary didn't upset Isaac anymore. If he couldn't make ends meet somehow, he would move to Texas and work for his brother.

He also didn't mind losing the position of sheriff. Mind? He was almost overjoyed. There was not one single, solitary thing about this job he would miss. He could walk down the street right now, give Judge Parmiston the jail keys and the badge, and go whistling happily on down the block to the barbershop. Losing this thankless job would not faze him one bit.

But losing this killer? Now that *really* irritated him.

***

When Isaac walked into the Jenkins service station, Cyrus was sitting on an overturned milk crate, a pan of turpentine on the ground in front of him, cleaning sparkplugs with a dirty rag.

"Hey there, Isaac," Cyrus said. "Hot, ain't it? Twister weather, that's for sure."

"I'm interested in something that happened in Mountain Home a few years back. You grew up around there, didn't you?"

"Nope. Born in Flippen. Grew up in Turkey Neck. You're probably thinking of my wife, Cinda June. Or maybe A.J."

"A.J. is from Mountain Home?"

"More or less in that neighborhood."

"More or less where?"

"More or less north. Near Three Sisters."

"Three Sisters? Where is A.J.?

"Took the day off." Cyrus picked up a different sparkplug.

"He stays at your place, doesn't he?"

"When he's there, he does. When he's someplace else, he don't. Last night was someplace else."

"When did you see him last?"

"Saturday evening. At the carnival."

"Man disappears for almost two days, nobody worries about him?"

Cyrus shrugged. "It's A.J."

"Does he visit any women?"

"A.J. ain't paid no attention to women since his wife died. But I guess you'd understand that."

"Who would he go to if he was in trouble?"

"Me. But he didn't. So I guess he's not." Cyrus studied the sparkplug, trying to decide if he had already cleaned it. "Might be he's at Doc MacPhie's."

"Is he sick?"

"Aw, I found a note this morning. A.J. had come in last night and took all the ice out of the icebox. Said he burnt his face and couldn't work."

"Burned his face?"

"Man spends his life underneath cars. Probably got careless and rubbed up against a hot tail pipe."

"The minute you hear where he is, tell me immediately. I want to talk to him."

"Hell, Isaac, so do I. He left a gearbox in pieces all over the workbench, and I need the job finished. Hey, might be he's resting on his boat down at the bridge."

"A.J. has a boat?"

"Boy, I'll say. He rebuilt a big 'ol Red Wing Arrow engine for it. Boat don't look like much, but damn, it's the fastest thing on the water. When he moves out, can't nobody catch him."

"Interesting," said Isaac. "One more thing. What is A.J.'s full name?"

"Albert James Stricklin, but you better don't ever call him Albert to his face. Bert, that's okay. But not Albert."

Isaac hurried back to the jail. There was no reason now to wait for the newspaper editor to phone. Isaac would head down to the river with several armed men beside him. He wanted to get to A.J., alias Bert Stricklin, before the man could kick over that Red Wing engine and move out.

342

CHAPTER 60

Louise made her smile wide and her eyes twinkly. In a fairly credible British accent she said to the teller, Elmo Johnson, "On second thought, twenty ones will make a frightful bulge in my purse. Let's trade again, eh what?" Deena still hadn't come through the vent yet, and it was getting harder to stall. "This time make it, um, two fives, nine ones, and eight quarters. You know, if you took off the glasses and grew a mustache, you'd look exactly like Douglas Fairbanks."

At the back of the bank, Bernard Fieldman took some papers and a ledger from the safe, pushed the door closed, and walked toward his office. The influx of customers today pleased him even though he couldn't remember ever having seen any of the three women before. As he approached Freda, standing near his office, he smiled and said, "My secretary, Ida Mae, mentioned the unique opportunity you want to offer our town. However, there's a phone call waiting that I need to take first. I won't be a minute."

As Freda waited near Bernard's office door, she cleared her throat hoping that Edna, who was sitting across a desk from an older lady, would see the ledger the bank manager was carrying.

"You don't understand," Ida Mae was saying to Edna. "We can't open an account for you unless you tell me how much money you want to put in. It's simply not possible."

Inside the heating shaft, looking through the grill, Deena made sure none of the bank staff was in a position to see her. She braced her thighs against the sides of the shaft, slipped her fingers through the grill, and pushed. When it came free, she held it tightly as she slid it silently down the wall. Then she pushed herself out of the opening, did a forward tuck, and dropped to the floor.

At the teller's window, Elmo Johnson thought he heard a thump and started to turn his head. "Ooo, my dress!" Louise squealed. Look!" She shoved the wad of dollar bills into her cleavage. "Do you think it's safe for a girl to keep money between her fronts? I saw it in a movie."

As Deena tried to scamper across the floor, she had to slow down to keep from slipping. The bottoms of her feet were oily from standing on Leroy's hands. Reaching the safe, she looked at the dial. It wasn't black, as Leroy had thought, only dirty. *This isn't an old model. What if I can't open it?*

Up front, Edna worked to hold the secretary's attention. "I thought bank accounts were confidential," she said. "I don't want people knowing how much I have in the bank. Why do I have to tell *you?*"

"Madam," said Ida Mae. "I work for the bank."

Louise, still flirting with the bank teller, gave a cute little squeal even Clara Bow would envy. "Golly! The money slipped down too far!" she said. "That extra bump looks like I have three bosoms," she giggled. "I look like I should be in a carniv...in a comedy."

Crouched in front of the safe, Deena touched the dial. Her fingers were shaking. *Am I scared or just freezing? If they see me, I'll never get to the shaft in time. Hello prison.*

She felt her feet slipping again and took hold of the lever on the door to steady herself. When she did, the lever moved.

People are so careless, she sighed as she pulled the door open. *Nobody remembers to spin the dial when they close a safe.*

***

Sitting in the driver's seat of Elaine's car in front of the bank, Hutchins wished he had a drink to steady his nerves. That jail looked awfully close. It was midday, and more people were on the streets now. A customer might walk into the bank at any minute. In fact, glancing into the car's mirror, he could see a man going up to the door.

"Hot damn!" Hutch murmured as he reached under the seat.

***

Deena's relief was replaced by a queasiness in her stomach. Inside the safe were several bundles of cash, each wrapped in a paper titled "Daily Cash on Hand." There was a stapler, a box of staples, and an unopened box of new 2-B pencils. There was nothing even close to being a ledger.

***

Isaac leaned against his desk, waiting for Bernard to pick up the phone. He was tired from lack of sleep lately, but too much on edge to sit down.

"Last week," Isaac said, when Bernard finally came on the line, "you offered to organize a posse to back me up. Well, I'm ready now. How many men do you think you can have here in an hour?"

"Honestly?" said Bernard. "Heck, Isaac, I doubt if I could get a dumb ten-year-old and a yellow pup dog to stand on your side of a chalk line on the sidewalk. You should have taken me up on the offer last week. I'm afraid it's too late now."

"What do you mean, 'too late'?"

"Isaac, for crying out loud, you let a suspected killer out of jail, the only suspect you had. What harm would there have been in keeping him locked up a couple of days, then sending him on his

345

way when the carnival left?"

"I've already told you, the evidence..."

"And Saturday at the carnival was a near riot. People storming the stage. Guns going off. You couldn't control it. You couldn't get even the local people to pay attention to you."

"That was an unusual situation..."

"Then you got into a fistfight with Philo Napker, a member of the Town Council, right in front of a crowd of Mercer County citizens. The Town Council is your employer, for gosh sake!"

"You said people want me to arrest someone. Well, I'm..."

"Yes, but that was before all the nonsense yesterday. You know what I'm talking about. People from town saw you out in the woods, running around half naked! I mean, what do you expect people to think?"

"I can explain that."

"And you'll get your chance. I hate to break this to you, but the Town Council has decided to hold a recall election."

"So I've heard."

"I'm sorry, Isaac, I really am. But I'd be a laughing stock if I tried to get anyone to support you now. You have nobody to blame but yourself."

346

CHAPTER 61

Ida Mae glanced toward her boss's office, hoping Bernard would finish talking with Miss Stone and come help her deal with the tiresome woman in front of her. "List our revenue produced by accrual assets?" Ida Mae said to Edna. "Madam, I don't even know what that means. You're only opening an ordinary savings account!"

At the back of the bank, her search for the ledger a failure, Deena jumped up and grabbed the opening in the shaft. Her legs and feet were too oily to get any purchase against the wall. She could climb it if Leroy pulled the rope, but with fifty feet of slack, she had no way to signal him. She dropped silently to the floor and quickly hid behind a desk. Tilting the desk chair, she rubbed her oily hands on the bottoms of the legs so she could slide it quietly to the wall.

Bernard Fieldman was still holding the ledger as he ushered Freda out of his office. "It's a fascinating plan, Miss Stone, Sister Cities with Sister Bridges. Mercerville and Merchantville. Unfortunately, even for the bargain price of nine-hundred-ninety-nine dollars and ninety-five cents, buying a bridge that's located in New Jersey is not exactly…"

Freda took a sudden violent coughing spell trying to attract Edna's attention to the ledger. Bernard turned to get Freda a glass of water from Ida Mae's desk and as he did, he saw a dark motion on the floor near the back wall of the bank. *Not rats,* he thought. *Anything but rats.*

Suddenly, the front door of the bank flew open. The roughneck Ace—recently fired and banned from the carnival—rushed in, holding a sweat rag wrapped around something

347

resembling a Stillson wrench.

"I got a gun! Stick 'em up," he yelled. "This is a robbery." Seeing everyone frozen in surprise, he clarified his order. "A bank robbery, I mean. Stick 'em up!"

Crouched at the back of the bank, Deena saw Ace and figured Elaine must have made a last-minute change in the plan. *I hate being so young. Nobody tells me anything!* As she climbed onto the chair, she gave a frantic wave to Ace, signaling him to stall for time while she crawled into the shaft.

At that moment, Ace would have called the feeling he was experiencing "glorious," if his vocabulary had attained that level of refinement. Here he was, in complete control of things for the first time in his life. People were treating him with respect. The customers had their hands up. The teller had his hands up. The secretary had her hands up. A naked girl was jumping into a hole in the wall.

Ace stood there, mouth open, watching Deena's legs disappear. He wondered if there was something wrong with the bottle of gin he had stolen from Hutchins' trailer.

"Excuse me, sir. Are you going to rob the bank, or not?" said Elmo Johnson. "Because if you're not, we'd like to get some business done today."

Ace saw Bernard with one hand in the air, still holding the ledger under his other arm.

"I said throw up your hands. Both of 'em!" Ace snarled and pointed the wrench at Bernard. "Unless everybody does what I say, I ain't going to rob nobody."

Bernard raised his other hand, and the ledger fell on the floor behind him, right at Edna's feet. She looked down, but didn't dare reach for it.

Ace heard the front door open behind him and swung around.

"Get inside!" Ace yelled. "Shut the door!"

Herbert Hutchins did just that.

"Now what the hell exactly do you think you're doing?" he demanded.

"Uh...nothing, Hutch," Ace stammered. "I was just..." Then, remembering that *he* was the man in charge now, Ace shoved the cloth-wrapped wrench toward Hutchins. "Gimme everything ya got!"

Hutchins did reserve a little, but not much. Most of it he gave to Ace with a lead pipe across the side of the head.

As Ace crumpled, Ida Mae screamed and covered her eyes with her hands. Edna seized the moment and the ledger.

Bernard Fieldman, his trembling hands still above his head, smiled at Hutchins. "My good man, you've saved us all. You're a hero!"

While all eyes were on Hutchins, Edna slipped the ledger under her white middy blouse. Suddenly the door opened and in walked the Professor, who had seen Hutchins follow Ace into the bank.

"All part of the show, folks! All part of the show!" Seeing Ace on the floor, he motioned to Hutchins to drag him out. "Great performance, wasn't it! Let's have a round of applause for two fine actors. Come on, everybody!" He clapped his hands loudly as the puzzled bank employees looked to Bernard Fieldman for leadership. Bernard lowered his hands, began clapping, and the others joined in.

"Everybody out!" Freda hissed and the carnies left quickly, Edna with her arms across her stomach keeping the ledger under her blouse, and Louise holding her chest to prevent the wad of bills from falling through her dress. The last person out was the Professor.

"Be sure to visit the Ten-in-One," he said as he went through the door. "Education, entertainment, and more excitement than a barrel of...ah...bank robbers."

***

As they waited at the rendezvous spot for Hutchins to return from dropping the dazed Ace off at the highway out of town, the Professor asked Deena, "You're certain there was nothing else in the safe?"

"I told you. Some cash," Deena said. "And papers listing how many fives, how many tens, and so forth. But no ledgers."

The Professor looked again at the ledger Edna had given him.

"Sorry, Professor," Edna said. "But I warned you all ledgers look the same."

"It's okay, honey," Louise put an arm around Edna's shoulders. "How could you know it was only the record of the office supplies?"

"The old lady's the embezzler," Edna said. "She's the manager's secretary, but she pretended she didn't know the first thing about bookkeeping."

"I think it's the teller," said Louise, "He never looked at anything below my eyes. That's not normal."

"My money's on the manager," Freda said. "If anyone's exploiting people, you can bet it's management."

"Just a blasted minute!" the Professor said. "You have no idea what management does. Look at this ledger! The man was reviewing expenditures on office supplies. Ninety percent of the time, management deals with boring, nit-picky details so the business can squeeze out a profit, and the employees don't lose their jobs."

"But the other ten percent, they're robbing us blind." Freda's eyes flared.

"You've never had to meet a payroll!" The Professor threw the ledger on the ground.

350

"It's time this carnival had collective bargaining," Freda said to the others. "Who's with me?"

"Carnivals don't unionize!" the Professor shouted. "Being organized runs contrary to everything carnies stand for!"

"Hey!" Seesla said sharply. "Elaine said no unnecessary attention, and here are half a dozen people standing beside the road yelling at each other."

"Not to mention," said Leroy, "we've got a dwarf in a yellow suit, a widow in a black veil, and a girl wearing nothing but my shirt and a quart of thirty-weight oil."

"You're right," the Professor said. "Everybody get back to the show. You'll all have to squeeze into Hutchins' car. I'm taking Otto's dispatch case to the sheriff. We have no choice but to join forces with the enemy."

CHAPTER 62

Isaac read the letter from Judge Parmiston one more time. He wished he had Sarah to talk things over with, but he had only a voice in his head saying, 'It's all over. You did your best. Put it down, and move on with your life. Let go of it, Isaac. Just let it go.'

I will. I'll let it all go, and gladly, he thought. *But not until midnight. Until then, I'm still sheriff.*

He stood up, put on his hat, and turned toward the door just as the phone rang. Isaac grabbed it before the second ring. "Bernard?" he said. It was MacPhie.

"I'm still at the hospital," MacPhie said. "Otto's throat started hemorrhaging, so they've taken him back to surgery to correct it. Anyway, when he began to cough up blood, he attracted the attention of the nurses by grabbing the little bedside table with one hand and throwing it against the wall."

"Pretty impressive for a man choking on his own blood."

"Not bad even for a healthy one," said MacPhie. "Anyway, when the nurse came, he stuffed a piece of paper into her hand."

"A note?"

"Yes, but in German."

"Can't they find someone..."

"I'm one step ahead of you," said MacPhie. "Turns out one of these doctors studied in Germany. As soon as he's out of surgery, the nurse will ask him to translate the note. Shouldn't be long now."

"Good work, Shep. I'll be at the boarding house. Phone me the second you know something." Isaac had absolutely no intention of taking Rachel with him to confront A.J. Stricklin, but she was

352

well-known and well-liked in town. Perhaps she could persuade a few men to go with Isaac and back him up. Even one or two would be an improvement over zero.

It was unusual for the Sheriff's Office telephone to have two calls in the same month, never mind the same sixty seconds.

"Hello, Isaac," Miz Russell said. "I'm so glad I caught you. This nice man from the carnival wants a chat. Don't you hang up now. Here he is."

"Chat? Listen, I don't have…"

"Sheriff? This is Desmond Pinckney. I need to show you some documents immediately, but I don't want to be seen going into your office."

"What documents?"

"It appears Otto has been trying to trap a criminal on his own."

"I'll be right there," Isaac said.

For the next half hour, Isaac and the Professor sat at the table in Miz Russell's parlor, hardly touching the iced tea she had brought them, focusing instead on the letters and papers from Otto's dispatch case.

"If only I had been able to read German as well as you can," Isaac said, "when I saw these letters the first time in Otto's tent."

"Then you agree?" asked the Professor.

"I sure as thunder don't want to," said Isaac. "But you make a compelling case."

"Naturally I knew that Otto is Jewish," the Professor said, "but it never seemed to be a factor in his life. Someone can hardly be an observant Jew and a carnival performer too. Consequently this scenario didn't occur to me." the Professor said, tapping his finger on one of the bundles of letters.

"You're very popular today, Isaac," Miz Russell said as she came in from the hallway. "Doctor MacPhie's on the phone and has

353

some surgeon to talk to you." Isaac hurried into the hallway and picked up the phone.

"Sheriff, I'm happy to report that Mr. Gieseking is showing good improvement," the surgeon said. "He is in such excellent physical shape, that in a week, or perhaps…"

"That's great to hear," Isaac interrupted, "but please don't make that public yet. I'd rather let people think he's near death. Now, did you look at the note he gave the nurse?"

"I did. It says, 'I was killed by a peasant.'"

"That's all? You're sure?" Isaac said.

"Translating it was simple. In German, it's only five words. 'Ich war von feldman getotet.'"

Isaac paused only a second. "Thank you, Doctor. You've been a great help." Isaac hung up, then dialed again.

CHAPTER 63

Bernard Fieldman stepped out of his Packard and entered the barbershop briskly. "I got your phone call just as we were closing. What's so important?"

"Shave and a haircut?" Isaac said. "Bay Rum?"

"Isaac, if this is about the Town Council's letter, I'm afraid nothing I said would change their minds," Fieldman said.

"It's fine. I never felt like a real sheriff anyway. Sit down. I'll give you a free touch-up while we chat." Isaac motioned toward the barber chair. "I'd like to review the recent crimes."

"Free? Well, everybody has to watch their pennies nowadays." Fieldman hung his hat on a peg and sat down.

Isaac fastened the striped cloth around Fieldman's neck and said, "Has anyone told you Otto is dead?"

"How awful!" Fieldman said. "Any clues?"

"Sort of." Isaac combed the part in Fieldman's hair. "Otto wrote a note accusing you of shooting him."

"What! That's preposterous!"

"He claims you were supposed to pay him some money. Listen, Bernard, I can't help you unless I hear your side."

Bernard was silent for a moment. "I'm embarrassed to confess this, but we're both men of the world. Otto was blackmailing me. Remember that banking conference I mentioned? And the snake dancer girl? Well, I invited her to my hotel room. It turned out to be a setup. Otto took photos. Nothing happened, but the photos look bad."

"The old badger game, eh?" Isaac began clipping the back of

Fieldman's hair. "Tell me something else."

"Sure. What?"

Isaac spun the chair around and looked Bernard in the eye. "The truth!" Isaac said. "Otto caught you embezzling from the Verein fur Hilfe."

"Never heard of it," Bernard said.

"Otto's account ledger proves otherwise! And his testimony in court will clinch it."

"You said he was dead."

"No, that's how you wanted to understand it." Isaac swung the chair back around and smoothed down Fieldman's cowlick. "Your tonic is making your hair brittle. I can sell you something better."

"So that's your game. Shaking me down." Fieldman was having trouble sitting still. "Okay, I'll buy whatever you're selling. Lots of it. I'll cancel your mortgage, too. In exchange for the ledger, of course."

"It would be foolish to go into partnership without knowing all the details. Start with the Verein."

"Okay, okay," Fieldman said. "At that conference, a famous financier invited me and another banker to dinner to hear a proposal. I was astounded when the carnival's strongman walked in wearing a nice suit."

"Otto," said Isaac. "Making a pitch for donations to the Verein."

"Exactly. Austria became a dictatorship last year, so Otto organized the Verein to raise money to help people escape. The Verein needed a banker to sneak money into Austria."

"Couldn't the big financier do it?"

"He's one of those Washington dollar-a-year men you'd know about if you read the financial pages instead of Police Gazettes," Fieldman said. "He needed an out-of-the-way bank with very few employees."

"Who are the people that are trying to escape?"

"Jews. The Nazis in Germany have passed oppressive laws restricting Jews from working or going to school," Bernard said. "Jews expect it will spread to Austria soon. If the Austrian government learned money was being filtered into the country, it would confiscate the money and accuse America of undermining Austria. The scandal would hit Roosevelt's closest associates."

"So you two bankers agreed to help. You deserve credit for being compassionate."

"Hardly! The other fellow said no. Afraid his employees might catch on," Fieldman said. "But I'm no fool. That financier could be a powerful ally, and I plan to run for governor someday. Those Jews are half a world away. I'm more concerned about *my* people here. Ozark people are decent and hard-working, but they're being crushed by the Depression!"

"So your bank got all the money."

"It was peanuts at first, but the volunteers were soon collecting impressive donations, and I was the only one who knew how much. I realized I could slow the disbursements enough to invest the money while real estate was selling for bargain prices. The Jews would still get their money—eventually. In the meantime, it would generate profits I could use to save Mercer County citizens.

"How did it backfire?" Isaac asked.

"Roosevelt, the Genius of Hyde Park, turned a slump into a major depression," Fieldman said. "The world's economy is delicately balanced at the best of times. Even a chicken farmer's son knows that when people lose their jobs and default on their mortgages, it has a disastrous ripple effect on financial institutions. If Washington had just kept out of it, market forces would have corrected, and the economy would already be improving. But as property values kept dropping, my bank got stuck with properties I

357

couldn't sell. I tried to spread the risk with more conservative deals, but eventually the paperwork was overwhelming me."

"I suppose embezzling isn't something a banker can delegate to his secretary," Isaac said.

"Fundraisers brag about how much they raise," Fieldman continued, "but normally they don't monitor exactly how the financial officer disburses it. Except Otto kept records on everything! Typical Kraut efficiency! He wrote people in Austria, asking how much money was getting there. A small discrepancy didn't alarm him because my job was to filter money in using difficult-to-track methods. But the discrepancy kept increasing. Five thousand here, six thousand there."

"When he caught on, he threatened to turn you in."

"He said he'd give me one chance to return the money, but it had to be immediately. Impossible! I didn't have it!" Fieldman said. "First I offered to skim a percentage off the top, but Otto wouldn't take it."

"You couldn't stall him," said Isaac.

"Show business people don't understand money. He was unreasonable. Traders can't speculate effectively if people expect us to repay them every time we make a mistake with their money," Fieldman said. "The Depression will be over next year. Nobody's stupid enough to reelect Roosevelt. When property values bounced back, I would have paid Otto every penny, with interest! Naturally I deserve a commission for being their banker, right? The Bible says the worker is worthy of his hire."

"I'm not sure God had embezzlers in mind."

"Rescuer, you mean! Who's keeping Mercer County families afloat? Me! Bernard Fieldman! I'm using Jewish money to cover past-due mortgages for twenty miles in any direction."

Including mine? Isaac thought. "So you searched Otto's tent for the ledger."

"He had shown it to me to pressure me. Originally I went there to beg for more time, but everyone was at a party. When I saw Otto's car beside a tent, I figured if I stole the ledger, he'd have no proof. But I didn't kill that skinny freak. He just pushed into the tent, turned around and yelled, and the next thing I knew, he was bleeding all over my best shoes. I ran like hell. Later, I realized Otto saw the freak sneaking into his tent and knifed him. Typical Teutonic warrior mentality. Once you arrested Otto, I wouldn't have any more problems. Except you didn't."

"Naturally you couldn't admit you were there, so you encouraged everyone to put pressure on me." Isaac stopped clipping. "Thanks a lot!"

"There was a corpse in his tent, for heaven's sake, and you wouldn't even arrest him! Anyway, he phoned me and demanded a meeting. I was terrified, but Friday night we met in the alley behind the bank. I promised to raise the cash."

"Now I understand that important duty Otto kept talking about." Isaac began clipping again.

"Afterwards I followed him and saw him shove a note under your door. I read it and knew he was double-crossing me. He would tell you everything. That scoundrel!"

"What's the world coming to when an embezzler can't trust an honest man?" Isaac said.

"When you finally arrested him, I thought you'd send him to Little Rock for trial. But like a fool, you released him."

"Sorry for thwarting your plans."

"Plans? Bankers don't make plans to kill people! We think of customers as the goose that laid the golden interest rate. Anyway, I went to the carnival Saturday afternoon. I lied and promised to deliver the money on Sunday morning. I couldn't think clearly anymore. My mind was totally overwhelmed. By last night I had realized that if he didn't die, I would go to prison, so I went to the

359

jail…. Well, I wanted you to think he was shot by a madman."

"That's exactly what I think."

"There's still a way to fix this!" Bernard said. "Look at me while I'll explain."

As Isaac swung the chair around to face Bernard, he felt a gun being pushed into his stomach.

CHAPTER 64

"Drop the scissors!" Fieldman dragged the barber cloth clear of his nickel-plated .25 automatic as he jumped out of the chair. Then he moved around so the chair would be between him and Isaac.

Isaac dropped the scissors and backed up. "I guess that's the gun you used to shoot Otto."

"I was serving justice on a murderer. Even though his victims were only freaks."

"They were men trying to earn a living in hard times."

"By pretending to be half of a woman? What kind of career path is that?"

"Turns out Otto didn't murder anyone. The killer is a man obsessed with freaks. Tomorrow he'll be behind bars."

"A lunatic! Perfect! That's our way out!" Fieldman said. "Tell people that he also shot Otto. The killer's going to be executed anyway!"

"Our little secret, huh? Doesn't shooting Otto bother your conscience?"

"He's German! We killed each other during the war, and the way Europe's headed, we may soon be killing each other again. The important thing is to save America from the power-lusting bloodsuckers our careless voters elect. Give me time, Isaac. I can make this pay for both of us."

"I don't know any law against bribing barbers. But believe it or not, I'm also the sheriff."

"I've seen you with Rachel Barlow! No sheriff could give her the things she deserves. Well, some sheriffs could, just not an honest

361

one. Think, Isaac! Beautiful wife. Big house. You could even move to Little Rock. Join high society!"

"Somehow the thought of high society in Little Rock never entered my mind," Isaac said. "Anyway, why should I trust you?"

"I never cheated a partner. That's as trustworthy as any real estate speculator gets." Perspiration beaded Fieldman's forehead. "Time," the banker said. "I just need more time!"

"Bernard, I hope the court gives you as much time as possible."

"Listen to me, Isaac! I hold deeds to big chunks of Mercer and Baxter counties. Potential commercial sites! Riverfront properties for resorts!" Fieldman's gun hand shook nervously. "I'll share it all, fifty-fifty. No! Sixty percent! I'll give you sixty percent!"

"No deal." Isaac wondered if he could reach his straight razor lying on the counter beside him before Fieldman could pull the trigger. He wisely decided against trying it. *Besides, if I did manage to cut his throat, nobody would ever trust me to give them a shave. I'd have to close the shop anyway.* "Face facts, Bernard. It's over!"

"I have cash in the bank safe. A lot! I'll give it all to you if you let me go."

"Money stolen from Jewish refugees? No thanks! All I want from you is a signed confession," Isaac said. "But I want it tonight, and I want you to arrange to get as much money as possible back to Otto's organization immediately!"

Bernard's shoulders slumped noticeably and his gun angled down toward the ground. "All the cash plus sixty-five percent of the investment properties?" he asked softly. "Sixty-seven point five?"

Isaac didn't move or even blink.

"Net?" Bernard said.

"All of it! Returned to the people you stole it from. At least as much as you can raise." Isaac leaned toward the counter and the

362

straight razor, just in case. "That's the only deal you'll get. You're down to just two options. Number one, give the money back to Otto, get the best lawyer you know, and I'll recommend leniency at your trial."

"And option number two?" Bernard's arm dropped and Isaac could see the banker's finger begin to slide off the trigger.

"Shoot me and spend the rest of your life on the run, a murderer."

"Everything I've ever cared about is here in Mercerville. Where would I run to?"

"I don't know, Bernard. But I'm pretty sure you won't be able to stay on the run for long."

"How did this happen?" Bernard said softly "I'm a *good* man." His arm dropped below his waist level. "Everybody *knows* I have a fine reputation," he said, almost to himself.

"Put it down on the chair, Bernard," Isaac said quietly, but firmly.

Fieldman slowly laid the gun on the seat of the barber chair. Isaac reached out smoothly but quickly and picked it up.

"I was must have been crazy. Temporary insanity," Tears welled up in the banker's eyes. "Don't lock me up yet, Isaac. I'll write a confession. And I'll go back to the bank and transfer all my assets, except my house and life insurance, to the immigrant's fund. It will fully cover all Otto's losses, I swear! Sending me to prison could destroy my wife and children, but if I make amends, maybe people will sympathize. It'll make it easier for my children. I'm begging you."

"You expect me to just let you leave here?" Isaac said.

"Here's the key to my car. I'll walk to the bank right now and do the paperwork. I'll phone Ida Mae to come back and notarize everything. By midnight, maybe one a.m., it will all be done and legal."

"I'm thinking I should lock you up right now." But what Isaac was really thinking was that every moment with Fieldman was giving Bert Stricklin more time to recover from his injuries enough to make his escape.

"Think, Isaac! A good lawyer could make hash of that ledger. Ledgers can be faked. Without my confession, the trial will come down to the word of a highly-respected bank president against that of an Austrian carny. Don't depend on getting a conviction from people I've saved from bankruptcy and starvation. This way is better for your case. Please!"

"Bernard Fieldman," Isaac said after a moment, "I order you to surrender yourself at the jail at eight o'clock tomorrow morning to be arrested for embezzlement and attempted murder. I'll overlook the bribe and pulling a gun on me."

"You're a good man, Isaac. Thank you." Bernard shook Isaac's hand vigorously.

"Make no mistake, if you aren't there by eight sharp," Isaac warned, "I'll strap on my gun and bring you back, dead or alive."

Bernard grabbed his hat and opened the door. "My way will be best for everyone," he called over his shoulder as he broke into a fast walk. "You'll see." Then he was gone.

CHAPTER 65

Isaac stepped on the truck's starter button and the gas pedal. The engine turned over but didn't start. *Careful! Don't flood the engine!* He sniffed the air but didn't smell gasoline. Maybe it would start now.

Not yet. Give it a full minute. Sitting in the truck counting the seconds, Isaac became aware that the pin back of his sheriff's badge was still in his coat's side pocket, poking him in the hip. *Well, I'll probably never have the chance to get used to wearing it.* He took it out and pinned it on his chest anyway.

Three blocks ahead, in the glow of the last hour of daylight, Isaac could make out the silhouette of Bernard Fieldman unlocking the door of the bank and going inside. *We made a deal and shook hands on it. Whatever else he may have done, in all the years I've known him, I've never known Bernard to go back on a promise.*

Isaac stepped on the starter button again, and the truck fired right up. As he headed north, he saw dark clouds spreading across the greenish-black sky. It was beginning to sprinkle. He slowed passing the filling station and saw Cyrus still inside, but no A.J.

***

The Professor stood looking out Miz Russell's rain-peppered front window as she placed a fresh pitcher of iced tea on the table. "Are you certain the truck that just passed was the Sheriff's?" the Professor asked.

"I can't imagine where he was rushing to," she said.

"Nothing out there except the bridge. Could be he's meeting someone with a clue about these crimes."

Not the bank president, the Professor thought. *He walked into the bank just before Cash drove past. Then who?*

***

For anyone using the hiking path, it was less than a mile cross-country from downtown Mercerville to the river. However, in a pickup, it was a hundred feet of asphalt gradually breaking up into patches, then surrendering to two winding miles of gravel. Finally, when an unwary driver would least expect it, the road turned sharply to the left to avoid the steep embankment sloping down to the railroad bridge and the river below it. Miss that turn and you could end up on the tracks saying hello to an oncoming locomotive.

Isaac pulled off the dirt road onto the wide spot overlooking the river. The wind was hotter now, in spite of the drizzle beginning to fall. He hoped he was mistaken in his belief that the clouds in the west were becoming a wall near the earth. He wasn't. They were.

Parked under a tree was a pickup truck Isaac recognized as belonging to the suspect, one Albert James, aka "Bert," Stricklin. He pulled up beside it close enough to see that it was empty. There was no one on the bridge or the rugged path leading down to the river.

At the bottom of the slope, a boat was tied fore and aft to the bridge piling. It wasn't the kind of fishing boat Isaac had expected, just an ugly assemblage of trash lumber twenty-five feet long, ten feet wide, and flat like a miniature river barge. The boat's draft was so shallow that a powerful engine could send it skimming across the top of the water like those fancy speedboats in newsreels. Unsightly though it was, it was a formidable escape vehicle.

Centered on the deck was the cabin, a homemade board shack barely large enough to sleep five fishermen, provided they were exhausted and tolerant. If Bert was on board, he would be inside that shack.

Sitting in the pickup, Isaac analyzed Bert's possible escape routes. There was only one path down to the riverbank. It was rocky and narrow and Isaac would be on it. Trapped between Isaac and the river at Bert's back, the man's only escape would be to his left or his right.

Running to the left would put Bert in the trestles supporting the bridge. If he stayed under there, a clear shot would be difficult, but Bert would be cornered. If he ran between the trestles to the other side, he'd have to slog across a broad stretch of muddy river bank. That would make him an easy target.

However, if he ran to his right, he would be in heavy brush that came almost to the water's edge. To an experienced backwoodsman and river rat, that thicket wouldn't be nearly the challenge it would be to a barber and part-time sheriff.

Okay then, expect him to break to his right, into the brush. From there, unless Isaac got a lucky shot, Bert could head into rough country and freedom.

On second thought, don't expect that. Expect the unexpected. Bert Stricklin was a killer. He was hurt, desperate, maybe insane. There was no predicting him.

Isaac got out and slammed the door hard. There was no obvious response to the noise. *If he's around, he knows I'm here. If not, I guess I'll just get my shoes muddy.*

For the first several yards, the path was steep and uneven, forcing Isaac to move slowly. He tried not to look down at the ground, but didn't have much choice. The drizzle was increasing, making the slope slippery. Isaac wished he could draw his gun, but there was too much chance he might stumble and drop it. *Probably shoot my big toe off.*

Halfway down, the path leveled off for a few feet. Isaac

stopped, caught his breath, and looked around. He heard the river's rush and the wind lashing the trees, but nothing else. If Bert was inside the shack, he had already missed his best chance for escape.

On the other hand, if he plans to shoot me through the heart with a rifle, this would be the ideal time.

CHAPTER 66

Gusts battered Isaac as he reached the waterline near the boat. At the bow end of the cabin, a lighted coal oil lantern was hanging from a hook. Half an hour ago, the sun was still out. That meant the lantern had been lit within the past few minutes as the clouds darkened the sky. And that meant the boat's owner must be somewhere nearby.

"A.J.? Bert? Are you in there? It's me—Isaac Cash." He listened for a reply, but none came. "Come on out, Bert. I just want to talk."

A sharp crack made him wheel around, drawing his gun as he did. On the path behind him he saw a tree branch, snapped off by the increasing wind. *Dang! I turned my back on him.*

Isaac wished he could have slept more than one hour last night. The only thing keeping him awake was the same adrenaline that was making him jumpy and clumsy. *Next I'll probably blow some Blue Jay to smithereens.* He remembered Sheriff Alsup's warning, "Bert never made any sound at all."

Might as well keep the gun drawn. If Bert was watching, he knew now that Isaac hadn't come to ask if the fish were biting.

Isaac stepped onto a foot-wide plank from the bank up to the deck. The drizzle had become pelting rain, and the clouds were a dark blanket stretching to the horizon. Isaac walked across the deck to the shack. Beside the door was a Mason jar full of raw honey and a bucket of coal oil.

Backwoods remedy, Isaac thought. *Clots the blood and prevents infection. He's treating some bleeding wounds.* A trail of weakening sunlight slid across the doorsill. Other than that, the inside was darkness.

"Bert? You in there?" he said again. "Come on out, Bert." No answer came. *If I try to slip through that doorway, I'm a dead man. In the cowboy movies, Tom Mix would put his hat on a stick and wave it in front of the door to draw Bert's fire. I don't have much faith in that trick.*

Isaac quietly bent down as low as possible. *He'll aim for the center of my chest. I have to keep way below that level.* He did a sort of one-handed pushup to get his head almost down on the deck and quickly stuck his head around the doorframe and pulled it back again. *Could I have missed him?* Isaac repeated the action, his eyes now better adjusted to the gloom inside. *Not there. Where could he be? Hiding in the bushes on the shore maybe?*

The rain pounded on the corrugated tin roof like snare drummers from a hundred high school bands. If he went inside to look for clues and someone crept up to the doorway, Isaac would never hear him coming. *Clue hunting will have to wait.*

As Isaac took one more look, he saw a cloth lying crumpled just inside the doorway. At first he thought it was an old oil rag, then recognized it as a man's shirt. He reached into the cabin and pulled the shirt out onto the deck. It was crusted with red. Isaac visualized blood spraying the front of the shirt as Bert hacked at the dying Half-and-Half's body. If the blood type matched, this shirt—along with Bert's injuries—might be enough to get a conviction.

Isaac stood up, the wadded-up shirt in his left hand, his Colt revolver in his right. The darkening sky had become a greenish-black tent, and the pelting rain had turned into the machine-gun rattle of marble-sized hailstones hitting the deck. Isaac looked up. The cloud cover was rotating. *Oh, damn!*

The funnel had formed to the west, but the hills made it impossible to tell for certain which direction it was heading. Using

Meekam's Hill as a reference, Isaac guessed the tornado was three or four miles away. As twisters do, it was following the path of least resistance.

If that thing hooks onto the river, it could be here in six or seven minutes.

Isaac heard a splash and a groan behind him. He turned to see Bert pull himself out of the water and onto the deck near the cabin. He was plastered from the waist up in cooling mud. In his hand was a massive knife. He lunged, slipping a little on the wet deck as he swung the knife. Isaac jumped back and instinctively thrust his left hand out in front of him. The wadded-up shirt snagged the knife, and the slash missed Isaac's face by a short half inch.

Too close to aim his gun, he pulled the trigger anyway, not sure where the long barrel was pointed. The shot passed over Bert's shoulder and smashed through the lantern, spraying burning oil across the wall of the cabin.

As Isaac pulled the trigger again, Bert's left hand grabbed for the revolver. The gun's hammer slammed down on the webbing between Bert's thumb and forefinger, preventing the cartridge from firing. Bert was on top of Isaac now, driving him backwards and down. Isaac, tired from lack of sleep, might as well have been wrestling a rodeo bull.

Pain shot across Isaac's spine as they crashed against the low wooden railing and tumbled over the side into the roiling water. Isaac fell at the muddy water's edge, his gun knocked from his hand. Several feet farther from shore, Bert was struggling to stand up.

Isaac's muddy footing was slightly more solid, and he leapt for the wooden plank on the end of the boat. As the hail and driving rain beat his face, he grabbed the board and swung it, aiming for the shadowy figure coming at him through the downpour. The blow hit Bert's arm, knocking the knife into the churning river.

Bert grabbed the other end of the plank, ripped it from

Isaac's grip, and threw it to one side. He looked down at the water only long enough to realize there was no sense trying to locate his knife. Isaac used that second to run for his life. A metallic glint caught his eye. A few feet ahead, his revolver was half buried in the mud. He dived for it, rolled onto his knees, and sighted down the long barrel as hail stones pelted him in the face.

"Stop right there!" Isaac shouted. Ankle deep in edgewater, Bert stopped. Behind him, the roof of the boat's cabin was now dotted with flames. *Fool gun is plastered with mud. Probably misfire and blow my head off.*

"Turn around," Isaac said, struggling to his feet. "Put your hands behind you."

Bert only stood there, water moving quickly up his calves toward his knees. To his left, the boat was now tilting sharply. The lines tying it to the bridge were taut and straining as the water rose. The tornado had hit the river, and the flash flood would reach them soon.

For the first time, Isaac got a clear look at Bert's face. It was bleeding, swollen, and heavily mottled crimson and purple, with long streaks seared black, and a gaping wound down his cheek. The shirtless man's shoulders and chest looked almost as bad. After being scalded by boiling oil and beaten with a cast-iron skillet, Bert Strickin no longer cared if some sheriff with a gun blew him to Hell. He was already there.

Bert charged, and Isaac pulled the trigger.

The gun didn't explode.

It also didn't fire.

Soaked to the skin, Isaac turned and ran across the muddy riverbank, then clambered up the slippery embankment toward the railroad bridge. Halfway up, Isaac thought Bert had caught him and was beating on his back. Then he realized that the hailstones were getting larger, the size of plums now.

Nearing the top, with Bert gaining on him, Isaac realized he needed both hands to scramble up the slope. He threw the revolver forward. It landed on the boards at the end of the bridge with a thunk that seemed unusually loud. The wind and hail had suddenly stopped. The air was graveyard still.

Isaac stumbled onto the bridge and tried to sprint across, but his foot slipped between the wet railroad track and the bridge planking. Bert jumped on Isaac's back, knocking him to his knees. He pounded Isaac on the shoulders and head, trying to beat him to the ground, but Isaac drove both fists into the man's lower belly as hard as he could. Bert pulled back a step, looking up over Isaac's head. Then he leapt forward, grabbing Isaac's neck as Isaac grabbed his.

The sudden silence was just as suddenly broken by a continuous roar. The noise didn't fade, so it wasn't thunder, and it didn't change pitch, so it wasn't a freight train. The black funnel was fifty yards wide and moving perhaps ninety miles an hour when it connected with the far end of the bridge. The ironwork crumpled as the tornado made a ninety-degree turn away from the struggling men and toward the opposite bank of the river.

The high winds at the edge of the funnel swept over the bridge, lifted the men ten feet into the air, then slammed them against the iron bridge truss.

As they fell back onto the tracks, a huge rectangular shadow twirled past over their heads. The boat had been ripped from its moorings and was spinning through the air, shedding bits of burning lumber onto the bridge in a circle around the two men who were stunned, but still trying to strangle each other. In a moment, the boat crashed into the treetops along the south bank and became trapped in the upper branches, its flaming cabin serving as a torch to light the battle on the bridge below.

In that distracting moment, Isaac managed to break free of

Bert's grasp and stagger to his feet. He tried to run down the bridge, but his legs betrayed him and he stumbled. Bert caught up with him and threw him against the bridge railing. The man's hands viced around Isaac's neck and slammed Isaac's head into the metal I-beam. As Isaac sank to the ground, he heard Bert scream. Isaac's blurred vision made out Bert staggering backwards from the impact of a wind-blown branch that had smashed into his burned face, carrying with it fingers of flames from the tree-imprisoned boat.

Floating into blessed unconsciousness, Isaac didn't think it at all remarkable to imagine he was seeing a white Chrysler Imperial Le Baron, apparently driverless, slide rapidly down the muddy hillside and crash into the bridge railing.

CHAPTER 67

Isaac remembered that time in Texas when he stepped off a caboose and found himself lying on the ground, surrounded by a cloud. A black hand reached through the fog with a metal dipper of water. Someone was asking durn fool questions. Of course Isaac knew what his own name was. Give him a few minutes, he'd think of it. Eventually.

"Bossman!" a voice insisted. "What day is it?"

"Did I trip?"

"Naw sir, the train jerked and threw you off. You hit your head on a tie."

Then the crew had helped Isaac over to the telegraph shack, and laid him on the army surplus cot until he felt better.

The fog now was like then, except now it was raining, and Isaac was face down on a bridge. This time it wasn't a dipper his eyes focused on, but his mud-caked Colt, lying on the planking five feet away. Isaac raised his head and saw a third person on the bridge, a short person, standing between him and the killer.

"Come get me, you hillbilly Frankenstein." The Professor was holding his little New York belly gun level with his eyes, which also meant level with Bert's heart.

"Closer, you damned freak," The Professor taunted. "Oh, you don't like being called a freak. You hate freaks! Well, you're the most deformed freak I ever saw! Step right up, freak. I'll put you in my sideshow!"

Dragging himself toward his revolver, Isaac understood why the Professor wanted Bert closer. His Derringer belly gun held only two small bullets, and a mere flesh wound was not in the Professor's plans.

"Get down, Professor!" Isaac yelled as his fingers closed around the grip of his Colt.

"Closer, Monster Boy!" the Professor shouted. "We're going up to the Big Show together."

"You're in my line of fire!" Isaac yelled louder. "Drop!"

Bert stopped and looked over the Professor' head, directly at Isaac.

Suddenly Isaac understood. Bert Stricklin was willing to meet death, but not from a freak.

Isaac raised up on his elbows and tried to aim the revolver with two shaking hands.

"Think how much science might learn," MacPhie had said, "if we could capture this guy and study him." Isaac had never shot a human.

"Throw up your hands. You're going to prison." The gun weighed a ton, and the trigger seemed welded in place. Was it physical strength he lacked? Or moral resolve? Squeezing harder only made the long barrel dip.

Suddenly Bert lunged at the Professor, knocking him off his feet. The belly gun and the Professor went sliding in opposite directions on the wet bridge.

Isaac pulled the trigger once, consciously, but the gun fired twice more after that. All three bullets hit Bert in the center of his chest. He stopped and staggered backwards against the bridge railing. Then, losing his balance, he went over.

Clinging with one hand to the outside of the railing, forty feet above the rocks, Bert looked through the upright supports at Isaac. It wasn't the glare of an enraged killer or the stare of a mortally-wounded animal. It was the look of a confused and abused boy wondering why. Why does all the world want to hurt me?

Bert let go and dropped into the torrent. After a lifetime of wondering whether there was a God, Albert James Stricklin was now going to learn the answer.

The Professor scrambled to the railing and looked between the uprights. "He's face down. The current's got him...wait, now he's underwater. He's gone." The Professor turned and looked at Isaac. "He *was* the killer, right?"

Isaac struggled to his knees and put the Colt back into the holster. He stood up, walked very shakily to the railing, and looked down at the rocks below. "Life really is strange," he whispered hoarsely.

"What? You okay?" the Professor said. "Your head took a pretty hard bump."

Isaac steadied himself against the girder, catching his breath as he watched the turbulent waters for any sign of a body. "I'm okay, I guess. Just thinking about a mother and a baby and a different bridge."

After a moment, Isaac pulled out his handkerchief and wiped his mud-streaked face. "Well, let's hope the tornado left my pickup where it was. Otherwise, we have a long walk." It hurt a bit to walk, but he started anyway. "I'm still feeling stupid. Tell me why you happen to be here."

"I came looking for you," the Professor said. "The landlady says it's time for dinner."

CHAPTER 68

Rachel put two pills into the hand Isaac wasn't using to press the ice bag against his head.

"Nurse Rachel, prescribing aspirin for this thing is like spitting on a campfire," Doctor MacPhie said, lifting Isaac's eyelids and checking his pupils again. "Looks okay so far, but tell me if you start feeling nauseated. By the way, you may also have a cracked rib."

"Glad to hear it," said Isaac. "I was beginning to think I'm just getting old."

"I'm going to give you some chloral and put you to bed upstairs."

"No," said Isaac. "I'd rather go home and take it."

"Be sensible, Isaac," said Rachel. "You're much better off staying here." But Isaac just shook his head.

"Well, if you're adamant," MacPhie said, "But I'm happy to drive you home and stay with you awhile."

"No need," said Isaac as the doorbell rang. "I'm feeling better. I'm okay to drive."

A moment later the Professor walked into the parlor.

"Your good wife is outside in the car, Doctor. She said there's no hurry," the Professor said. "I appreciate her driving me out to the carnival. Hutchins is bringing a generator-powered spotlight and roughnecks with trucks to haul my car up the hill."

Isaac gave everyone a short version of his experiences with Bernard Fieldman and Bert Stricklin. "It could be days before Stricklin's body turns up," he said. "As for Bernard, I'm swearing all

378

of you to secrecy until he's locked up. But I believe he'll keep his word, and the money will be back under Otto's control very soon."

"I'll go to the hospital tomorrow and tell Otto the good news," said the Professor. "By the way, Edna, Louise, Freda, and the others said they very much appreciate that you understand about their part in the bank…uh…deception I told you about on the way here from the bridge. They're grateful you won't take legal action against them. In fact, Freda says that if you ever see her in a carnival, she will happily offer you a free psychic reading. And the Hootchy dancers said they would…um…well, they send their love."

"Professor," Rachel said, "was it a coincidence, your carnival coming here where Bernard lives?"

"Not exactly. Otto read our booking schedule in *The Billboard* magazine. That's the bible of the outdoor amusement business. He telegraphed me that he wanted to join us for the rest of the season. We had become friends years ago in an indoor circus in New York. Otto kept the marks from harassing me, and I kept the dwarf clowns from annoying him."

"How could dwarves annoy a strongman?" said Jeremy.

"Like anyone else, dwarves have all kinds of personalities. Those guys were pretty aggressive."

"I know it's not much consolation, Professor," Dr. MacPhie said, "but I believe science will someday learn how to prevent your condition."

"You think we should be prevented? That's what fanatics like Bill Berkeley want."

"I apologize. I made a bad choice of words," MacPhie said.

"No apology needed. What *really* needs serious research is people with small minds and tribal attitudes. People like that cause a huge amount of suffering, and they come in all sizes, shapes, colors, and political parties."

"Professor, did Otto tell you in the beginning about Bernard

Fieldman?" Isaac said.

"No. He only said he needed to meet with people concerning his refugee organization, but didn't have travel money. He's a great performer, so I said yes," the Professor said. "And speaking of performers, Leroy will pick me up soon. The tornado missed the carnival, but we had a blowdown of several tents. We'll repair things tomorrow, and Wednesday we'll make the jump to Springfield, Missouri."

"I wish Otto had talked to me as soon as he arrived," Isaac said.

"Would you have believed some Austrian carnie who appeared out of nowhere and accused the town's leading citizen?" the Professor said. "Otto couldn't take that chance."

"Do you need someone to replace Otto?" Jeremy said. "Maybe I could be an acrobat. Mom, what could you do?"

"I'd help Seesla sew costumes to cover the dancing girls a little more," she said.

"I couldn't afford that," the Professor laughed. "The more you covered them up, the fewer tickets we'd sell. Anyway, your mom's only joking about joining a carnival."

"Am I?" Rachel said. "What's here for me? I'd like more from life than dusting other people's furniture. And I'd like a husband who would be a good example for Jeremy. So maybe I *should* travel. Meet new people. It's better than sitting around getting old and sad."

The room was quiet for a moment, then the clock on the mantle chimed ten-thirty.

"Ah. 'We have heard the chimes at midnight.' Or close enough." The Professor looked out the parlor window. "Leroy has just pulled up in front."

"Jeremy, you may walk the Professor to the door," Rachel said. "Then go to bed. It's past your bedtime."

"Past mine, too." Dr. MacPhie stood up and walked into the hallway. "Isaac, phone me immediately if you start feeling worse."

Isaac and Rachel stood looking at each other for a moment. Isaac cleared his throat, but couldn't think of the right words to say.

"I will, Shep. Thanks," he called out, picking up his hat. "Goodnight, Rachel. And thank you for everything."

***

Isaac threaded his pickup through the debris from the near-miss tornado. An empty rain barrel. A sheet of corrugated tin from someone's chicken coop. Plenty of broken branches to give him unpleasant memories. Sure enough, as he neared home, the headlights fell on a large chinkapin limb lying in his front yard.

He pulled the pickup into a tight turn so the headlights would illuminate the front window. Immediately he saw a fist-sized gouge in the wooden frame, only half an inch from the glass. The glass itself was perfectly fine.

Isaac put his head down on the steering wheel and for the first time in ages, he wept.

CHAPTER 69

Three days later in Springfield, Elaine spread her skirt across the carousel's dragon-shaped bench as she sat down. Except for her trailer, the Flying Jenny was her favorite place. It reminded her of children. "Beautiful sunset," she said.

"Yep," said Willie, perched on the basswood rump of a nearby red and yellow Herschell stallion.

"You've been a good friend, Willie, and a great help to me. So I wanted you to be the first to know. When the season's over, I'm leaving the show." Elaine said. "I became a woman much too young, and it's been a merry-go-round ever since. But something always told me I should create my own destiny."

"You've got a special person inside you, Elaine," said Willie. "More special than being a sideshow attraction."

"Thank you. I think so, too," Elaine said. "So I've decided to try for the big time at Coney Island. But not as a fat lady anymore. People say I have a beautiful voice, so I'm going to stand up and sing songs that will cheer up everybody who listens."

"The Professor knows lots of people. Maybe he could find you a job."

"I don't want anybody to do it for me, thank you. A letter of introduction would be fine, but nothing more. Someday everyone will be saying the show isn't over until the fat lady sings. In two years you can write a letter to 'Elaine Cranbrook, USA,' and it'll get to me. If Kate Smith can make it, so can I! I'm twice the woman she is. At least in pounds."

CHAPTER 70

Later that week, as Mercerville coped with the unfortunate news about Bernard Fieldman, life slowly began to drift back toward normal. Cyrus eagerly began telling anyone who stopped at the garage that he had always suspected A.J. was touched in the head, and that Cyrus himself had warned the sheriff that "A.J. was fixin' to make his getaway to the Florida swamps. Maybe even Cuba."

For twenty-five cents—"one good ol' American quarter"—Cyrus would take you down to the river and point out the trees where "that twister set the boat right on top, and it hung there two full days until the wind come up again, and the boat fell on the river bank and smashed."

Cyrus also offered for sale—"while supplies last"—six-inch squares of the actual wood from the boat. And he would autograph them "for only one additional dime, the mere tenth part of a dollar, folks."

As word spread that Isaac had solved the murders and killed the murderer, he became considerably more popular, and people started dropping by the barbershop. Some of them even got haircuts.

On Thursday, Elmo Johnson came in to tell Isaac the bank was rescheduling his missed mortgage payments to the end of the mortgage period, according to a revised payment plan placed in the files by Bernard Fieldman. After Elmo left, Isaac wrote his brother Carl.

"Your offer of a ranch hand's job is much appreciated, but I believe I'll turn it down. The county bigwigs have decided to make the sheriff's job a three-quarter-time deal and keep me on. With the

383

increased salary and the change in the mortgage, I believe I'll manage okay."

That evening Isaac stopped by the boarding house. On the telephone table in the hall was a copy of yesterday's *Mountain Home Sentinel* with the headline—

"Local Leader Confirmed Dead"

"The body found Tuesday by volunteers searching the swollen White River has been positively identified as local banker Bernard Fieldman. As there were no signs of violence, local authorities have labeled it an accident.

"One possible explanation, according to Sheriff Isaac Cash, is that after working late at the bank doing pro bono work for refugees, Mr. Fieldman walked on the hiking path down to the river in order to evaluate tornado damage to some riverfront property the bank owns. While standing atop a boulder on the riverbank, he slipped and fell into the raging current. This newspaper sends its condolences. Mr. Fieldman did a great deal of good in this community."

Illusion can bring truth to life, the Professor had said. *Well, I suppose letting people hold on to a positive illusion is sometimes the best thing for everybody.*

Lower on the front page, an article was titled "Reverend Pulls Hat Out of Ring."

"Highly-respected clergyman Bill Berkeley today withdrew his bid for Congress. 'It is urgent,' he said, 'that I continue educating America about the need for laws preventing defective births. Under the National Socialist Workers Party in Germany, for example, the Genetic Health Courts are far ahead of

384

America in passing sterilization laws much better than ours. We owe it to ourselves not to fall behind in purifying America's future generations.'"

Isaac put the newspaper down and walked into the kitchen where Rachel was washing dishes. He picked up a dish cloth and began drying. After some small talk, he came to the point.

"You weren't really serious, were you? About leaving town, I mean. Not the part about being lonely. That part I understand."

"I know you do," Rachel said. "For a while I could hope that my husband might come back. You had no hope."

"No. At the funeral home, I closed Sarah's coffin with my own hands." He kept wiping even though the glass was now bone dry. "You're an incredible woman, Rachel. I think the world of you. But if you're thinking there's a future for us, I can't make any promises right now. I need time to get my head clear."

"Relax. I'm not an Elsie Harkens beating the bushes for a new husband." She turned toward him. "The only man I'd look for is a man who is seriously looking for me."

"But you *were* joking about leaving town, right?"

"I wasn't talking just to hear my head roar. Other women have lost their husbands and still managed to live fulfilling lives. I've decided not to stay put anymore."

"What does that mean?"

"Did you know I always wanted to be a nurse? No, I guess not. You barely noticed me before last week. Well, Dr. MacPhie knows a nursing school that might give me work to support Jeremy and myself until I graduate. Shep says that even at my age, I can still become a Public Health Nurse."

"MacPhie's a good man, but..."

"Yes, and we're lucky to have a good doctor here. The Ozarks are full of people who can't get decent medical care because the distances are so great, and they're too poor to go where the medical services are. In spite of what that crazy preacher said, the real problem for mountain people isn't heredity. It's poverty and lack of education. I believe I can do something for them. Wish me good luck, Isaac."

Isaac hung the damp towel over the edge of the sink and touched her hand. "Rachel, I wish you everything that's good. Everything!"

***

Isaac tossed and turned a lot that night, but woke up feeling surprisingly optimistic. Change is a fact of life, he realized, a necessity, and you have to let it happen.

What with folks still stopping by to congratulate him, it was noon before Isaac got around to locating the leftover can of paint in the storage room. As he walked out of the barbershop, the sun was coating the new window with light, and the tree-covered hills were beautiful in a way he hadn't appreciated in a long time.

He was kneeling beside the truck, stirring the paint, when he heard footsteps. He turned just as Jeremy knelt beside him.

"What'cha doing?" the boy said.

"Painting a sign on my truck." Isaac pointed toward the box of stencils he had borrowed from Hansen. "You reckon your hand is healed enough to help?"

"You bet!" Jeremy said.

"Then hold that letter 'M' stencil against the door and don't let it move even a smidge."

"Are we going to paint a sign on both doors?" Jeremy asked.

"Yes, and when we're finished, we'll drive down to the boarding house and show your mom," Isaac said. "Maybe even drive out for a short picnic. If she has time."

"What's the sign going to say?"

Isaac dipped the brush into the white paint. "Mercer County Sheriff."

Epilogue

The Professor— Desmond A. Pinckney, Jr. (not "the Third"), married Seesla shortly after the start of the 1935 season. It was not a carny carousel wedding, but a formal ceremony in an Anglican church in Toronto, Canada, where they were appearing. They left the carnival world in 1942, and Pinckney spent the war years working in the cramped confines of airplane nose cones at the Bell Bomber plant in Marietta, Georgia. In 1946, Pinckney died of a sudden cerebral hemorrhage while reading a book about ancient Carthage. They had no children.

Seesla, the Snake Girl— After the Professor's death, Cecile Hampstead moved to Gibsonton, Florida, winter quarters for many circus and carnival performers. There she started a small company designing and sewing costumes for circus and carnival acts. (Some of her costumes were used in the 1952 Cecil B. DeMille epic, *The Greatest Show on Earth*.) She never remarried and died in her sleep at the age of 76.

Baby Elaine— Elaine Cranbrook never made it to Coney Island, but in New York she joined a show going on a tour to England in 1935. After the tour was completed, she remained in London and began singing in English music halls under the name "Elaine Brooks, the Yankee Songbird." For a time, her popularity was exceeded only by the British singers Gertrude Lawrence and Vera Lynn.

Over the next four years, she lost a good deal of weight (partly by eating only baby food for a year), but was still a large woman. During the London Blitz in 1940, Elaine repeatedly went into the London Underground bomb shelters and kept people calm by singing songs and telling stories. She was a great favorite, especially with children. On one such occasion, the lorry taking her to the shelter received an almost direct hit, killing both her and her driver. Elaine had never married.

The Original Wild Man from Borneo— Willie Carter continued his act until sometime in the early 1940s. In 1943, he tried to enlist in the U.S. Army Air Corps, requesting duty with the 99th Pursuit Squadron (later called the "Tuskegee Airmen"), but was rejected as being too old for military service. He used his savings to open a men's clothing store in Philadelphia, eventually adding two more stores after the war. Carter married and had five children. He died in his office one afternoon of a heart attack. On his desk was a glass paperweight containing a small metal strip attached to a chicken bone.

The Great Houdeena— Deena MacRae gradually added escape tricks to her act, including escaping from a locked Cary safe. In 1937, her mother died, and Deena went home to care for her ailing father. Then in 1939, Deena heard that an abandoned well had collapsed, trapping an eight-year-old boy twenty feet underground. Excavation equipment would not reach him in time. Deena drove there, handed one end of a long rope to some people who were standing around gawking and went into the well headfirst. After twenty-five minutes, she had squirmed down close enough to free the unconscious child. Unfortunately, as the men dragged them up, the rope twisted around her left leg and broke it in three places. The child survived, but Deena was left with a pronounced limp for the rest of her life. She eventually married, moved to Arcadia, California, and raised a family of three, all boys.

Ivan the Terrible— Otto Gieseking recovered and increased his efforts throughout World War II to aid Jewish immigrants from Austria and Germany. The relief group he started is credited with having raised almost a million dollars in donations. He died of cirrhosis of the liver in December, 1945.

Dr. Shepherd Tingely MacPhie practiced medicine in Mercerville until his retirement at the age of seventy-eight. For the last twenty-five years, he also served as the county's Coroner. He kept extensive files on cases of death by foul play. Dr. MacPhie never bought another pipe to replace the one he had used to save Otto's life.

Leroy Anderson traveled with the show for one more season, then returned to his home in Duluth, Minnesota, where he was active in forming the Duluth Shakespeare Players. After the attack on Pearl Harbor, Leroy enlisted in the U.S. Navy. He was twice awarded the Navy Cross for exceptional heroism in battle. He was killed in the Battle of Okinawa in 1945.

Jerome "Jeremy" Barlow enlisted in the U.S. Army in 1942 and was eventually assigned to Military Intelligence in Washington, D.C. Following the war, he joined the FBI, had a distinguished career, and retired as Special Agent in Charge of the FBI field office in St. Louis, Missouri.

Isaac L. Cash is buried in a cemetery near his birthplace of Cotter, Arkansas. On one side is the grave of his first wife, Sarah. On the other side is his second wife, Rachel. In his will, he instructed that these words be engraved on his headstone:
"Dreams keep us alive."

* * *

THE AUTHORS

Robert McGraw has had several professions, but his most difficult job is convincing his wife he's actually writing even when it looks like he's only staring out the window. He is the author of numerous magazine and newspaper articles, as well as five books. Two of his television scripts won awards from the International Television Association.

A former professional symphony musician, Robert has a Ph.D. (all but dissertation) in music. He also studied art at The Ruth Prowse School of Art in Cape Town, South Africa.

Darrin McGraw graduated from Stanford University and received a Ph.D from UCLA. His professional work has included writing, editing, teaching, managing a public library, and supervising the Fallbrook School of the Arts. He served for eight years as the writing director of the Culture, Art and Technology Program at UC San Diego.

Also by Robert McGraw and Darrin McGraw

Animal Future

In a near-future full of mentally-enhanced animals, a Vietnamese-American policewoman, a well-dressed chimpanzee, and a fast-talking spy join forces to stay alive as fanged assassins try to keep them from uncovering a terrorist plot.

What reviewers say—

–BEST. BOOK. EVER. … Forget about writing until you've read ANIMAL FUTURE … [The McGraws] crack me up. – http://www.marianallen.com/2015/02/best-book-ever-animal-future/

--There's **action, drama, secrets, mystery and adventure**. There were parts that made me laugh and others that made me think.... I couldn't put it down.
 http://melsshelves.blogspot.com/2015/02/book-review-animal-future-by-robert-and.html

–**A rip-roaring ride** with a lot of great people, only some of whom happen to be human. ...there's plenty to keep you turning the virtual pages. -- Eugenia Parris

Excerpt from *Animal Future*—

Mack crossed his legs for the seventy-eighth time and laid the plastipage magazine down beside him on the bus stop bench. The readout in the top left of his ViewGlazzes showed it was a quarter to six in the morning. If someone had been watching him as carefully as he had been watching the tailor shop, they would have been justified in wondering why he had let four different shuttles pass him by. They might have assumed that "Classic Bimbo Weekly" had riveting editorials.

At this hour the street was empty. Most of the signs were targeted to elevated animal consumers, with huge lettering to reach species with poor eyesight. There were a variety of languages, but the majority of signs targeting animal customers were in Spanish or English.

UpRite Primate Shoes, All Sizes
Vocoder Fitting for Less—Specializing in Hard-to-Fit Species
Clínica Médica Nocturna Para Ciudadanos Provisionales
Parfumerie des Bêtes Elites...

Down the street, a polisec horse turned the corner and headed Mack's way. He remembered she had trotted across the same intersection more than thirty minutes ago, and if she recognized him, he could be in for some trouble.

In the old days before the Elevation, when police horses had riders, there was an even chance of talking yourself out of a situation. Now their riderless saddles carried only armaments: freeze gas to immobilize you until a burstcar arrived, or, if you were too far away, stop-rockets to bring you down and keep you there until the horse got close enough to gas you. Horses could walk a beat for several hours, and they had a great awareness of changes in their surroundings. However, they weren't flexible thinkers. Trying to talk a horse out of arresting you was a waste of logic.

She stopped in front of Mack and gave him the big-eye. "Miss bus?" she snuffled. The vocoders provided by polisec were barely adequate for communication.

"Yeah, well, you know." He tried to make borderline panic sound like mere embarrassment. "I guess I was too engrossed in reading an article." He nodded toward the plastipage. The horse lifted her head to bring her binocular vision into play, then turned sideways a little to focus on the title of the mag.

"Mmph! Right!" she snuffled as she saw the girlie gifs cavorting across the page.

"No, really," Mack said. "A story about this year's Olympic Marilyn Monroe Team. Nine absolutely perfect clones." He swiped his finger across the plastipage, trying to get the article to come back up. "And four alternates."

The horse tossed her mane and snorted hot breath in Mack's direction as she checked his face against her memory of mug shots.

After a longish moment, she said, "Pay more attention to bus!"

* * *

394

www.ingramcontent.com/pod-product-compliance
Lightning Source LLC
Chambersburg PA
CBHW022204030726
47494CB00019B/248

9781942409069